Praise for *Nappily Ever After*

"Trisha Thomas's debut novel is a fusion of humor, a fast-paced plot, and characters we care about. Venus Johnston's journey is a familiar and compelling one that will have satisfied readers craving an encore."

—Patricia Elam, author of *Breathing Room*

"Thomas refuses to let her characters slide into stereotype, and she keeps the pace fast and funny."

—*Publishers Weekly*

"Thomas offers painful but amusing insights into the politics of beauty, black culture, and male-female relationships; her first novel places her in a league with Terry MacMillan and Bebe Moore Campbell."

—*Booklist*

Also by Trisha R. Thomas

Nappily Ever After
Roadrunner

WOULD I LIE TO YOU?

A NOVEL BY

Trisha R. Thomas

 THREE RIVERS PRESS • NEW YORK

Published by Three Rivers Press, New York, New York.
Member of the Crown Publishing Group, a division of Random House, Inc.
www.crownpublishing.com

THREE RIVERS PRESS and the Tugboat design are registered trademarks of Random House, Inc.

Originally published in hardcover by Crown Publishers, a division of Random House, Inc., in 2004

Printed in the United States of America

Design by Leonard Henderson

Library of Congress Cataloging-in-Publication Data
Thomas, Trisha R.
Would I Lie to You? : a novel / by Trisha R. Thomas.—1st ed.
1. African American Women—Fiction. 2. Los Angeles (Calif.)—Fiction. I. Title.
PS3570. H5917F56   2003
813'.6—dc21   2003007057

ISBN 1-4000-4903-2

10 9 8 7 6 5 4 3

First Paperback Edition

To the readers who loved Venus
from the beginning
and brought her to life

WOULD I LIE TO YOU?

A woman who doesn't know what she wants
will never have what she needs.

HERE COMES
THE BRIDE

THE light hum of the cello set the mood for the joyous day. A wedding. Venus Johnston, do you take this man as your *awfully* wedded husband? Lawful, not awful, as she'd always thought the preacher was saying during TV ceremonies when she was a little girl. Yes! Yes, finally she would get her chance. Lawfully wedded bliss. Clint smiled, but showed no teeth. His lips delicately turned up, a smirk. A grimace? No. He was truly in love and about to make Venus the happiest woman alive. Her man. Sexy. Successful. Fine. All three characteristics a girl could only fantasize about. But for Venus it was now a reality.

"If there is anyone who knows of a reason why this union should not take place, let them speak now..."

Venus hated this part. When the nightmare began. The most dreaded moment when *the woman* actually stands up and says, *"I do. I know of a reason."* Venus knows the voice. It's played in her head a thousand times. She turned around slowly to see the gorgeous actress Vivica Fox, a picture of beauty in a stunning flowing wedding dress. A glorious shimmering diamond hung around her neck, almost blinding the guests.

Clint loved Vivica, that's what he always used to say. But she could never be a real threat because she was only in the pages of glossy magazines and in Hollywood movies. Yet, here she was, extending her elegantly gloved hand to Clint. "Come along, dear. You've played outside long enough. You know you need a real woman, someone who's going to love you and take care of you and put you first at all times. Tell her, sweetie. It's time for her to let you go. How many times must we go through this?" Vivica's voice echoed off the church walls.

"Please no... not again." Venus couldn't tell if she was thinking it or saying it out loud. Her panic was rising. Boy, it's getting hot in here. The music switched abruptly. She looked over where the cellist was replaced by a hip-hopper with a bandanna and a gold tooth. *It's getting hot in here... so take off all your clothes.* "Shut up, shut up." She felt Clint release her hand and start toward Vivica Fox.

"Wait, no!" Venus grabbed his sleeve. He shook her off and began walking again. "Somebody stop him!" Venus screamed. "Clint, she's no good for you. Can't you see through all that Maybelline... it's not real, can't you see that she's fake? She's not real."

Clint put up his hand. "It's too late," he said with ease. "You had your chance and you blew it." He turned and slipped his hand into Vivica's glove-covered one. They began to walk away, waving like the king and queen of the ball.

Venus hiked up her wedding gown and chased them outside.

"Clint!" she screamed. She turned and watched Vivica and Clint climb into a shiny white Range Rover with a bunch of cans tied to the back and the words *Just Married! But Not to Venus* spray-painted all over.

"NOOO, not again!" she tried to scream, but the words smothered her, making her struggle for air.

"Hey, you all right?"

She snapped out of it and found herself staring into Airic's face, concern and panic written all over him. The rest of the wedding party stared at her with confusion. She was confused too, standing next to Airic with the scent of gardenias and stargazer lilies fragrant in the air, listening to the light hum of the cello. The sun was high above their heads and the breeze was gentle enough to keep a nervous bride cool.

Wasn't it perfect? What wedding isn't? Regardless of the amount of money spent, the blood, sweat, and tears, for the bride all that mattered was walking down the aisle seeing the light in her future husband's eyes. The small details, like her satin heels sinking into the grass, the cake arriving slanted, or the ice statue of Cupid's bow melting into a dripping phallic symbol, or the mother of the bride chanting, "Thank you, Lord," were inconsequential on this monumental day. Getting to the altar, hearing that last "I do," and the crowd cheering as if a touchdown had been scored...that's what it was all about. Venus, the maid of honor, and Airic, a groom's man by default, were the only ones not clapping or throwing rose petals when the minister announced, "You may kiss the bride."

They ignored the organ pressing out the cue for them to fall into procession with the rest of the wedding party. Instead, they remained standing opposite one another, Airic pulling at the black satin noose around his white starched collar; Venus twisting the engagement ring hidden underneath the small bridesmaid bouquet she held, unable to shake the nightmare that had haunted her like a black cloud for the last two years. Each and every time she went to someone else's wedding, she felt cursed. And the conversation she and Airic had on the way to the ceremony hadn't helped matters.

Riding along the edge of the Occoquan River in the northern valley of Virginia, they'd traveled quietly most of the way. Swaying green grass surrounded the tall stretch of trees for miles along the highway. Venus kept her attention on the serene view, trying to remain calm. "...all I'm saying is that we're not getting any younger. By the time I finally get to walk down the aisle, I'm going to need a cane."

"Why is it my fault?" Airic responded without a pause. "How many times have I told you, name the time, name the place, I'm there. I think you're the one with cold feet." He steered with one hand while his slender fingers pushed relentlessly on the tuning, unable to get a radio station to come in clearly. He shut it off, giving her his complete attention. "Name the date," he said almost as a dare, cutting his eyes in Venus's direction. "What's wrong? Calendar a little tied up?"

Her frustration came out in a completely opposite form, putting her hand over her mouth to stifle the laughter.

Airic gripped the steering wheel until his pale knuckles lost color in his already fair skin. "I'm serious. Name the date."

"Sure, I'll name a date and then the week before the ceremony, you'll say, 'Oh, I thought you were talking about 2002. You meant April of *this* year.'" Venus deepened her voice to mock his. "'Can you reschedule, dear?'" The sun beamed relentlessly on the passenger's side. She was hot. She was irritable, and not just from the dress pinching her in the back where the zipper stopped. Her hair was so tightly pulled back from her face to create a bun effect that her eyes hurt. One more of the bride's many requests, including the heavy layer of fake pearls that felt like a knotted rope around her neck. She tried to adjust the cheap necklace and snagged a wispy strand of hair that was too short to stay put. "Shit."

"Name the date, Venus!" Airic thought the expletive was directed toward him.

"No...it's—"

"Name the date," he demanded again, his graying temples creasing at the sides, the skin tightening around his eyes.

"Right, pencil me in for June first of 3003." Venus responded with as much sarcasm as possible, no longer just pissed at the uncomfortable dress, the snagged hair, or the necklace choking her.

Airic's foot pushed harder on the gas, speeding into the opposite lane to pass a small white Jetta. Venus always checked when she saw the small foreign car, looking for the personalized license plate that read BABY-DOC. Of course by now Clint would have moved up in the world, driving something a bit more sophisticated, but she always checked. Always.

"See what I'm saying? Happens every time I tell you to pick a date. This is what I get, silence."

"Right." It came out louder than planned. Venus gave the hair and metal clasp one last chance to part on friendly terms, then gave it a tug, unafraid of the consequences. "Sure, Airic...whatever."

°   *   *

SHE was tired of replaying the conversation in her head. Setting a date. Tired of picturing herself in another white gown like the one worn by the bride, with the splendid train that flowed effortlessly up the aisle. Tired of the whole business. How she'd managed to be standing witness to yet another ceremony was beyond her.

She'd only met the bride, Felicia Meadows, a year and a half ago when she'd been hired as her assistant. Felicia didn't talk much during their interview and only answered questions when she was asked. She'd kept her hands folded on her lap without one fidgeting episode, a sure sign of diligence and focus. At the time Felicia hadn't even a boyfriend, no prospects for the future. Simply moved to the northern Virginia area fresh out of college without a plan, without a strategy, determined to get away from her southern roots in Memphis. Now she was married to Joseph, a friendly financial analyst who insisted on coming all the way up to the tenth floor to pick her up for lunch instead of waiting downstairs in the no-parking zone.

With forced steps, Venus moved closer to Airic. They were standing on the very spot where Felicia and Joseph had just taken their vows underneath a flowered trellis with streams of ivy. "I'm sorry." Still holding on to the compact flower arrangement, Venus stretched to reach around his lean shoulders. The white ribbons cascaded down the back of his tuxedo. "Whenever you're ready. No rush." Her soft brown eyes smiled out of duty. Always her last words... *no rush*. She was only thirty-six. Considered an old maid at one time, but not now. Statistics showed she was right on schedule to give birth to her first child in her first marriage at nearly forty. Plenty of time, *no rush*.

"Let's get out of here." She kissed Airic on his narrow chin, inhaling his scent.

He kissed her back, whispering near her ear, "That's the best idea I've heard yet." He swayed her gently back and forth. "One day left to get all the good loving I can." His jaw line creased deeply with a smile.

It was true. By Monday morning there would be two thousand miles between them. Working in opposite corners of the country, she in Los Angeles and he in Washington, D.C. A few months earlier, when Ron Chadnum had invited her to lunch and placed the L.A. account on the table, she didn't think twice before grabbing it and declaring herself the winner. She rode home singing along with Mary J. Blige at the top of her lungs. "Like sweet morning dew... I took one look at you... you were my destiny." Only thing, she wasn't singing about Airic. Her destiny and sweet morning dew was the new account. Fashion had always been her first love and finally she'd be in the center of it with the JPWear clothing. She'd prepared a list of reasons why it was a good move: spending time with her parents in Los Angeles, enhancing her career, and opening the door for other opportunities. Turned out, none of the excuses were necessary.

Over dinner she'd told Airic of the offer—the offer, not the acceptance. "Will you take it? Sounds like an incredible opportunity," he'd said, a little too excited for her taste.

"It is, but what about us?" Venus had asked cautiously over microwaved lasagna that still had cold spots in the middle.

"*Us* is solid as a rock, two thousand miles can't put a dent in us." Airic had made it sound so simple. Part of her wanted him to throw drama, plead for her to stay, maybe even pout a little. What would it hurt to show that he cared, needed her? He didn't always have to be so understanding, so mature. But tomorrow was the big day. It came quick and painless. She was already packed, already had an apartment, and Airic was already used to the idea of her being gone.

She felt a warm surge of anticipation for the night to come. A send-off like no other. Going-away sex was the best kind. They'd have to go at least three rounds to hold them over until they saw each other again. Airic scooped her up effortlessly like she was being carried over the threshold. Venus called out to her best friend who was wearing the exact same shimmering silver bridesmaid's dress, making it look sexy and glamorous while Venus felt like a foil-wrapped chocolate bar.

"Wendy, catch!" She threw the small bouquet and blew a kiss.

Wendy caught the bouquet and now held two, shaking them in front of her like pompoms. Her rich brown skin gleamed against the shiny gown. "Call me when you get settled in L.A. I'll keep an eye on your man for you, don't worry."

Venus grinned, revealing a set of just-whitened teeth, feeling light in Airic's arms. "This man doesn't need watching, he's in love." She kicked her leg out as she was being whisked out of the wedding garden past the idle crowd of well-wishers. For the moment, she felt like she was the bride. She blew kisses to no one in particular while Airic carted her off. She snuggled into the sweet, heavy scent of his cologne. No rush, she thought. Her day would come.

RED LIGHT, GREEN LIGHT

From the street, the design studio looked like one of many smog-coated buildings in the downtown garment district of Los Angeles. The cloud cover tinted the entire city with a gray haze. The sky had been heavy and dense since she'd arrived in L.A. a week earlier. Venus faded in and out of thought, a dullness blanketing her mind while her heels rubbed against the concrete, her feet moving blindly to her destination. Legend and William strolled ahead in their corporate suits and silk ties, with the confidence of Morehouse grads with a long string of alphabets after each of their names. It was a look Fortune 500 companies would appreciate if not for the silver studs climbing up William's ear and the thick twisted dreadlocks hanging down Legend's back. William was the studious one, with his intense, light hazel eyes that bore straight through her to get his point across.

Legend, on the other hand, refused to offer anyone, especially Venus, that much power by giving his undivided attention. He always managed to look off to the side or over her head as if he was bored and had other places to be.

The two men reached the double glass doors, appropriately pausing and standing off to the side with the door pulled open for Venus to enter. Legend's slate gray suit complemented his dark, well-oiled skin. "After you." He swung his hand open to improvise the right of way.

"This time don't save your best idea for last," Venus instructed while slipping past the two men. For one so small she was fast on her feet, and her high heels didn't slow her down. Neither did her fitted skirt encompassing the neat little package both men appreciated when they thought no one was looking.

"I've heard this guy, Jake Parson, doesn't play. He won't hesitate telling us to take our marbles and go home. We have to give him everything we've got right up front."

"No problem. You're the boss." The words came out in Legend's mock thespian voice. His lackadaisical attitude infuriated Venus about five times a day, but it was also what kept her on her toes.

They were on their way to a meeting with Jake Parson, a onetime rapper who now owned and ran one of the largest fashion empires in the country in spite of himself. He'd bought his way into the clothing industry but now had hit a roadblock, unable to reach the market he'd originally captivated. He'd brought the thug life into the mainstream with oversized pants and baggy jackets. Only these thugs were being dropped off at school with lunch pails and skateboards. The young street look was now owned and coveted by middle-class suburbanites who'd never seen the ghetto life up close and personal. The life they saw in rap videos and on covers of CDs told them no thug was complete without his JPWear.

It wasn't what Jake Parson had envisioned when the company started six years ago. The young women's line was the biggest hurdle. No upstanding around-the-way girl would be caught in JP jeans. It was almost as bad as being seen in a pair of Kathie Lee Gifford's spandex jeans.

IN the lobby, Venus scanned the framed pictures of music artists in brightly colored oversized clothing emblazoned with the JP logo on the front. She recognized most of the artists even though she'd started her private boycott of music video channels over a year ago. The half-naked women shaking their asses had sunk to an all-time low and she'd decided to turn it off instead of becoming enraged and disgusted. Still, rap and hip-hop music was now like baseball and apple pie, the all-American way.

She walked to the receptionist's desk, which was nothing more than a curved glass top on a clear base, matching the rest of the minimalist decor, soft lighting, chrome accents, and pristine white walls. The leggy brunette, with lips as dark as her hair, stood up with the phone still attached to her face. After hanging up, she escorted them to a spiral staircase that hung on steel wires. Not very practical, Venus thought, holding on for dear life. Legend and William came up behind her, no doubt staring at her round derriere with each step.

"Have a seat. Mr. Parson will be right with you." The receptionist left the three of them in the conference room, which held a series of straight metal chairs and a long, narrow frosted glass table in the center. The clear wall looked down onto the sample makers' studio on the first floor. Fit models walked around topless, or bottomless, depending on what stage of pinning they were in. JPWear had gone truly commercial, using skinny waifs as fit models, for the men as well as the women. Venus made a mental note: *Need real models with real bodies.*

"Wassup!" Jake Parson entered the room, slapping high fives, moving into a loose huddle with Legend and William. He turned toward Venus with the same excitement. He smiled, his eyes roamed her face. The ex-rapper slash clothing mogul held her hand in a tight professional grasp, but Venus still noticed the softness of his palm. "You must be Venus Johnston. I'm Jake Parson. I hear you picked my boys up when they were facedown on the curb."

"Ah, we like to see it as down but not out." Legend did a few raise-the-roof gestures. "It ain't over till it's over." Ever since the two men reluctantly had to sign on as employees instead of the entrepreneurs they started as, they weren't the happiest campers. Urban Assault, their old company, was underresourced and ran out of the capital to stay in the competitive business of advertising and marketing. When Venus heard Legend Hill and William Marks were looking for partners, she relayed the information to Chadnum Mass Marketing and proposed a buyout. Robert Chadnum wasted no time bringing them into the company, but not as partners—just plain old-fashioned working stiffs with plain old-fashioned paychecks.

Jake Parson ignored the rebuttal. "Pleased to be working with you." He wore a loose-fitting suit with a thick turtleneck underneath. Not even he wanted to wear his own line of clothing. His wide smile made him look boyish, too young to be running a multimillion-dollar company. "My boys here never let me down when I was on the rap circuit. The original PR masters. Came through on several gigs. Nice to know they're in good hands." He still held hers in a firm grip.

The thin hairs on the back of her neck rose. She suppressed the shock that had now risen to anger. She didn't like being the outsider. Legend and William conveniently failed to mention the buddy thing with the president and owner of the company. This meeting had been planned well over a month ago, and they had not said one word.

"Nice to have references." She slipped her hand out of his and stepped around Legend and William, eyeing them long enough to make them as uncomfortable as she now felt.

Jake Parson turned back to his boys. "Let's get this party started. How about we head out, get something to eat? We don't need to stick around here when we could be at Links nursing some Lemon Drops...and I'm not talking about the candy." They slapped hands again, the three of them looking like a football team rally with high fives and shoulder bumps. It had been a long time since she felt this way, ignored and irrelevant. Which had always been the case when she worked for Donnelly and Kramer. Seven long years and not one promotion. It took a mental breakdown for her to get the hint and move on. Within a few months she'd landed a job with Chadnum Mass Marketing where she now wore the badge proudly, *Multicultural Marketing Director.*

The power was only in the title, since at this moment she felt small and insignificant. A tight knot formed at the top of her stomach.

She looked to Jake Parson. "You know, I'm on a tight schedule. I have a few conference calls to make this afternoon, so I need to get in, get out, and then you guys can reminisce and have your play time afterward." Venus pulled her sleeve back to check her watch for emphasis. The last thing she needed was to head to their old stomping ground where she'd have to sit back chewing the inside of her jaw while they went down memory lane. From the looks of things, they had a good long history and plenty to catch up on.

"Oooookay." He moved to the far corner of the table like a reprimanded child. He slipped into one of the swivel metal chairs. A distinct chuckle floated to the head of the class. Venus turned around to glare at Legend, then began to speak in her managerial voice.

"Well, first off I'd like to thank you and congratulate your choice of Chadnum Mass Marketing. I'm excited to be working with you—"

She was interrupted by someone making a big deal of clearing his throat. Her bet was on Legend, having once witnessed him do a mastur- bation gesture during a corporate meeting. His way of showing someone what he thought of them, trying too hard to suck up. She ignored the muffled cough and continued.

"The way I see it, your company has a lot of catching up to do. JPWear took the entire wave of urban fashion to a new level, but all of a sudden, it's become general goods, the kind of clothing you can pick up at any de- partment store. The key to getting back on top of the streetwear game is creating a mystique, the allure that comes with being exclusive. If you're kicking it in JPWear you gotta feel like you're the shit." She paused, un- easy with her use of slang. She awaited Legend's second attempt to em- barrass her.

"There is no uniqueness to the brand. People want to be able to get it, but they need to work for it. Nothing good comes easy . . . or cheap." Venus recalled the sighting of a few JPWear hats on a rack at a local Chevron gas station. "I think you're going to have to create an entire new line, make it exclusive," she continued. "Bottom line, JPWear can be bought anywhere and everywhere. It's not cool anymore. I suggest JPWear create an alias, a new name, a new brand to attract a new following."

Legend burst out, unable to contain his disagreement, "JPWear can easily cut back on the number of retailers. Starting an entire new line under an entirely new brand is ridiculous, not to mention expensive. Why in the world would he need to start over from scratch?"

Venus found herself once again glaring at Legend, wanting to pounce. Wasn't it just this morning they'd agreed with the direction to approach JPWear's overhaul? Now he was saying the complete opposite. She main- tained a dignified stance, doing her best to control the situation. "Being oversaturated in the market does three things to a fashion-forward brand. One, it dilutes the edge factor; two, it kills your profitability; and, three, it creates a guaranteed slide into oblivion." She turned to Jake, with her back completely to Legend. "So the question is, can you put the horse back in the barn after it's run away? I say many have tried, but few have succeeded. I would be interested if anyone can give me an example of a successful line that has brought itself back from overexposure. Levi's jeans? Tommy Hilfiger?" She shook her head. "...And now we have Nike, struggling to get back the crown. It's not going to happen."

"Maybe not for them, but JPWear's got the juice." Legend kept his attention directed at Jake and William, not so much as a glance in Venus's direction. "As much money as it would take creating a new line, the marketing, the advertising—hell, we could throw half as much at JPWear and get the same results. Change the image, step up the media. It can be done." Legend looked directly at Jake, waiting for confirmation that he was in the lead.

"It's definitely something to consider." Jake Parson looked between the two competing forces, bemused by the rivalry.

"Mr. Parson, how long do you want to be in this business—three, four, or five more years? That's the question. If the answer is yes, then Legend is right." Venus frowned with the thought. "But if you want to create, as we say in the business, a 'going concern'—something that has longevity—you have to think about introducing a new line, with a new brand. I agree that it costs just as much money to turn around an existing company as it does to start a new one, but the latter usually yields better results."

"And exactly when did you ever run your own company? You've been hiding under the corporate sheets too long, you're out of touch." Legend had let his contempt slip out once before and Venus had put him in check with finger wagging and head bobbing, but not in front of the paying customer. She bit down hard, catching the inside of her cheek.

"Don't hate Legend, it's not like you brah: We're talkin' business here, and all ideas need to be heard and considered." Jake Parson turned his attention back to Venus with apologetic eyes. She wanted to tell him not to sweat it. She'd make Legend pay later.

Venus continued, "When you first talked to Chadnum, the discussion revolved around the fact that the Macy's buyer threatened to pull your line. Did they tell you why?"

A brief moment of embarrassment swirled around Jake. "JPWear clothing was going in a direction that they might not agree with."

"Which means they're tired of sharing the same styles as the other stores. Your company pulled in $80 million last year. Your closest competitor did six times that business. Do you know why? Because they're exclusive."

Legend was shaking his head. "... then cut back on some retailers and focus on the high end."

"Cut back on retailers, cut back in profits, period. He needs to keep the existing line at the general department stores and create a separate one for the high end." Venus rolled open her palms to show the end of her magic trick. "It's not complicated."

"Well, why didn't you say that?" Jake interrupted.

Venus looked as if to say, brotha please, hoping that Jake was asking a rhetorical question. These things had to be hashed out; even the simplest solutions needed dialogue. "I like the direction." Jake stood up, running a hand down the lean muscles of his abdomen. "I like it a lot, now let's eat."

Venus looked at her watch again, indicating her need to keep things moving. "I think I'll pass."

Legend gave Venus a defeated glance before leaning back. His thick dreadlocks hung over the back of his chair. He ignored Jake's offer of food and libations as well, trying to deliver his own message, "I'm just saying, JPWear is still the hottest thing going. That's plus positive to have everybody walking around with the *JP* on their jackets and T-shirts. What's important is building on what we already have. We don't need to start an entirely different line."

Jake nodded his head; he'd take it all under advisement. It didn't slow Legend down any. William sat silently, writing down notes. His usual tactic was to sit back and listen, collecting information, drawing a conclusion that made more sense than all the rest. This time he had nothing to add, afraid to side with Venus in the presence of Legend.

"Have I ever steered you wrong, man?" Legend stood up, straightening his tie and adjusting his suit.

Jake stood up and leaned over the table, slapping hands with both men, "That's why you my dogs. Who else was I gonna call?"

The conversation turned into a boys' session regardless of how many times Venus tried to interject, their large shoulders huddled together as a wall to keep her out. She tried talking over them a few times, their voices becoming louder, their laughter thicker.

She picked up her purse and briefcase and left the room quietly, unnoticed. She opened her small Nokia phone as she elbowed her way out the double doors of the JPWear studio. She dialed and listened as the phone went into the fourth ring.

OPEN SEATING

"Hello, sweetness." Venus let out a sigh of relief when Airic picked up. She climbed into the leather seat of her car.

"Hello, Buttercup."

"Hello, Ever Lovin'." She peeled off her high-heeled boots while sitting in the front seat.

"Hello, Kissy Face."

"Okay, that's enough. How are you?" She put her hot exhausted feet on top of the steering wheel as she pressed the button to guide the seat back as far as it would go.

"Needing you," Airic breathed into the phone.

"Are you going to be able to come this weekend?" She was on the verge of whining but didn't want to alarm him. She after all was a woman. Real women didn't whine.

"Venus, I left you a message. You didn't get it?"

"No. What message?"

"I've got a proposal sitting in front of me that has more holes than Swiss cheese. I've got to have it together by Monday morning. I won't be able to come."

Venus squeezed her eyes shut. It took everything she had to stay light. "I miss you, that's all. This long-distance love thang is puttin' a hurtin' on me."

"I miss you, too. You know that."

"Another week without you. I don't know." She wiggled her toes, staring up at the windows of the JPWear studio, picturing the three men inside the stucco building laughing and chuckling it up, not knowing whether she was alive or dead.

"Well, doesn't Chadnum need to see you? You can fly back here. You can't do everything over the phone and computer, can you?" he asked in a telling voice.

"The only thing I can't do through e-mail or on the phone is what I want to do with you."

He laughed. Airic had an enormous sense of humor. Love and laughter were two of the same as far as Venus was concerned. Once the laughter was gone, so were the good times, closely followed by the love.

She sat up straight when she saw the three men file out of the large double doors of the building. If she didn't know them personally and have a deep yearning to run them over with her car, she would've classified them as handsome. Now there were three of them. Solid, refined, educated—jerks.

Men didn't like working for women, as much as they tried to hide it. They could pretend that all was fair, but there was still major dissension. She knew sometimes she came on a bit too strong, what she called her Napoleon complex. Trying to make up for her slight size and stature. She should've known Legend and William were going to stage an uprising, not wanting to be bullied by a woman. All men could secretly hear their mothers yelling at them to take out the trash or cut the lawn.

"I'm not promising, Venus," Airic said, breaking her concentration on the Three-Live crew heading her way.

"I'm asking you to try. I have to go now. I'll call you tonight when I get home."

"You know where I'll be."

"In my heart," she said quickly before hanging up. She slipped back into her camel suede boots, pulling them over her calves. Flipping open the mirror on the back of her sunshade, she checked her makeup. Eyes still neatly lined with the soft brown pencil, her brows still sculpted to perfection, courtesy of Gina the Korean dynamo at Picasso's Salon. Her coral brown skin never needed foundation; instead, she pressed a light powder for the shine. She touched up her lipstick, then stepped out of the car.

The clouds had parted after a heavy shower, leaving the downtown streets wet and steamy. She walked quickly, sidestepping the potholes that were filled with rainwater. She caught up to them, hurrying until she was by Jake's side.

Startled, his hands flew out of his pockets like they could possibly do damage. "Lady, you shouldn't sneak up on people like that in the downtown streets of Los Angeles. We've got protocol out here."

"I called out, you guys didn't hear me."

Legend and William turned around with a dampened spirit. The mean teacher was back ruining their field trip plans. "You're joining us for lunch, Ms. Johnston?"

"Don't mind if I do."

"I don't mind at all." Jake Parson extended his arm and waited for her to take hold. Venus tapped his arm down lightly.

"I think I can manage."

They walked five or six blocks up Broadway passing several restaurants on the way. She stayed silent, listening to their conversation range from homelessness to interest rates to Betina Grayson, *I know ya'll remember Betina*...

She zoned into her own thoughts—when would be the next time she saw Airic, what to do with her empty weekend. This was the second one in a row they'd missed being together. Days were long, nights even longer. Even though she'd spent the first half of her life in Los Angeles, it wasn't home anymore. She could have only so many dinners with her mother and father before it felt like she'd moved back in with them. The guest pleasantries had already worn off. Now, her mother asked her questions like when she and Airic were going to get married since she'd been wearing a ring for well over the required get-to-know-you period, if she'd considered having her eggs frozen, seeing how she'd celebrated her thirty-sixth birthday a month ago. And the hardest questions of them all—how was Clint doing, did she ever talk to him, when was the last time she saw him... was he happily married?

She wished she could answer that question. But then again, she was grateful to not know. Clint was a part of her life she tried hard not to think about. One of those it-could-have-been-me stories. She'd pushed him out of her life for his lack of commitment and then stood idly by while he married another woman less than a year later. The past that always resided in her ever present state of mind.

"Here it is." Jake opened the door of the restaurant for everyone, then slid in behind Venus. Once the restaurant door shut behind them, the daylight was closed out completely like a lid-covered box.

She could feel Jake behind her in the darkness of the entrance. It took a moment for her eyes to adjust. Before that she was following the muted sound of dining, plates connecting to forks, voices in light conversation.

"How's this?" The hostess stood to the side for the four of them to examine.

"Perfect, thank you." Jake pulled the chair out for Venus and sat down next to her. Legend and William took two seats directly across.

Jake Parson had been a household name, a rap artist who'd made a million from one silly little song. Then turned his attention and his bankroll to clothing and made another million and then another. She'd found as much information on him as possible before their meeting. He was one of the few entertainers she knew who had actually graduated from college. After reading his impressive dossier, she'd still written him off as a hip-hop accident, falling into good luck and fortune.

Though she must admit, she was impressed with his restaurant selection. Restaurant choice said a lot about someone's personality. This one was subtle, quiet, but still humming with a vital energy. She could see him in her peripheral vision. Confident. Appealing. Stop that, she told herself. Watching the moves of a man she'd just met (she checked his left hand that held up the menu), an unmarried man, was not smart. Neither smart nor considerate. She prided herself on being both. She'd made plenty of mistakes in her lifetime, with men mostly the source. She was at the pinnacle of her professional career and love life, so why did she feel the heat of Jake Parson's shoulder every time he bumped her slightly? Answer.

Lonely. Here in big old Los Angeles without her baby, her kissy face, her sweetness. Nothing more to it than that. She missed Airic. This new person was merely an image, a mirage. No one could make her laugh the way Airic did. No one could sing the words of "One in a Million" by Larry Graham in its entirety, hitting the long notes and all. No one could give a good horseyback ride like Airic, twirling her around until she was dizzy, then dropping her onto the bed, and diving in shortly after. She bit her lip. Plain old-fashioned horny.

"What do you say, Venus?"

"Excuse me?"

"Vitro Cabernet? A red wine, not too dry." Jake was leaning into her face as if she were hard of hearing.

"Perfect. I'm sorry."

"Where'd you go?" He searched her eyes.

"Probably back to work. All work and no play, that's the motto, right, Ms. Johnston?" Legend pulled the knot free that was housing his locks. "Try to relax. Chadnum doesn't have a wire on you, does he?" He loosened his tie with one finger.

Venus was about to lash out at Legend before being trumped by Jake.

"Work is going to get the job done. I have no problem with playtime, fellas, but when it comes time to roll up the sleeves, I expect nothing less than what you'd give Mr. Smith, or Mr. Tom. You know what I'm saying?" It was a professional tone she hadn't heard until now.

"Always." William spoke up, putting his hand out for a soul shake, then a knuckle butt.

Venus crossed her legs under the table. That did it. She'd wait it out. The warm rush. She would not be taken over by such a small gesture. Speaking up for her, taking a stand in her defense. She was too old to fall for chivalry. She worked hard to suppress the acknowledgment but it came out anyway; "Thank you," she breathed out in a whisper, then put her face back into her menu.

"Anytime." Jake stroked his goatee.

"Let's order." Legend's tone took on an edge. That alone was enough to make her smile.

She was used to Legend's and William's sarcasm, but growing weary by the moment. No one understood their frustration more than Venus. She'd experienced her share of working for people she considered less qualified. After ten years of climbing and groveling, she was finally where she wanted to be, deserved to be—director of multicultural marketing, in charge of helping the big companies connect with their brown brothers and sisters without offensive toe-tapping Bo Jangle ads. She wore the title like a badge of authority and honor. Although Robert Chadnum was an African American himself, he surrounded himself with a staff of the majority consensus, white males. Venus was one of the few female managers, not to mention the even fewer black women, at the corporate headquarters in Washington, D.C. After two years, she still walked into her own office and stood in awe of the sweeping view of the Potomac River, the beautiful teak wood desk and furnishings. The art that she'd picked out herself. Romare Bearden collections full of vibrant yellow and blue hues. She had an expense account that allowed her to take clients skiing in Vail or sailing down the coast instead of to a simple lunch or dinner. She'd done her time and was now enjoying the perks of her servitude.

That's how she'd ended up in Los Angeles, going the extra mile, doing what was expected, and exceeding those expectations. But what had it gotten her? A one-way trip to Lonely Town, USA. Los Angeles was filled with people. Five million at last count, and there was still something so isolating about being here. Everyone drove around with their faces forward, blind to what didn't involve them. Seeing only their immediate connection. The various cultures, black, white, Asian, Middle Eastern, all sectioned off like miniature countries on one land. You had to find a clique, a group, a club, or something, or simply fall into the shadows. She looked up and watched the interaction between the three men, their Adam's apples rising and falling, and realized she wasn't going to be a part of this club either.

"Are you ready to order, or do you need a few more minutes?" The waitress stood over them with her white shirt buttoned to the neck and her black apron snug around her conservative-fitting black pants and still managed to look charming. Venus guessed, student. The ones who wanted to be actresses usually worked closer to the west side, Century City, Santa Monica.

After her first glass of wine, Venus excused herself to the rest room. Jake stood up, as a gentleman would, then William and Legend followed suit as if it were a game of Simon Says. In the dim lighting, she moved carefully around tables and in between seated patrons. A door pushed open and light escaped. A sharply dressed woman walked out. Before the door closed, Venus caught a glimpse of a mirror and sink and beelined it to that direction. The bathroom was lit but still required a flashlight if she wanted to touch up her makeup. She went into the stall and closed the wooden shutter door. She stood staring at the slats in the door casing, trying to remember if it was up or down, when people could see straight through to the other side.

It didn't matter, she didn't really have to use the facilities. She just needed a minute to figure it all out.

If it was only the lonely bug that had bitten her, why then did she find Legend and William so completely undesirable? They both had the looks, the style, the manliness guaranteed to get the job done. Since they had been working together she'd felt nothing, not even a twinge of possibility. Not a flash of wonder when the two men walked into her office on a bright hot July day making every other female, and a few males, track them as they passed. Nada. Zilch. Not even a flicker of fantasy. The entire office had buzzed after they left. "Who was that? Umph, girrrrrl," was all she'd heard the rest of the day. She'd been impressed as well on first arrival, she'd heard so much about them, seen their photos in a couple of business articles, but their cockiness had reared its ugly head two minutes into the interview. Legend with his smug attitude and brass bullets of truth. The truth as he saw it. William sitting there, confident and all knowing. Nada. And yet, here was Jake Parson, a perfect stranger, triggering waves of heat in her elbow every time he accidentally nudged her to reach for the bottle of wine or the bread. The instant high when his leg widened, touching hers. Excuse me, excuse me, she should've said, you're in my space. She should have, but no protest, verbal or otherwise.

Venus shook her hands out. The tingly rise of anticipation. Instant attraction was normal. It happened all the time. It didn't mean anything. The human mind was stronger than the pheromones that lurked, seeking and hunting constantly for a new mate without authorization. I didn't order this ... send it back.

She took a long minute of meditation in front of the sink while she washed and rewashed her hands. An extra minute to strengthen her resolve before going back to the fire.

*   *   *

BY the time lunch was over, so was the day. The sky was dark, filled with clouds ready to burst. It had been unusually rainy and cold in Southern California. Venus was beginning to think she'd brought the heavy clouds with her from the East Coast, following her like a bad attitude. *You can run but you can't hide from yourself.* Venus stepped outside as the door was held open for her. The others filed out behind. The air was thick with car fumes and misty rain.

"Why don't we go back to the studio and put some of this down on paper?"

"Sure." Venus tightened the belt around her leather coat while she watched Legend and William stride up ahead. There was a heaviness to her step from the two glasses of wine.

Jake Parson stayed, walking by her side. "They're not your biggest fans, huh?"

"What gave it away?"

He smiled, showing a straight set of teeth and cocked his head to acknowledge the obvious.

Venus walked with her eyes on the subjects. "I was the one who brought the two of them to Chadnum's attention. But instead of being grateful it's like they blame me for making them aware they'd failed. Like if it wasn't for me, they'd still have their pride. The big entrepreneurial struggle could go on."

"I think you hit it. They have some pride issues... definitely wouldn't take it personal, though. They're good guys. They respect you."

"Lucky me." Venus slowed to create more distance between the men walking ahead. "Why didn't you just hire them to come work for you? I mean, this is obviously an inside job. They could have easily left Chadnum and come and worked for you without the middleman."

Jake stayed quiet.

"What's that look? If they're your *boys,* you didn't need me here.

Right?" She stopped him, touching his arm. "Oh, God. You're trying to say I have defective merchandise."

"You sure do read a lot into silence." His lips parted into a smile. "None of the above. It was you."

"Me?"

"You, Venus Johnston. I got wind of you about a year ago. I probably should have sought you out then, but I thought I could make wine out of water, gold out of dust, continue doing what I'd started and everything would take care of itself. Then I saw the nice write-up about you teaming up with Legend and William in *Black Enterprise* and I thought, three birds, one stone. I get the best of both worlds. I trust these guys, I know them, but they need balance."

"Balance, as in a mother-hen type to keep them in line?" Venus rolled her eyes to the gray sky above.

"No. There is nothing motherly about you."

She crossed her arms over her chest. "What's that supposed to mean?"

Jake threw up his hands. "I can't win here. All I'm saying is that you guys complement each other. It may not look that way now, but I know what I'm talking about." There was an awkward moment of silence, only the sound of their shoes against the pavement, cars passing in the wet street.

They reached the corner of the JPWear studio and stopped for the light. Jake looked down at her where she only came to his shoulder. "We should probably call it a day. You seem beat."

"Yeah, beat down." She dropped her eyes for a minute, stopping to look up at him, and noticed a dark line in the center of his throat along the edge of his turtleneck. The scar was as neatly placed as the rest of him, as if it were drawn with a felt pen. She quickly diverted her eyes, but too late, he pushed his leather collar closed around his neck.

"I think I'll go home and sink into a big tub of bubbles."

"I'll walk you to your car." They crossed the street without Legend and William noticing they were no longer following.

"So where's home?"

"An apartment on Wilshire, the 9000 block."

"Chadnum must pay well."

Venus didn't answer, happy to let her lifestyle speak for itself. She pulled out her keys and pressed the unlock button to her leased BMW. "You've been a perfect gentleman. I hope some of it wears off on your boys."

"I'll see that it does." He brought his hand up for a warm shake, even softer than in the office when they'd first met. His hand swallowed hers.

"See you Monday." She opened the car door.

"Why do we have to wait until Monday?"

Venus rolled her eyes. "I think you know the answer to that question, Mr. Parson, colleague, client, sir." She gleamed a smile while taking her hand back.

He leaned on the open car door, grinning. "I'm all that, huh?"

"All that."

"See you Monday." Tapping lightly then closing the door for her without a fight. She figured Jake Parson had to try, page two in the player's handbook.

BUTTONS

LUNCH was still heavy on her mind. Her stomach as well. She threw off her work clothes and grabbed the gray flannel shirt hanging on the chair. She put her face into it before putting it on. She loved the comfort and smell of Airic's shirts. The worn-out buttonholes came undone as quickly as she'd buttoned them. Only one, midway down, stayed closed. She picked up the phone and carried it with her while she scooted between the cool sheets of her bed.

For the third time she dialed Airic's number. He wasn't in his office or at the house that still held her blue toothbrush and favorite weekend jeans. The white terry robe hanging on the back of the bathroom door. It was three hours later in D.C. and Airic was nowhere to be found.

The phone rang while it lay in her hands. She answered quickly, "Hi, Honey."

"Hi."

Venus paused for a quizzical second. "You're not Honey."

"No, but stranger things have happened."

"Who is this?"

"Someone who asked you out earlier this evening and you turned me down."

"Mr. Parson, how did you get my phone number?" She sat up against the pillows.

"That was the easy part. I've been contemplating this call for the last hour. I wasn't sure if you'd be too happy about it. But then again, you called me honey."

"That's because I thought you were Honey." She couldn't erase the smile on her face.

"So Honey hasn't called?"

"He's probably trying to call right now, but you're tying up my line." She picked at a tiny feather that made its way through the down comforter's duvet.

"I feel really bad about that. So what's the real reason behind turning down my invitation, besides you and your honey?"

"Isn't that enough of a reason?"

"No. I wouldn't think it's all that serious."

"I'm not going to do anything that's going to jeopardize our working relationship."

"I just wanted to have a bite with you, talk shop."

"We just had a bite, and a drink. Lunch lasted nearly three hours; wasn't that enough?"

"Obviously not or I wouldn't have asked for more. Didn't want our creative streak to have a chance to die down come Monday."

She could already feel the tone change, his voice slowing into a soft rhythm. "I thought two days was a long time to wait since we were on a roll."

"Mr. Parson, I'm not stupid. I know what I know."

"What do you think you know?" He attempted to formalize his voice.

"Trouble."

"So now my name is trouble?"

She pictured him running a hand across the silky hairs on his face that matched his neatly cropped Afro.

"You know what I mean. I don't want to play this game." This time she pulled two of the light feathers, digging for more.

"Really?" He took a long deep breath. "I love your smile, reminds me of sunshine, bright and beautiful."

"Is that the best you can do?" She coughed out a laugh. "Aren't you the one responsible for 'luscious lips and fat juicy hips...c'mon baby I want to ride'?" Venus smirked to herself, remembering the song that played on the radio every hour, every minute of the day.

"Those were my younger days when I didn't appreciate the finer things in life."

"Thank you, Mr. Parson. You have a good night."

"You too. And I hope Honey calls soon."

Me too, Venus thought, while hanging up the phone and kicking the hot covers off her feet. She went into the small kitchen, checking the cabinets for comfort food. She opened a can of salty Campbell's soup but then dumped it down the drain. She watched as the soft noodles slithered into the mouth of the garbage disposal.

The company Airic, or in this case, *Honey*, had built from scratch was now a mega player on the World Wide Web. He'd patented software that provided virtual private networks, allowing companies to keep their employees' web surfing under control. Venus had put together the marketing material, a picture of a businessman sitting in front of his computer screen with glazed eyes staring at a fleshy woman on a porn site, the caption underneath, *A mind is a terrible thing to waste. Protect yours.* Airic poured his heart and soul into the company. But Venus never complained about feeling neglected or played as a second fiddle. She didn't have to. She had her own career to keep her busy, one she enjoyed immensely. It was a two-way street. Numerous times she'd been unavailable to Airic. He never once complained. It was only fair that she now comply with the rules. Their relationship was based on mutual respect, mutual admiration, and a mutual love of work.

Like every other relationship Venus had experienced, she looked to the long term. Anything good was worth working and waiting for. If it came too easy, it had no value, empty calories like the package of popcorn she had just stuck in the microwave. She stood in front of it watching the numbers count backward.

The phone rang at the exact same time the microwave bell went off. She pulled the hot bag of popcorn out, tossing it to the counter then chasing down the phone receiver.

She used her fake groggy voice. "Hello." She didn't want Airic knowing she'd stayed up waiting for his call. It was nearly midnight, East Coast time.

"Has Honey called yet?" The voice was light and familiar, but not Airic's.

"No. Not yet." She gave serious thought to being angry but it wouldn't be genuine. She wasn't truly annoyed. "Exactly what do you want to talk about? Let's get it over with." She pulled the bag of popcorn open, ignoring the hot steam and tasting a buttery kernel but leaving the rest behind as she paced nervously around the apartment.

"Okay, what does Honey do, what's he look like, how'd you two meet?"

"Sizing up the competition?"

"Always gotta know what your competition is up to. Number one rule of business."

"So this is business, Jake?" She added his name almost as an afterthought.

"My philosophies serve me well in all aspects of my life. So you're going to answer my questions?"

"He's a delectable six foot two inches tall, wide shoulders, tight abs, kind of a Tyson Beckford thing going for him. He's a self-motivated businessman who's done quite well for himself. He's sent me flowers every Friday since I've known him, regardless of where I am, what I'm doing. He sings to me and makes love like a Harlequin hero. I don't believe I've left anything out."

"Okay, let me read this back to you. He's around six feet tall, too slim for your liking but there are more important things to be mad at. He's on the light-skinned side, but if he were as chocolate as Tyson Beckford he'd be near perfect. He works himself into the ground and sends you flowers to apologize for not having enough quality time. He keeps you laughing so you won't notice the bigger issues. He's a little stiff in bed but you've read enough romance novels to keep you going. Did I leave anything out?"

A part of Venus wanted to laugh, the other part wanted to hang up before he delved any further. Was she that transparent?

She sucked her teeth. "So you've scoped out the competition; now what?"

"Define the plan of action. Zero in on the weakness, build from there."

"Sounds like it came out of a playbook. We're talking about a relationship here? That's how you go about things?" Venus was walking around her apartment, the phone cradled against her ear while she straightened pillows and not-quite-centered art on the walls. She'd straighten, take a step back, straighten again, a nervous habit.

"Absolutely."

"And will you let me in on this plan, or is it a secret attack?"

"Oh, you'll definitely know what's going down. Won't be a question." He laughed with invigorating confidence.

Venus stopped pacing and found herself in front of the long maple-framed mirror that hung on her bedroom door. Reaching out to straighten it, she realized it was she who was crooked. Not quite centered. Wearing nothing but Airic's flannel shirt that stopped above her knees, she leaned in closer making a confrontation with herself. Caramel brown skin year-round. Honest eyes. Direct. No lies. No tricks. Smart and savvy, especially when she wore her DKNY suit, the black one with the tight-fitting slacks. She was power in that suit. She pulled back to examine herself all the way down to the toes. Nice ankles and calves. She'd come to appreciate her legs, give them the respect they deserved. So what if they weren't long and sensuous. More like an undersized gymnast. But they worked well with her spiked toe pumps, the ones that made her calf muscles stay in permanent flex.

"Tell me what you're wearing."

Her breath caught in her throat.

She listened again, while his voice went lower, softer, "Don't be shy, just tell me." A perfect mix of titillation and fear began to rise through her. She placed a finger at the base of her clavicle and trailed down the center of her chest until it stopped at the closed button. The worn hole released easily. She let her hand travel the length of her nude front, down the flatness of her tummy. She walked back to the bed and climbed underneath the down comforter. "Why are you doing this? Is there some kind of bet on the table?"

"You're beautiful." He paused, his voice swirling in her head. "You're intelligent and sexy, an unbeatable combination. Now your turn. Why me?"

She tried to tighten her breathing so he wouldn't know the unsettling war he was causing. "You're the one who called me. I didn't call you."

"You asked me to call. You didn't say it out loud, but trust me, the point was made."

"I'm going to hang up now." Venus said it lightly and without resolve, waiting for him to protest, a small plea for her to stay on the line. He responded with only silence. Daring her, challenging her to walk away. She slid her finger to the large middle button on the phone. "I'm going to hang up now," her final threat.

The phone hummed then screamed in her ear before she could press the button... *if you'd like to make a call please hang up.* She lay there confused, her pulse erratic from the stimulation of Jake Parson's voice in her ear. "Idiot. Fool," she whispered to the unmoving ceiling fan above her head. She wrapped the pillow around her face, encasing her scream. Women were so gullible. A little attention, an ounce of wide-eyed enthusiasm, and out went all logic and reason.

She jumped when the phone rang, this time lifting herself up to see who was calling on the small white box. Her own name appeared in the digital readout, Johnston Venus.

"Airic," she breathed out in relief, the one and only, *honey.*

"Yes, hi. Sorry it's so late. Did I wake you?"

"I wasn't asleep, just daydreaming with my eyes closed."

"Good news. I can make it out there this weekend. I'll be there first thing in the morning. I'm actually on my way to the airport now."

"What happened? I thought you had to work," she asked cautiously.

"Nothing's right without you. I'll work tomorrow after dinner knowing you're in the next room instead of miles away."

"Okay." Hesitating. "See you in the morning." She let the phone slide out of her hand and squeezed the cool comfort of the pillow to her face, pushing it hard against her mouth. Her thoughts were still defiant, *why didn't you call earlier, what keeps you from picking up the phone just once before one o'clock in the morning?* It happened more frequently than she liked to admit since she'd come to Los Angeles. Airic forgetting to call, then calling as if he hadn't forgotten anything at all. His work, his schedule.

The phone rang again. Venus pulled herself up on her elbows. Unknown name. Unknown number. She snatched the cord out of the wall. She wouldn't be a fool twice.

GRAVY AND BEANS

She'd dreamt of kissing him, his hands holding her tight around the waist. Venus usually only had crazy dreams when something was weighing heavily on her mind. Too much to handle while awake so it had to be dealt with on a subconscious level. Like she and Jake Parson sliding all over each other in a full embrace at the edge of a sandy shore. Rolling around until the water soaked their bodies, causing her to gasp for breath until she'd awakened.

She was an awful person who didn't deserve a fiancé who would fly five and a half hours just to see her. She slid a hand under the cover, between her legs, curious if it was all the workings of her mind, if her body had participated in the betrayal as well. She was greeted by warm moistness. Deliciousness wasted on an arrogant man. She removed her guilty fingers, wiping the evidence against her thigh.

That's all it was. Boredom. Jake Parson wasn't anything new. Nothing she hadn't seen before. Washington, D.C., was full of them—good-looking black men with charisma and charm, deep voices and lively personalities. Jake Parson wasn't special. Just because he was rich and sexy and had a good phone-sex voice didn't mean he was a prize. Besides, she had Airic. What more could a girl ask for?

*   *   *

Airic looked like he'd stayed awake through the entire night flight. His eyes were laced with red spider veins. Underneath were pools of darkness that made an appearance whenever he was heavily stressed. Venus hadn't seen him look this tired in a long time, not since last May when his company had its initial public offering. The nerve-racking expectations. He'd hired a squad of high-tech cubs with promises of great returns, stock options dangled as carrots before their eyes. If the IPO didn't produce the results he was expecting, he feared his young staff would take their bat and ball and go home, play for another team, a winning team.

All the worry turned out to be a waste of time. The stock was released at $24 a share and climbed to almost $200 at the closing bell. She remembered the way he picked her up and spun her around, a kiss that left her breathless and dizzy. They were rich, at least he was, for a whole three days before the stock eased down to a comfortable $120 a share. It was still more than he'd anticipated. He now boasted a staff of twenty. The raft was stable in angry waters. The company was doing well, at least that's what he continually reassured her. She didn't know what to believe on days like this when he looked like he'd been run over and left on the side of the road.

"Long ride?" She tippy-toed to reach his face, kissing him softly. "As soon as we get to my place I'm going to run you a hot bath and fix you some tea. You're going to take a soak, then climb into bed."

"Yeah, that'd be nice." His eyes stayed fixed and straight ahead.

She was speechless. Where was his protest, his jokes about pampering being another marketing ploy like Valentine's, Mother's, and Father's Day. Just another excuse that required a trip to the mall. Where was the comic influx? It's not that bad, honey, I still have enough energy to make you scream like a girl. Then she'd say, I am a girl, and he would say, well then, my work is done. None of that. Only his sluggish lean body pressing on her as if she had to carry him the last mile. She stopped and turned to face him. "Baby, are you all right?"

"I'm fine. Tired. I didn't sleep on the plane." He pursed his lips and kissed her forehead. The lines more defined around his eyes. Older than Venus by a solid ten years. Neither one of them had any time to waste. Although he'd already experienced fatherhood, a marriage, and the divorce that followed, he'd made it clear that it would be all fresh and new again. A partnership, 50–50 right down the middle when they had children of their own. Why should she have to give up a career that she loved? They agreed on just about everything, even wrote it out. It made sense.

Now, when she looked at him, his head leaning slightly against the passenger window, a frosted mist forming near his open mouth, she couldn't see how things could be split down the middle. He was working so hard.

What had she done last night? Listen on the phone while a man seduced her. Cried her eyes out until she fell asleep feeling like a lecherous pig for betraying Airic's trust. The man who'd touched her life in more ways than she could name, standing by her when she needed a wall to lean on, underneath her when she needed a stable foundation, and too many times, simply a hand to hold.

"I love you, baby." She reached across letting her hand glide softly down his cheek. She traced his ear and stroked his fine soft hair. He needed a trim.

The hostage line in the parking lot began to move. She was next to pay her ransom. She pulled out a ten and waited at the open window before she realized there would be no change. The Ethiopian parking attendant sat patiently while she daydreamed and smiled at her when she finally snapped out of it. The orange-and-white-striped gate had lifted. She put the car in gear and sped off.

What was she doing here in Los Angeles, her on one side of the world, Airic on the other?

He needed her, she needed him, but now they were miles apart from each other. Was it some kind of death wish she secretly harbored for the relationship? Why had she taken the assignment so quickly? She guided her shiny white BMW over the concrete bridge and joined the five-lane traffic jam on the 405 freeway. The sky was a dim, flat gray. The sun was nothing more than a smoldering haze, no circular shape or definition to it. Not like back home. Oh! She said it again. Back home. Then what was she doing here in Los Angeles? She'd asked herself that question numerous times. Her answer always straight from the pages of *Essence, O,* and *New Woman*...unleashing her career potential, setting goals and overcoming fears. She was, after all, the millennium woman. You can have everything, right, she said to herself while tilting the rearview mirror for an eye-to-eye look at herself. Underneath it all, she simply wanted to be loved…unconditionally loved. A husband, a baby, a home with a cuddly little dog. Well, she was halfway there. She had the house in D.C. and her precious little Sandy, a pretty brown cocker spaniel, a constant reminder of Clint Fairchild. The gift that kept on giving like a Post-it note on her forehead reminding her of what she'd lost.

*   *   *

AT home Venus massaged Airic's back and shoulders, her petite brown hands working hard but not seeming to cover enough square footage of his long narrow torso. Her fingers covered with lavender oil stretched and kneaded his skin. When she was too tired to rub another muscle, she pulled the sheet up around his glistening shoulders. His eyes, covered by the thick curved lashes, remained still. She leaned over him wondering if he was in dreamland. Was she in there? Did he have his arms wrapped around her waist? Was he pulling her chin up, awaiting a kiss?

She was too old for romance. Good grief, she knew romance was about as useful as a paper towel. It did a fine job on first use, but it was temporary. Nothing worked like an old-fashioned cotton towel. Even when the edges got ragged, frayed, and thin, it did the job. Yet she couldn't help but feel like something crucial was missing. She couldn't help thinking of Jake Parson.

The phone rang loudly next to the bed. Airic's body lay still, not even a twitch. He stayed on his stomach, his head resting on his crossed arms.

Venus bounced off the bed and carried the phone into the living room without looking at the caller ID.

"Hello."

"Hey there. Just checking to see if you can pick up some peppermint extract on your way over for dinner."

Her eyes widened. Venus had forgotten about dinner at her parents' house. There was no way she could drag Airic out for an excruciatingly painful Q & A session with her mother, not as exhausted as he was.

"I can't come. I'm sorry, I should have called earlier, but I've been playing nursemaid over here with Airic. He's tired. Not feeling well." Venus looked around the room as if another excuse could be found.

"Well, if he's that tired, why'd he bother to come?"

"Guess he needed to see me, just like I needed to see him." So there. Her mother was constantly waiting for the other shoe to drop. Maybe it was Venus's track record that concerned her. The inevitable ending.

"I'll bring over a couple of plates. If he's not feeling well, he certainly doesn't need to eat any of your canned specialties."

Venus bit her lip to keep from saying something rude. Her mother wouldn't tolerate it.

"What'd you fix?"

"Brown rice, stripped beef, asparagus."

"With thick gravy?"

"Same way you've been eating it for thirty years."

"I'm sure he'd appreciate it. I know I would. Thank you, Mom."

Venus looked around the apartment and started working quickly to put it into mother-inspection shape. She picked up the magazines and moved them into a stack on the glass coffee table. When she leaned over to pick up Airic's socks and shoes, she saw a manila folder peeking from underneath the skirt of the couch. She leaned over and picked it up. Something Airic must've been looking at while he waited for Venus to run his bathwater. She looked around for his briefcase to put it in so he wouldn't leave it behind when he left Monday. It was a natural habit to look inside.

She opened it to the yellow-lined paper filled with notes, jotted numbers, and dates. She scanned the single sheet, then closed the file and was about to slide it into the black attaché before it hit her; those were future dates, with future earnings and stock prices. How would he know what the prices would be before the date happened? He had no control over that kind of thing. She opened it again and studied the dates. It was some kind of formula that calculated probability. Ah, her specialty. She always helped when she could, and he respected her business opinion and advice. She set it aside and planned to tackle it after dinner. She picked up his socks and tucked them into his shoes, threw his jacket over her arm, and grabbed his overnight bag. She took everything to the bedroom where he lay sleeping. When she passed him a second time, she pulled the chenille throw over his shoulders. He didn't stir.

•   •   •

THE telephone rang in two short bursts, signaling the intercom outside of her building. She picked up the phone quickly so it wouldn't wake Airic.

"It's me, Venus." Her mother's voice always gave her away, whether she was tired, disgusted, or in a really good mood. Today qualified as tired.

"Do you need some help, Mom?"

"I need you to open this door before I drop these hot plates." Then again, maybe it was disgust.

Venus overheard the sound of the electronic lock releasing. She hung up the phone and raced down the elevator to meet her mother.

"I got it." Venus stuck her body between the elevator doors and reached out for the bag. Pauletta was wearing her favorite black exercise pants that she never exercised in, with a long white T-shirt that said BERMUDA, accentuating the spread of time she was trying to cover.

"Airic's still sleeping."

"Oh, okay, well I'll see him another time." Her mother stayed on the lobby floor.

"No, Mom. That's not what I meant. Please come up."

She snapped her purse closed, leaving the keys in their place. "Are you sure? 'Cause I don't want to disturb him."

"Trust me, it would take more than the two of us to wake him."

Her mother came in and walked straight to the living room. "I like what you did with that wall."

Venus had painted one side an eggplant purple just a few days ago. Her mother inspected the job, looking to the corner of the ceiling and then to the floorboard. Venus lingered behind, while noticing the gray edges of her mother's hair, way past touch-up. Which was unusual since her mother had a standing appointment with Ruby every two weeks for a wash and set; and on the sixth week, whether it fell on Jesus' birthday or her own, she was in that chair for a touch-up. Maybe her mother was finally seeing the light and had plans to go natural. Venus started to mention it, then thought better of it.

"What's the landlord going to say about you putting these wild colors on the property?"

Venus set the plates on the table and came and stood by Pauletta's side. "It's just paint, Mom. They can always paint right over it. I can't stay here with white walls, it'll drive me crazy. On this side, I'm going to do a deep mustard yellow for contrast."

"That'll be interesting."

Venus wasn't sure if it was her mother's usual sarcasm and had no time to care. She was famished. She turned to the plate of food. She pulled the foil back, inhaling the aroma of steaming gravy and beef. She grabbed a fork and didn't wait to sit down at the small glass table with seating for only two. It was a simple café set she'd bought at IKEA to fill space. Temporary like the rest of the apartment.

"Ummmm, delicious." Venus ate like it was her first real meal in twenty-four hours. Which was true. She hadn't eaten a bite since yesterday sitting next to Jake Parson at the restaurant. Even then she played with her food, chewing sporadically to look like she was having fun, fitting in. "Umm. This is sooo good." Her mother seemed to be in another world, ignoring the praise, still staring at the purple wall.

"I've got to go. You know your dad won't eat if I'm not there to fix his plate." She turned and headed for the door.

"I'll walk you out." Venus said through a full mouth of beef and gravy. She wiped with the purple napkin that was sitting on the place setting to match the purple wall.

"Thanks, sweetie." She turned and hugged Venus nice and long and gave her a kiss on the cheek. "Why don't you and Airic do something special this weekend? Life is too short to be sitting around. Don't waste it."

Venus almost choked on a small piece of beef. Okay, who is this sweet woman and what has she done with my mother? "Mom, is there something wrong?"

Pauletta turned and hugged Venus again, this time tighter. "Nothing's wrong. Just try to enjoy your weekend. You deserve everything good this world has to offer. I love you."

Again, she found herself feeling off balance, the center of things that she knew and comprehended falling from underneath her. First Airic, now her mother, acting out of character.

She went back to the table, no longer feeling the surge of hunger. She tucked the edges of foil back over her plate and set it on the counter. Maybe it was her, maybe she was the one lost in space while everyone else was growing and evolving. Venus was stuck in her usual expectations. Needing her mother's sarcasm and Airic's lightheartedness. Things change, people change. But then where would that leave Venus?

EMPTY FOLDERS

THE worst part of a Monday morning was knowing she had five solid days to go. She slid underneath Airic's long arm and snuggled close. His eyes did a butterfly dance, then opened completely.

"What time is it?"

"Five-thirty." Venus didn't need a clock to know that. It was precisely the time the sun started peeping through the large window directly over her bed. "I'll make coffee." She started to get up. He stopped her.

"I feel bad."

"Don't. You were tired, you needed to rest and that's what you did. Don't feel guilty about it." He'd spent the entire two days sleeping, eyes closed, lids sealed. Although he had opened them temporarily on Saturday night in an energetic mood to make love that just as quickly sizzled out like a match in the rain.

"I think everything is working again." He lifted the sheet slightly to give her a sneak peek.

"But your flight leaves—"

Airic kissed her in midsentence. "I'll catch the next one." He pressed himself on top of her, his long body stretching across hers. She wrapped her arms around him, giving him the encouragement he needed to follow through, even though that was the last thing she wanted. Her mind was somewhere else. Driving Airic to the airport, not knowing when she'd see him again. Having to face Jake Parson. The silent battle among Legend, William, and herself. None of it she wanted to deal with.

Venus needed to be touched, to know that there was more to life than the discourse in her head. Airic moved with ease between her thighs, making her heart beat faster, sending waves of O_2 to her center. She shivered against his warm chest where his heart beat solid and strong. He was her life, a cord of rope that kept her from falling over the edge. He kept her sane. How could she even think about anyone else? Here was the only place she wanted to be. She moved with the rhythm, grinding her pelvis against him, needing the friction and the heat. She dug her fingers into the flesh of his narrow hips and directed him to drive the thoughts away one stroke at a time. She lifted her hips as far as she could with the weight of him, begging for more. She needed for him to go deeper, to love her harder.

Her mind swam to an uneven balance, leaning to a quiet space. White light, white noise. Airic's heavy breath in her ear, the rush of his heartbeat. She was sinking, falling for sure to reach the other side. She arched her back giving him endless access, letting him know she was his to do with as he willed. He let out a moan of appreciation. Then she felt his body go rigid.

"Oh God, oh baby." Hoarse whispers crept from his throat and into her ear. She urgently took her last chance to reach the other side, moving her hips into position, cupping her own breast, closing in on the outer circle of her nipples, kneading until they were ripe to the touch. For Venus it was as simple as breathing. Capturing as much fuel for the moment until her breath was caught. When she stopped, the plane would shift, rolling her down the hill, into the light place. She held on waiting for the collapse of pleasure into each other's arms... then the precious solid five minutes where they would cuddle in each other's arms, then pop up like dual bagels in the toaster.

Time to go.

*   *   *

"VENUS, have you seen a file that I had lying out... right here?" Airic was walking around in a frenzy, the collar of his coat twisted inside, his tie angled to the side. His bony fingers dug through the magazine stack on the coffee table.

"Right here." Venus held it up. "I was going to take a look at it for you."

He took it out of her hand before she could finish, packing it away. "Did you?"

"No, I never got a chance." Bewilderment set in. Her eyes followed his movement. "What's wrong?"

"Nothing. I don't want to be late. I can't miss this flight." He threw his bag over his shoulder and leaned over to kiss her.

"You seem a little agitated. If you don't want me looking at your stuff, just say so."

Airic grabbed the smooth point of her chin so she couldn't pull away again, kissing her lightly on the lips. "That's not it. I just can't be late." Another kiss between the eyes. "Ready?"

"Sure." Venus pulled the door closed and followed him out of the apartment to the elevator. While they waited, she turned toward him and began fixing his collar and tie. "I hope you're taking care of yourself better than this when I'm not around."

"Nothing can replace having you around."

The elevator doors opened. The mirrored walls made the elevator feel crowded with only the two of them. "Do you mean that, or are you just making kissy talk?"

He pulled her close. "I mean it." He pulled away just as quickly when the doors opened, making Venus skip to keep up with him to the car. He took the keys and reminded her that she drove too slow. She moved to the passenger side grudgingly, thinking about his hard pedal-to-the-metal driving.

Thank goodness the traffic was steady enough to keep him below eighty miles an hour. Venus chewed on her inner cheek the entire way to the airport as he stop-and-goed.

"Kiss-kiss," he said, standing at the curb of the gate. She puckered up and threw her arms around his shoulders. Airic began to pull away before she could finish the thought. "I'll call you."

"Okay." She waved with one hand. "See you."

He mouthed the words *I love you.*

*   º   *

THE first face she saw was Legend's. His deep strong smile faded when he saw her coming through the glass doors. He ended the conversation he was having and closed his cell phone.

"Good morning, Sergeant," he said, saluting her.

Good morning, asshole. She made a half grin. She looked at her watch. "Where's the rest of the crew?"

"Jake is on his way. I was just talking to him before you walked in."

"Well, time is his money." She pulled out empty folders and fanned them before putting them back. If Jake Parson said one word about his little phone tag, she would kill him. Venus opened her briefcase on the oversized glass table. She restacked, reshuffled, and redid everything in arm's reach. Legend sat across from her, watching silently. His smugness was a sure sign that she was the topic of conversation between him and Jake, whether it was only moments ago when she entered the room or right after his test flight a couple of nights ago. Surely, she was the cause of Legend's cheery mood. Venus swallowed hard, not comfortable with the smug grin on his face. She had intended on blasting him first thing, for not telling her of their existing relationship with Jake. First-degree sabotage. Now she felt powerless.

"What did you guys do after I left Friday? Get anything done?" She measured her breaths, working them in slowly, in-out.

"Not really. Just more brainstorming." He leaned back, letting his dark long locks hang independently of his shoulders. "So how was your weekend?" Legend asked.

"Good, thank you. How was yours?"

"Couldn't have been better."

"And why was that?" Venus kept her face in an empty file.

"Hung out with some friends I hadn't seen for a while. Kicked it at the Lakers game. Then went to an after party. You?" Again, the know-it-all smile.

"Nice and quiet." She slid a yellow notepad across the table. "Do you think you can recall any of the conversation you guys had on Friday? It would be helpful." She rose and pulled on the heavy glass door. "I'm going for coffee, want any?"

"No, I'm cool, but thanks for—"

Venus was already out the door and headed toward the stairs. She had to step out of the room before she jumped over the table and swung Legend around by his woolly locks.

"Is there some place I can get some coffee around here?" Venus asked the new receptionist, a stick man dressed in all black. He had a phone wrapped around his head like a helicopter pilot.

"Yes, ahah, airight. No problem." He pushed a button on his hip.

"Now what were you saying?"

"Coffee."

His bones almost looked like they hurt under his black knit turtleneck as he pointed across the way. "First open space to your right, make a right, make another right and there's a full-fledged Starbucks attached to the end." He turned away from her, pressing his hip. "This is me, is that you?" He laughed into the tiny mouthpiece.

Venus followed the shiny palette of colored tiles, similar to the yellow brick road, only it was pastel pink, green, and orange. She just wanted a simple cup of coffee. She stepped in line behind a smorgasbord of spray-colored hair, pierced ears, and people who had no business claiming to be fashionistas.

She felt a bump as the herd moved closer to the happy Starbucks cashier. She felt it again, turning around abruptly.

"Good morning." Jake Parson stood over her, his goatee crisply outlined on his face. His lips equally arched in perfection.

"You mind backing up a little?" Venus put her small hand in the center of his chest and held steady while her knees tried to give way. Solid. Thick and hard—his chest, that is.

"It's kind of tight in here. Sorry." He lifted his hands to show he was doing no harm, then laced them behind his back. Still, he scooted closer. She was being molested in a public place. She should hold up her hand and scream for security. Instead she stayed put, determined not to be moved. Not to budge. Her boots were rooted, solid in one spot.

He tapped her on the shoulder, pointing ahead. "Your turn."

There was no one in front of her, a space as large as three people served. She stepped up. "A double Grande Espresso."

"Going for the gusto, huh." Jake Parson stood on her right side, fishing into his wallet. "These are together; get me a tall, whatever's on tap." He handed the cashier a twenty.

"A pastry or cookie, Mr. Parson?"

"Not today. Too much work getting it off." He patted himself, making a point to smooth his hand over his silk sweater, leaving the imprint of his tightly muscled chest and stomach.

They moved together to the left as the unwritten rules dictated, waiting patiently for their special blends. Jake kept a good two-inch distance. Venus reached for a couple of napkins to pat her nose and forehead. He grabbed both coffees and started walking. She followed.

"You have mine." She skipped closer, carefully reaching across his chest.

"Right, I just thought we were headed to the same place."

She unhinged the coffee from his manicured nails. "I can carry my own, thanks."

"I like your hair this morning. Did you twist it or something?"

He caught Venus off guard. He had no idea what dangerous waters he was treading with this subject. Hair had been her driving force for the better part of her life. At one time, she defined herself by her ever glossy relaxed strands, making sure they received all the loving care her salary could muster. Now, this man was standing in front of her, eyeing her natural finger-length style, looking at her like she'd done something special just by waking up this morning and spraying Kiehl's Moisturizing Spritz, working it through with a few quick tugs and swirls. He was messing in dangerous territory. Mighty dangerous territory.

"Thank you," she said dryly, recovering, not believing she'd just fallen for it. She started walking again with a mission.

"Ah, Miss Johnston."

She stopped, pivoted around on her riding boot heel.

"We're this way." He was ahead once again.

*　　*　　*

WILLIAM and Legend were inside the conference room, both standing at the wall-sized windows looking down on the sample-cutting floor.

"Hate to interrupt," Venus said, sliding into her seat.

"Hey, man." William reached over Venus's head, shaking Jake's hand. They stood over her, two well-dressed pillars. Either direction she turned, she'd be staring into someone's crotch. She sipped her coffee. "Can we get started?" She slipped on her black-rimmed glasses, trying hard to stare straight ahead.

Finally, everyone took a seat around the table. All hail the queen, she was thinking. She would not be squashed today. If they tried, they'd be eating her size sixes.

She looked over the notes Legend had scrawled illegibly. Something about a test market, maybe; she turned the pad upside down, then back again. Not today. Not today, she chanted in her mind. She would not let Legend make her look foolish. She was beginning to wonder if it was all worth it, working with the dynamic duo. Sure, they'd done the best ads Nike had seen in five years. Sure, they'd turned Jack Daniel's reputation around from being a brown bag beverage to the urban beverage of choice. Did that mean she had to endure this insolence? She'd produced her share of miracles, too; Legend and William weren't the only ones. She'd made the Avon lady more than a ding-dong housewife. She'd made the company understand that women—black, white, Spanish, or Asian—wanted to feel strong. Believe in themselves. Who better to represent that than Venus and Serena Williams? A $15 million ad campaign with nearly $70 million in newly generated sales. Damn right she had made a miracle happen.

"I think the first thing we're going to have to do here, guys, is make a commitment to work together"—she looked over at Legend then to Jake—"as a full-fledged team. And by that I'm just saying that every team has a captain, which in this case happens to be me...if you don't think I'm qualified to be in that position, I will surely step aside and make room for whomever you feel is worthy." The silence that followed was hollow and uneasy. Venus didn't blink, tried real hard not to fall out in laughter. God, she loved power.

"Absolutely. I have every confidence in you, Ms. Johnston." Jake looked over to the other two men. "I'm sure we're in full agreement."

"No doubt." Legend placed both dark hands on the table, strumming lightly.

"I have the utmost respect for you, Venus." William smiled, twisting one of the many rings on his fingers.

"Okay ... then let's get started."

That was easier than she thought. Too easy. They could be appeasing her to throw her off guard, or they could mean what they say. She deserved their respect. Just as Jake had reasoned, whatever chips were sitting on Legend's and William's shoulders were not put there by her and they knew it.

For two solid hours they threw ideas on the wall. It was a bull-run session; they all agreed a new brand for the young women's side was necessary, but the men's line could stay under JPWear. Jake liked the name *Feline* and had been carrying it around for some time, something about an ex-girlfriend who took no prisoners. The young men's line needed to come out strong and represent JPWear with a sophisticated style for the high-end stores and keep the general line going into the low end. They needed a superpower to represent the new brand. Slick, sharp, and hot.

"Lila Kelly." Venus tossed it out like they were playing Pictionary.

Everybody gave it a minute, rolled it around like a wine-tasting class.

"Too new."

"Too soft."

"Too cuddly."

"Guys, you're making her sound like a plush toy." She jumped up. "That's it. That's JPWear. Isn't that what we want? That's what it's all about. Lila Kelly is all that and more. She's young, sexy, and mysterious. She can sing her ass off."

"She's fine as hell," William of little words added on. His light eyes grew misty, thinking of a pretty face and expensive extensions. Venus rolled her eyes.

"Anyway. She's first choice, really the only choice. She's hot right now. She's going to milk that number one spot for at least another year, straight through the Grammys and the other slew of awards shows. We've got to get her now. Hopefully Kani didn't think of it first; he's working his way into a women's line, going after Baby Phat."

"That line's got no sex appeal; I've seen it," William chimed in.

"They wouldn't want to pay for Lila Kelly," Jake added. "She's going to be pricey. I already know that. Number one on the Billboard charts for four weeks in a row. Just tack on a million per week."

"No way." Venus leaned on her knuckles. "First thing we offer her is a chance to design a couple of pieces. Young girls are a sucker for that. Hell, old girls are a sucker for that. There's not a female in the country who hasn't dreamed of designing her own clothes; you can thank Mattel for brainwashing us with Barbie and paper dolls. Then we'll offer her a small piece of the company."

"Ah, Venus, I think you're forgetting…paper dolls were a product of the seventies. She probably wasn't even born." William apologized with his eyes for having to bring the bit of truth to her attention. Lila Kelly was young and Venus was not.

"Paper dolls, or computer-aided design, it's still the most exciting thing for a girl to do, plus she'll be part owner."

"Oh hell no!" Jake leaned back in his chair. "Stock? I'm not giving away my company."

"Everybody's doing it, Jake." Legend's thick soapbox voice now sounded like music to Venus's ears. "A small slice of the pie. The risk is far lower than up-front cash and prizes. JPWear offers stock options, just like Microsoft. If the campaign is successful, everybody wins. If it's not, nobody loses."

"See, y'all going to mess around and get me kicked outta here. First the lights, then I won't be able to pay my rent. Then all four of us are going to be looking for gainful employment." Jake let out a nervous laugh. He was half serious, half joking. But he was in, Venus knew.

"Don't even think like that. If anything, this is going to get your crown back. This is going to be so hot!" She tapped her pen on the edge of the table.

They wrapped up the day with a delegation of tasks. They needed to get Lila Kelly to tentatively agree so they could start the media attention. They needed the media attention so Lila Kelly would agree. One big circle, which came first, the chicken or the egg. Each and every step depended on the last and the one before.

*   *   *

"SMART and sexy, see I told you," Jake whispered, catching up with Venus.

She'd just made it down the roller-coaster stairs and was still trying to catch her breath and thank her creator at the same time. She stopped walking and eyed him over her glasses. The excitement of the meeting was a turn-on, she had to admit, but she wanted to combat his enthusiasm with a dose of reality.

"What do you want? No, seriously," Venus asked, seeing his grin get bigger. "Tell me where you see this going. Let's save ourselves a lot of trouble here. Is it the challenge, the excitement of going after a hard case? Is it my miniskirts, the boots... what?"

He started laughing. A full onboard, deep belly laugh. "Dinner. Just dinner."

Venus shook her head and walked away. Must be the miniskirts, she thought. Gotta go shopping. She couldn't help but smile. The fun was always in the chase.

TESTS

Her apartment was dark. When she walked through the door, the red light on the answering machine was blinking furiously. She pressed play while she dropped her Bergdorf bags to the floor. Shoes, her only shopping weakness. Two neatly boxed pairs hit the carpet while she ran, fumbling with her clothes. She listened to the messages play through the open door of the bathroom. The first two were Jake Parson. She knew, even though they were hang-ups.

"Hey, Precious, it's Dad. Uh..." The machine cut off. "Hey, Precious, call me when you get in, it's important."

Venus tried not to panic. The last time she'd received one of these cryptic calls her father only wanted to ask if she'd help him shop for her mother's birthday. After forty years of marriage, you'd think they'd know what each other liked. Not wasting another moment, she came back to the living room and dialed her father.

"Daddy, hi."

"Hey, Precious."

"What's going on?"

Her sweet, strong, and loving father, Henry Johnston. As a child she'd almost forgotten her own name because he only called her Precious. She could feel him walking while he was talking, going somewhere for privacy. The movement of being transported on the phone made her dizzy.

"What is it, Daddy?" she asked again, pressing her fingers to her temple.

"Hold on." He continued walking.

"Sorry about that. Had to move to my room." That meant he was standing up against a wall with his hand in his khaki pants pocket with his shirt hanging over his fifty-year-old belt. His room was a hobby station for his model train collection. The massive display took up the entire center of the room, complete with tiny towns, railroad stations, and farms.

"It's about your mother. Tests. She didn't want you to know. She didn't want anyone to know. But I need to tell you."

"What kind of tests?"

"The doctor found a cyst in her breast."

Venus held her breath. She could feel the heat flush through her cheeks. "A cyst?" Her mouth turned dry and her knees buckled. The couch in the living room was only a step away if she could make it.

"They want to go in and take a sample, find out what kind of cells they are."

"Oh, God, when did all this happen? What do you mean, she didn't want me to know? Oh God!"

"Hold on, now. We both can't be wrecks. I need you to tell me everything is going to be all right. I can hardly see straight right now. I'm scared out of my mind. I need a calm head here."

"Oh, I know, yes, of course, everything is going to be fine. When is the test?" Venus swallowed the urge to cry.

"In the morning. I don't know what I'd do if I lost—"

"Daddy, no. Don't think like that. I could tell by the way she was acting when she came over Saturday something wasn't right. Oh, God." Venus was trying to hold on to herself, but it was difficult. What if it was cancer?

"A biopsy?" She wrapped her arms around her stomach. She needed to be strong for her father. "What time is the test?"

"First thing in the morning. You can't come, Precious. She'll be mad, full of shame, and I don't want her more upset than she already is."

"I'm not, I wouldn't show up like that. But I want you to call the minute, the second, you are out of that doctor's office with the results."

"This is bad, pretty bad. I've never loved anyone like I love your mother." His breathing slowed, as if remembering something. "We may have our problems. We've always had sort of a shaky thing going from the outside, people probably wondered how we made it this long, but I wouldn't trade a minute, not a day, with your mother. I love her."

"I know you do, Daddy. I love her, too."

"No, Precious, I don't think you understand. Pauletta and I...your mother is my soul. If I lost her, you may as well bury me, too."

Venus almost tripped over the shopping bag, not seeing from the blur of tears in her eyes, trying desperately to get to the bathroom tissue roll.

*   *   *

SHE hung up feeling wrung out of shape. Nothing worked, her arms and legs stayed frozen as she stood in the middle of the floor, the purple wall pushing toward her. She thought about her mother staring at it, pictured her standing in the exact same spot. Possibly feeling the same way, as if it would fall forward, crushing her, stopping her from taking another breath. She picked up her coat and ran out of the apartment.

The cold night air felt good. She could breathe out here. Pray and God would hear her, out here. She stopped at the corner and pushed the pedestrian signal. She hurried across the street in front of the line of headlights, waiting impatiently. On the other side she didn't know which direction she wanted to go. Wilshire Boulevard was an endless stretch of restaurants, boutiques, and office buildings. What she really craved was open space. A rural thicket of trees, a park bench to sit on, somewhere she could beg for God's help in private. Break down and ask for mercy, ask that her mother be all right. It'd been a while since she asked for any favors, wanted any special attention. She didn't ask for much, never had. A promotion, a safe trip as she boarded a plane, a blessing to the mother of a missing child on the news. Simple things. But this required concentration, hands clasped, eyes shut tight. Dear God...

A bus stop with large Plexiglas panels surrounding a bench came into sight. Venus sat down and inhaled cautiously, spent from walking. She put her head down and put her hands together. She felt the air move briskly in front of her face as cars passed by, the sound of traffic graphically loud.

Soon she didn't hear anything but her own thoughts, her own words.

Her own fears, and desires. She'd figured a long time ago that there was no difference between the two. Fear and desire came from the same deep place of the soul, wanting something so badly that it surpassed all logic and reasoning. She understood the consequences of both but couldn't stop herself from asking...dear God...please make my mother okay. I can't lose her. Please, God. She sat still, letting a spray of dust surround her face while a bus stopped, then took off again. I can't lose her, Daddy can't lose her. Tim wouldn't make it either. You've got to help, you've got to make this right. Venus stayed in one spot until she heard God concede, a confirmation letter very plainly written, ask and you will receive. She'd been taught that in the days of patent leather and pigtails, *ask and you will receive.*

*   *   *

SHE sat in front of the TV chewing on the inside of her cheek. A long night awaited her. She'd already called Airic three times, two pages, and nothing in return.

Just like Daddy, now she needed someone to tell her it would be all right. Funny how people needed to pass the burden of information, as if it weighed too much in their own possession. It had to be shared to feel relief. Spread around and thinned down as if it would lose potency if one more person knew.

The phone shook in her hand. It had to be Airic on the cell. "Yes."

"What's going on, what's so urgent?"

"I thought you'd never call. I'm sitting here going crazy. My mom is going in for tests tomorrow. There was a spot on her mammogram."

"Babe." He stalled for a minute. "I'm sorry. You all right?"

"No. I'm not all right. Why is it that you can never be found? This is just so ridiculous, you out there and me out here. It wouldn't be so bad if you were reachable, but it's like you're underground or something."

"Hey, hey, now, calm down." Airic's emotional reserve could only fill a glass halfway. His first reaction to anything was to look at it logically, what could be done to *fix* the problem. "Your mom's going to be fine. No matter what the results show. It's not 1980, not even 1990. This is 2000; medicine has come a long way. First things first, finding the best doctor for her case. In the morning, get on the horn, check into doctors in the area who specialize in women's breast issues."

She sniffed and wiped using the sleeve of Airic's flannel shirt.

"Your mother isn't the type to let something happen to her, she's a fighter. Just like her daughter, a fighter. This thing doesn't stand a chance against a Johnston. There's nothing conclusive, right?"

"Right." Her sarcasm made it obvious it wasn't the only thing making her cry.

"Listen, there is nothing, or no one, more important to me than you. Don't ever think it's not you I'm working for. I'm trying to get to you like you're trying to get to me. It's a constant work in process. When I've got all these business issues tied up, we're taking a long vacation...alone. Might even make use of that ring I put on your finger."

Venus stared down at the solitaire diamond she'd been wearing for two long years. It looked far bigger through the kaleidoscope of her tears. "Everything is going to be fine, baby," he reassured her before she rolled over in an exhausted ball. "Your mom is going to be fine. You know it. Tell me you know it."

She stayed quiet, not knowing if she wanted to partake in such a simplistic thought. Not knowing if she wanted to be an accomplice to such naïveté. "She will," she said quietly. Then, "She'll be fine," strong and loud in a definitive declaration. Venus held on to Airic's words of encouragement. As soon as she fell asleep the phone rang again. She opened the cell phone in her hand, still scrunched in a fetal ball on the couch. "Hello." Somewhere, a phone was still ringing. She closed her cell, then reached for her home line.

"Did I wake you?" Jake Parson sounded quiet and humble.

"Now's not a good time." Her words came out as thick as her tongue.

"Oh, I see. Okay."

"No. Wait. Can I call you back? I just need to regroup for a minute."

"Sure."

Venus ran to the bathroom and threw water on her face. She studied her eyes in the mirror. Tired. The news about her mother had already sucked ten years off her life. She pulled out her toothbrush and dabbed a little toothpaste on it. She brushed, grateful for the tingling spearmint.

When she was younger, she and her brother each had their own box of Arm & Hammer baking soda, sticking their wet toothbrushes in and coming out with white caked powder. The gritty powder made her want to rinse and spit before she got the job done. Her brother...she closed her eyes. She'd already had her allotment of tears for one night. She'd call him tomorrow.

She slid into her bed, bringing the phone and Jake's number with her. "Hi, now what can I do with you, I mean for you?" Venus squeezed her eyes shut, cursing herself for the faux pas.

Jake was polite enough not to take notice. "What do you think about going to Lila Kelly directly, skip the agents, skip the management? My friend hooked me up with two tickets to her concert, backstage passes, after party, the works. We could—"

"We?"

"Of course. You think I'm going to give you the tickets and let you kick it with honey while I'm sitting at home playing solitaire? I don't think so." He coughed the words out.

Venus rolled over on her side. "I don't know. Isn't there some kind of ethics line we'd be crossing? Approaching someone without representation?"

"We're not talking dollars, not trying to get any contracts signed. We'll just get in and see how it sits with her. Look, I just don't see the point in pushing this idea without a willing participant. I need to know where she stands. What she's about."

Venus thought...what harm could it do? She already worked with him daily. One added night wouldn't hurt.

"I'll go with you." She faded off, closing her eyes.

"Good deal. The concert is Thursday."

"Jake."

"Yeah?"

"Will you do me a favor, a huge favor, and not discuss this with anyone?...Legend or William."

"I wouldn't think of it. I have double the reasons that you do."

"Oh yeah, like what?"

"Like one, I don't need anyone accusing me of sucking up to the pretty lady with the pretty smile, accusing me of preferential treatment. I wouldn't want anyone to think we were on a date. I have my standards."

"Ohhhh, yeah, right." Venus rolled back over, staring up at the ceiling fan. She'd been here before. "I'll talk to you tomorrow."

"See you in the Starbucks line."

Venus hung up with the *pretty* smile on her face. For a minute she'd forgotten about her mom and dad. But only for a minute.

STRAWS

VENUS was in a fog, right along with the fuzzy layer that surrounded the morning air. The traffic didn't faze her. She looked straight ahead, then shifted her vision to her cell phone every time she inched forward. She was waiting for her father to call with news about her mother. The longer it took to get downtown, the better. She'd be no good anyway with the anxiety that was crawling up her spine.

Pauletta Johnston, and her no-nonsense take on life, was all Venus could think about. She could only imagine her mother's way of dealing with this...she was either going to live or die, period. No middle ground, no brighter side. Things are what they are. If the tests came back positive, she would simply throw up her hands and claim that it's her time. There would be no chemotherapy, no radical surgeries, no visits to healers. It struck Venus how different she and her mother were, complete opposites, seeing things from extreme sides of the fence. But then again, that straight line between them, she on one end and Venus on the other, had served more as a link, a true connection that led to deeper understanding.

Venus believed in every abstract theory known to humanity, while her mother kept herself grounded in her Baptist beliefs, no time for the free spirits of the world. But what about the power of positive thinking, the ability to change the outcome of things? Venus had come home from college filled with questions about the universe after a trying first semester. A load of twenty-eight credits, an affair with her computer class instructor, rooming with an eccentric roommate who lit candles and incense all day while the teachings of Krishnamurti played loud on the tape player. She'd closed her door, but it seeped in anyway. Venus had absorbed it through the air, the burning incense, through the walls, the words and theories, freedom of the mind. She'd tried to explain to her mother the concept, the power of the mind. Pauletta simply shook her head, not bothering to look up while she prepared the corn bread stuffing for Thanksgiving, "God set those plans in motion long before you could believe in anything. The only thing you do with all that thinking is take the long way."

VENUS stopped and looked up at the JPWear building. The outside stucco appeared gray, matching the sky and her mood. She'd made it here by some strange force. She hadn't paid attention to one exit, street sign, or stoplight. Maybe her mother was right... Regardless of what she did or believed, she'd end up where she was meant to. It was out of her hands. She picked up her cell phone and slipped it into her platinum leather bag, left unzipped for easy access. She got out and locked her car, strategically stepping around the potholes in the downtown street.

"Hey, I was getting worried about you." Jake Parson met her at the base of the wobbly stairs. "Double espresso, that's two shots." He handed her the Starbucks cup.

"Sorry I'm late." She took the cup from his hand, careful to avoid contact with his perfect brown fingers. "Thank you." She was taken aback by the small gesture, pausing to stare at the cup to make sure it was real. "I guess this is to make up for waking me in the middle of the night."

"Absolutely. Anything I can do to keep our little project moving smoothly." His smooth skin creased at the sides of his mouth with his smile.

She led the way up, realizing he wasn't going to go first. She was grateful she wore her new midlength skirt instead of the micro-mini still laid out on her bed. William and Legend were sitting across from each other at the long conference table, both on their cell phones having similar conversations.

Jake signaled for them to hang up, doing a roll with his hand. They both closed the small black casings at the same time.

"Wassup?" William stood up and slapped hands with Jake as if he hadn't just seen him yesterday, or the day before. "This is the deal. Arista is going to let us license the picture of Lila from her new CD for the T-shirts. We're going to do a test market, see how those sell with a close net distribution in D.C., Atlanta, and of course NYC. We get the numbers back on that and we got proof that the deal is profitable."

Venus looked between the two men. "Proof?" She chastised Jake with her eyes.

"Actually it was something Legend wanted to pursue, and I didn't think it was a bad idea."

"It makes sense to get some real numbers on paper, Venus. You know that more than anybody," Legend said with a calmness that made Venus want to hurl her coffee toward him.

"Real numbers? The fact that she sold a million records in five weeks, that's proof. The T-shirt thing is going to tip off every manufacturer and distributor in the business. We're going to have a bidding war on our hands. It's a waste of time, and money."

Legend stood up and walked to the other side of the room to make his point. "By the time the competition even knows what we're doing, our line will be off and running."

"So you intend to run the T-shirts with Lila Kelly's face when we don't have a shred of communication between her and us."

"It was your great idea to base this entire launch on one woman; now you don't even know if she's coming aboard." Legend's words came out accusatory. "Aren't you supposed to be the great rainmaker?"

"Wait a minute . . . calm down." Jake moved between the bickering couple. "This is getting a little out of hand. Table this until cooler heads prevail. Venus is right about one thing, the risk of launching a test campaign without any communication with the Kelly management might not be a good idea."

"We've got Arista's permission," William interjected.

"But we're trying to work directly with Lila Kelly for the entire line. That's like going to her father for her hand in marriage first and asking her second. Women just don't play that anymore. We're talking about getting her directly involved, then we go around her back? Come on."

Legend's tone was intact but his face showed signs of defeat, something he would never get used to. He excused himself while Jake and Venus continued the conversation. William followed, like a child caught in a divorce war.

The studio was airy and empty on the main floor. Now that it was just she and Jake in the room, she let the sadness override her. Jake came and stood by her side. "Don't worry. Lila Kelly is not going to pass this opportunity, I can feel it."

Venus stared down at the cell phone she still held tightly in her hand. The blank face screamed at her, no missed calls, no message from her father. "I'm not worried about that. I mean, I am, but..." She plopped into one of the Martian-shaped chairs by the corner window, feeling exhausted. The small battle with Legend had depleted what little energy she had left. She wanted to know what was going on. Her heart would burst and roll away if something were to happen to her mother. Cancer was such an ugly word, something people dealt with every day. But this would be a first for Venus, first for her immediate family. She couldn't think of anyone down the family tree who'd had cancer, a lot of close calls, but never the actual demon. Her uncle Gordon had some lymph nodes removed from the inside of his throat from a tobacco-chewing habit, but as soon as he had the scare he gave up the dirty business and that was the end of it. There'd been sickle cell for one of her cousins, the exact same age as Venus—well, who would have been if she hadn't died six years ago as soon as she hit the thirty mark. She'd been fighting the disease all of her life. Jenie.

Venus put her hands over her face. Death was an inevitable part of this life, but it never made it easy. Her many aunts and uncles were starting to pass away in old age. It was inevitable. But not her mother. Not now.

"Hey, hey... what's going on?" Jake walked away, coming back quickly with tissue.

Venus wiped, and blew. "It's not about you, JPWear. I'm dealing with some other stuff right now. I'm sorry about the outburst."

He pulled up a chair and sat down. "You want to talk about it? I know I'm not *honey*, but I can still listen." He remained quiet, waiting in vain for the humor to set in.

Venus peeked at him from her bloodshot eyes. "No, this is pretty bad." She whispered, tearing the tissue into a rat's nest in her lap.

"Tell me."

She sniffed, then wiped again, shaking her head.

"I have a suggestion, let's get out of here, get some fresh air."

"I'm waiting for a phone call, important news." She blew again with the tissue he'd supplied.

"Whatever news you were going to get sitting here in this corner, you can get somewhere quiet and peaceful." He helped her up like a rag doll. "Come on." He picked up her bag. "Good grief." He pretended to be weighted down then suddenly able to stand straight when she took the bag out of his hand. Once again the stab at humor was wasted on Venus. For now, there was no good to be found in the world.

*   *   *

THEY drove in silence with the top down in his small two-seater. The wind whistled in her ears while they sped down the Santa Monica freeway. Midmorning there was no traffic. The sky was gray with overcast appearing as a threat of rain, but it would burn off by lunchtime. Venus kept her phone pressed against her rib cage so she would feel it vibrate.

"Where are we going? I don't want to be too far out of the city. I might have to get back fast." She spoke above the music and the car racing through the wind at full speed.

"Not too far, I promise."

Before Venus had realized it, she had fallen asleep. Car travel did that to her when she had the privilege of feeling safe on the passenger side.

She opened her eyes when the car stopped moving. They were parked. The distinct sound of seagulls and waves filled her ears. The beach was a few steps away.

"I can't get out," she told him, leading his vision to her camel suede boots that the moist sand would surely destroy.

"Take them off. Little sand between those toes will do you good. Sand is like an instant pedicure. It sloughs off the dead skin and massages your feet."

Venus looked at him strangely.

"What? I'm not supposed to know about that kind of stuff?"

"What do you do, read *Glamour* and *Essence* in your free time?" she asked, peeling off her boots.

"Actually, there're men's magazines out there with better advice than your girlie periodicals any day of the week. I thought you were in the know, Miss Johnston." He picked off his shoes one at a time, sliding the socks inside. His feet were nice, she had to admit. He rolled up his pant legs, then looked for Venus to start her stripping session.

"I have panty hose on, go wait over there," she instructed.

He got out of the car and stood with his hands in his pockets facing the water. She raised her skirt high enough to get a hold of her stockings, working them down around her ankles. She peered back at him. He was still staring out in the opposite direction.

"Okay. Ready." Her first step sank deep into the warm sand. She wanted to cry out in delight. It had been at least a year since she'd been to the beach. The shores of the Pacific had always been a source of solitude and peace for her. A place to come and let all the worries glide away with each roll of the tide.

"I love the beach," he said to the open air, reflecting what she was feeling at that very moment. They both took a deep cleansing pause. "You all right, you need my jacket?" Jake touched her shoulder, as if testing the reliability of her sweater coat. His tight square jaw reminded her of the romantic heroes in fiction. Coming to the rescue with love and goodwill. She had to force herself to turn away from him.

"No, I'm good, thank you." Even though the sky was a serene gray, the air was still a comfortable temperature, the sand was still warm.

He slipped his arm through hers and they started walking, "I grew up in Los Angeles, all my life, and you know the first time I ever went to the beach I was seventeen years old. Damn near a grown man, and I had never been to the beach. I couldn't even swim. When I went away to college, and people found out I was from California, they used to talk to me like I was some surfer dude, saying stuff like gnarly and surf's up. They had no idea that I grew up in Central Los Angeles, on dry land, locked into my neighborhood, with no way out."

Venus walked close by his side. "I know, people find out you're from Los Angeles, and they have these immediate pictures of big-tit women from *Baywatch*. I guess the same way we think people from Oklahoma ride horses to work or New Yorkers don't know how to drive, period."

"I never thought that," he said, leaning down to pick up a shell. "I didn't know anything except what was happening right in my own neighborhood. People getting shot for no reason, girls I thought were pretty turning up pregnant before I even got a chance to ask them out. Friends doing time for selling a joint, getting out of prison more a criminal than when they went in. I pretty much thought it was going on the same way everywhere."

Venus bent over and picked up a shell, too. This one large, glistening white. "Listen." She put it to his ear. The hollow sound of wind passing. He closed his eyes. Venus knew what he was feeling, the escape. The sound that transported her on so many occasions. Unlike Jake, she had spent a great deal of time at the beach. On picnics with her family, she, her mother, father, and brother would set up camp on a grassy hill area. Her mother, who hated the sand and never got into the water, preferred sitting on the wide-spread blanket in her hot-pink one-piece bathing suit with her dark square sunglasses, the entire time. She kept watch over the foil-covered fried chicken and Tupperware containers of potato salad and sliced watermelon, so the seagulls wouldn't attack. Venus and Timothy would play around in the salty waves with her father nearby, practicing his breaststroke. After a couple of hours her mother would walk to the shoreline, standing with her thick legs and solid waist, and wave them in, "Time to come eat! Come on now, get out of that water."

Venus had drifted off, too, now realizing Jake was holding her hand, his hand helping her press the smooth shell to his face. "I like that, like it a lot. That's why I bought my place over here. Trying to make up for lost time."

"You live here?" They stood in front of a row of tall slender condo-miniums, each one painted a sunny pastel color. His was a soft sea blue.

He took two steps at a time getting to the front porch. He unlocked the sliding door and pushed it open for her.

"My feet are all sandy."

"I own a vacuum. Come on." Jake held the door open for her.

She padded her way into the spacious entry. One entire wall on the first floor was windows looking out toward the sea. "This is nice." Venus wanted to tell him it was breathtaking, something she'd wished for herself a time or two, but her strength was ebbing lower by the minute. She sat down on the plush leather couch, feeling every bit as exhausted as she probably looked. Last night she'd slept in two-hour pockets, never really getting any rest.

"I'll get you some water." His soft padded steps fell silent against the hardwood floor.

She looked around the modern decor. The light tan walls mixed with red and black accents. African art sat on the shelves and on the walls. The leather couches. The candles strategically placed around the side tables. The stereo system with speakers built into the walls. This was a bachelor's web. She couldn't help feeling like the unsuspecting fly who'd fallen into his trap.

"Here you go." He placed a plate of fruit and cheese on the table in front of her. "I bet you don't eat breakfast."

Venus shoved two red grapes into her mouth. Sweet, succulent, and tender—she was referring to the grapes but thought the description equally fitting for Jake. His sleeves were folded back, and his forearms had caught her attention when he set the tray down. She could easily imagine what the rest of him looked like, the even magenta brown tone of his skin. The ridges of his muscles, tightly flexed.

"What's your favorite music?"

Venus stopped fantasizing long enough to answer, "Mostly old-school mellow stuff, Isley Brothers, Al Jarreau. None of the so-called Nu Soul have anything on their sound. You knew what time it was when an Isley beat came on the stereo. Time to just kick back, let the groove steal you away." She picked up the plate and laid it in her lap, using both hands to pick the grape cluster clean, leaving a bare vine. "I needed that." She dusted the cracker crumbs off her skirt and into the empty plate while he fumbled with his CD collection and shifted things around in the disc tray.

The sound of an Isley Brothers song came out quietly, unpronounced, filling the space where she sat like another source of air. She pressed her knees tightly against each other when the first bar sailed out softly ... "I've been thinking of you, and you've been thinking of me ..."

"Where's the bathroom?" she blurted out, standing up abruptly.

He pointed over her head. She turned around, feeling almost drunk, and wandered off. When the warm walls of the bathroom surrounded her, she closed the door.

"You look mahvelous, dahling," she said to the mirror. She leaned in close over the sink. Her lipstick was eaten off, eyes bloodshot. Not the picture of seduction. The medicine cabinet beckoned to be opened. She wasn't surprised to find it completely empty. It was the first place women went to check out a man's personality, his hygiene and habits. She closed it, looking around. The bathroom was spotless. He probably never came in here anyway. It was the guest bathroom, neat and classy like the rest of his place. A copy of *Black Man's Quarterly* displayed from the top of the chrome magazine rack. She picked it up to stall time. A red sticky extended out, marking a page. She opened it to a small picture of Jake Parson looking suave and sexy in the center of the article. Guess Who's on Top, read the title, announcing his company as a top-grossing urban outfitter. She flipped it closed and looked at the publication date. Three years ago. She rubbed her finger across the page, circling his face. The eyes were risk free, the smile charming. His tightly cropped hair as dark and as black as the sweater he wore in the photo. Shame on you, Venus. She slapped the pages closed and tossed the magazine back in the case.

"I should get back," she said, standing on the edge of the living room rug with her bare feet. The music still played softly. She didn't dare go back into the comfort zone.

Jake stood up, holding her phone. "It rang. There's a message." Venus rushed forward and grabbed it from his hand. She pushed the button and listened, intently.

"I've got to get back." She snapped it closed, nearly brimming over with tears.

⋅   ⁚   ⋅

JAKE didn't respond, only driving like a professional, zigzagging through traffic, making her know that he understood how desperately she needed to be by her mother's side. When she'd hung up the phone and he asked what happened, Venus quietly said, "My mother, she's in the hospital." He picked up his keys and told her to wait there. Venus watched him jog in the sand to his car parked the distance of their leisurely stroll. He drove the car back to his condo where she was waiting outside in her bare feet. They sped away and hadn't slowed since. "The hospital is on our way; why don't you let me drive you? It doesn't make sense for you to go all the way back downtown, then backtrack."

Venus looked at him and nodded. Right about now, nothing made sense. Not the bubble in her throat, the sweat beading on her forehead and under her armpits. The message her father spoke into her phone. "It's bad, Precious. It's worse than we thought."

"Okay, but you don't have to stay. My father can give me a ride back to my car." She took in a long deep breath. "You don't have to stay." She announced for the second time.

⋅   ⁚   ⋅

HOSPITALS were such cold places. Venus had thrown on her boots without putting her panty hose back on and now she was freezing, shivering, while she stood in front of the elevator waiting for it to come and transport her to her mother's floor. She felt Jake's smooth hands run along the sides of her arms, up and down. When the elevator door opened, he escorted her inside, holding her close.

"This way." He led, for which she was grateful. She couldn't have read the numbers of the hospital signs if she'd tried, her eyes completely clogged, stale with tears.

"Daddy!" Venus ran to her father who was standing outside the hospital room. She threw her arms around him and realized how slight his shoulders felt. She'd only seen him a few days ago, at least it felt that way, and in that time he'd lost weight. How long had this been going on and she not known a thing? "What did the doctor say? Tell me everything, right now. Tell me."

"Well, they're going to have to take the whole breast. Maybe the other one, too; they're not sure yet. Not sure if it's moved to anyplace else in her body. They don't know. But they're moving fast, Precious. They're going to take care of her. I trust Dr. Prah on this. She's your mother's doctor. She's been up front and honest about everything the whole time."

"What do you mean the whole time, how long has this been going on?"

"It's been a few months. Your mother never suspected a thing. She was going in for her blood, you know the diabetes check that she gets once a year. The doctor asked her when's the last time she had a mammogram, Pauletta said, never. You know your mother, look only when you intend to find. Sure enough, they found something. They showed me, too, on the X-ray screen. Looked like a dot, no bigger than a pinhead. So tiny. How could something so tiny be so dangerous? They wanted to see if it was going to shrink, thinking maybe it was the estrogen that she'd been on; so they changed the dosage, but it didn't go away, just got bigger..." He broke down in tears.

"Oh God, Daddy." Venus held him while his shoulders rose and fell in her arms. Her father had always been supportive, agreeing to whatever his mother presumed right. He'd probably just gone along when he should've demanded answers. A few months, a precious few months.

The doctor came out of her mother's room and tried to introduce herself. Venus didn't want to waste time hearing what the woman had to say. She moved straight past her to Pauletta's side.

"Don't come in here with those big boo-boo tears. I don't need that right now." Her mother's eyes followed as Venus moved slowly toward the bed.

"Mom, what is going on? I can't believe you didn't want to tell me. I could've helped, somehow."

"Are you a doctor? I know you studied those medical books right alongside of Clint, but I don't believe I remember you getting a degree in medicine."

Venus wiped her eyes. She'd have to straighten up. Her mother didn't respond well to emotion considering it a waste of time. "Okay, so what's the plan?" Venus said, pulling up a chair next to the bed. She swallowed the next wave of tears.

"The plan, Dr. Prah is going to remove these saggy pitiful things that have given me nothing but trouble since the day they finished nursing your brother. They'll probably take the lymph nodes, too. Then run me through a grueling bout of poisonous drugs to make sure they got everything. Simple enough, Venus. I don't want to drag this thing out any more than it's already been. I asked them to cut both breasts off when I first found out about the cyst, but they thought it was drastic. Now look at me. This is drastic, talking about the survival rate, like I may as well check my bags at the door. Did you bring any gum? My mouth is so dry. Who is that fella out there talking with your father? No, don't tell me. I don't want to know. The less I know, the better."

Venus held her mother's hand and squeezed it tight, placing the cool inside of her palm to her cheek. "I love you, Mom."

"Oh, Venus. I told you. Please. Please, don't cry. I don't need that right now."

Venus stood up and leaned across her mother for a hug, careful of the thick white bandage on her chest, letting her mother's tears soak the top of her head.

         ✦   ✦   ⁿ

THE doctor had already left, but Venus was ready to burst. She had questions. This all seemed so sudden. Right breast, both breasts, lymph nodes. Wait a minute, she kept telling herself, while Jake escorted her down the hall. She looked back at the empty corridor where her father was no longer standing. He'd resumed his place by her mother's side, promising that everything would be all right. "Go home, Precious. I'll be right here, don't worry. The surgery's not till tomorrow morning. Come back in the morning." Henry patted her off, then gave Jake a look as if they'd come to some sort of gentlemen's agreement.

Jake drove slowly; there was no need to rush now. There were no words exchanged. He let Venus find her own thoughts. It was evident she didn't want to talk about her feelings.

They pulled up behind her car, abandoned on the empty street. Business hours were long over downtown where usually people were strolling on foot and coming and going in cars. The streets now were quiet and idle. The bright moon seemed suspended behind the Bank of America building. She closed her eyes for a minute before opening her door.

"Thank you, Jake."

He jumped out of his side of the car and came around. He helped her out, then escorted her to the lone automobile on the street. He waited while she got in. "I'll call and check on you, if that's okay."

Venus started the car and was startled when the loud hard beat came out blaring. She quickly turned it down and apologized to him with her eyes. She'd just sworn her allegiance to old-school R & B.

He smiled down on her. "Love me some DMX. Drive safe." He tapped the hood of the car and stayed behind as Venus pulled off, slowly. She watched him from the rearview mirror. Jake Parson. She planted his name somewhere deep, hoping that it wouldn't escape.

GLUE

TIMOTHY took the first flight he could get out of Boston. His lanky tall frame could be seen over a string of heads coming off the plane before him. He and Venus were exact opposites in the body form department. She was short and curvy, he was tall and skinny. His soft eyes lit up when he saw her, and smiled.

He dropped his carry-on bag and picked her up. "Hey, Shorty."

Venus had already decided that she wasn't going to cry, but in her brother's arms she felt she had a right to. He had been the one she ran to when anyone messed with her in school, even though she was the oldest. He was the one who stood up for her even when the bullies themselves were bigger than both of them. He kissed her forehead and put her back on the ground.

Timothy threw his slender arm around her shoulder, and they started walking, "You know she's going to be fine; I've yet to find a wife and Mom will refuse to die before that happens."

An involuntary laugh came out of Venus. She felt immediate guilt for the betrayal of her spirit in this time of sadness. But he was right. His mother would not rest until both of them were securely tied into knots with their future spouses. She held on tight to his waist while they walked through the airport.

VENUS drove straight to Kaiser Hospital. The two buildings on opposite corners sat smack dab in the middle of worn-out Hollywood. Venus tried not to find fault in the facility based solely on looks and location. She knew that the quality of care was based on the doctor, not the building. As soon as she showed Timothy to their mother's room, she was determined to find Dr. Prah and get some answers.

Venus and Timothy walked down the corridor, looking straight ahead. Neither one of them had ever been hospitalized for anything. Not a broken bone or a removed tonsil. It had to be the worst possible place ever created by man. A conglomeration of misery and misfortune all housed under one roof. Malady, disease, and depression.

"Guess who's here, Mom." Venus pulled Timothy's hand and put it in Pauletta's. She was out of it, already prepped for the surgery that was scheduled in less than an hour. Her hand was limp, the pulse slight.

"Hi, pretty lady."

"What are you doing here?" Her words came out groggy and slow. "Don't you have that dessert thing to do?"

"It's a dissertation, Mom. And I finished, so I have plenty of time to stay here with you."

She opened her eyes wider. "Oh Lord, not you, too," she mumbled, looking up at Timothy's freshly twisted locks.

"Mom, my hair was like this the last time you saw me, it just grew some more."

Pauletta's grunt came out as a snore. She was back to sleep, her mouth partially open.

"How's she doing?" Dr. Prah came to the foot of the bed and whispered to neither one of them directly. Venus looked to her, then to Timothy.

"This is Mom's doctor."

Dr. Prah was a brown-skinned Middle Eastern woman with thick glasses and short hair. She put out her delicate hand. "Nice to meet you." Timothy had been filled in on the way over about Dr. Prah's shortcomings. He shook her hand, almost feeling sorry for her and the grilling she was about to receive from Venus.

"She's groggy, but is that enough? Are they going to give her more anesthesia before the surgery?" Venus stroked Pauletta's forehead.

"Yes, of course. She was just given something earlier to relax her. She had a bit of anxiety."

Their father walked into the room holding a vase of flowers in each hand. He set them down on a corner table near the window before he realized the room was filled by people.

"Tim-boy." He reached out and grabbed Timothy's shoulders. They hugged a long time. Since Henry had lost weight, she could see the resemblance in their faces. Her father and brother both had sharp chins, slanted eyes, and fine sculpted noses, like African royalty. When she was growing up, Venus never had liked the width of her nose, always wishing she looked more like Timothy, like Henry. She looked down at her sleeping mother; she'd never wish that way again, she wouldn't trade in one thing that reminded her of Pauletta Johnston. The deep coral brown of her skin, the fullness of her lips, the high cheekbones, and the width of her nose. She was perfect in her skin.

Two nurses came in ready to take her mother to surgery. The short, thick female nurse stood with her hands on her hips, waiting for the room to be cleared so she could get around to the side of the bed. Dr. Prah shook their father's hand and told him everything would be fine. She smiled in Venus's direction, then Timothy's. They watched the bed become mobile as it was being rolled toward the wide door.

"Wait a minute, Dr. Prah." Venus grabbed the raised metal bar on the bed, "I want to know why you waited three months before you did a biopsy."

"Venus, not now." Her father's tone didn't derail her, nor did the use of her actual name.

Dr. Prah faced Venus, her mouth a straight line. "We were monitoring the size and growth of the cyst very closely. The only thing I can tell you is that we make decisions on a case-by-case basis. What one does for one patient doesn't necessarily work for another. Your mother's breast tissue is very dense, and the odds of us getting a good sample from that cyst were slim. As it was, for this test, we had to go through nearly four layers of tissue to get to the cyst. We didn't want to put your mother through all of that if there was a possibility that the cyst would dissolve on its own."

Which came first, the chicken or the egg? And what's this *we* crap? Venus hated when doctors used the term *we*, as if no decision was theirs and theirs alone. Never wanting to take responsibility for their actions.

"So in other words, *you* made the decision to risk my mother's life on a guess that it was purely an estrogen-charged cyst because you didn't want to put anyone through any trouble. Well, now we've got trouble, wouldn't you say?"

"And we're dealing with it, Ms. Johnston. I understand you're upset, but if you'll excuse me, we've got to stay on schedule."

"My question still hasn't been answered. Why didn't you do a biopsy from the beginning? I mean, you can be honest, it's about the money, right? Would it have cost any more money from the HMO than all these other tests, the ultrasounds, the mammograms? I mean wouldn't it have come out about the same if you'd done the biopsy right then and there? Now we don't know what could have happened in that span of time. The difference in the cancer spreading..." Venus's voice rose to a peak before cutting off. She watched the nurses wheel her mother down the hall. She could barely breathe, the fluid running from her eyes and nose and past her mouth.

Timothy grabbed her wrist when she tried to follow Dr. Prah. Venus kept talking, she wasn't afraid of doctors. They weren't saints or great keepers of hope. Her ex-boyfriend, Clint Fairchild, was a doctor, with her help she liked to add. She'd supported him for four years while he went to medical school, then as soon as he graduated, she was expecting the big ·engagement ring, a big pow-wow sitting around deciding on the date of their nuptials, maybe even a promissory note for late delivery. But there was nothing. After four long years of opening her refrigerator to find urine samples, slides of blood samples, and a host of other disgusting containers, nothing.

It would be safe to say Venus had a propensity to judge them—doctors—harshly. They were simply people who often made mistakes. Just like the one Clint made by marrying someone else instead of her.

Doctors were people who made mistakes, but it always seemed someone else had to suffer the consequences.

Timothy and Venus walked hand in hand, following slowly all the way to the elevator. Their father stayed by Pauletta's side, waving as the doors closed. Timothy looked down on Venus's head, "We're going to look back on this day and think of it as nothing more than a memory. You won't feel what you're feeling now. The mind tries to re-create the same emotion, but it'll never be as real as it is now. So let it happen. Roll around in it, let it smother you, don't be afraid to feel."

Venus looked up at him. "You have too many psychology degrees. You need to stop going to school and join the rest of us down here on earth." She swung her body around and hugged him hard before the second convulsion of tears washed over her.

THEY waited downstairs in the cafeteria. Venus looked around the staid environment and wondered why they didn't use something cheerier on the walls. Yellow or bright orange would have fought off the gloom that hovered in the air. If you found yourself in the hospital cafeteria sitting for hours, fretting and worrying, the last thing you should be staring at were depressing bland walls.

"So, how's Airic doing?"

Venus poured another packet of sugar in her lukewarm coffee. "He's fine, I guess."

"Uh oh, what's that mean?" Timothy leaned forward on his pointed elbows.

"Means I haven't talked to him today, at all. He knew I was going to be worried shitless and he hasn't called once."

"Maybe he figured you'd call him, if you had any news. Phone works both ways, V."

Venus nodded in agreement. She didn't want to worry about Airic right now. Worrying about him would be selfish.

"So I heard you tell Mom you finished your dissertation. What's next on your list?"

"I don't have a list. I go where my interests take me."

"Well, where is your interest taking you next?" Venus said with her face leaning on her open hand.

"Africa."

Venus sat up straight. "You're kidding, right?"

"No. I'm seriously considering spending a year there, maybe more, depends on how it goes. One of my buddies is in the Peace Corps. He e-mails me these incredible stories; it sounds like a great experience."

"So what would you do . . . I mean what does your friend do?"

"He's a doctor of sociology, but he's helping build schools, literally, with his hands. Plus he's teaching in one of the schools already finished."

Venus looked hard into Timothy's face. She thought about what she was about to say. She understood that people only asked questions when they already had the answer, but in this case, she truly wanted to know. "What are you running from?"

He looked up at her. "Running?" He smiled, but his eyes had flatlined. He took a simple breath. "I haven't figured that out yet." A sadness seemed to overtake him. A sure sign that he knew, but it was no one else's business.

Timothy was quick and intelligent, and Venus knew she was no match for him. But she had to ask. Even knowing he'd already covered that angle somewhere in his mind, analyzed his own motivations, and justified them in one full sweep. "Let's go somewhere else, get out of here. This place is beyond depressing." She grabbed her purse and scooted out of the hard vinyl seat.

*   *   *

"DAD'S probably looking for us by now." Timothy looked at his watch. They had been walking for at least an hour. They looked up to see which corner they were on and realized they hadn't wandered off as far as they thought. A few blocks at the most. It was mostly the window shopping and people watching that had slowed them so.

Venus stopped and turned on her heels to face Timothy. "Just a little longer." She was scared of what was waiting back at the hospital. The thought of entering those large double doors, riding up the elevator to the fourth floor, and seeing her mother made the bile rise to her throat.

"Come on, we'll walk this way, guaranteed to take another hour."
Timothy looped his arm through hers. "I'll even stop to pretend I'm tying
my shoes once or twice."

Her mood lightened by the time they made it around six square blocks.
The hospital lobby was filled with signs, directions, and rules. She felt
sorry for anyone who couldn't read English and was bleeding to death.
Venus led the way to the north end elevators. As soon as she turned the
corner, she saw a good-looking black man coming toward her. She was
about to politely say "hello" as she did to all men of color just as a show
of respect, but quickly realized that wouldn't do.

"What are you doing here?" Venus touched Jake's elbow, perplexed and
excited all at once. "This is my brother, Timothy."

"How ya doing? How're you holding up?" he said, turning to Venus and
sliding a hand down the side of her arm.

"Okay." She was still stunned by his presence.

"I just saw your dad. He says your mom is doing great, came through
like a champ."

Venus felt a pang of guilt. She'd assumed the worst and hadn't wanted
to face it, out strolling the boulevard as long as possible, and here a perfect stranger had found her mother and delivered news of safety.

"We better get on up," Timothy said behind Venus. "Nice meeting
you."

"Do you have to leave?" Venus said before Jake could say his good-bye.
"Can you come back up with us?"

Jake hesitantly followed. In jeans his look was softer, more casual, but
he still looked like he'd forever have to fight the image of the one-hit-
wonder rapper instead of the businessman he'd become. All three of
them took separate corners of the elevator and rode up quietly. Timothy
stepped off first in the wrong direction.

"This way," Jake instructed, as if he, instead of the two of them, had
spent the entire day at the hospital and knew the lay of the land.

The lighting in the hospital room was dim, the curtains closed to block
out the sunlight. Venus walked in and kissed her father on the forehead as
he sat next to the bed. Pauletta lay quiet with a trail of tubes in both arms.
The sight of Pauletta calm and resting scared Venus. She'd never known

a day that her mother wasn't in full fighting mode, ready to argue over the injustice of being charged a completely different price at the register than the tag or sign posted at Kmart, or the credit card statement showing duplicate transactions. Venus had spent enough time at her mother's elbow watching as she pointed out the rudeness of a salesperson or the unfairness of a store's policy.

Pauletta's hands lay still at her sides. Venus held one and traced the lines of her mother's palm. The same nurse from earlier came in behind them. "She's going to sleep for a good eight hours." Her words came out loud even though it was intended as a whisper. Her thick roundness scooted past Venus where she could get to the machines. They all stood around feeling awkward, like they'd been told to leave but were not quite sure.

Henry looked up with worn, tired eyes. "I'm going to stay a little longer. You guys go on home. The nurse is right, she's going to sleep all day and probably through the night."

Venus smoothed a hand over his shoulder. "We can take shifts, Dad."

"No, no, that's not necessary." He spoke in a hushed but firm voice. Something told Venus that he preferred to be alone with Pauletta. The same way they'd lived for the last fifteen years, their nest free and clear except for the two of them.

Timothy acquiesced first, giving their father's shoulder a squeeze. "See you in the morning, Dad. Call if you need anything. I'm staying with Venus." He looked up to confirm. She nodded her head. "Okay." Timothy kissed Pauletta on the smooth pat of skin between her closed eyes. He motioned let's go.

"I wanted to talk to Dr. Prah," Venus said as Timothy escorted her out. Jake took the other elbow. Venus felt like a Looney Tune; was she the only person who saw this whole situation as wrong? She shook them both off and stopped in her tracks. "I'm not leaving until I talk to the doctor." They stood in the hallway outside of the door.

"What's that going to do, V? What's it going to solve? Let Mom get some rest. You're tired, too. The only thing we can do is help Mom recover." Timothy wrapped a soft hand around her neck. "I know you want to blame somebody for this, V. There's nobody to blame." He pulled her in close. "Mom's going to be fine. All that matters is that she's going to be fine." Venus let Timothy sway her back and forth, her neck twisted up with the length of his body. She'd forgotten Jake was standing there.

"I probably should go" were the first words out of his mouth when Venus finally turned around to see him.

"Nah man, let's go get some coffee, real coffee, the kind with steam coming off of it." Timothy looked to Venus. "You in, V?"

She hunched her shoulders as if she had no choice.

*   *   *

THE three of them filed back into the elevator, taking their respective positions in each corner. It stopped on the second floor, and a young woman carrying a baby got on and took the corner closest to the door as if instructed. They all rode down in silence. Venus stared at the bundle hanging over the edge of the mother's shoulder. Small and innocent. Wide round eyes, taking everything in, so sweet and soft. She couldn't remember the last time she'd held a baby. Her policy had been to stay as far away from them as possible, knowing the pain they could inflict on an unmarried woman over thirty. Venus turned to face the panel of buttons, her head now pounding. She squeezed her fingers to her temples.

"So you and Venus work together?" Timothy's voice may as well have come out of a megaphone.

Jake answered, then asked Timothy where he lived, what he did for a living. Venus was grateful when the elevator doors whisked open. The woman and baby got off first. Venus thought about reaching out to touch the billowy fluff of hair on the baby's head. Just one feel couldn't hurt.

"This is the lobby." Jake's voice stopped her hand from rising up out of her coat pocket.

She watched the baby bob up and down with the movement of its mother until she couldn't see them anymore. "My car's this way." Jake was leading the way. He and Timothy made more small talk walking a few paces in front of her. He wore his thin sweaters always slim against his body, proud of his lean washboard stomach. He had a nice butt, too, firm and slightly curved. She was delirious; there was no other excuse for watching this man gliding in front of her.

"Here we go." He pointed his laser key at the big utility vehicle and pressed the locks open.

"I was wondering how we were all going to fit into that two-seater you drove me in yesterday. How many cars do you have?"

"Only this and the one you rode in yesterday," Jake said, proudly. He didn't live in excess. He used the SUV whenever there was going to be anyone else in the car. His mother and brother were the main reason he'd purchased the large vehicle in the first place. His brother, he explained, was six foot seven and a basketball guard playing for UCLA.

Timothy had already slipped into the backseat, hidden behind the dark tinted windows. He'd taken the red-eye from Boston, probably hadn't slept in twenty-four hours.

"Jake, I know it was Timothy's suggestion, but he's really tired. Maybe we should take a rain check."

They both turned to look at the subject, slouched over in a drooling sleep.

"Told you. Now what are we going to do? I'm not carrying him." She smiled, shaking her head, remembering the days when she'd tried. He was only three years younger, but when he was little, she did her best to carry the lanky toddler from one spot to the other, his arms and legs flailing, nearly touching the ground.

They rode down Sunset Boulevard with a sleeping Timothy in the backseat. The stores and office buildings lit, vivid and twinkling, as if co-ordinated with one another. Venus caught Jake in her side vision, his confident chin tilted up, his muscular arm guiding the steering wheel with precision. Timely as it was, Jake's presence only made her feel worse. She bit the inside of her cheek, chewing softly. Airic still hadn't called, and here Jake, whom she'd only known a short while, was by her side offering support, sticking like an amazing new glue that only worked as long as you needed it, then slipped away without leaving a trace.

"I'm sorry I bailed on you."

"Are you kidding, with this kind of emergency? Besides, William and Legend have it handled."

"They must, since you have time to baby-sit me." She didn't look at him. "Thank you," she said, watching out the side window where the lights began to stream together, everything in slow motion. Nothing in the last few days seemed real. From the moment her mother came over Saturday with the hot plates of food, time seemed to have stopped, like a broken tape getting caught in the mechanism. Chopped and spit out with worn-down sound.

"You know, I had no idea about what was going on when I asked you to that concert. I'll understand if you can't go." Jake turned down the stereo to make sure she was listening.

"No. If anything, I could use the fun. A concert." She smiled. "Last concert I saw was Ashford and Simpson."

His laughter was loud enough to have awakened Timothy, but when she looked back, he hadn't stirred.

Jake swiped at his eyes, still trying to recuperate. "What year was that?"

"I don't know. I guess 1985, '86. The only reason I remember that concert was because the guy that took me thought he looked like Nick Ashford. The long greasy hair." She put her hand over her face, embarrassed by the memory.

Then the question she knew was coming. "How old are you?" he asked, still in a half-believing state.

Venus smiled. "How old do you think I am?" Blinking unconcerned, knowing how often people thought she was far younger than her midthirties, but that was all before now. Before life had struck her with the most gripping fear she'd ever imagined. Age comes unannounced one day, striking like lightning. She remembered her aunt Quena, vivacious, sweet, always with a smile on her face offering her and Timothy fresh sticks of Juicy Fruit gum out of her purse and smelling of it when she'd leaned over to kiss them hello. Then Uncle Robbie died. Someone had shot him straight through the heart in their very own living room. No one knew who did it. Everyone was a suspect because Uncle Robbie dealt drugs. The stress of having to stay in that house, live there under the very roof where her husband had died because she couldn't afford to go anywhere else, right along with the open wound of not knowing who was responsible for the tragedy, left her drained. Venus would never forget the time she'd looked up to that sweet voice, the scent of Juicy Fruit popping in her mouth, and saw a twisted, tired Aunt Quena. Her eyes sagged deeply, her mouth turned down at the sides, unrecognizable but for her scent.

Venus inadvertently touched the plump skin that had sprung up underneath her eyes, the result of too much crying last night.

"Never guess a woman's age. Just tell me." Jake's voice snapped her back into reality.

"I'm thirty-six." Venus felt the shift where his foot tapped the brake unexpectedly. "Don't worry, I left my cane back at the apartment. I promise not to embarrass you."

"You look good," he said with reserve, trying not to let on that he was blown away.

"Now your turn. How old?" she said teasing.

"I don't think that's pertinent information," his voice in a false bass.

"I told you, now you tell me. I'll guess. I'm not afraid to guess."

"No. None of that."

"What's wrong, think I'll insult you? Let's see. You're friends with William and Legend, old school chums I gathered by the handshake and shoulder knocks. You've got that great smile, where you still expect good things to happen . . . definitely a sign of youth. I'd say, twenty-six."

"No way. You already knew."

"That's part of the profession, making assessments, making assumptions, identify and attack," she mocked from one of their previous conversations.

He parked the car on the street in front of a small restaurant then leaned against the door panel. "Have you assumed anything else?"

She understood the question but avoided a real answer. "My assumption is that you like trendy little spots for coffee," Venus said while looking out the window at the small café. She took another look at her brother in the backseat. The streetlight shone down on his peaceful face in dreamland.

"He'll be fine," Jake reassured her.

Venus opened her door and felt like she was on top of Mount Rushmore with no way to get down.

"I'll help you, hold on." Jake trotted over to the passenger side, extended his hand, but it wasn't enough. He grabbed her by the waist and hoisted her down slowly.

Venus slid the length of his body before feeling her feet touch the ground. She stood staring into his chin, his smooth brown throat to the V-neck of his collar where the scar she'd noticed before sat perfectly centered. He closed the car door behind her and took hold of her hand. "Watch out for that puddle."

"You sure we can park here?" Venus asked, looking back on the shiny hood and black tinted windows, "I don't want the car getting towed with Timothy in the backseat."

"He'll be all right. We can see the car from inside."

The small café, with its earth-toned interiors and soft lighting, felt warm and cozy. A glass case full of scrumptious desserts greeted her at the door. Cheesecake, coffee cake, her favorites. She realized how hungry she was as she stared at the desserts. A young man with a white apron stopped and grinned at her, "Which one you want to try?" His accent was freshly south of the neighboring border.

"If I had my choice, I'd take one of each, but I gotta keep my girlish figure." Venus heard Pauletta's voice come out of her mouth. Her mother used to always say that, *gotta keep my girlish figure,* even though she'd never had one in the first place. "The cheesecake," she said, this time more subdued.

"To drink?"

Jake spoke up, ordering for them both, "Go find us a table; I'll bring everything over."

The place wasn't large, but it seemed to be the happening spot. Every seat was occupied. Venus wandered over to the glass entrance and looked out to the empty table and chairs out front. It was probably too cold for everyone else, but it would be just what she needed. A dose of cool reality. She and Jake were falling for each other. Not like earlier, when it was a game of cat and mouse. She couldn't be sure if it was the circumstances. A time of vulnerability and crisis. What she was certain of was that she had to stop it from going any further.

"Out there is fine with me," Jake's voice came from behind her. Her mind took a sudden dive, then up again. She was reminded of the night he called her on the phone. The deep sexy tone of his voice, the way he controlled her with his seduction.

Venus pushed the door open and let the cool dark air snake around her face, breathing in for clarity. He set the tray of coffee down and pulled back her chair. The screech of the metal against the concrete sidewalk sent chills through her body.

"You're cold?"

"A little." Venus couldn't stop shaking. She was cold, she was nervous, she was scared.

"This should help." He slipped out of his jacket and wrapped it around her shoulders. He put the small cup of coffee in front of her. The wide saucer of cheesecake sat in the middle of the table. He nudged it toward her. By the time he got around to his seat, she was halfway finished.

He gave her a disbelieving eye.

"It's good. I couldn't help it. Taste." She offered up a heaping serving. His lips wrapped gently around the fork. The cake slid into his mouth. His eyes maintained a direct line to hers.

"It is good." His eyes hadn't let go of her yet.

"Jake." Venus put the fork down, turning her head away. She didn't want to look at him when she said it. "I like you, a lot. I haven't known you but a minute and it feels like a lifetime of friendship. This..." She paused, looking down at the ring on her finger. "This whole thing with my mom being sick, you being here for me. I thought I had everything figured out...I had it all figured out. My life finally made sense." She took a long deep breath. "Now there's you, my mother, I've been thrown out of my safety zone. I'm scared. I don't understand what's going on. I feel like I'm being tested or warned, or both. It doesn't make any sense."

"What doesn't make sense?"

"You." She looked around, taking in the glare of the light bouncing off his shiny car. "The fact that you're here and *honey's* not. Remember him?"

She caught the sullen expression on Jake's face.

"I haven't forgotten." He leaned back in his chair, holding the large mug of coffee close to his chest. "I just hadn't given it any thought."

"How can you say that? What does that mean? You don't care that I'm engaged?"

"Basically."

She threw her face into her hands.

"You care." He took a sip of his coffee. "I think that's enough for both of us."

"I think we should just stick with the plan. Work together, that's it. I appreciate you being here for me, with all that's going on with my mother. But after today, we have to go back to business relations."

"When had it ever left? As far as I'm concerned, it's always been business relations. I enjoy the people I work with or I don't work with them." He tilted his head a little to the side. His wide eyes were warm and steady.

Venus didn't believe a word he said. All signs pointed to attraction, mutual. "Fine." She pulled the plate of cake back in front of her but had no desire to eat. "I'm ready to go."

Jake stood up and came around the back side of her chair and pulled it out. If this is what he meant by business relations, she couldn't imagine personal. A little toe sucking, full-body massages, and whipped cream maybe. He didn't budge when she stood up, sharing the same air space. Her purse vibrated against her hip. She reached in and pulled out her phone.

"Yes." Venus breathed into the receiver, still sharing Jake's space. Her voice went soft, her eyes lowered. Jake backed away one step at a time, realizing it was *honey* on the line.

⸱　　✦　　✦

THE drive back to the hospital was quiet and empty. Venus had a strange isolated feeling, even with Jake right beside her and Timothy asleep in the backseat. She wanted to apologize, but she didn't know what she'd be apologizing for. The SUV pulled to the curb, Jake put the gear in Park, and continued to stare straight ahead.

"Thank you," she said, opening the car door. "Timothy, wake up." She reached back and tugged on his arm. "C'mon, Timothy."

He sat up and wiped a slender hand across his face. "Sorry about that, guys."

"No problem. We'll have to get together under better circumstances." Jake got out of the car and gave Timothy half a hug. The same way

Venus felt that she'd known Jake all of her life was the way he and Timothy looked together. Like old friends. True friends.

She walked up to Jake and kissed him on the cheek. "I'll see you later."

He dug up a smile from somewhere deep. "Give your mom my best."

Venus watched his SUV pull away. She didn't understand what was happening here, or why. Just as she'd tried to explain to him, her world had changed overnight, in one blink of the eye. Nothing gradual or slow about it, just a complete shift.

SHIFT

SHE and Timothy drove over first thing in the morning as their father had instructed. Pauletta was half sitting up, sipping water from a straw, when they walked into her hospital room. Her father steadied the cup in one hand and supported Pauletta's head with the other.

Venus felt a major change happening in the Johnston family. Her mother would have to let someone help her, when usually it had been the other way around. Pauletta had always been in charge. As long as Venus could remember, her mother had been the disciplinarian and the decision maker. Pauletta paid the bills, analyzing the paychecks that were brought home by Henry each month, making sure it was all accounted for. He didn't seem to mind. It was an easy way to get along, no arguing, no fighting. That is, until he'd started collecting trains. He wouldn't let Pauletta, who called it immature and a waste of money, dissuade him. He explained to Pauletta, he'd never asked for one thing for himself while the children were small, in need of the best school clothes and being driven in the best car. Venus usually listened to their conversations uneventfully, knowing it would be the same, her mother having the last word, but for the first time she'd heard her mother say something endearing, "Okay, Henry, you're right. I couldn't have asked for a better husband, I know that's for sure. Hell, buy the whole train station, you deserve it." That summer, Venus started seeing her father differently, understanding differently; it wasn't that he'd been weak, or small—he'd been the complete opposite. He'd been the strong one, doing what was necessary to keep his family together, keeping the pieces whole and healthy. Sacrificing. That was what love was all about, making compromises.

"Hey, Mom." Venus pressed her lips on the side of her mother's head. Her skin was cool, dry. She winked at Venus and gave a half smile.

Dr. Prah walked in as soon as Venus had pulled out her lotion to rub on her mother's face and arms.

"How's our patient doing today? How're you doing, Pauletta?"

Venus stood up from the side of the bed. "How do you think she's doing?"

Dr. Prah ignored her. "Good news, you get to go home tomorrow."

"Home!" Venus walked around the side of the bed. Henry stuck his hand out. "Precious, you sit with your mother. I'm going to go talk to Dr. Prah, outside."

"I know she didn't just say 'home.' "

Timothy stood up, cornering Venus. He was smart to do so. She felt a surge of something dangerous, clawing. "How in the world is she supposed to go home that quickly? She just had a mastectomy, or weren't you there?"

"Ms. Johnston, your mother would not be released if she were not able. Everything is going very well. Her blood pressure is normal, her platelet count is good. She's definitely doing well, and two days is standard after this type of surgery."

"What happened to, every case is treated for individual needs? Now we're back to standard."

Pauletta grunted, pushing herself up, slightly.

"Mom."

Henry rushed to her side. "Sweetie, wait a minute, now. Let me help."

"Venus, go." Her mother's voice was light and scratchy, but there was no doubt about what she'd said. "Leave, just go."

Venus stood in shock, her heart racing. She wanted to slap some understanding into Dr. Prah, make her see this was all her doing—her mother, sitting up in pain asking her only daughter to leave.

"No, Mom. This isn't right. You shouldn't be going home this soon."

"Get out!"

Venus jumped with the tone of her mother's voice, the awful way her face had turned into one sharp stab. She picked up her purse and stormed past Dr. Prah. The elevator wouldn't come quickly enough. She hit at it again and again, pushing, holding. "Son of a bitch, hurry up." When the doors opened, she saw her brother trotting toward her. She stepped inside and pushed the Lobby button so the doors would close.

"Venus." He called her name and attempted to stop the doors from closing, but too late.

*   *   *

THERE were times when the Los Angeles coastline looked like a painting, full of purple and fucshia swirling around the yellow sun. Venus had been told that the smog and pollution in the air created the majestic sunsets. She didn't know how it could be true, that something so completely beautiful and perfect could be caused by something so foul.

She drove along Pacific Highway, keeping an eye cautiously on the road while still staring into the fiery dusk. She parked the car and sat, watching the white foam of the ocean waves rolling into the shoreline. With the moon high and the sun finally set, the waves could still be seen dancing in the distance. She picked up her phone and pressed the redial button.

"I'm here. Right out front." She closed the phone and waited. The lights in his house popped on in the downstairs area. She could see him through the window, shirtless, walking to the balcony. He waved her over. Venus only stared. He leaned on the balcony with both arms extended. Venus threw her head back, imagining those arms around her waist. "What am I doing?" she whispered.

She opened the cell again. She saw him go back into the house and pick up the phone. He was back outside, standing with the phone to his ear.

"I know you're going to think I'm crazy, but I can't stay. I'm sorry. I'm sorry for the false alarm."

"You're here, you might as well come in." It was odd, sort of strange to watch him talking to her at a distance. The wind blew in a steady stream making his long white pajama pants cling to his muscular thighs, his smooth chest brilliant with the sheen of light from the moon, just like the waves in the ocean.

"I reassessed the situation. It's not smart, even if we planned to just talk."

"Can I come sit with you in the car?"

Venus looked at him, standing on the deck, "Only if you put a shirt on."

"I'll be right down."

"So how is she?" Jake slid into the seat and buckled himself in, probably out of habit.

"She's good, I mean, as well as can be expected after losing a body part. Is a breast a body part? I never thought about it till now. I mean it's not like they're organs, like a liver, a kidney. You need all of those parts. A lung…" She trailed off, she was in tears again. She'd driven halfway there with her eyes foggy and sightless. She thought she was through. Now here she was crying, again. It seemed she hadn't stopped since she'd met him.

"Let it out," Jake whispered in her hair while he hugged her. She felt his arms pull tighter. She knew how good it would feel to stay in those arms. It would be the easy way to do things. This was crazy. She sat up, feeling an immediate void when she separated from the heat of his chest.

"My mom is doing well, really. I'm the one that's a mess. She acts like this was just one more thing on her to-do list. One more day in the drudgery of life. 'Gotta keep moving, Venus. You won't get nothing done by standing still.' That's what she's always told me. But I feel paralyzed. How can she just think this is another day?" She cleared her airways with a tissue from the large box of Kleenex she had to stop and buy on the way over.

"Today, she asked me to leave. She sent me away, told me to get out of her hospital room, like I'm the one that's crazy. Just because I want answers, some justice. I have a right to be angry, to grieve."

"Why do you use that word? No one died, Venus."

"I feel like someone has. I know she's still here, but a part of her, a vital part of her, is missing. If I was the one in that bed, in that hospital with tubes coming out of me, with bandages wrapped around my body, I assure you, it wouldn't be business as usual. I couldn't take it. How can she sit there and act like nothing's happened? How she isn't mad at the world is beyond me. And then to tell me to get out, to leave because I wanted answers...she kicked me out of the hospital room." She said it again with an incredulous frown.

Jake grabbed the hand that gripped the steering wheel. He rolled it into his, smothering it with his wide smooth palm. "Your mother's going to be fine. Sounds like she wants to put all of this behind her. There's nothing wrong with that. It sounds like you're angry, and you want her to be mad, too; but she's accepted it. You're going to have to do the same."

Venus snatched her hand back. "Why? Why do I have to accept it? Why can't I try to do something about it?"

"What exactly would that be?" Jake looked at her. His face was half masked by the darkness and half lit by the moonlight.

"I don't know, but there has to be something. Don't you see how wrong it is, to take something like that away from a woman? And it keeps happening over and over, not just my mother. Millions. Women. It's like some awful punishment. Who's next? Our lives aren't even our own. We could be struck down by this awful disease, that serves no purpose...at any moment. You know, you're moving along thinking you're in complete control of your life, you've finally got the life you've worked for, the career of your dreams, the house, the family, the entire package, then zip, bap, boom! It's destroyed! It's not fair!"

"That's the way you see it. Maybe your mother doesn't see it as the end of the world."

She took a deep breath, speechless, unable to respond. Yes. Certainly. That was it, her mother saw it as one more pothole in the street. Just keep moving. Go around them if you have to, just keep it moving. *Come on, Henry.*

Then where did that leave Venus? Who was going to help her get past it, the fear, the unknowing? She'd never had that ability to just keep moving, to run over roadblocks, to jump over potholes. Venus had to understand why the obstacle was placed before her, its mission and cause. Understand its meaning.

The cell phone rang, creating an unsettling tension in the car just as it had the night before outside the café. Venus looked at the lit screen but didn't reach for it. Jake stared at it, too, as if it were some alien that landed near his lap.

"You probably should get that. I'll be inside if you need me." He stepped out of the car and strode in long steps, creating an amassed distance between them before Venus could ask him to wait.

She got out of the car and hurried behind him. "Jake!" He turned around. If it was annoyance she saw, she ignored it. "Can I stay here, with you ... tonight?"

"I don't think that's a good idea."

The wind pushed his words over her head, soaring, floating out to sea. She stepped closer, "It's not complicated. I just want to stay."

"It will be complicated. I do things no other way."

She caught those words and their meaning. She took a few more steps toward him. The sand swallowed her deeper. She put out her hand.

"You've been forewarned," he said, taking her hand, pulling her to follow him inside.

•   •   •

VENUS didn't care about the danger signs, the hidden curves or slick terrain. She'd taken the safe route all of her life, doing what was right, doing what was best. The same road her mother and father had taken for nearly forty years. She didn't want to end up that way, never having taken a chance, a detour. If her destination were predetermined, it didn't matter. She'd take the long way.

The sound of running water kept her in a semiconscious state as she lay in the center of the large bed. Jake touched her on her shoulder, telling her to get up. He led her from his bedroom to his bathroom where there was a huge tub filled with steaming water and a continuous flow of bubbles moving in circles. He turned around and left, closing the door behind him. The music flowed from an invisible source, the votive candles burned in the corner.

She slipped her sweater over her head, then unzipped her skirt. She unsnapped her bra and let it slide down her arms. She turned and looked at the door once more, then quickly slid her panties down around her ankles, kicking them off. She bent over to run a trail in the water with the tips of her fingers.

She climbed the tiled steps to the tub, cool underneath her feet, then sank into the perfect warmth. The water caressing her skin overwhelmed her for a moment. She cupped a handful and rinsed her face. She was being cared for. A bath had been run for her. Candles lit, lights dimmed. *For her.* She laid her head against the smooth curve of the porcelain. She closed her eyes and let the music and the flutter of the bubbles calm her spirit.

*   *   *

A quiet knock at the door interrupted her reverie. She'd been soaking for a while. The water had cooled. Chill bumps rose on her skin. She sat up then grabbed a towel off the rack. "Come in."

"You all right in here?" Jake came inside the bathroom, covering his eyes. "Here's a robe." He pushed the thick terry fabric on the chrome towel rack.

"Okay" was all she could think to say. She felt entirely helpless and, with that, completely dependent on him, his kindness.

Jake fumbled for the doorknob, still with his eyes closed. Venus got out of the water as soon as he closed the door, pulling the robe tight around her wet body. It hung on her like a man's robe should, large, oversized. If it had fit perfectly, she would have gone into a panic, having to acknowledge that he dutifully housed and bathed women all the time, a normal practice for him. One more wasn't a feat.

The bedroom lighting flickered with the movement of the candlelight. Venus saw the covers pulled back, the burgundy sheets folded back to a corner. She looked around for Jake. The same sweet music played through the walls. Small candles burned on each side of the bed. She climbed into the cool soft linens, sliding her feet into the tightness. She inhaled the covers, knowing they'd hold Jake's scent. Crisp, light, sweet.

A knock, then the door opened partially. He stuck his head in. "You look good sitting there." He walked to the edge of the bed.

"Bet you say that to all the girls that find their way into this spot."

He tilted his head, analyzing the question and all that she implied. "Nope, only to the ones who actually look good." He pointed his finger at her. "Don't ask a question if you don't want to know the answer." He'd been prepared for the direction of this conversation.

Venus pulled her knees close to her chin. "But I have to ask."

"Then ask and be quick about it." He sat down next to her and pulled her legs across his lap. She was glad she'd painted her toenails, even though she'd given up on the whole daunting war of keeping her fingers and toes sparkling. Out of boredom one night, she'd dipped the brush in the half-empty Petal Pink polish and painted them, making it a project, just as she'd paint the walls, or a mural.

"Are you seeing someone, as in a mutually agreed upon relationship?" she asked, being quick about it and getting it over with as he'd suggested.

"Do you really want to know?" he whispered, before reaching across her into his nightstand and pulling out a small jar. He unscrewed the top and dove right in. He slathered her feet with the moist cream, rubbing and massaging. She squeezed her eyes closed and bit her lip so not to moan or let the words *I love you* leak out involuntarily. Because she did, at that moment, love him.

He worked and kneaded the heel of her foot with his palm, pressing his thumbs to the center of her arch, then moved to the base of her toes, sliding, rolling, pushing. She slid down deeper. He moved around and positioned himself directly over her feet. He dipped for more cream, warming it in his hands before starting again, then moving up the firm part of her calves, circling her knees, then higher to her thighs. She tried to remember that tomorrow she would wake up and still be on earth with a real life, with real problems, that regardless of his answer, she was the one obligated. She was the one in a committed relationship.

His hands smoothed with a light friction to the rise of her hips, then down again. He motioned for her to turn over, edged the robe off her shoulders and began to massage the tenseness around her neck. Venus took a deep long breath, but didn't exhale, afraid it would come out, a heated cry for help. She concentrated on breathing out slow and careful.

"That's better, let it go." Deeper penetration came with his words. He rubbed the base of her skull spreading his hands into her hair and scalp, taking full control of her mind and thoughts. She would scream if he stopped. His hands in gentle claws trailed down the length of her torso, taking the robe with him. Before she could comprehend the coolness on her exposed body, he was back, gliding his hands from her head to her toes. She turned over to face him. The rhythm of her heart was pounding wildly in her head. He wet the skin of her clavicle with his mouth. Venus kept her eyes on his refined face. The noble line of his chin, the bridge of his nose rising into the sculpted line of his brows—he would age gracefully.

She grabbed his head and pulled him down on top of her. His tongue, his lips, the kiss, washed her ashore leaving her weightless. She wanted to disappear inside him. He let the weight of his body fall on her, still managing to move his hand against the length of her waist, trailing the bones of her ribs to her breast.

Her breast.

Venus gasped, rising up with strength she didn't know she had, pulling the robe tight around her chest. Jake rolled off, to the side, shocked. "What happened?" He reached to touch her. Again, she flinched. "What's wrong?" He blinked confusion.

The panic elapsed as quickly as it had come, but she knew the culprit could be identified easily if it returned. She took a deep breath, letting out an I'm-sorry-it's-not-you.

Jake sat up and touched her cheek. He scooted closer and pulled her into his chest. "It's okay. Relax." He kissed her on the forehead. Venus curled up underneath him, closing her eyes, trying to block the picture of her mother, the bandage wrapped so tightly around her body, she wondered how she could breathe. The dry edges of her lips moving slowly to tell her to get out, to leave!

"I got you," Jake whispered into her hair. He rocked her a tiny bit while Venus took in shaking breaths with each sob. "I got you," he whispered.

REVELATIONS

BLAND grayness covered the room. Rain fell with a dull thud to the outside deck. From where she lay, looking out the window, the sky and the water all appeared as one thick fog. She lifted her lids high enough to see Jake's chin above her head. Her eyes caught on the small scar in the center of his throat. Higher still, she saw his lashes flutter, but he was still asleep. She laid her head back on his firm chest and listened to his steady pulse. She wanted to slip her hand underneath his shirt to feel his skin. Pull on the drawstring of his pants and slip her hand down to feel his solid thighs.

It was all for the best that nothing happened last night. The regret would have swallowed her whole. But if she never got another chance, she would regret that, too.

Pauletta was going home today. That was how the head-butting began, the announcement that her mother was being kicked out of the hospital to fend for herself. After such a brutal physical attack, she was being sent home as if she had nothing more than a few stitches instead of the barbarism that was perpetrated on her body.

Venus felt Jake's arm tighten around her. "You up?"

"Yeah." She rested her head on her fist, balancing to stare at him. "Hope your neck is okay, you slept in an awkward position."

He tilted his head side to side. "Think I'll live."

The small conversation was feeling forced. Venus raised up, and threw her feet over the edge of the bed. "I should go in today."

"That's not necessary. We've got it covered. Legend knows the situation. We're all on the same side. He's not going to do anything you wouldn't approve of." Jake reached out and stuck his hand through her hair, pulling a strand and letting it bounce back.

"You mean, like the T-shirt test." She rolled her eyes and self-consciously stuck a hand through her hair where he'd touched. It was dry. She usually braided it at night to keep it tame for the next day. Ever since she stopped straightening her hair, she was on constant duty to keep it from frizzing too badly. Her natural curls only acted right with a handful of goo and moisturizers. The steam from the bath last night didn't help either. Right now she was representing Buckwheat to the fullest. "I hope you have something I can work with."

"Plenty of goodies." He hopped out of the other side of the bed. "Really, though, we got things handled. Shaun is back."

"Who's Shaun?"

"My senior designer and right-hand man. Plus, what you're dealing with is way more important." He pulled on the drawstring of his pants that Venus had been eyeing. "Nothing crucial is happening today."

"You're just saying that cause you like me."

That was a start. One solid chip of ice broken.

"I'm going to hop in the shower downstairs. You can use the bathroom up here."

"I'm still coming with you to the studio." She stood up. "Separate cars, of course."

"Of course," he said, before pulling the bedroom door closed.

*   *   *

VENUS followed Jake all the way downtown, changing lanes when he did, shifting and dodging the slow pockets on the 10 freeway like experts. She parked on the street while Jake took his spot in the monthly parking garage. It made sense to take separate cars. Later on, she'd planned to go straight to the hospital to check on her mother, even if she wasn't wanted there.

It felt good being at work, having some type of control. Here, she was Venus Johnston, marketing genius and queen of the one-liners. There was nothing to hide, she kept telling herself, checking her makeup one last time. The only thing she'd had in her purse was a lip pencil and lipstick. She used the dark pencil on her eyes. After filling in her lips with the Cinnamon Stick color, she used it on her cheeks, smudging it in lightly. She played at her hair and hoped she looked like a stressed-out daughter dealing with a sick parent, versus a one-night-stand hoochie who'd spent the night at a man's house without a change of clothes. She was both.

"Hey, Venus! You're back?" William stood straight and tall in his steel-colored suit that matched his eyes. His usual neat cropped hair was filling into thick curly chunks. Did this man ever have a bad day? She hugged him for some unknown reason.

"Sorry to hear about your mom. Jake's been keeping us updated. Our thoughts were with you all the way."

"Thank you, William."

"You want to see what's going on in the studio before we go up?"

"Yeah, sure." Venus pushed her bag strap closer on her shoulder, glad to be inducted so quickly into the brotherhood. She followed him into the studio where the sound of whizzing sewing machines and cutters filled the air. The hum of voices giving direction, yes, no, too much, too little. An excitement ran through her, she too had been bitten by the Barbie craze at one time, wanting to be a fashion designer. Walking among the real thing was invigorating.

"Check this out." William walked over to a group of women who didn't look like the usual model types. They were thick sisters with tiny waists and bubble bottoms. Hips. Oh my!

"Ladies, this is Venus Johnston, the marketing coordinator for the new young women's collection." They all turned around and spoke hellos. Their eyes turned quickly back to William. He blushed enough to maintain his shy act.

"New fit models, just like you said."

"Impressive," Venus said, looking over the statuesque women; then it hit her, maybe they were too good-looking. "Has Jake seen them, I mean, it was his decision I'm assuming?"

"Oh yeah."

"Great." Her toes felt crushed. She had a major complex about her size. Women stacked with fullness in all the right places made her feel small and inadequate. "That's perfect. It's going to make a huge difference in how the line sells. Gotta have real bodies."

"And they do." William waved baby bye-byes to all the models. They responded in kind.

"There you are." Another model, Venus assumed, came toward them. She was a little older than the rest but still had all the other requirements, long legs and thick thighs. Her crop top revealed a lean belly with a gold loop piercing.

"Venus, this is Beverly Shaun. She's the senior designer for JPWear."

Venus stammered, "Hello, nice to meet you." She stuck out her hand for a strong, confident shake even though she'd been thrown by the realization that this beautiful woman was Jake's *right-hand man.*

"Oh, I'm so glad to finally meet you, too. I was out of town for those first days you were here, then you were out of circulation, so finally, great, we meet." She shoved her mass of honey-brown hair to one side of her shoulder. Her hair, eyes, and skin all seemed the same color, like a bronzed statue. "Jake told me it was your idea to change the fit models. I can't tell you how long I'd been suggesting that very thing, but no one would listen to me." A smile appeared, then faded.

"I know how that is." Venus turned quickly to William. "We better get going; it was nice meeting you, Beverly."

"Oh, I may as well come up with you guys. I usually sit in on the morning meetings."

"Right, okay." Venus found herself leading the way to the conference room, a strange cloud of jealousy trailing her. The fit models, and now this bombshell who was working directly underneath Jake, made Venus suddenly sick.

Legend was already seated, going over a report in front of him. He got up when he saw Venus. "I didn't expect to see you for a while. Your mom doing okay?" His words held more sensitivity than she thought possible.

"As well as can be expected. Thanks for asking."

He touched her hand. "Glad you're back. It's a lot of work running the show."

"Yeah, right," William let out in sarcastic agreement.

Beverly Shaun came in behind them and took a seat. Her ample breasts seemed to stay afloat at the table. "Are those the numbers from the T-shirt run?"

"Yep." Legend slid them over for her perusal. He glanced toward Venus. She felt obligated to say something positive.

"That was fast. So how'd it work out?" Venus sat down across from the two of them. William found his place at the window overlooking the studio. "Sold out in every market. Definitely a winner."

Venus took in a deep solid breath. It felt good to be confirmed on the choice of spokesperson although she much preferred being taken at face value. She only hoped she wasn't right about the SOS alert to the competition that Lila Kelly T-shirts would surely send.

Jake walked in. He looked over her head and then right through her. "How's it going? You guys getting started without me?" He sat down with his one container of coffee.

Legend and William looked at him oddly, then looked at each other. He was being too obvious by not even acknowledging Venus after being MIA for the past week. C'mon, she was thinking, get it together.

"Venus, it's nice to see you. Glad your mother is doing better."

"Thank you. I appreciate that." Venus swallowed as if a large dry ball were lodged in her throat. "Looks like everything is going smoothly. I like what you've done here. The models, very crucial to how this is going to play out. And the T-shirt test, wow, Legend said it was a smash." Her words were chopped wood.

Jake leaned back in his chair, a little more at ease. "So I've got what I need to move forward. But we'll still need the dotted line signed."

"I'm working on that." Venus pushed her glasses up on her nose. "Lila Kelly will be in town and I've scheduled a personal meeting." She felt better saying it, even though it was Jake's setup. He understood. She needed her leverage back quickly.

"Excellent. And Beverly, how's it going on your end?"

Venus looked between the two for hidden tension, checking the air for invisible lines and cross-communication.

"All the patterns had to be recut and regraded for the new models. The ad shoots are going to be pushed back anyway, right?"

"Nah, nah. Whether we get Lila or not, we've got to be ready. You will meet your deadline. Don't even think like there's leeway. Keebler elf style if you have to."

Venus shot a look at Beverly to see how she took the reprimand.

"No problem." Beverly smiled. She slid the print out down the length of the table. "Some exciting things are about to happen." She looked like a little girl on her fifth birthday.

"Absolutely." Jake caught the flying report down at the other end. "Absolutely."

Venus stared between them, how ridiculous she must look, sitting there trying to pick up invisible clues about Jake Parson. What she truly knew about him could fill an aspirin bottle. She had no idea of his true motivations. What made him tick. She'd only assumed it was the status quo. Every man liked a good challenge. A solid brick wall to kick down so they'd feel victorious in the end. Thank God her cement was still intact. She'd almost fallen for the sweetness. The tender loving care.

"I'm sorry, I hate to interrupt, but what's the Magic Show?"

"It's the trade show for the urban sportswear scene. One giant show-room so the buyers don't have to hunt you down."

Venus felt silly for not knowing this information. She jotted down a few notes. "Is this something I should attend?"

"We got it covered." Legend's eyes shifted to William and Beverly, responding to the silent question of "who is we?"

"I see. So what's the strategy for the show? Are you planning anything special or are you just going to hang clothes up on a hook?"

"Luckily, I secured a place in the runway showing. We get a ten-minute spot. That's gold in itself; but no doubt, we'll have our area hooked up. Billboards, standing models wearing samples, and best of all, me doing a lot of grin and grip."

Somewhere in between Legend boasting about his ability to sell ice to

Eskimos and sugar in a cane field, Venus blanked out. She was overtaken by visions of Jake massaging her body, smoothing rich warm cream onto her feet and legs, his soft firm hands trailing the length of her back. She could still feel him holding her through the night while she lay on his chest.

"It's not going to make us or break us, whether our presentation is dynamic. It's more out of respect, kind of a religious ceremony for the club of urban fashion, marking territory." It was Jake's voice, the only one that could have snapped her out of the scene she was reliving.

"Okay. Sure." Venus could care less at this point. She looked at her watch. "I'm going to have to get a move on. Beverly, it was good to meet you. Glad you'll be here to keep these guys under control." Her delivery was a little slow, and no one responded to her attempt at satire. She turned to Jake, "You have my cell number if you need to reach me. Don't hesitate to call if you want to discuss anything." She rethought the wording. "Keep me in the loop especially if you get the call from Lila's agency." There, that was better. She slipped out of the double doors feeling like she was leaving something behind.

"Hey, where you headed?" Jake caught up with her, touching her elbow.

"It's still early, I'm going to see if they released my mom yet."

"I'm through here as well, I'll tag along."

"Oh, no, Jake, that's not a good idea. It's such a tense situation right now. Plus, I left Timothy with my parents all day yesterday, and he's going to want to get out."

He didn't blink once, only waiting for her to run out of excuses. "Give me a call when things lighten up. Glad you confirmed our date to see Lila Kelly. I was getting a little worried."

"Oh, no. I wouldn't let you down. I'm in, definitely."

Venus moved swiftly out of the building. She didn't like the way she felt. What was that all about? She had a man. A good man, who loved and honored her. Airic was too busy to do much more than that. She certainly didn't have to worry about him with another woman. Not like Jake who was a flame to the multitude of moths flying in the night. Little fluttering winged insects like Beverly Shaun. Any woman with two eyes would find

Jake Parson attractive, and if they couldn't see, they could surely hear the mating call in his voice.

She pounded the car when her key didn't slide in perfectly. It was so irritating, feeling this way. She had a man. She slammed the door shut and started the car. One was enough trouble, she certainly didn't need to worry about two.

PARTS

VENUS drove straight to her apartment. She planned to change clothes before she saw her mother again. Even under duress, her mother had the ability to see disorder, things that were afoul and not quite right. Pauletta would notice that Venus was wearing the same red sweater, the same black skirt. Yes, she'd spent the night over another man's house while she was engaged to be married to someone else. She wished she could say that to her mother—How come you know when something's rotten in Denmark when it comes to me, but you can't see how rotten things are with your own life?

Pauletta's life, what Venus knew about it, had been textbook migration from the South. Venus's grandmother Mimi had moved her four children, Pauletta, the oldest, Aunt Kat, Uncle Mike, and Uncle Jackson from Oklahoma to California in the late 1950s with no husband. They moved in with Albert, a cousin who had "done good for himself" working at Northrop as an assembly worker. Albert helped Mimi get a job doing the same work at night, leaving twelve-year-old Pauletta as the overseer of the house with her three siblings. She cooked, cleaned, and helped everybody but herself complete their homework for school the next morning.

Pauletta met Henry when she was eighteen, when he walked into the corner market and bought a pint of cold milk. He peeled back the foil seal and drank it right there at the cash register. Pauletta was impressed that a grown man still drank milk and hadn't graduated to Jim Beam like the rest she'd known. They were married three months later. Figuring the math on that one, Pauletta had to be carrying Venus at the time. She and Henry moved to a small apartment where he finished his education in the day and worked at night. Pauletta started working, too, as a cashier at the May Company department store but had to quit after a few months because of an aching back and swollen feet. Pauletta liked to brag about that being her first and last job. And Henry liked to brag that the only important job was taking care of him and his new baby. The end, at least to their version.

Pauletta conveniently left out the part where cousin Albert had been messin' with her, trying to make a woman out of her since she was already doing the lion's share. She couldn't wait to get out of that house, away from Albert. Even though Henry Johnston wasn't her dreamboat, just the fact that he'd docked by her side was enough. Pauletta jumped on board and sailed away. Henry was considered a good catch, educated with a future ahead of him. But he was never what anyone could describe as handsome. He had all the right ingredients, the rich chocolate skin, the sculpted nose and chin, but in all that, there was a goofiness about him, an okey-dokey-type personality that made his intelligence seem questionable, even though he was an honor student in the top percentile of his class. The bits and pieces of conversation Venus had assimilated over the years from Pauletta and her Sunday visits with her sister made it clear that Henry wasn't the man she dreamed of, but he certainly made her dreams come true.

Venus would toss that around in her mind, the full meaning. *Settling* was such an ugly word, so she tried not to use it when telling their story. She tried not to use it when telling her own story as well; Airic wasn't her first choice, but he was the choice she'd made. It wasn't settling if happiness came in the long run.

＊　　＊　　＊

HER apartment felt empty and lonely with the curtains drawn closed in the middle of the day. Venus guessed that Timothy was still with her mother and father at the hospital, where she should have been. She pushed the button on the answering machine and stood over it in the middle of the apartment as she began to undress, one of the perks of living alone. She peeled off the red knit top and slung it over the back of the couch. "Hey, Venus, it's Wendy. I saw Airic downtown. I'm so sorry to hear about your mother. Call me. We should talk. I love you. God bless."

The next message was Airic's. "Hey baby, just checking on you. I won't be able to make it there this weekend. I know that's the last thing you want to hear with all that's going on with your mom, but I can't get around it. Maybe you can come here. You probably need a break from all the stress. Um...okay, let me know what you decide. Love you."

His messages were always left on her cell phone. If he really wanted to reach her, he knew how to do so. Venus stood over the answering machine like it was a living, breathing thing of contradiction and confusion. What was this telling her, that he knew she wouldn't be home and it was safe to call because he really hadn't wanted to talk to her anyway?

She felt waves under her feet. This was something she never expected out of Airic. But then again, she couldn't have predicted the last few days. Nothing had been as usual. Things were falling apart like an earthquake, consistent rumbling underneath the earth's core. A bubbling up of all that hadn't been right.

Calm down, she tried to tell herself. It was just a message. After all, she was the one who didn't answer her phone last night, sitting in the car, watching it ring like an alarm bell, telling her to do the right thing. She'd ignored it and chased after Jake instead.

She pulled a fresh T-shirt over her head and noticed that it clung to her firm round breasts, molding her every curve. She took it off quickly and found another top, large and floundering. Something that wouldn't remind her mother of what she'd lost.

*　　*　　*

"It's me." Venus held the cell phone close to her ear while she drove, maneuvering on busy Wilshire Boulevard.

"Girl," Wendy blew into the phone. "I bumped into Airic downtown. I

couldn't believe it when he told me about your mother. How're you holding up?"

"Not good. No, I shouldn't say that. I'm good. My mom is doing okay.
The doctor removed her right breast. She's supposed to get out of the
hospital today and she just had the surgery day before yesterday. It's just
a trip. This whole thing. She's still Pauletta, you know. She's acting like
everything will be okay, so I'm trying to hang in there and feel the same
way."

The words crept like small bruised animals in her throat. But she kept
going, "...because, I mean...the fact that a breast is gone doesn't take
away your soul, doesn't make you less of a person, right? What the hell is
the big deal? She's still alive and that's all that counts." Her mouth was a
garble of words while she rubbed at her eyes. Venus couldn't help it,
pulling over and nearly running up the side of the curb. She tried to plug
her tear ducts, stop them from rendering her blind. She'd met people who
didn't cry and claimed to have never shed a tear they could remember.
Their ducts must've been removed, or they'd already cried a lifetime's
worth of sadness and had no more to give. Soon, she'd fall into that cate-
gory.

"Oh, Venus, oh sweetie. I'm coming to Los Angeles. You're all alone
out there, dealing with this. I'm coming."

Venus wanted to tell her no, that's okay. It's just a breast, the part nobody wants on the turkey 'cause it's too dry. She wanted to tell Wendy that
her mother was fine. She was fine. It wasn't necessary. Crying over a stupid lost breast.

"I'll make arrangements for the kids. Sidney will understand. He needs
to spend some time with them anyway."

A pool of silence wavered between them. Venus knew Wendy would
do it, fly all the way from Washington, D.C., just to be by her side. Hadn't
she been there when Venus cried thirty days and thirty nights over losing
Clint Fairchild, and swore she'd never tell a soul?

They dubbed it Black Saturday, the day Clint married Kandi Treboe.
Venus attended the wedding, she'd wished them both well, and why
shouldn't she, she had Airic. But in truth, Venus hadn't been ready. An

eclipse began the morning after, a sudden darkness that encapsulated her world. The cloak was thick and heavy with shame and embarrassment. Why she even went to the wedding was a mystery. Her only excuse was that she had believed the freedom was real. The lightness and forgiveness of her heart were real. But deep down inside she'd been miserable, and Wendy was the only one who knew the truth. She held her, rocked her, and kept the liquids flowing like caring for a lingering flu. Only it was heartache. Clint had married someone else right under her nose.

"I'm okay, really. I'm fine. You can't drop your life over this. My mom is going to be fine." Venus sniffed, trying to get a hold of herself. "I think everything is going to be okay. Timothy is here. My dad." Somehow, they both knew not to mention Airic.

"If you need me, Venus, you know I will be on the first thing smoking. Do you hear me?"

"I do, loud and clear."

They hung up. Venus was once again exhausted. She flipped the rearview mirror down to face herself. She dug in her purse and pulled out the Visine. She squirted a few drops in her eyes and let her head fall against the headrest while her eyes burned with more tears. She listened to the steady movement of traffic. The swish of cars tearing by. She pictured herself opening the car door and stepping out too far, being hit, slammed in her center and carried away. Destroyed, no longer whole. Was it she or her mother? It felt like there was no separation between the two; she placed her hand over her breast and began to weep and mourn their loss.

* * *

THE hospital bed was empty when Venus came around the corner. First appalled, then relieved, she stepped back into the corridor. The nurses' station was partitioned off, only allowing the tops of their heads to be seen where they were seated. Venus walked over and leaned in on her elbows. "Did Pauletta Johnston check out already?"

A soft smile appeared on the Asian woman's face, "Pauletta, yes. You're her daughter?"

Venus nodded her head, guessing that nurses gossiped like every other work pool. Venus being kicked out in favor of Dr. Prah was probably worth at least ten minutes of lively discussion.

The nurse pulled up information on her computer screen. "It's not in here yet," she said as she shuffled through papers in a tray, then came up with a bunch of paper-clipped forms. "Hold on; yep, she's checked out. I thought I saw her being rolled out not long ago. 11:56, is the time stamp." She looked at her watch. "You probably missed her on your way up."

Venus mouthed the words *thank you* and turned and left. It was true. Always a step behind, she chastised herself, pushing on the elevator button. She couldn't figure out if she'd planned it that way. A true sign that she was never going to catch whatever she was chasing.

The elevator pulled open.

If the heels on her boots weren't four inches high she would have fallen over backward. Venus stepped back and gave a second thought to running in the other direction.

Clint Fairchild. Wait, no, *Doctor* Clint Fairchild, crisp and starch fresh in his powder-blue shirt and gray slacks. His dark skin even darker, healthy and glowing.

His eyes squinted with recognition. He pushed the button to open the doors back up that had begun to close. "Venus?"

She paused, as if she didn't know who he was. "Oh my goodness, is that you, Clint?" She stretched out her arms. "What are you doing in L.A.?" They hugged long and hard.

"This is me, I'm on staff. Pediatrics." His mouth stretched in a wide smile. "Man, this is wild, how're you doing?" Genuine joy spread across his face.

"I'm fine." She blinked too many times.

"What's going on? What're you doing here?"

"My mom, she had a mastectomy."

"No. V, I'm sorry." He took a deep breath. His smile completely faded. "How's she doing?"

"I'm on my way to find out. She checked out today. Probably home by now."

"I'm sorry." The incredulousness of the situation weighed in his tone.

Venus switched places with him and punched the elevator button. "I better get going. At least I know where to find you. I thought you were back in D.C. practicing at Greater Washington."

He got back on the elevator too. "Oh, yeah, I was. I just took this spot about three months ago. I'm actually the head of the department." His chest puffed up with pride.

"Of course," Venus said, before she could stop herself, feeling the old tensions rise. She scanned his left hand quickly. "So how do you like it?"

"Serious work, here. Crack babies in neo. I thought it was bad in D.C., but L.A. just might have the upper hand in that department."

"Really, wow, that's sad."

"Yeah." He watched the lights count down to his floor. "So we've got to get together, V. Play catch-up. I know we've got a lot to talk about so don't even pretend like you're too busy, or make any excuses." The curve of his mouth in a half smile, his eyes lowered. "Where're you staying? Your mom's?"

"No. I have my own place, I'm here on assignment. This whole thing, the cancer, my mom, I just found out about it. I guess God puts us where we're supposed to be." She put her head down. "I would be sick if I was stuck in D.C. while all this was happening. Not doing so good here, either."

The elevator stopped. "She'll pull through, V." He touched her chin, lifting her face slightly as if he had a right. "We'll sit down and talk about it, okay? Meanwhile, I'll look into what I can. Find out what's what."

"Sure, yeah. I'll give you a call, maybe we can do coffee or something. Not here, though, it's terrible." She tried to make light before the doors closed.

"I'd like that—"

As soon as the sliding doors sealed, she felt the nausea kick to her stomach. A harsh burning that made her stumble slightly out the hospital entrance.

Clint was in Los Angeles.

She made it to the parking garage and found her car. She got inside and dropped forward with her head on the leather steering wheel. "Clint here, in Los Angeles, the same hospital as my mother. Here," she whispered through the round hole of the steering wheel. She started the engine and sped out of the parking garage, winding in a spiral until she reached the street. She swung out into traffic, barely missing another car. She could still feel the cool tips of his fingers on the point of her chin. He wasn't wearing his wedding band. She saw it with her very own eyes, the day he and Kandi had been pronounced man and wife, the ring exchange. But he wasn't wearing his.

So what.

She came to a stoplight and took the spare minutes and laid her head down on the steering wheel, holding her stomach. The car behind her honked. She stepped on the gas quickly and sped through the light as it turned yellow.

Clint's here.

So what. So what. So what. So what! she finally yelled at the top of her lungs. So what he looked good, so what he wasn't wearing a ring, and so what if she had thought about him at least once a day for the last two years? It's not like they were good thoughts. Half the time she'd pictured herself pouring something cold and thick over his head, or walking up to him out of nowhere and landing a hard right across his face. That's what you get . . . for walking away from the best thing you ever had.

She was doing twice the speed limit. So what. She ran a light that turned red while she was in the middle of the crossing. So what. She turned a corner on nearly two wheels. She slowed when she saw the orange and green sign of a 7-Eleven convenience store. She needed something, anything, to squelch the uprising in her stomach. She came to a stop, parking crooked and on the edge of the curb, and jumped out and ran inside. The water bottles sat low in the corner of the refrigerated compartment. Venus squatted with her skirt tight around her thighs. She opened the Evian bottle, taking a swig, drinking for survival.

It didn't mean a thing. Her life would not be altered one iota. Her mother was still sick. She still had Airic. So what. She still had a career that she loved. She still had Jake. The water bottle tipped past comfort and spilled down her blouse. She stood up, wet and flabbergasted. Had she just thought that... *she still had Jake?*

"Hey, you plan on paying for that?" The cashier behind the counter waved to get Venus's attention.

She wiped her mouth and patted at moistness on her chest. "Yes," she said, feeling a sudden and unnerving relief. Unwarranted, unfounded relief.

SLOW DANCING

A line of people packed in around the Pantages Theatre. Bodies pressed against each other. Rain still poured with a fury past the overhang where the words *Lila Kelly Tonight* were written on the marquee. "I think we can bypass all these people." Jake took Venus by the hand and pulled her through the thick crowd. A petite young woman with thick blond braids held up her hand.

"We're not admitting yet. Wait behind the yellow rope, please."

Jake held up his tickets and the backstage passes.

"Okay." She softened immediately. "Go straight to the end and make a right at the stage." Venus heard the gasps and moans from the waiting crowd when they appeared to receive special treatment. The young woman unhooked the yellow rope for them to pass.

"It's raining, they should just let everybody in."

Once inside Jake still held on to her hand. The red interior was old-fashioned and eighteenth-century heavy. The chandeliers, high ceilings, and wood moldings were beautifully maintained, shiny rich oak with intricately carved designs. "I saw *The Wiz* here." She looked around, reminiscing about the day she and her mother saw the African American play with Stephanie Mills as Dorothy. Nearly front-row seats. The majestic colors of the costumes, the dramatic songs and acting. It was the first time she'd ever seen such a thing. An ensemble of black singers and dancers, the giddiness of that day, the exuberance recalled with so much clarity. Her grip tightened around Jake's hand.

"I only saw the movie. I was a little embarrassed watching Michael Jackson ease on down the road, I must say."

Venus smiled. "It's a classic. I'd show it to my kids if I ever had any." They reached the dark corner at the end of the aisle. The giant red velvet curtain was closed on the stage. Venus followed, still eyeing the first few rows, remembering herself as a child beaming with wonderment.

"You want kids?" Jake asked, making more than trivial conversation.

"Yes, I would like to have kids." Venus held her head down as if there were shame in that confession. "You?"

"Definitely." He rethought his answer. "But if I couldn't have them, it'd be no big deal."

"What do you mean?"

"I mean, if the lady that I fell in love with couldn't have kids, I could live with that." He was fishing. She stayed quiet. "Does Airic want children . . . with you?" It was the first time he'd used his name, the first time he'd acknowledged him with more than the euphemism *honey*. Venus tried not to let it shake her. She continued walking, following the dark maze with spotlights shining up from floor level. She'd told Jake about Airic having two daughters from a previous marriage. They'd talked about all sorts of things the day they'd spent together, the night. She wasn't sure, but she thought she mentioned the fact that they were nearly grown, and Airic could be looking into the face of grandfatherhood shortly. But yes, he'd wanted children . . . with her.

"I'm sorry. I guess that's personal." Jake slowed and let her go in front of him. They finally came to the end of the trail. Two large bounty-hunter-looking guys came up and towered over Venus. Jake stuck his passes in front of their large round faces.

"You need to wear those, around the neck, money." One of the men lifted his fat finger, making a ring around his neck area. "Gone mess up your look, dawg?" He grinned.

Jake pulled the tag over his head. Venus did the same.

"Oh shit . . . I know you. Whassup man, you ain't makin' no more hits?" He started doing a little dance. ". . . *I like them luscious lips and those fat juicy hips.*"

Jake saw Venus from the corner of his eye ready to fix the bodyguard's incorrect version of the song. He stopped her. "Nah, man. I'm outta the game."

"Right...you make them T-shirts and shit. My little cousin likes your stuff, man. That's cool."

This time Jake's chest puffed up. Venus intervened. "JPWear is a multimillion-dollar company. It's more than T-shirts, I can assure you. That's why we're here to talk to Miss Kelly, to see if she's interested in representing the preeminent force."

The bodyguard tilted his head like a puppy who didn't understand. "Yeah, okay. Miss Kelly only allows five minutes per visitor. Ya'll want to go in individually or together, five minutes together or five minutes each way. Your call."

Venus felt like she was visiting a prison ward. She scrunched up her nose to show her distaste for the way they were being treated.

"Together," Jake commanded, needing to get his grounding back around the oversized men.

The one wearing his black cap backward turned around and started walking. "Follow me."

Venus was thinking this was a tad much. But then again, this was Lila Kelly, the hottest new diva. Fans—men, women, girls, and boys—were probably her worst nightmare at this point, pulling and scratching to get a hold of her. She probably needed bodyguards just to make a trip to the corner market, probably couldn't stroll down the feminine hygiene aisle without being spotted. It was embarrassing enough carrying the large brightly colored boxes to the checkout, Venus couldn't imagine having to do it with people watching intentionally.

"You ready?" Jake had to tap her twice before she reacted. The vision of wearing sunglasses and a London Fog hat and coat, reading the quantities on the boxes, deciding between light flow or heavy, still on her mind.

"Five minutes," the perspiring bodyguard said before stepping off to the side and opening the dressing room door.

The pretty young woman was sitting on a leather couch looking through a magazine. "Hi." She smiled brightly. Her tanned skin flush with makeup and dark heavy eyeliner. Underneath it all, Venus thought, she looks like a baby playing dress-up. She stood up and put out her hand like she'd been taught to do.

"Jake Parson. This is my associate Venus Johnston. We wanted to talk to you about an offer to be a spokesperson for JPWear."

Venus chimed in. "Actually, it's a new line called Feline, an offshoot of JPWear, targeting the young hot urban crowd like yourself. It's an awesome line of clothing; I can tell you'd love it."

Lila Kelly smiled brightly again. She sat back down on the couch. "You guys are the ones that put out the T-shirts with my face plastered on 'em. You know I hated that cover shot of me? My eyes looked too close together. Now I hate the T-shirts."

Venus went into auto-damage control. "That picture of you happened to sell half a million T-shirts. You are beautiful, intelligent, and incredibly talented. That's what people are buying. All of you. Not just a pretty face. You're so much more than that, Ms. Kelly. JPWear knows that. That's why we want you to head the new line."

Her voice was husky, lower than the soft mellow singing voice on her records. "Cool. Would I get to pick out what I wear? Design some stuff?"

"That's something we'd have to work out—"

"Of course," Venus countered. "Of course. We think your style is incredible."

"Someone picks my clothes for me. Well, not everything." She lifted her foot wearing a pointed-toe boot. "I got these on Fifth Avenue when I was in New York. They were screaming my name right through the window. Had to have 'em."

"Nice." Venus sincerely appreciated a good boot, or any shoe for that matter. "Do you think it's something you could do? I know you aren't allowed to make those kinds of decisions without representation, but is it something you'd like to do?"

"Of course, I can make that kind of decision. I'm eighteen. I can do whatever I want to do."

Except pick out her own clothes, Jake's eyes said. He pulled out a business card. Venus snatched it from his hand and pushed it into her own pocket. "Okay, great. We'll be in touch. Wait till you see the jeans with the fur on the sides, you are going to fall backward for these. They'll go with those boots, too."

"Could I keep some of the clothes, after I model them?"

"Of course," Venus said before Jake could get technical. She could see him putting together small print in his head. Decisions always came with a cost.

"So you guys going to stay for the concert or did you just come to ask me about the clothes deal?"

The question threw Venus. She zeroed in on the bright eyes underneath the heavy makeup. She was a smart girl. Intuitive and shrewd. Funny how those traits got overshadowed by beauty and talent.

"We came to hear you sing. You have a beautiful voice," Venus said assuredly, waving good-bye while the large escort used his body to cut off the conversation. "We'll be out there." Venus squeezed the words out before the door was closed in her face.

Venus put an arm around Jake's shoulder, then quickly removed it. Caught up in the moment. "That was perfect. Wow. She's something else. I really think this is going to work out. Print ads, commercials. With a recognizable voice like that, we could even do radio."

"We?" He blinked cautiously. "You thinking about staying with my company?"

"No. I am not thinking of staying with your company. I have a very good job that I enjoy, thank you very much."

"Well, what if Lila Kelly's only willing to follow through if you're with JPWear? What if she only wants you? You could stay here and take care of your mother." He nudged her with his elbow.

"Good one, but I don't think I'm the lure here. And that's a low blow trying to use my mom. She doesn't need me anyway." Venus slipped into a moment of sadness.

The seats of the theater began to fill. People were mulling about, trying hard to find something to do so they could be seen before the lights went down. Flash and glitter, miniskirts and furs. Venus felt matronly in her skirt, sweater, and leather jacket, even though fashion had always been her strong suit.

"Our seats are over here."

"Umph." A woman cleared her throat and made her girlfriends look in Jake's direction, ignoring Venus altogether.

"You have a devilish effect on women."

"All except the one I want." The curtains bumped around with movement. Lila's band was getting into place. The lights dimmed; "Got to Get You into My Life" started playing loud enough to make people think for a moment Earth, Wind & Fire themselves were on stage. The beat moved through their seats. The excitement was building. The audience started clapping, calling out her name, L-i-l-a, L-i-l-a. Venus found herself joining in, looking at Jake while he did the same. His face was lit with energy. Another side of him, free of concern.

The music switched; this time it was Lila's music. The curtains pulled back and at the same time, mini–smoke bombs went off onstage behind the drummer and three guys with horns. The crowd roared. "Ladies and gentlemen, the incomparable Lila Kelly."

The voice boomed out of nowhere, and then she appeared. Dressed fully in white leather jeans with studs down the side, a leather vest that barely closed showing her flat tummy and belly button, and to top it off, her leather boots, the only thing she hadn't changed out of since they'd met earlier. Her smile opened with her arms. The crowd felt the invisible hug and let out sincere appreciation. "How you doin', L.A.?" She went to the other side of the stage, strutting in her tight jeans. "I said ... how you doin'?" The left side of the audience screamed louder. "Now, that's what I want to hear." The band kicked in with heavy drums and horns; Lila spun around and started singing her number one song.

Before Venus knew it, she was up on her feet, dancing to the music, feeling the deepest rhythm played from the bass guitar, the drums, the beat fully through her body. Jake was next to her, dancing in his space. The entire theater had turned into one big nightclub. "Thought you didn't do concerts," Jake screamed near her ear, the only way she would have heard him.

Venus beamed a smile, doing the last dance she remembered, and doing it well. Some things you never forget. She'd needed this, to laugh and throw her head back, letting her tonsils show. The exhilaration of not caring whether she looked sleek and sexy, only pure movement. But she must've been doing something right, because Jake stopped watching the stage and started watching Venus.

When the music slowed to the next intro, the crowd screamed again. "Someone Like You," the slow ballad that had women, young and old, believing in love again. Lila's soft crisp voice sailed out over the speakers, filling the room, commanding full attention. She addressed the audience, "Have you ever stopped and asked yourself... where did love go? Why has it passed me by?" Lila hummed again, and women from the audience screamed, Tell it, girl. "But then he came along. Oh yeah, the man that stopped your breath, made you feel sexy when you hadn't done a thing. Hadn't changed a thing, no new clothes or teeth brightener, no fancy workout outfit"—the women laughed on cue—"but he saw it. That spirit, that ecstasy... that deep down well full of love, been there all along, waiting, waiting, for someone like you..." She broke into the song.

"She's good," Jake turned to Venus, but stopped short when he noticed her eyes full of sadness. Or hope? He took her in his arms and held her. Held her while the tears soaked the crease of his chest. Venus held on, like it was a dangerous ride with long yielding curves. She let him move her from side to side, her arms wrapped around his neck.

"Well, let me tell you boys and girls, anything good is worth waiting for. And when it's damn good, you'll be thanking the heavens above that it took so long." Lila's backup singers fell into chorus.

Venus coughed a laugh mixed with sadness. What did she know, this girl-woman? How could she know about this burden of heart and soul? It took Venus a lifetime and she knew she still hadn't gotten it right.

Jake swayed her from side to side. She closed her eyes, letting her heart and mind get swept away.

BRIGHT LIGHTS

THE concert with Jake had been fun, a little good-time relief she'd needed desperately. Yet walking in and seeing her mother propped up on pillows watching television erased all memory. She'd come in fully prepared to tell her mother about meeting Lila Kelly. More important, bumping into Clint at the hospital the other day. But none of it mattered. Venus didn't feel the urgency once she walked into her mother's bedroom.

At one point, Pauletta would have lived for that kind of drama. Today she looked calm and unconcerned. Not worrying about covering her azaleas for the winter mornings. Not checking on Daddy to make sure he wasn't eating in the living room. Not talking on the phone giving firm advice to her brother or sisters about their grown children.

Her parents' bedroom was exactly the same way as it had always been. Beige walls. Dark teak dresser and headboard, thick tarnished brass mirror with a blue dried flower display hanging with a large wired bow in the center. A huge antique frame housed an old black-and-white wedding portrait of Pauletta and Henry. Venus had studied that picture like it was the Last Supper with Jesus and his disciples. The stiffness of her mother and father as they stood side by side, he in a heavy wool suit, and her mother wearing a sharply tailored gown with a square neck and half sleeves. Simple, no frills. There was a hint of joy in her mother's eyes. A sense of relief.

Venus used to stand on the bed, holding on to the headrail, on tiptoes, to kiss her father in the picture, "I now take you as my awfully wedded husband." Lawfully, her father would correct her while scooping her up in his arms. She'd asked him a hundred times, what lawfully meant. He'd explain, "When you're bound by the laws of marriage to love and protect that person, just like I do with your mother." The word *awfully* still stuck in her head, some sort of Freudian slip.

The scent of her mother's Jergens lotion lingered in the room. Even now, Pauletta was still on the left side of the bed, nearest to the wall where she'd always slept. Venus sat down in Henry's space.

"Hi, Mom." Venus kissed Pauletta on the forehead. "Can I get you anything?" She ran a hand across her cheek, kissed her mother again.

"Can you turn the channel? Last thing I want to see is *Judge Judy*, those people spewing nonsense."

"The remote's in your hand, Mom."

"I know. Your daddy put it there, but I'm not feeling like I can push the buttons."

Venus looked down at her mother's fingers limply wrapped around the remote. She slipped it out of her hand with ease. "Did you feel that, Mom?"

"I didn't say I can't feel anything, I just don't have the strength to push the buttons."

"Is that normal?" Venus stood up and didn't wait for an answer. "Daddy," she called out twice. Henry and Timothy both came running up the stairs in a short burst of panic. The weight of them both caused the floorboards to creak.

"What's going on?"

"Is it normal for Mom not to be able to move her hand, her fingers? I think we need to call the doctor."

"Venus, it's normal," Timothy offered, a little frustrated by the anticipation of a real crisis.

"She's going to have therapy three times a week to start her muscles moving again." Henry reached across and touched Pauletta's shoulder. "You need anything, sweetheart?"

"I think we should call the doctor. She can't even change the channel. How much strength does it take to change the channel?" Venus presented the question looking for a reasonable answer.

"Oh, Lord. She's been here all of fifteen minutes and here we go."
Pauletta let out a sigh. "Push my pillows up a little, Henry."

Venus stood with her arms crossed over the wet spot on her blouse.
Her father came around the other side of the bed and scooted the pillows
higher.

"You don't want me here, Mom? Is that what you're saying?"

"Not if you're going to keep up this neurosis," Pauletta said, now
propped high enough to look Venus in the eye. Crinkled white hairs were
edging from underneath the silk scarf tied tightly around her head. "I
can't take any more of you making things out to be more than they are.
Quit being so wound up."

Venus looked over at Timothy, standing with his hands pushed in his
faded jean pockets. Then to her father, flipping the channel. Her mother's
eyes were still focused on the television, all three of them acting as if all
was well.

"I have to go." Venus grabbed her purse. Pauletta didn't respond, only
stared straight ahead.

"Oh, now, Precious." Her father followed her down the stairs.

"I'm upsetting Mom. She needs to rest. She's right, I'm doing nothing
but complaining, making her feel worse."

Henry stayed close as she went out the front door. "Now wait a minute,
that's enough. I've never known you to be so selfish. Where's this coming
from? Seems like the last few times I've seen you, you've had your fists
balled up."

"I can't stand it. You guys acting like all's well that ends well. This is a
tragedy and I want something done about it. She's up there like a rag doll;
she's half there, Dad, and you guys are just taking it in stride. Am I the
only one disgusted by all this?"

"Taking it in stride. Have you lost your mind?"

Venus focused on the thick line running across her father's forehead,
the intense glare in his eyes. Surprisingly, his voice still came out even
and calm. "Nobody is taking this lightly. Especially not me. But I'm not
going to sit up there trying to make her feel bad. You don't know what
she's feeling deep down, that's Pauletta's way. She's not going to sit there
quivering and pitiful waiting for someone to save the day. 'Cause nobody

can do it. Not me, not Timothy, and not you. Support, Venus. That's what she needs. Not the constant searching for something wrong, something to fight about. The doctor did the best she could, and even if it wasn't the best, it's done now. We've got to deal with it."

"Now," he said, gathering a second wind, "it's very simple, you're either in or you're out. I'm not going to have this anymore. You either come with full support or don't come at all."

Venus watched him turn and walk away. His angled shoulders moved in one full motion to swing the door open to go back inside. Timothy managed to slip out before the screen shut. He gave her a look to let her know he wasn't next. He'd spare her the lecture.

"You all right?"

She and Timothy stood in front of the pink stucco house with the brown composite roof, both staring out past the perfectly manicured carpet of grass.

"I can't stand it," she said, hoping the impending tears understood the consequences of showing up again. "I love her so dearly, and what's happened is so wrong. I'm angry, Timothy. I don't know any other words for it. I'm mad, and there's nothing you can say to make me feel any different."

"You're angry at Mom, or the disease?"

Venus turned away, her arms folded over her chest. She didn't want him to start up with the psychoanalysis.

"If you can't tell me," he said, stepping closer, "at least think about it for yourself."

She knew there was something deep-seated at the root of her anger, but it didn't lessen the facts. Her mother had been treated like a second-class citizen. If she'd had money, the kind that could buy a doctor's second opinion, or a third, they wouldn't be having this conversation. Mostly, she was angry that her mother had felt like it was something to be ashamed of, a dirty little secret like cousin Albert wanting to make her his child bride. Or maybe it was only Venus who Pauletta hadn't wanted to know. Fear that, after all these years of posturing, her daughter would find out that she wasn't perfect, that she was merely human.

She leaned on Timothy's narrow chest, still trying not to cry. "I'll see you tomorrow." She started down the concrete path to the street where her car was parked. She passed the handprints that they'd made in the concrete. Venus and Timothy, 1974. The flower Venus had drawn with a stick now looked like a crab missing its claws.

"I'm leaving in the morning," Timothy called behind her.

Venus stopped on the stairs and turned around. "Africa?" she said in jest, but unable to put a smile behind it.

"No. Not yet. Heading back to Boston."

"I'll take you to the airport. What time?"

"Eight o'clock flight."

"I'll be here at six." She blew a kiss and waved.

Her cell phone rang as soon as she buckled her seat belt. It restricted her from leaning forward to fish it out of her purse. She unsnapped herself and grabbed it too late. *Missed call.* She clicked to see who it was. Airic. She pressed the button to call him back, closing it before it could ring.

*   *   *

FEELING helpless was the worst part. She had questions that needed answers. The hospital looked empty, abandoned, as Venus drove by. The entryway, the double glass doors were a reflection of black. The lights in the hospital had been put on reserve, conserving energy for the California fuel crunch. She parked her car in the even darker parking garage and sat for a moment. She wanted to get her questions together for Dr. Prah. She couldn't make it a war; like her father said, what's done is done. But not in Venus's mind; she was sick to her stomach about the whole situation. The way her mother had been handled. It infuriated her, the thought of Dr. Prah tossing her mother's file aside to look at the next, and the next, as if a life, a beautiful full life was not at stake.

The information desk was in the center of the lobby. A security guard sat on a stool, not truly securing anything. His head rested on the side of his fist. He tried to look alert once he saw Venus coming toward him.

"The directory doesn't list Dr. Prah. I know she's in this hospital. I don't remember her office number, can you look it up for me?"

He tapped a few keys and waited for the screen to open up. "Dr. Prah is no longer with Kaiser." He put his finger on the screen, then twisted it around so Venus could see for herself. "Not available HS location 10/22 forward PATs to Dr. Lamb."

The look on her face indicated that she didn't understand. He flipped the computer module back toward him. He began reading. "Not available at the Hollywood/Sunset location as of October 22; forward patients to Dr. Lamb. That's what that means. Dr. Lamb is in 206." He pressed a button to make the screen fade, then fell back into his security stance, head perched on bent elbow and fist.

Venus walked, stunned, to the elevator. She had just seen Dr. Prah today, or was it yesterday? She couldn't really say that she'd actually seen the doctor. Not physically. She pressed the button again. This was adding insult to injury, a hard stiff poke in the eye, and any other cruelty beyond comprehension. Dr. Prah butchers an innocent woman and then bolts. God! Did Pauletta know? Probably, yes. Why tell Venus anything? What could she do about it, except make things worse?

Once inside the elevator with the doors closed tight, she swung her purse around, knocking it into the handicap bar. Shit. What kind of doctor just ups and leaves patients who are in her care? Maybe she'd been fired. Maybe someone found out she was a walking liability, giving bad medical care and advice, and sent her packing. The elevator opened up directly to the new doctor's office. Venus walked in and went directly to the partitioned window. There was a beige-skinned Latina woman sitting with the phone pressed against her ear. She held up one finger and smiled. "Yes... okay, no problem, we'll see you then." Her accent was thick and happy.

"My mother is a patient here, she had a mastectomy, courtesy of Dr. Prah, and now I find out she's no longer here and Dr. Lamb is the referral." It came out more as a question than a statement; Venus was still trying to understand herself.

"Yes, we have Dr. Prah's patients. Let me see. What is your mother's name?"

"Pauletta Johnston."

"How do you spell that? Oh, never mind, here she is. Yes. We have her scheduled for a follow-up on the thirty-first." After reading the rest of the file, she looked up with a compassionate frown. "How's she doing?"

Venus had to think about it for a minute and realized she'd never asked her mother that question. Never once simply asked, "Mom, how're you doing?"

"She's home. Resting. She has weakness in her hand and arm. I wanted to talk to someone, I have a lot of questions. There's so much going on, and I don't understand how to help. I want to help, but I'm afraid of what's going on." The receptionist's facial expression was Venus's only clue that she was losing it, speaking in hiccuped phrases, unable to maintain the front of calmness and reasonability.

The receptionist rushed from around her square box and put an arm around Venus. "Come. Come with me." She pushed the door open and took her inside. Venus could feel the eyes of the waiting patients witnessing her breakdown, watching her being escorted away to the private ward for the distressed. She maneuvered Venus around the maze of halls, stopping in front of a closed door.

"Here. Sit down. I will get you some tissue." The door closed. Venus was alone inside the exam room. At least the walls were a sunny yellow with soft pastel pictures of meadows and woods. But she was still cold. She rubbed the sides of her arms, afraid to let go even for a moment to wipe the liquid draining from her nose and eyes.

"Here you go." The small hand appeared with tissue. She grabbed hold. "I'm sorry, this is the worst feeling, not being able to help or to do anything for my mother."

Venus blew and wiped while the receptionist pulled up a chair next to her. "Dr. Lamb is going to stop in and talk with you. He doesn't have a lot of time between his patients, but I'll make sure he sees you. Everything is going to be fine." She rubbed Venus's back. "You're shaking." She walked over and stood tiptoe in front of a cabinet to pull out a plastic wrapped blanket, similar to the airplane blankets. She opened it and spread the blanket around Venus's shoulders.

"Thank you." Venus blew again and dabbed at her tired eyes, the double-crossers.

"Do you want something to drink while you're waiting? How about some tea, or coffee?"

"Water would be fine."

"Okay, be right back." The receptionist moved quickly.

Venus took the window of time to calm herself. She hated being pathetic. She'd had enough of that to last a lifetime. She took a moment, telling herself to shake it off. She had real questions that needed real answers. She didn't want someone patronizing her, telling her everything would be all right. Go home, be patient, wait your turn...the cancer would find you if it needed you.

"Here you go." A Dixie cup filled with water appeared. Venus nodded a thank-you. She was quickly alone again in the brightly lit room. She looked up to study the source, wondering why they weren't conserving energy in here, too. Fluorescent lights. Tricky. Designed to not work unless all of them were working. Like the lights on a Christmas tree, connected and intertwined, all dependent on the other. Sort of like a family. The blood was the cord that bound each to the other whether they liked it or not.

The doctor knocked before coming inside. Venus looked up to see a gentle-faced man of color, not sure which culture, his fine curly hair graying at the temples. He wore a white coat, old-school style. Most doctors ditched the lab jacket for business casual these days. He was a welcome sight.

"How're you doing today? I hear you've got some questions for me." He sat in the chair the receptionist had planted beside her.

She nodded a yes.

"Why don't we start with the most important one; your mother's surgery was considered a success. A dye scan was performed during the operation that shows where the cells may have trailed and it appears the cancer hadn't moved beyond the right mass." He looked up to assure her, "Dr. Prah removed the lymph nodes just as a precaution. When your mother comes in next week, we'll discuss how we're going to continue to fight this thing, radiology, chemo. There's a lot of new therapy, new options that are available now that weren't accessible even a few years ago." He bounced back in the unsteady small chair, probably forgetting he wasn't in his doctor's office, closed the file, then asked. "So now, your questions."

"I was concerned about me." There, it was officially noted. Venus was worrying about herself at a time like this. She wanted to know the chances of her getting cancer, too. Mother, daughter, the link of blood and genetics, heredity, and lights that completely broke down from the weakness of the other. "Tell me," she said as if they shared a secret, "what's going to happen to me?" Venus twisted the used tissue around her index finger, forming a mock cast. She squeezed it tight, putting enough pressure to remind herself that she wasn't an unfeeling shrew.

He sighed, as if it were a common fear. "A while ago, the medical community believed very strongly that if you had an immediate relative like a mother, grandmother, or aunt with breast cancer, the likelihood of cancer was substantial. That's different from what we're finding out these days. Your odds are just as good of not getting cancer as they are of getting it. Does that make sense? What I'm trying to say is, there are no definitive prediction markers for breast cancer. As hard as we like to assign numbers and quantifiable data to everything, this disease still remains a mystery as to its causes, as to its targets, who will be affected, who won't. Same goes with the genetic analysis. Finding the so-called cancer gene doesn't guarantee cancer. In fact, from that study alone, it's proven not to be the case. Maybe it has something to do with caution. Once those people find out they're at risk, they may take better care of themselves, better diet, exercise, rest. The fact of the matter is, no guarantees. The best thing you can do is be aware. How old are you?" Dr. Lamb asked, leaning forward to get her attention.

"Thirty-six."

"You're already doing something right." He smiled.

Venus returned the smile appropriately. Pauletta looked younger than her age also. What had it mattered?

"The first thing to do is get a baseline mammogram, just to have it on record, something to use as a reference mark. Then have follow-ups every other year, and do your home exams. There's a lobby full of reading materials to show the proper way to do them. I think you're on the right track by being here. Understanding this disease and keeping a watchful eye is the only defense at this point." He put a light hand on her arm before standing up. He pulled a card out of his front coat pocket. "If you need anything, have any questions, you can always call." He handed her the card, then grabbed a pen off the counter with Pauletta's file. "Same last name as your mother?" He began to scribble doctor scratch, looking to her for an answer.

"Yes. Venus Johnston."

"Okay, Venus Johnston, we're now friends; don't hesitate to call for yourself, or your mother."

Venus nodded her head up and down, still wavering on shaky ground.

"You go on home and take care of your mother. I bet you can cook, make some old-fashioned chicken soup, or my favorite, gumbo. She needs to be healthy when we start the preventive medicines." His gray temples creased with his smile. "I'm depending on you."

Venus stood up and walked to the door he held open. "Thank you," she whispered, or what sounded like a whisper to her congested nose and eardrums. "Dr. Lamb, I know this is probably a normal thing, to switch patients, but what happened to Dr. Prah?"

"She's moved on to a private practice. It's not in our best interest to make referrals outside of our medical group, but I'd be happy to pass that information to you as a personal favor, if your mother would like to see her instead. I wouldn't be offended at all."

Venus had the urge to hug him. "No. That's not necessary. My mother is going to love you. I was just curious."

"Take care, now," he said, as he moved on to his next crisis.

Doctors weren't so bad, at least not all of them. She stood in front of the elevator, smashing her thumb into the steel round button, suddenly feeling like it was stronger than she and attempting to push back. Amazing how things were meant to be. If Dr. Prah hadn't ditched her mother, there wouldn't have been a Dr. Lamb to save the day, to save her mother.

A very pregnant woman came and gave it a just-in-case press, then waited right alongside of her. Obviously a nurse, from her flowered smock and white pants.

"When are you due?" Venus looked down at the wide tummy, still wiping at her nose with tissue.

The woman wore blond synthetic braids around her dark skin. "Six more days; it's scheduled. I'm not leaving this in the hands of Mother

Nature. My doctor and I decided to induce. Didn't want to take any chances. You haven't seen crazy, till you've seen a hospital on Halloween night. No thanks. My baby is scheduled to grace this beautifully mixed-up world on schedule and in an orderly environment."

The elevator arrived. The doors opened. Venus let the very pregnant woman go first, then attempted to take a step in. She grabbed the metal bar and slumped down. It felt like the square box was tipping on its side.

"Whoa, you all right?" The woman's blond braids hung over her shoulder, tickling the bridge of Venus's nose. "I'm a nurse. Look at me." She took a hold of her wrist, checking her watch at the same time. "Too low and your eyes are way glassy. When's the last time you ate?" She helped Venus stand.

Venus felt like telling her, since the nightmare started with her mother diagnosed with cancer. Since that day she'd predicted her own demise; death was imminent, so why eat. "I haven't had anything all day."

"Well, first stop, the cafeteria." The woman pushed the basement button. "Is there anything else wrong with you, a condition? You are here at the hospital." She squeezed her wrist and checked her watch at the same time.

"Not for me, I'm here for my mother. I'm fine."

The elevator stopped at the lobby. The very pregnant nurse tapped the button again. "I'll see you down."

"Oh no, you don't have to."

The doors closed. "I'll just make sure you get something good. Don't try the fettuccine or tortellini, they use real butter, for God's sake." The elevator stopped, sending a light dizzy wave over Venus. She followed the compact woman to the cafeteria.

"Got an emergency here. Excuse me." The pregnant nurse reached past a couple of white shirts and green scrubs. She sniffed a mound of cottage cheese, then put it back. She picked up a bright green cup of Jell-O squares with whipped cream on the top. "6112, Vera. Put it on my account." She waved at the cashier and came back to the table with the wobbly green glob. Venus looked at it, poked, then ate.

"That's a safe warm-up. Then you can try the mashed potatoes. It's good to start out slow when you haven't eaten in a while. So what's your

story? You certainly don't look like you're broke. Food just not an appealing part of your day anymore?" She snapped her finger and pointed at
Venus. "Maybe you're going to look like me in about seven and a half
months. You pregnant?"

Venus nearly choked on the mouthful. "No." She swallowed. "My mom
was sick. Food was definitely the last thing on my mind."

"Oh, yes, I understand. So, how's she doing?"

The question again. How was she doing? She looked the perfect
stranger in the eye and wondered how she would react if she simply said,
I don't know, never bothered to ask, too busy worrying about myself.

"She's doing okay, as well as to be expected after a mastectomy."

"Ooooh, I'm sorry." The woman curled a soft frown. She sat quietly
watching Venus eat, realizing there was only so much she could do for this
one. Her work was done. She looked at her watch. "My husband is probably parked out front waiting with his panties in a bunch." She stood up,
not that much taller than when she was sitting. "Try the mashed potatoes.
They use real butter too, but not a crateful like in the fettuccine."

"Thank you." Venus stood up, reaching out and having to stand nearly
a foot away from the protruding bundle of joy to give the woman a hug.
She didn't want the opportunity to pass again, the pull of waiting arms
from someone with an open heart. So many things people took for
granted.

"You take care." The nurse did her best to hug Venus back but her arms
only reached halfway.

"I will. Thanks." Venus slumped back in the vinyl seat. She finished the
Jell-O and cleaned the sides of the bowl with her spoon.

THE late lunch crowd was beginning to file in. Chirping voices and echoes
of laughter. The drab dark cafeteria was coming to life with the people
who took pride in their jobs, the caretakers, the healers. She spotted Clint
talking with a small crowd. He dismissed himself when he spotted Venus.

"Come here often?" He leaned over on both knuckles, giving her a
peck on the cheek. The man had gotten better looking with age. His pure

chocolate skin was even darker, probably from the California sun. There was nothing like watching the change, a boy transformed into a man. When they'd lived together, she didn't think he could get any more good-looking than he already was. His heavy-lidded eyes tilted downward when he smiled. His serious athletic body from running track and playing football in high school and college was still maintained. This was more than looks or his gorgeous physique. This was about confidence, a self-maturation that gave him a new appealing air. He was comfortable filling his man shoes.

"Gotta love the excellent cuisine." She looked down at her empty Styrofoam bowl.

"Can I sit?" His even jawline rose and fell with the question.

"Sure. So how have you been, Dr. Fairchild?"

"No small talk, okay. Uh uh, you were my best friend, V. I'm not about to sit here and waste your time or mine with bullshit chitchat."

"You were mine, too." Venus said, softly. "So then, no small talk. Where's the woman you dumped me for?" She folded her arms over her chest.

He smiled, the lights in the cafeteria brightened. "You dumped me first." He shook his head like he should have known better than to ask, will the real Venus Johnston please stand.

"How's your mother doing?" His tone quieted.

"She's home, resting."

"I wish I'd known she was here, I would have checked in on her. Who's her doctor?"

"Who *was* her doctor, you mean. Dr. Prah suddenly no longer works here. I mean, are you guys in a union or something? You just up and quit or move on like it's no big deal. People's lives depend on you guys and you act like it's just a job, off to the next best offer. I'm glad she's gone anyway."

Clint let her say her piece as he'd been trained to do many years ago. He shook his head. "Who's her doctor now?" he said it slowly, making it clear he wanted a straight answer.

"Dr. Lamb."

"I've heard of him but haven't met him yet. I'll make it a point to talk to him, let him know it's all in the family."

"So you have to have a reference, be from good stock to get good care?" She asked, feeling the heat rising in her face again.

"This line of business ain't no different from any other... putting in a word can't hurt and it always helps." He leaned back and crossed his arms over his wide chest. "Is that okay with you?"

"I've already talked with Dr. Lamb. He's a good man. I don't know what else you could add."

"Still trying to play tough, huh?"

Venus shook her head no. That was the last time they'd met. Not now. Here she was a raw open wound, seething and leaking hopelessness. There was no energy for pretense, no will for it.

"Fine, I won't talk to him."

"I didn't say not to, I just feel like I can already trust him, without your recommendation." Venus pushed the hair off her neck, feeling too warm and a little uncomfortable.

"That's a good thing. I'm glad to hear it." He leaned forward on both elbows. His eyes softened, folding at the corners. "But if you need me, you know where I am."

"Not really," Venus said, finding the center of his pupils, even with his hooded lids, there was a reflection of light. "What are you doing here, in Los Angeles, slumming? I thought you were going to stay in Washington, D.C., forever, you and your new bride."

"I was wondering when it was going to come up, when you were going to bring her up again."

"Well, you did marry the woman."

"Yes, I did." Clint leaned closer on the table. "So what about you, did you make it official?" He eyeballed her ring finger. Venus touched it, remembering that it was there, that she was indeed engaged to Airic. That she indeed loved him, though she couldn't remember the last time she'd told him so.

"Not yet. Airic's still in D.C. I'm here working on a project. We've both been busy, too busy for nuptial planning."

"Couldn't squeeze it into your schedule, huh?" The mocking didn't feel harmful. She understood what Clint was saying. After she'd put the gun to his head, marry me or else, he had a right to assume she was in a hurry to make the run down the aisle. "I never got the scoop on…"

"Airic. He's a software engineer by trade. He started his own company. Doing very well."

"I have no doubt about that."

"He's a good guy." She wouldn't go any further. Men and their doggy traits, sniffing for imperfections, chinks in the armor. Not another word about Airic. "So, does Kandi like L.A.?"

"I wouldn't know." His expression withered into the old Clint, sometimes sullen and menacing. There was a hardness about him that came from the streets of the D.C. neighborhood he grew up in. A crack-addicted father, and a mother who abandoned him at age ten. The hardness that was needed to overcome those obstacles also kept him at an arm's distance.

"As in, you haven't asked?" Venus treaded lightly but could feel her bottom lip hanging in anticipation.

"She's still in D.C."

"So, she's coming later?"

"I doubt it."

She folded her arms over her chest to stop the chill bumps from rising with her curiosity. "You're not together anymore?"

"I don't know what we are." He shook his head. "The last straw was when I told her I got the job out here. She thought it was some kind of plan to get away from her. She'd just got on as an administrator for the Prince George County school district. We were having problems, some issues, already; this was just the final nail."

"Final as in the big D word? Why would she rather stay there and work? I thought she wanted to be married, babies, the whole nine. You can do that anywhere. L.A. is just as good a place as anywhere else." Venus found herself way too excited. She drew in a long deep breath that made her head sway in warp speed, this new information swirling around her. "I'm sorry to hear it, Clint."

He blinked, and Venus thought she saw a twinkle of moisture.

"I hope it works out. I really do."

"You know what, I believe you. Isn't that a trip?" Clint looked around the cafeteria for a minute. "I'm sitting across from the only lady that's truly ever wanted the best for me."

A lump built up and swelled in her throat making her unable to respond.

"Ain't that a trip? You tried to tell me, didn't you? What's that old saying—set it free, and if it comes back to you, it's yours; if it doesn't, it was never meant to be? And here I am sitting right before you, you before me. That's a trip." He shook his head again. "What do you think this means? You said yourself that God puts us right where we're supposed to be."

"Something my mother used to always say," she said carefully so not to disturb the dry ball lodged in her throat. "I don't know if it's true." She stared into the empty Styrofoam bowl.

What was she saying? Hadn't she dreamed of this day? No, not dreamed, predicted it, like some clairvoyant. Played this moment out as if she'd written it herself, the day Clint would come groveling back in her life. Funny, though, she couldn't remember her lines. She couldn't remember if she'd said, "You and I belong together, always have. Our paths will continue to cross because we are connected." Maybe she'd even reached out to touch the dark smooth plane of his cheek, whispering in soft words an angel would use, "We're spiritual beings, drawn to one another but not in this lifetime. In this lifetime it's too late for us," then disappearing like a cloud of smoke.

"Venus, you all right?" He was up and next to her in the booth before she could respond. He nudged her face to his. He looked into her eyes, more as a doctor than a missed lover. He flicked a miniature flashlight, shocking her into real time.

"Ooooh." She blinked, squeezing out the assaulting light. "Charming." She shoved his hand away with the offending tool.

"You looked like you were dazing out on me."

"Still a little shaken from everything going on with my mom. And now you show up. I could definitely crawl into a nice warm bed and space out for a couple of weeks just to sort it all out."

She felt his firm thigh against hers. Shoulder to shoulder. Friend to friend, she thought.

"I know you're going through hell with this, what's happening with your mother. It's got to be driving you crazy. I know. I know exactly how you are. But she's going to be okay. You got to believe that." Clint licked his bottom lip, a nervous habit. She looked at him, studying his face, amazed that she still trusted everything he said to be true. Even after what he'd done to her in the past, his words were gold, sacred and valued.

"You want to do something to get your mind off it? We could see a movie, go to dinner. I get tired of this place sometimes."

They both looked around the staid hospital cafeteria.

"I don't know how you can stand it," she said, relaxing a bit already.

"I get out of here around six. I can pick you up at seven, after a quick shower."

Her mind was screaming *No,* but the words "That's fine" easily slipped from her lips.

He pulled out a pen from his chest pocket. She wouldn't tease. The same way he knew all her quirks, she knew it bothered him to be sitting here with his starched collar and bland tie, and good grief, a pocket protector.

"Write your address, phone, any pertinent information that won't get me stomped on by your boyfriend, or excuse me, fiancé."

She smiled. Just friends. Just dinner. Relax.

"You can reach me on my cell phone." She wrote everything but her name. "Same to you. The day when Kandi finally does come around, I don't want any incriminating evidence found linking me to Your Greatness." She handed the pen back. "Do you have a card, Doctor?"

Clint pulled it out and wrote his home number on the back. He touched her arm, patting then squeezing before standing up. "So I'll see you tonight."

"See you tonight," she confirmed. He walked away. He'd filled in around the edges, his body was still muscular and tight. He walked with the same loose swagger, kicking his pant legs out hard before each step. He stopped near the crowd he'd originated from, patting shoulders and waving good-byes, then left the cafeteria empty-handed. He'd forgotten to eat. He turned one last time to wave at Venus.

She mouthed, "See ya," calm, cool, and impossibly stupid. What was she doing? Going to dinner with Clint? Her list was stretching long with bad decision making. First Jake, now Clint.

ATROCITIES

THE main library in downtown Los Angeles felt like Grand Central Station. Large dome ceilings, people from every walk of life going in different directions. Venus wandered through the stacked bookshelves, looking for the numbered section in her hand. The librarian hadn't needed to look up the area where the books on breast cancer were housed, as if she'd directed hundreds of worried women to this section every day. It was endless. Three rows, filled with books about women's health. The majority concentrated on the breast cancer war. Venus grabbed as many as her arms would carry and found an empty seat at a large mahogany table.

The slap of the book pages echoed through the high ceilings. It made sense to start with the history of breast cancer, to start from the beginning. The need to understand had always plagued Venus. Where there was no logical explanation, she applied her mother's handy faith of preordination. But only after concentrated effort, fierce and steady dissection. This, she had to understand. She was a long time away from accepting what will be, will be. Even though Dr. Lamb had made it clear that after billions of dollars of research, uplifting fund-raisers, and an awareness movement unmatched by any other, there was still no definitive cause or solution.

She still had to see for herself.

The Cancer Journals by Audré Lorde, *Breast Cancer* by Anne Kasper, and two others by Susan Sontag. By the third book, Venus was convinced she was going to die, and soon. The constant nonaffirming causes were everywhere. From pesticides in the foods to the plastics of containers. All types of carcinogens that replicated estrogen in the body, causing the breast cells to grow rapidly out of control. The worst possible cause— Venus stopped breathing when she read this one—remaining childless past the age of twenty-five. "Early menstruation—along with late parenthood is considered a classic risk factor for breast cancer in women. Breast feeding for at least six months also proved to reduce the risk factor." Yes, that was her, and millions of other career-driven women of the 1980s and 1990s who had made a choice. A woman who wanted to raise a child "with a man," a father, in the home they'd created on equal ground. Was it her fault she hadn't found him by the age of twenty-five? She slammed the book closed. But then how would that explain her mother, who had given birth to both she and Timothy before the age of twenty-five? Nursed them at her breast, a homemaker who didn't have to breathe in high levels of carbon monoxide in the city streets when traveling to and from her job.

Maybe it was the laundry soap, or the ammonia she'd cleaned the floors with, or the shampoo, or even the Lysol spray Pauletta lived and breathed. It killed germs.

Life was unfair. That was the only conclusion. If women knew for sure that having a baby before the ripe old age of twenty-five was an effective risk reducer, would they have opted to forgo careers and settle on the first man who came knocking?

She shoved the books randomly back on their shelves, realizing it may have been better to leave them on the table for a librarian to replace correctly for the next woman who needed to know the odds of her demise . . . and why. But she had no time. She needed to get ready for her meeting with Clint, the only other man besides Airic whom she'd ever considered having a baby with.

SHE felt like such a fool. By the time she'd pulled the third change of clothes out of the closet, taking off the gold sleeveless cow neck in exchange for the black Lycra V-neck, she was sure. A certifiable fool. All this for the man who'd made it clear she was not worth having. Not worth caring about. Not worth marrying. She could have shaved off two years of risk and been with child if Clint would have gone along with the program.

She slipped her pointed toes into the black slingbacks, standing in front of the mirror. The skirt too loose. The last time she'd had it on, it hugged and gripped her hips showing off two perfect cantaloupe halves. This time it looked like an ill-fitting slip. She pushed it down and kicked it off.

Standing there in her black thong panties, she stopped to stare. Now this would knock Clint off his feet. Bastard. She wouldn't give him the satisfaction. He'd never get his wide dark palms around her body again.

She pulled out the black dress that stopped high on her thighs. Sleeveless, with a draped neckline—the dress Airic had picked out for her for a dinner meeting with one of his potential investors. Seeing it in one of the mail-order catalogs she received daily in the mail, he'd stuck a folded piece of paper in it with a note, this one. When it arrived, it was lopsided and big. She didn't have time to start shopping again, so she started chopping. Cutting the length, using safety pins on the shoulders. She took it to the dry cleaners and asked them to fix it. The seamstress wanted Venus to try it on so she could pin it correctly. No. It's just how I want it, she'd told her. Please. Fix it. She hadn't worn it since that night she walked into the restaurant, knowing she fulfilled the beauty quotient when Airic's face lit up and his investor signed over the check.

Now, in front of the mirror, Venus did a full model's turn, the bottom flounced up, flashing the cusp of her ass. Perfect. She smoothed her hands down her flat stomach, sucking in even more. A victorious grin rising on her cheeks. "Someday...the one you gave away will be the only one you're wishing for." Mariah Carey's song came out loud and off-rhythm. She kept singing anyway... "just think again 'cause I won't need your love anymore. Someday, hey, hey." Her anthem for Clint Fairchild fit perfectly the many nights she'd climbed into the shower, head held high to the pulsating water. Her voice never cracked in the insulated walls, the tears neither weighed nor acknowledged as they trickled down the drain.

The phone rang. She ran toward it before realizing it could be Airic; Stopping in her tracks, she stared at the contraption. She peeked cautiously at the caller ID—unknown. She picked it up slowly, faking a groggy "Hello."

"Did I wake you?" Clint's voice was still a reason to smile, still sounding of hope, and strength, the characteristics of the imaginary prince in Cinderella's syndrome. All promise, all fantasy.

"No. I was just sitting here, waiting for you." Venus couldn't help the girlish giddiness, even though being nonchalant had been her goal.

"You sounded like you were napping. Guess I don't create that much excitement these days."

Venus tapped her pounding heart. Her nerves jangled from knowing what she was doing was wrong. "Do you want to come up, or I can come right down? I better just come down. I'll be there in a minute. Oh, what kind of car are you driving?"

"Come down and see."

She closed the phone and dropped it into her purse. She pulled it right back out and pushed the power button off. The last thing she needed was for Airic to call. In the two years they'd been together, she'd never committed as many atrocities as she had in the last few days. Kissing Jake, nearly making love to him. And now, singing and dancing in front of the mirror waiting for Clint, her long-lost prince, to arrive and take her away, at least away for the night. She was bad to the bone. Guilt without shame, or shame without guilt. Either way, she knew exactly what she was doing and it was flat-out wrong.

"Well, look at you." Venus leaned into the passenger window of the sporty-style Mercedes.

"About time, right?" He flashed a smile. The triangle-cut diamond hanging off his earlobe caught her eye. She wondered if it came with the car, a package deal.

She let herself inside, striking off points for him not opening her door. The leather felt good on her thighs. Cool, soft. She leaned back. "It is nice, Clint."

"Yeah, for a while I felt like I was only working for the student loan administration. Paying them back was a full-time gig. Thought it was about time I got something for myself." He leaned over and kissed her on the cheek. "You look beautiful, V."

She thanked him, taken aback by the coolness of his aftershave, comforting and familiar. "You look good, too." Spoken only as the truth, not just a response.

"So does *he* know where you're at tonight, who you're with?" Clint directed the steering wheel with one hand, barely holding it but in full control.

"That's a strange question coming from you." Venus turned back to the glittering boutique windows that for a while held her in a hypnotizing glare. She had been daydreaming before she heard Clint's voice. How funny he should ask that, when she'd been thinking the exact same thing, wondering how all of this would play out. If she would go home and confess that she'd gone out with her ex-live-in lover, that they'd had a wonderful night laughing and talking about old times, but that was it. One glass of wine and then a polite good-bye kiss. Intentions were always for the best. No one ever woke up with a plan to be conniving and two-faced, a long-term plan to end up staring into the eyes of an old lover, claiming that now they could be just friends. No one ever predicted these things; they somehow just happened.

"Why is that strange coming from me?" Clint leaned toward her a little.

"I guess, I thought we had a clear understanding. This night wasn't anything more than two friends catching up on old times. Getting together, as you put it, for dinner."

"No doubt. But dinner or no dinner, friends or no friends, my lady wouldn't be out with another man wearing that dress. You get what I'm saying?" He eyed her crossed legs.

"There lies the misunderstanding; I'm not your lady." She pulled the length of her dress to cover her exposed thighs. Mariah's song played in her head... *Some-day-hey-hey*...

The ride was shorter than she'd liked. She wanted to savor the quietness, the mood. Her response about the dress had put a damper on any further conversation. Clint pulled in front of the restaurant and let the valet park the car. The Moustache Café was a small Italian restaurant decorated to look like a street café in Rome. Soft twinkling lights hung from the silk trees. The sounds of night, chirping frogs and humming cricket wings, played as a subtle backdrop. The table they were escorted to was in a dark corner with large burning candles surrounding the area.

The host pulled her seat out and helped Venus into her chair. "I'll be back with fresh bread and a sample of our house wine."

Venus was already softening, the ice slipping off the edges of her shoulders. She had intended to be tough and unshakable. She came here to make him feel remorse and rub his face into the facts. Fact. On the night of her thirty-fourth birthday, he brought home a puppy instead of the engagement ring she'd purposely showed him in the window at Zaire's a few weeks before. When the proposal didn't materialize, she'd concluded that he'd been using her for the last four years to get through medical school and had never intended to marry her.

Fact. Yes, she had indeed kicked him out of her house, but she'd apologized for that, and they were on the narrow road of recovery when she'd found another woman's pitiful pancake number nine in his bathroom and overheard him whispering sweet nothings into the phone. Fact. Their reconciliation was further sabotaged when he showed up with said owner of that horrible color of blush at an event he knew good and damn well Venus would be attending. Fact. That woman had been dating a married man right under Clint's nose, and he still chose her over Venus.

Fact. Said woman was his punishment for life.

Her leg kicked up involuntarily, a reflex of memory shooting across her knee like a doctor's gavel. Clint was lifting a glass of wine to his lips and didn't notice the table's quick vibrations tickling the plates and flatware. A glass filled with a sample of wine was sitting in front of her while the server stood patiently by waiting for a thumbs-up or -down. She grabbed the glass and swallowed the blood-dark liquid. Her eyes burned and her throat threatened to seize. Clint smiled, knowing she'd drunk it too fast. He pushed a glass of water toward her.

"I think we'll look at the wine menu."

"Yes, sir." The waiter conveniently pulled it from behind him like a magician doing his best work. "Everything on this side is available by the glass, and this side is by the bottle only."

Clint squeezed out a thank-you and a have-a-nice-day smile. Venus was still recovering from the firewater.

"That was awful. Eeew."

"I forgot, you like that sweet stuff," he said over the menu. "Let's see, no Boone's Farm, wait, I see some Gallo. Oh no, I'm sorry, that's Galileo."

This time she kicked intentionally with a dead-on target.

"Ouch, I'm just playing. We'll get anything you want. Shit, I'll drive to the liquor store if I have to, make it back here for the second course."

"You're not funny," she said through her watering eyes. "I think I'll pass altogether on the alcohol." She folded her napkin in her lap.

"There's got to be something. How about the Riesling, light, citrus flavor with a touch of sweetness?" he read out loud from the menu.

She shook her head no. "My mom's illness has put me on a quest for good health. No alcohol. Beginning now. Not even a glass of wine with dinner."

"Well, if you're not having any, I'll pass, too." Clint put the menu down. "So how's she doing?"

"You asked me that earlier, remember?" It was the best she could do, seeing how she still had no answer.

"Okay, then, how're you doing?"

"Fine." She leaned back in her chair. A slow operatic tempo played through the hidden speakers. The outdoorsy sounds of crickets and frogs were starting to get on her nerves. Maybe she would give up the wine starting tomorrow. She needed something to calm her down, relax her, or she'd never make it through the rest of the night.

Clint took a deep breath. "Okay, no small talk. I think I made that rule. Tell me what we're doing here. Is this the I-just-wanted-to-see-if-I-still-felt-anything-for-him date?" He blinked slowly, his eyes locked on to hers. Sliding his hand across the table, he beckoned her to meet him halfway, tapping, creating a beat to the music that had none. "Tell me what's on your mind."

Venus put her hand on the edge of the table, forcing him to travel the extra mile to get to hers. "I know how I feel about you, Clint. I don't need an evening out for that."

"And that would be...?" He leaned forward, giving his full attention. He'd changed like Clark Kent to Superman. No longer the mild-mannered doctor he was earlier with the starched buttoned collar. Now his soft silky shirt clung to his defined chest and arms. His face and neck glistened with a fresh shave and splash of cologne.

Venus leaned her elbows on the table, pulling her hands away and using them to support her story. "You were the one who got away. I'm the one who sent you out there, young, single, and free. I take full responsibility for that. I cried a long time wondering how stupid I could be to let someone like Clint Fairchild get away from me, Dr. Clint Fairchild. For a while I actually waited for the call, the message on the machine that said, 'I can't go through with it. I can't marry this other woman, you're the one I want.' When you didn't call, it finally dawned on me that this wasn't a bad dream that I was going to wake up from. This was my life, this was your life, and we truly were over. But in all that time, I never stopped thinking about you." Venus blinked several times seeing herself then, waiting.

"I'm talking about now, V. Not yesterday, or two years ago. Now. How do you feel now?"

The room temperature went up a few notches. Her eyes darted across the room to the stone fireplace with red arched flames shooting up that felt an arm's reach away, the heat smothering her face, no room to breathe. She picked up her glass of ice water and worked it down her throat with short careful swallows, hoping the water could wash away the vivid memories.

"Is there anything left for now?"

What was he asking her? If she still loved him? If her heart still shattered into a million tiny pieces with the mention of his name? If she was still waiting for the call?

The cool slickness of the glass she held felt like it was slipping from her hand, melting with her heat, the frustration. The anger. She gripped the glass tighter, not wanting it to slip away.

"Venus, just give me a simple answer. Have you considered—"

She felt a new strength pulsing around her fingers. She shoved the water with one thick push toward Clint's face. It spilled around his lashes as he blinked in shock. He shot up out of his seat, grabbing the napkin and wiping at his face taking in much needed air. "What the fuck is that about, V?"

"That's for having the nerve to ask!" Venus was on her feet too, her finger in Clint's face. "The nerve to sit there and ask me how I feel. The same way I felt then, pissed off. Pissssssed off!" She grabbed her purse off the back of the chair and moved through the obstacle course of table and chairs with openmouthed patrons who were hoping the show wasn't over, waiting for more crucial information. Was it another woman? It was always another woman.

"V," Clint called after her. "Venus."

"Stay back." She turned around and warned him. "Don't risk it, Clint. I swear. I don't know what I'll do to you. I've wanted to scratch your damn eyes out for two years, don't give me the chance." She made it outside and sucked in the night air, then let out a long slow exhale.

"V—"

She started walking, each step numb, the ground unsure beneath her feet. She already regretted throwing the water on him. She hated ignorant behavior. Especially public displays of behavior. All those people staring, watching while she made a fool of herself. She should have had the wine. At least it would have dulled her senses, made her less quick to react. "Now. He's demanding answers, now," she whispered through gritted teeth.

The sound of her heels clicking against the concrete came alive, as if the volume had just been turned up. The numbness wearing off, she could feel the chill around her. She stopped to see where she was, as if she really believed she could make it home in her spiked heels. She pulled out her cell phone. In the good old days, she would've had to find a phone booth and dig in her purse for the fifteen cents her mother had taped inside with firm words before a date, "Always be prepared to say no, Venus. You don't owe anybody anything."

"I need a taxi." She moved closer toward the corner to see where she was. "Wilshire and Melrose, could you send someone in a hurry? I'm freezing my ass off out here." Literally, she felt the cold air gust up and surround her nearly nude bottom. She smoothed the fabric of the dress down and pulled it into a ball around her thighs.

"Nice, V." Clint's silver Mercedes pulled up on the wrong side of the street. "Come on, get in the car." He waved her toward him as if that's all it took for his will to be done.

She started walking again. He trailed slowly on the wrong side of the street.

"Go to hell, Clint. You know, instead of standing there happier than punch, congratulating you and Miss Kandi, I should have told you then, got it out of my system. You suck! She sucks. You deserve each other."

"Oh, that's real mature. This is good. I remember all those years feeling like the young boy, not smart enough, not good enough, for the savvy Venus Johnston with her two degrees and her corporate climbing, bungee jumping, bourgeois friends. My, my, my, how things change." He was obviously trying to incite more violence.

Venus was feeling the urge to hurl her shoe, actually both of them, straight into his face. "I didn't make you feel that way, those were your own insecurities."

"I didn't make you kick me out either," Clint retorted dryly. "I wasn't the one who lost her mind, coming home without a stitch of hair, talking about how you were cutting me out of your life by cutting off your hair. I didn't do that, V. You did it." The car stopped. She heard the door slam. He was walking up behind her, still daring to be close.

"I wasn't the one who stopped answering the phone, stopped taking calls, then all of a sudden, you're over it. So then everybody else is supposed to be over it, too. You're ready to put the pieces back together... just like always, Venus-way or the highway. What the hell did you expect me to do?"

She turned around and walked back to him, slowly, each step a little more threatening. Clint hesitated, meeting her halfway. Eventually they were nose to nose. Venus stood before him. "I didn't expect you to turn around and marry somebody else. Not her. Not so soon. Not ever. I expected you to be there, like love. Do you remember asking me if I ever loved you, really loved you? Well, I want to know your answer to that question. Did you ever really love me? 'Cause if you did, if you truly did, you wouldn't have married her. Not like that." She pushed his hand away when he tried to smooth her shoulders. "Answer me, Clint. Did you ever really love me?"

"As much as I knew how, V." He tried to lean in and pull her into his embrace.

The yellow taxi pulled to the corner just in time. She took off her shoes and ran to catch it before the driver began to think he was being set up for a car jacking. She could feel Clint's pull, the energy of his eyes watching her get into the cab, the same way he'd watched her at his wedding when she'd stepped away after wishing him love and luck. What choice did she have, then or now? She had to walk away.

QUICKSAND

V ENUS wasn't through her front door before the sound of the ringing phone sent her already overworked adrenal glands into high gear. She paced, thinking of what she'd say to Airic. She'd avoided him long enough. She picked up the receiver and carried it to her bedroom, peeking at the caller ID box. It stopped ringing but the readout remained. Unknown caller. She picked up the little plastic casing, then slammed it back down. "Identify the gah-damned caller! What good are you?"

She moved back into the living room, where the machine kicked on. She waited, holding her breath, listening.

"Hey you, just checking on my girl. Sidney gave his blessing for me to fly out there, so holler if you need me. Plus, I could use the getaway. There's some stuff going on at this end; either way, I think—"

Wendy's voice cut off with the machine. Her tone was too low. She sounded tired. Venus wondered if her friend still cared to switch places as they often talked about. The Single life versus Married with Children. Which life was more consuming? More eternally exhausting?

The phone rang again. Venus assumed Wendy was calling back, planning to finish her message. She picked it up quickly.

"You're there." The warm touch of Jake's voice.

Venus sat down on the thick sofa, pulling her feet together on the edge of the cushion. "I'm here."

"Everything all right?" Jake sounded far away, an echo of space in his words.

"Everything?" She stared at the raggedy toe polish, wearing off at the tips.

"I must've caught you at a bad time. *Honey* sitting there beside you?"

"No."

"Just a woman of very few words tonight, huh? Okay, I see." The pause seemed longer with the air between them. "I was only calling to see how things went, how your mother was doing. How you're doing."

Finally, the sound of a crashing wave. She had a feeling he was outside, standing on his deck. The swift wind blowing, carrying his voice out to sea.

"I'm fine. My mom...she's at home. My dad and Timothy are taking care of her. We didn't have a good departure earlier, but I'm going to make a fresh go of it tomorrow."

"Good, she needs you."

"How do you know?" She managed to scratch off all the flaky polish on her big toe. She liked it better that way, natural, clear of trying to be something it wasn't. She ran her thumbnail over the rest of them, looking for another loose chip to pry.

"I know because you're easy to need. When you left the studio today, I found myself watching the clock."

"Hmm. Interesting. Why do men always proclaim their need after I'm already gone?"

"I couldn't figure it out either, why in the world I was missing someone who didn't miss me. Thinking about someone who wasn't thinking about me. That's not my style at all," Jake confessed.

"So what was your conclusion?" Venus felt the day's events drifting off like the waves in the background. Certainly the last few hours had turned into a distant memory.

"I still have no answer. It's all new to me." His bewildered reply was sincere.

"Oh yeah? I thought you were a strategist, had everything all figured out."

"I don't think that's going to work when it comes to you." Jake was doing it again, his voice traveling at a snail's pace, taking his time with each point.

She leaned back on the couch, closing her eyes, letting the lightness capture her mind, but only momentarily. She tried to pick up the tone. "You're trying to say I'm a hard case?"

"That's not what I'm saying at all. You're just a mystery. No, I take that back. More like a perfectly wrapped present sitting under the Christmas tree. Like when you're a kid, you know the present is yours. You know it's something good, so perfectly wrapped, every line and corner in place. The bow situated neatly on top with ribbon streaming off the sides. What's inside is a complete mystery, but you know it's yours, even though it doesn't have your name on it. The anticipation is the best part, knowing if you sneak a peek, unwrap the edges, the surprise will be ruined." He paused long enough to make Venus remember his hands up the sides of her thighs, massaging, caressing. "So I'll wait. Take my time. I'll wait for Christmas."

Venus had already turned on her side, curled up on the couch like a baby being held by loving arms. She could sit and listen to him all night, into the morning, into the day. She squeezed her knees together, trying to push down the pressure rising between her thighs. He may as well have been there beside her. She could feel her nipples pushing against the fabric of her dress, the tingling that would pull them into hard knots instead of the usual soft mounds of flesh. It wouldn't stop there; the tingling would move to the core of her being like a balloon filling up with warm water until she couldn't stand the pressure.

"Did you fall asleep on me?"

Venus popped her eyes open. "No. Almost. I'm tired." She hoped that would explain the throaty lull in her voice. The longing. "I have to get up early and take Timothy to the airport. He's going home tomorrow."

"What time is his flight?"

"Eight... I think."

"Can I come?"

"What? No. That's too early. Plus tomorrow's a Saturday; don't you have something exciting to do in the morning?"

"Waking up with you. Very exciting."

"Good night, Mr. Parson." Her voice was a lazy drawl into the pillow she rested on.

"I've been demoted, back to Mr. Parson. Okay, that's cool. But I want to see you tomorrow."

Venus hugged herself, burying her face in the smooth brown skin of her knees. She didn't want the universe to hear what she was about to say. The higher powers that absorbed wishes and intentions, making them into reality. "I want to see you, too," she whispered, feeling the chill of embarrassment.

"Do you?"

She didn't know what to say next. Careful not to be too quick with confirmation. Careful not to scare him away. Still, careful not to let him in. She let the movement of her breathing speak for her. The quiet careful inhale, the cautious exhale, dictating her actions. Moments passed. Endless time, the distance between making a decision that could change her life, alter her path. A swell of sadness overcame her, the surety that nothing could change her path or her life. Not even Jake.

"I better go." She waited for his response, afraid he would declare her ambivalent. A woman who doesn't know what she wants will never have what she needs.

"Until tomorrow, then."

She hadn't chased him away. Venus held her breath to contain her joy. "Until tomorrow."

Venus hung up the phone now wrung out, completely listless. Her mind was filled with thoughts, regrets, and a lifetime of choices. She didn't need to go back that far; she could have picked from an assortment of mistakes and experiences like a buffet table of chocolates. Her thoughts landed on her first year in college, where she'd started at the ripe old age of seventeen secure with the knowledge she had a boyfriend waiting back home—Tony Jones, a power forward who played his heart out on the basketball court. But more than heart was required for a college scholarship. They were both crushed when they found out she would be going to USC alone. The endless conversations on the telephone into the wee hours of the morning promising a lifetime of teenage love. Venus meant it at the time; she was certain college wouldn't separate them. Still in the same city, a thirty-minute drive to the central part of Los Angeles, where the University of Southern California campus clung to its heritage, forging on with its hundred-year-old brick buildings and bronze statues.

The college experience started out textbook style, standing in lines— lines to pay tuition, lines to get classes, lines to get on waiting lists for classes. Slowly a status quo emerged where learning and academics became a side note to parties and wild dorm nights. Staying up past two in the morning playing shots, popping quarters into small glasses of Cuervo Gold and taking a swig whether the quarter went in or not. The full assemblage of friendships that included openmouth kisses while six other people sat around deciding who would be next.

She'd meant it when she said she would love Tony Jones forever but had to admit that forever was relative, especially to a seventeen-year-old. Tony had shown up, knocking at her dormitory door, alarmed because Venus had no longer been sitting by the phone when he called. When she *was* home, she was shouting over Prince music and the voices that were too deep to be in a girl's dorm room that late in the first place.

"What are you doing here?" Venus had asked, over the loud music that seeped past her at the door. She was dressed to go skiing in the San Bernardino Mountains, a two-hour drive east. It would be her first trip. Her roommates had donated a piece here and a piece there, giving her a Salvation Army slash Benetton look. Her hair hung straight underneath a purple fleece hat. She wore a yellow vest over a polar white turtleneck and leopard print purple pants. It was important to look cute on the slopes, her roommates had explained. "Especially when you don't know what the hell you're doing out there. Men love to rescue, but only if you're dressed cute."

She stepped outside to hug Tony with shaky arms. Afraid she smelled like last night's party and a white guy who looked like a younger, thinner Alec Baldwin. They'd stayed up all night kissing on the floor, wedged between the sofa and the coffee table, his saliva dripping down the side of her mouth, falling into her ear. They were drunk enough to have gone all the way, but the Baldwin boy came in his pants before Venus got out of hers.

She had to force herself not to laugh at the memory while Tony stood in front of her. His freshly trimmed Afro in a shag, short in the front and thick in the back. She felt a little sorry for him in his letterman's jacket. Blue and white all the way, remembering three years in the stands, cheering for him, proud that she had the best-looking boy at John Marshall High School.

"What's going on, Venus? You haven't been answering my calls, you're never here?"

Venus nodded her head, yes, that was true. She pulled the door closed all the way to shut out Prince wailing "1999." "I'm busy; school is so much harder than I thought. The classes are time-consuming. Lot of time at the library, can't get anything done here with my roommates being so gothic." She'd just learned that word in her humanities class, but generally it was used to describe the students who wore only black, with large boots and overcoats even when it was a hundred degrees outside.

"You can't call? Not even between classes?" His hands were balled fists in his jacket pockets.

"I'm sorry, it's just been hectic." Another new word.

"Like now, you're too busy now, too." He could see the antsy pants she was wearing, needing to go back inside to let everyone know she was ready to go. Daryl and Michael were inside, too. Three girls and two guys. She could always deny neither one was there for her. "I can't talk right now, but there's some things we have to discuss, later."

His eyes lowered. "Like what?"

"Like we're in two different worlds now." She didn't mean to say two different worlds. He assumed she meant his job at the Stop and Go Gas center where he sat in the tiny red booth and took people's dirty dollar bills for gasoline and cigarettes. She knew what was coming before it happened. He'd been angry a long time over the fact she was there and he was not.

The thumping noise brought her roommate, Jessie, running out first. Her Asian heritage permitted her eyes to open only so far while she covered her mouth in shock. Daryl and Michael filed out behind her, each grabbing an arm and pulling Tony backward. Venus pulled the acrylic sweater from around her neck, straightening out what she could of herself. Ignoring the stinging knot growing near her eye.

"Let him go." Venus pulled away from her roommate's grip, breaking free, then pulling on Michael's arms to make him let go of Tony. They released him, still ready if he tried anything dangerous.

Tony yelled his good-bye so that everyone on the dorm floor could hear it. "Bitch, you ain't good enough for me! Not the other way around! You're only good for one thing"—he grabbed at his crotch while he was backing away—"and that's all you'll ever be good for."

Last words always hurt. Venus still carried them with her, vivid and defining. She wondered if Jake Parson thought that was all she was good for. Just a pretty box underneath the tree that he couldn't wait to get into. Whatever he thought or didn't think of her was of no consequence. It wouldn't make a difference in how things were going to turn out.

CHECKS AND BALANCES

TIMOTHY was standing behind the door when Venus let herself in with the house key she'd carried since she was twelve. The Johnston house had remained intact for over thirty years. A new roof, new carpeting, some cabinetry here and there, but solid. Unlike Mrs. Rayban next door, who'd never fully rebuilt after a fire her son caused while getting high with his friends. She also put bars on the windows to keep the boy out once he upgraded to crack instead of old-fashioned marijuana. Mrs. Rayban's house looked hard and unhappy. Trees and shrubs had been chopped down to eliminate any hiding places for burglars, leaving dry stubs like gravestones in a cemetery.

"Ready to go, I see." Venus reached around Timothy's lengthy torso.

"Yeah." He nodded with a sense of guilt.

Venus picked up his leather shoulder bag, and he grabbed another light suitcase. She looked back at him. Telepathy had been one of their games. They pretended to be able to read each other's minds. It started out as a card game like Dante the Magician; one would write it down, then the other would try to guess, queen of hearts, four of spades. Then it turned to real thoughts, hopes, and fears.

"I said my good-byes last night," he answered the unasked question. "They're still sleeping." He quietly closed the door.

Venus looked up and saw Mrs. Rayban peeking out her window. She checked for all noises, comings and goings, the unofficial neighborhood watchman. Venus thought about waving but decided not to spoil Mrs. Rayban's security by letting on she was seen.

"Whatever happened to Scotty?" She started the car, backing out of the driveway.

Timothy knew the drill as well, ignoring the face hiding behind the curtain. "I don't know. We would have heard if he died. He must be in jail, where it's safe."

"Safe?"

"People who do drugs die quickly, especially when they're on the street. In prison, he's got a better chance of getting sober and getting his mind back."

"So you still thinking about Africa?" She didn't wait for him to respond. "Do you want to stop and get a coffee or something?" Venus looked at her watch. "You know Magic Johnson's got a few more Starbucks opened up down here. He's trying to reignite the whole concept of black business in black neighborhoods. I admire him." She looked at her watch again. "I guess we don't have time to stop, really."

She continued not bothering to look over at Timothy. She knew he wasn't listening anyway, at least not right now. He'd call two or three days later with a delayed response as if he'd just read the e-mail. "The thing I admire is that he's trying to do things right here, things that make a difference. I mean, everybody doesn't have to travel back to Africa to make positive things happen. If you've got so much to give, time and money, there's plenty that can be done right here at home. Magic's proven that.

"How was Mom last night?" She changed the subject to maybe get a response.

"Good. I'd say really good. We just had a time changing her bag. Dad left me there and went out to pick up some food. Mom has this drainage thing still attached and I freaked out. But we did it. She's riding this thing to completion. You know, she's going to be fine." Timothy kept his face to the window. His hand went up to his face, once, then again faster, wiping.

Venus reached in the backseat where her life-sized box of Kleenex sat. She pulled a few sheets and slid them into the hand resting in his lap. She hadn't seen Timothy cry since he was a boy, when Henry gave him the spanking of his life for bringing home a D on his report card. Not just a D, a D minus. It was a sanctioned beating. Henry and Pauletta sat at the kitchen table over coffee trying to figure out the best way to deal with it. Their straight-A son nearly failing in math. Unacceptable. They'd met with his teacher earlier that day. Too much playing around. Inattentive, not turning in his assignments. His other grades had declined as well. A's to C's. But he'd never approached failure. It was one of those nights when everyone knew there was no choice in the matter. Success was measured by expectation.

A nine-year-old Timothy waited up in his room like a man waiting for execution. Pauletta started the vacuum so the neighbors wouldn't know they weren't perfect. Venus ran bathwater, pouring her Jean Naté body wash into the tub so Timothy could soak afterward. It was the only thing she could think of as an offering of help. It went quickly, the beating, because violence and anger were something Henry Johnston hated more than anything in the world. Even though his was a planned action, even though it was decided by logic and implemented with exactness, it was an act of rage nonetheless. The bathwater sat cold when Timothy hadn't come out of his room. Venus tapped on the door, then pushed a folded piece of construction paper under it, "You're invited to experience the luxurious Venus Spa. Your bath awaits." He never came out, the entire night.

"Are you going to go see Mom today?" Timothy asked, still staring out the window.

"Yeah, I plan to, soon as I drop you off at the airport, head right back over." She reached up to his frizzy locks that needed retwisting. "I'll take care of her. Dad and I both will."

He swallowed. The lump of his throat, bobbing, up and down, like he had more to say but it wouldn't come.

They hugged at the curb. The LAX airport felt like a vortex, a circling spiral of time travel. Wherever you were about to go would be so far removed from whatever you'd just experienced in Los Angeles. The swirling traffic, the thick dry air, the lifetime of sunshine. The atmosphere so completely different from any other place, from Mars to Earth.

She kissed him near his ear with extra effort since she was wearing her Reeboks instead of four-inch heels. He half-bent over to whisper in her ear. "I love you. Take care of Mom. She loves you, Venus. You don't have to be afraid of her."

Venus stayed on the curb until he was behind the glass doors of the terminal. A gust of pungent car exhaust blew around her face. She held her breath to let it pass, zipping up her sweatshirt and pulling the hood over her head. She didn't want to go to Pauletta smelling like taxicab fumes.

"No waiting; you're going to have to move your car, miss."

Venus turned around and looked at the police officer. "No problem. I'm going right now."

She turned back and blew a kiss to the glass doors, knowing that Timothy was giving her one last wave good-bye; even though she couldn't see him, she knew he was there.

*   *   *

PAULETTA still ate the middle out of the bread, something she'd been doing all her life. It didn't matter how many times Henry reiterated that the best vitamins, the best fiber, were in the crust. He finished cutting off the fine line of brown, leaving flat toasted squares.

"I'll do the dishes, Daddy." Venus got up from the dining table. She still had a slice of honeydew in her fingers. It dripped lightly into her open palm.

"No, I got it. I want you to take her this tray, visit with her while she's in a good mood. She's getting restless and it's not even midday."

"You sure?" Venus stayed planted, knowing she couldn't stay downstairs forever. Pauletta was sleeping when she first arrived. She hadn't been back up since.

Henry handed her the tray.

"Okay. I'm going."

He stopped and turned around. His graying sides widened to the center of his receding hairline. "She's not going to bite, Precious."

You sure?

"I know, Dad, don't be silly." She turned around and pushed up the stairs. When she reached the top, she realized it had been a few weeks since she'd been to the gym. Out of breath, she clung to the doorjamb of her mother's bedroom entrance.

"Venus?"

"Yes, Mom."

"What're you doing?"

Venus came inside and sat on the edge of the bed. "I was winded. I think I'm getting old."

"If you think it, so it will be." The sides of Pauletta's mouth were enclosed by two thick comma lines. Her face was shallow, her high cheekbones prominent. "Grab that bag for me."

Venus followed her eyes to the May Company shopping bag. She could see that it was dated, especially since the department store was now called Robinsons May. Venus set the tray down in front of her mother and went over to the bag. She knew before she picked it up. Bills. Envelopes with the utility company logos and a few credit cards. She sat on the bed. Venus reached in and pulled out the first envelope.

"You want me to write out the checks, just tell me how much?"

Her mother looked at her directly. "That's exactly what I was going to do."

"Good." Venus relaxed a little. They could work together. Mothers and daughters were nothing more than two different dresses cut from the same cloth. One wore hers short, the other long, one maybe wanted a zipper, the other, buttons. Style limited to accessories, but the foundation was the same.

"That one, there." She nodded to the yellow envelope Venus held in her hand. "Open that."

Venus opened it and took a few extra minutes scanning before handing it to her mother.

"You're not going to be all in my business now." Pauletta took the invoice with her strong hand.

"No, ma'am." It was a natural inclination to look at numbers. Any numbers. They were like puzzle pieces, orderly and magnificent, having only one answer. No confusion, no guessing of relevance. Always a yes or no, a positive or negative.

She opened up the next bill and wrote the amount her mother specified. The total was growing in her head. They were up to nearly two thousand dollars paying credit cards, insurance payments, and utilities. The house had been paid off a year ago. Henry had booked a cruise vacation in celebration. Pauletta said she didn't want to be stuck on a ship with a bunch of fanny-pack-wearing tourists who were older than she. Venus asked her mother how she knew they were going to be older than she was, and Pauletta replied, " 'Cause the theme of the cruise is Life Begins at Sixty."

Venus had to suppress the urge to look at the check register to see the balance of their account. "Mom, do you want me to add up what we've written out so far, make sure it's all covered?"

"No. I do not."

"Oh, look, that was the last check. Where do you keep the rest?"

"They're in the drawer downstairs next to the dining room entrance. Big blue box."

"Be right back." Venus got up and took the checkbook with her. She felt like such a lunatic sometimes, needing to know everything, constantly searching for things gone wrong.

She crept into the bathroom and stopped in front of the mirror. She smoothed a hand over her forehead. One day that crease would stay, the imprint of worry. One day it wouldn't just wipe away. She sat on the toilet and thumbed through the register one page at a time. The entries in her mother's handwriting were consistent—utilities, credit cards, and the Unity Baptist Church. Venus wondered why, if her mother claimed that all things were preordained, she needed to make payments on a ticket to heaven that had already been punched.

No way her parents had that kind of money on a monthly basis. Pauletta had never worked and Henry was retired, receiving less than half of what he earned when she thought they were rich. Then there would be the doctor bills. Those were waiting around the corner to jump out and scare the crap out of everybody when they were least expected. Unexpected incidentals that weren't covered by the insurance. She chewed the inside of her cheek. She wouldn't bring it up to her mother. Henry would be more reasonable. They needed someone to look at their situation. A financial planner.

She flushed the toilet for sound effect, then carried the checkbook downstairs.

"Hey, Dad." She reached around and kissed him on the cheek.

"How's she doing?"

"Great, we're paying bills. I feel like I'm playing with Monopoly money up there. Is this normal, like over two thousand dollars a month in expenses?"

Henry put the newspaper down, folding it in half. There was a large cartoon of the president on the page. She could blame him for skyrocketing inflation and inadequate health care.

"That's not been my department for some time."

"You don't look, ever? I mean, you don't look at the bank statements, the bills, nothing?"

"Your mother's always handled it, and I think she's done pretty well. Two kids through college; well, one who refuses to quit, but that's not on my dime." Henry smiled; it had been a while.

"I think you guys should sit down with a financial planner. Get some clarity on where you stand. I mean, you're both going to be around a long time. You have to manage your money very carefully, unless you plan on getting a job." Venus started naming off the payees and amounts. It all sounded a little ridiculous, like it was she who should be sitting at the table looking up, dazed and confused, instead of her father.

"Just what I thought."

Venus turned around to see her mother leaning on the kitchen entrance wall.

"I knew you weren't doing nothing but looking for trouble. Something to complain about or find fault in."

"Pauletta, what are you doing out of bed? Coming all the way down those stairs by yourself."

"I knew she was down here bothering you about something. That was enough to get me out of bed." She made a couple of slow steps to the kitchen table with Henry rushing to her side. He slid out a chair for her to sit in.

"What is it, Venus? Why are you always looking under rocks, and in crevices, always looking for the stink? Did I raise you that way, to be so negative?"

"That's not what I was doing. Mom, I was just trying to help. I want you and Daddy to see a financial planner; it's something that should have been done a long time ago. You guys are going to need..."

"What...? What is it that we're going to need? Let's see, if it's coming from your point of view, it must be money for the worst possible scenario—a full-time nurse, an oxygen tank. How about two burial plots? We should just go ahead and get those out of the way."

"Mom!"

"Is this my doing? Did I make you this way?"

Venus looked to her father. Somehow she'd done it again, even on her best behavior, she'd done it again.

"I'm not going to be an invalid anytime soon. Neither is your father. You just let us worry about us. You need to concentrate on your own life; get yourself together and stop running around here digging up bones."

Venus always heard her mother use that expression about people who couldn't mind their own business. Too busy digging up bones in other people's backyards, while theirs stayed buried deep hoping no one would ever find them.

"Okay, Mom," she whispered.

"Okay, what?"

"I don't want to make you mad. I didn't mean to upset you. Please, let me help you back upstairs."

"I'm down here now. Glad to be out of that room." She adjusted herself in the chair, her right arm limp at her side.

Venus knelt down and kissed her mother on the chin. "I love you, Mom."

"I love you, too. Now, you can start from the beginning and tell me what's really on your mind. You think your dad and I need help? We're not broke, if that's what you're thinking, far from it."

Venus stood up. "I just got nervous. You and Daddy are so proud and I didn't want that to get in the way if you needed anything. I know you wouldn't ask, and I can spare some cash."

"You bet you can. You still owe us for the down payment of that house you're not living in. Speaking of who is, where's Airic? Haven't seen him in some time." Her mother's raised eyebrow and pursed lips let Venus know her mother was indeed herself. The cancer, the illness, didn't stand a chance with Mrs. Pauletta Johnston.

Venus rolled her eyes. "Now who's digging in whose backyard?"

SOLITAIRE

SHE realized she hadn't talked to him in three days. That had never happened before. Airic was reliable, dependable, and honest. It wasn't her imagination or a case of happenstance. They truly had not made the effort to touch base with each other. Both ends of the candle dampened, unable to burn. No flame moving rapidly toward the middle. She tried to remember if any words were exchanged, any complication planted.

Airic didn't like complications. He'd had enough of that with his first marriage to Wanda. An eight-year stint that produced two children. Tionna and Kiva, two beautiful daughters that Venus only saw in pictures. They were both nearly grown, one in college, one about to start. They sent him cards that had only their names signed, no "I love you, miss you, wish you were here." He sent them cards with the same, signed "Airic." Not "Daddy, kisses and hugs." At first Venus thought it strange and pushed for more communication, prodding him to call, or at least pick out a gift instead of just sending a check. Airic made it clear that things were as they should be. No complications.

She pressed the auto dial for Airic's number as she steered the car out of her mother and father's driveway. She pressed the phone tight against her ear while she drove slowly back to her apartment. She listened intently, counting the rings until the answering service picked up.

"It's late there, I know. I just wanted to say I love you. Wanted to tell you that I miss you." She quickly hung up before she said what was really on her mind. She didn't want to let on that she was on the highest rung of the ladder and felt like it would topple over any minute. One bad thought after another pureed into a thick slush of sadness as she glided down the 110 freeway. Her mother's illness. The upsetting date with Clint. Work, and the thought of letting Jake down. If Lila Kelly didn't sign on, she will have wasted a lot of Jake's time and money. She thought of Airic, not being available to her now that she wanted to talk. She was making a mess of things as usual. Her mother told her to quit looking for the voids, the holes. Stop looking under rocks. It was a hard habit to break. She tried to think positive. Airic had obviously been preoccupied for the last few days. And to say she'd been a little preoccupied would be an understatement.

Her apartment still hadn't taken on a life. Growing up in her mother's home where something was always cooking, or the house had just been cleaned, Venus depended on the sense of smell. It made a house a home, bacon frying, cookies baking, a pot of beans simmering. She flopped herself on her full down comforter, inhaling but still coming up empty. Not even the scent of Airic from his last visit.

Venus lay in bed trying to relax in the quietness of her room. The sun had gone down, then stopped, threatening to suspend itself over the East Cascades. She'd will the sleep to come, knowing she'd feel better after an uninterrupted break from her own mind. The anxiety would melt by morning, transforming itself into something entirely different. A more harmless form of pain like yelling at a customer service operator, accusing a salesperson in the department store of racial profiling, or cutting someone off on the freeway.

She remained restless, curled up in a tight ball. The illuminated clock on her nightstand was a new source of light now that it was completely dark in the room. It was only seven o'clock, but the heaviness of the day's events had taken its toll. It hadn't turned out too bad, really. Venus smiled thinking about herself and her mother. They had lain in bed playing a game of Mancala before she dropped off to sleep. Afterward, her aunt Katha had come over armed with po-man's meals, as her mother called them—casserole, soup, and spaghetti, the kind of meals that could be stretched over a few days at a time. Venus made a big salad with healthy greens, tomatoes, and carrots to counter all the bread and starch her aunt had supplied. While her father tinkered with his trains she and her aunt cleaned the house. She'd kissed her sleeping mother good-bye, and thanked God that she was still whole, in her heart and mind. She would rather her mother be mean and ornery than quiet and displaced.

All in all, it had been a great day. She just needed to relax. She could at least claim no regrets, until now, she thought, as she reached up to answer the ringing phone. She knew it was Jake before she'd said "Hello."

"Get out of bed, I'm coming to get you."

"How do you know I'm in bed? And what makes you think I'm alone?"

"I'll be there in twenty minutes."

The silence was final on the other end of the phone. Venus sat up and looked around her dark bedroom.

Pauletta would have a quick painless antidote for what Venus was feeling. She'd say something simple like "anybody that has a choice has too much to choose from in the first place." Glib, effortless, and absolutely true. She had no business feeling like she had choices.

Venus threw off the covers and jumped out of bed. In the bathroom she sprayed moisturizer in her hair and tugged it into spirals. She uncapped the lipstick and rubbed it around her full lips. She slipped on the jeans that had been sitting in a ball on the bathroom floor. In the closet, she rummaged around for a sweater to pull over her head. By the time twenty minutes had passed she was effortlessly beautiful with her smoky dark eyeliner smudged from her earlier struggle for sleep. He'd think she meant to do that. She paced around the front door of her apartment and was about to change her mind when the phone rang.

"Your chariot awaits." Jake was smiling into the phone.

She laughed. "I'll be right down." She grabbed her keys and left her purse behind. As if by doing so, she carried none of the responsibility of being herself. Identity unknown. Jake was standing at the entrance, still hovering near the security panel. He wore a crimson red sweater with JPWear emblazoned across the front and a pair of dark denim jeans that hung loose and generous.

Venus pushed the door open. "What do you think you're up to, Mr. Parson? Is that to impress me?"

"What?" He looked himself up and down, following her eyes.

"I know who you are, you don't have to flaunt it." She tugged at his baggy jeans.

He turned a full circle. "Just wanted you to know what you're working with." Venus couldn't help focusing on his firm butt while he did his model turn. "I think I know what I'm working with. I like it."

"You do? I was beginning to think I was just a job."

"You're not just a job..." She smiled and frowned at the same time. "You're an adventure."

He grabbed her hand and led her out the second set of glass doors to the dark clear evening. She stood beside him while he unlocked the car door and opened it for her. Well of course he did. If nothing else, Jake was a gentleman. A well-studied gentleman, like learning how to speak another language, or to play tennis. His goal was to be everything a woman would ever want. Then why was he single? Stop that!

She shook it off. Besides, she didn't know if he was single or not. He'd never said.

"Okay, I know you're sick of this question, but how's your mom doing?" He started the car, the engine's vibration sending tiny ripples through her body.

"For the first time, I can honestly say she's doing well. Quite well. Her spirit is strong and accounted for. The surgery was really only the beginning. She's got the strength to make it through all the stuff that's coming next, the chemo and the side effects. I know she's going to be fine." Venus squeezed his hand back that had found hers. It was going to be okay.

"I'm glad to hear it." He took his hand back and shifted the gears of the sports car. They were on the freeway speeding in and out of line with the other cars.

"Now, are you going to tell me where we're going?"

"Don't panic, we won't call it a date. Please feel comfortable knowing that you are having dinner with Mr. Parson, a colleague and client." He looked at her and smiled. "Then, we're going to my place to make out."

She slapped his shoulder pretending shock. He chuckled, but didn't try to take it back.

Venus let her head fall against the headrest, riding to the bass rhythms coming out of his speakers. She closed her eyes and gave herself up to the beat as he glided the car's gear easily to high speed.

* * *

THEY were within walking distance of his condo. The restaurant sat on the pier, overlooking jagged rocks and crashing waves. Each setting was intimate, tables with room for only two. Couples dining by soft candle-light, peaceful, without pretense. The waiters laughed and talked with their patrons, taking their time, making sure everyone was taken care of.

Jake sat across from her, smiling, rubbing his well-manicured goatee after the hostess left the menus and water.

"I have to confess, I'm not hungry. I ate earlier at my parents' house."

"That means you came just to be in my company? You don't know how good that makes me feel."

"What must you think of me?" Venus couldn't maintain the eye contact without falling under his spell. She hid herself behind the menu but asked again, "What's going on in that head of yours? You worried about Lila Kelly?"

"Nope. Wondering if I should get the salmon or lobster bisque."

"Liar." Venus couldn't resist looking him directly in the eye now.

"I'm thinking how beautiful you are. I'm thinking I wish that I'd met you before this ring was put on your finger."

She put her hand underneath the table. She looked down, not knowing how to respond.

"Now, your turn, tell me what's going on with you. Did I embarrass you?"

"Am I blushing?" Venus put the menu down. "You shouldn't say things that might get you into trouble. What if I took this ring off right now? What if I said, you're right, you're the man I want to spend the rest of my life with? Let me guess, I bet you'd turn around and run so fast in the other direction I'd have to use a searchlight to find you."

He smiled. "You shouldn't say things that might get you into trouble."

"So what would you do?" She leaned forward, both hands placed underneath her chin.

"I feel like this is a dare."

"You're the one who brought it up."

"Why don't you take it off and find out?" Jake leaned forward, rising to the challenge.

She swallowed hard, giving it actual thought. She imagined slipping the ring off and into her pocket. "What would that mean for you? Really, what more could that mean? That I'm an unloyal woman, easily swayed by any smooth-talking, smooth-walking brother such as yourself."

"First of all, I'm not just any brotha."

The preppy waitress came over, happy and drunk with life. "You two looked so intense and in love, I didn't know if I should interrupt." She let a puppy dog smile fall on both of them. "That's a beautiful solitaire." She bent her knees to get a better look. "Wow, a beautiful cut. My husband is a jewelry designer, so I'm constantly looking and taking notes. That's a true beauty. Good choice." She turned to Jake with a smile.

"We need a few more minutes." He opened the menu for the first time.

"Okay, I'll keep an eye out." She bounced away, her ponytail swinging, without a clue as to what damage she'd done.

Venus was the one doing the staring this time.

He looked up, catching her off guard. "What's on your mind?"

"I want to know what you'd do, if I took off the ring. Tell me."

"Actions speak louder than words." He put his face back in the menu.

"What's that supposed to mean?"

"That means, try me."

She twisted the ring around until the diamond rested inside her hand. "I know this is what you do, Jake. This is your *thing*. But this is my life, it's real. Would you really mess with that when you know you're not serious?"

He leaned back in his chair with a confused look.

"What will you two have this evening?" The waitress came back, leaning slightly between the two.

"The check. We're going to head out," he said, reaching into his back pocket.

Venus flashed a polite smile. "Just give us a few more minutes." She waited until the waitress was out of earshot. "What're you doing?" The thought of going back to her apartment, having failed at something as simple as being pleasant, felt unbearable. "What happened?"

"I guess I'm a little tired of being told I don't have a sincere bone in my body."

"I didn't say that."

"That's exactly what you said."

Venus let her head rest in her hands for a moment. "I'm sorry. Okay? It's just that you don't even know me, and all of a sudden you're talking about us like"—she looked up at him—"as if we can be more than what we are right now. I enjoy your company, I guess that's obvious. You enjoy mine, but I'm in a committed relationship. Period." She turned the ring back around on her finger.

"Then why are you here?" Jake leaned forward on his elbows. "How committed are you when you're here with me?"

"I know my limits. I have boundaries."

"Really? Where were those boundaries when you were in my bed the other night?"

The air left her lungs and did not return. A low blow. Venus stood up and gripped the edge of the table. "You know what, you're right. We should go. Can I be honest with you? I was just sitting in the car on the way over here, trying to figure out why someone as perfect as you doesn't have someone in his life, and I just got the answer."

"Sit down, please."

She folded her arms over her chest. "I don't want to sit down. Are you coming or do I need to call a taxi?" The last thing Venus wanted was to end another night out being picked up on the street corner by a tired, condescending cab driver, but she'd do it before letting Jake disrespect her.

"Just for a minute, please, sit down."

She slid back in the chair and kept her attention on the burning candle in the center of the table. The flame dimmed, then failed completely, giving her no excuse to look down.

Jake scooted the candle to the side and reached for her hands. "I wasn't trying to insinuate that we would run off to the hills and live happily ever after just like that. I know with a woman like you, I'd have to earn that right. All I was trying to say is that, you came to me. When you stayed with me that night, I understood something was missing in your life. It's not too late to find out what that *something* is, that's all I'm saying. I didn't mean to imply that you were less than the person you are by being with me. It's an honor, a privilege that I don't take lightly, and I know you don't either." He covered her hand again with his. His palms were soft but firm, "I didn't mean to make you uncomfortable. I'm sorry for putting you on the spot."

Venus stopped avoiding his eyes and looked up slowly. "I have to apologize, too. Everything about you is sincere, and so real it scares me. Men like you are scary, dangerous. Women like me are afraid of men like you, that you'll break our hearts and steal our souls. So it's safer to not believe you, to keep the distance."

A sudden chill crept up her shoulders, remembering the way he held her at Lila Kelly's concert. She wanted nothing more than to believe him. It was always the case. No matter how self-assured and confident a woman appeared to be on the outside, on the inside, she wanted to believe, to trust, but was simply afraid.

"That's an interesting take. Especially coming from you. You come off like you've got it all together."

"Oh, yeah, right. Like falling helpless into your bed with my damsel-in-distress routine?"

He shook his head. "Forget what I said."

"No. You had a point. I mean I can't blame my mother's sickness anymore. Being scared and traumatized can make you do some crazy things, but I'm not feeling that way anymore. Things have settled down and I'm still here, no excuse." She finally had the strength to take her hands back. "Maybe something is missing, or wrong, in my relationship with my fiancé, but I learned a long time ago not to blame others for my unhappiness, or happiness for that matter. Either way, it's my responsibility. I've got to know what I want if I ever expect to have it." She stopped picking at the fine threads in the linen tablecloth. "I have to look within myself."

"So what is it then, why are you here? If happiness can only be found within yourself, that would mean you don't need anyone."

Venus looked around the restaurant to all the smiling happy couples, the toasts of champagne glasses meeting in the air, kisses being shared over the table, hands being held. The rituals and mating dances that spoke volumes of love, constant sweet emotions caught in the lenses of her eyes like a photographer capturing the shots for a lifetime of memories. She looked to Jake, still unable to find the words to explain. There was no explanation without a confession. She'd already told him that she didn't depend on others for happiness, she'd told him boldly that she was responsible either way the pendulum swung, so it would be foolish to tell him now a simple truth.

She was here with him because he made her happy. Indeed, hearing his voice on the other end of the phone made her smile, the warmth of him standing too close made her dizzy with joy.

"I guess you'll tell me some other time." Jake took her hand as he stood up. "Come here." They walked out of the restaurant holding hands. The dark wooden stairs of the restaurant led down to the pier. The Santa Monica beach crowd had thickened. By nightfall the pier transformed into a carnival with cotton candy stands, whirling Ferris wheels, and sandbag tosses.

"Where to now?"

"That's up to you." Jake stopped and turned to face her.

She didn't have a chance to respond before her lips met with his. His mouth felt like a warm treat. Sweet caramel dripping down the sides. She opened wide, her arms around his back, her tongue tasting the smooth inside of his lips.

His hands slipped underneath her jacket, pausing near the sides of her breasts before circling her waist, just how she pictured, exactly how she'd dreamt. It all came back to her, the dream, how they'd kissed on the beach, rolling in the wet sand.

Venus pulled her head away. She watched him; this wasn't a dream, or a fantasy. It was the two of them standing amid a full crowd of people, a crowd she couldn't see or hear. She found his lips again, wrapping her arms around him even tighter. Venus kissed him openly without reserve. She could stay in his kiss, in his arms; all she had to do was believe.

As much as she wanted to follow Jake home, fall into his large king-sized bed with the big soft pillows and silk sheets, she couldn't ignore the guilty voices in her head. He pulled up in front of her apartment to drop her off. He leaned across the gearshift and kissed her good night. "I understand," he said. His eyes shone in the reflection of the moonlight. It could have been the street lamps, but to her, it was the light of a million shooting stars. She walked up the brick steps of the entrance to her apartment feeling like lead weights were attached to her arms and legs. It was the hardest walking away she'd ever done. Jake waited in the car, making sure she got in safely. She turned and waved once securely inside. He put his thumb and pinky to his face, to say he'd call. She'd be ready when he did, in bed, warm and cozy, waiting for his sexy voice to lull her to sleep.

WET LIES

THE door of her apartment opened without her assistance. Venus stepped back, shocked to see Airic.

"I was starting to worry." He held out his arms. "Thank God you're here."

She automatically fell into his slim build. His heart was beating erratically. Or was it hers?

"I wanted to surprise you. I thought somebody kidnapped you. Your purse, your wallet, everything left there on the table. I checked the garage and your car was still parked. I didn't know what to think."

"I went for a walk." The lie tumbled out quickly. "How long have you been here?" Venus sensed him looking her over for clues.

Airic pulled the cuff back on his shirt and checked his watch, "A couple of hours." He gave it some thought. "That was a long walk."

"I stopped and had some coffee in a little espresso bar and read a couple of magazines. Just out wasting time on a Saturday night." She began peeling off her shoes, then her clothes, anything that would show traces of Jake or a sandy beach. "I think I worked up a sweat. I'm going to take a quick shower." She kept talking while she made her way to the bedroom. "Do you want to get something to eat, or are you full from that delicious airline cuisine?"

He didn't respond.

She turned the shower knob to full pressure. Her heart was threatening to leap out of her chest.

"The only thing I need is right here." Airic's voice startled her. She jumped, turning around to find him directly in her face. He kissed her. "It's been such a long week." He rubbed his narrow chin in her hair. The hair that probably smelled of sea air and garlic-brushed shrimp from the restaurant she never got to eat in.

The phone rang. Venus went rigid.

Airic zeroed in on her jangled nerves. "That's probably your dad calling. I spoke to him earlier, trying to find you. I think I got him worried. I'll get it." He hurried to the phone on the bedroom nightstand.

Venus could barely remain standing, surely she'd fall over. She reached out and held on to the sink, hoping, praying it wasn't Jake on the phone. She pushed the bathroom door closed and leaned against it with her ear. She couldn't hear a thing with the shower water beating against the porcelain tiles. She wasn't able to hear anything over the sound of her blood coursing to her brain. Jake, he would know better than to speak. He would know. She squeezed her eyes shut. "Please, know," she whispered.

A light tap at the door before Airic let himself in again. Venus was standing in her bra and panties feeling like her brother had just walked in on her instead of the man she'd been sleeping with the last two years.

"I told him you were safe and sound."

"It was my dad?" Her voice rose in a strange octave.

A resounding "Yeah." The kind that says, of course, who else would I be talking about?

She swallowed something dry and painful. Relief, fear, guilt. "Okay, good. I'll be out in a few minutes."

"Can I get in with you?"

This wasn't happening. Airic, her sweet, polished, no-nonsense older man, who carried out actions based solely on necessity, asking to take a long hot shower with her. What would be the sense in that? Neither one of them would get clean, absolved from the fate that was headed their way.

"I just want to get in and out, babe." She kissed him on his chin. "You can jet in after me." She stepped into the shower, pulling the frosted glass door to a close.

"Sweetie?"

"Yeah?"

"You forgot something."

Venus looked down at herself, wearing the soggy bra and panties, and couldn't help but cough out a hysterical laugh. She stripped off the wet panties and tossed them over the door; the bra followed, hitting the floor with a splat. She heard him pick them up, squeeze out the excess water, then hang them on the towel bar.

"Thanks, hun. I'll be out in a sec." She didn't talk like that, words like *hun* and *sec*. She didn't jump into a shower without testing the temperature first, and she certainly didn't do it with her bra and panties on. He'd know. Any fool would know there was something off-kilter. Maybe she was in luck, Airic wasn't anybody's fool.

The sound of the twenty-four-hour financial channel on the television came from the living room. She came up behind Airic sitting on the couch and kissed him on the earlobe. He put the pen in his hand down and reached up, touching a handful of wet hair. "Uummm." He pulled up, putting his face in for the deep scent of herbal freshness.

"Smells good." He held her hand while she walked around the length of the couch, then climbed into his lap.

"So what happened? I thought you couldn't make it here this weekend. This is the second time you've changed up like that."

Airic cradled her in his long arms, "I try to do the logical thing, stay and work, but then I start missing the woman I love." He kissed her nose. "You. You're important. You're here dealing with something real. Made me reevaluate things. Give some thought to what's important, and what's not."

Venus closed her eyes, remembering why she'd been attracted to him two years ago. How they'd met while sitting in an airport during the Christmas holiday. She didn't want him then. She was still hoping for a reconciliation with Clint. She eventually accepted fate and gave Airic a chance. They weren't a passionate couple, filled with starry-eyed hope. Just two grown people who'd had enough of life's curveballs, wanting stability and union. Honesty. No games.

"I'm glad you're here." She felt the angled hardness of his penis stiffen underneath her.

He searched her eyes. "For a minute it didn't seem that way."

Venus ran her fingers along the freshly cut hair at the nape of his neck. "You just caught me off guard. First I don't hear from you at all, and suddenly you're here." She zeroed in on his brown eyes. "Has everything been going okay? Seems like you've been busy." It was a natural course of action to turn the blame, a defense mechanism used by the guilty party.

"Been in the trenches, but no more than usual. I called and left a few messages but couldn't seem to catch up with you."

"My mom. I've been running around dealing with her and the doctors. It's been a mess."

He looked so tired. Venus couldn't help feeling sorry for him. She leaned in and kissed him on the lips. "Of course I want you here. I would have come to D.C. if all this hadn't been going on with my mother."

"Your dad says your mom is doing well." A perplexed look creased his already furrowed forehead.

"She is, actually, very well. Good enough to chase me down the stairs."

"What?"

Venus chuckled to herself. It hadn't been funny at the time, but now, she was glad to know her mother's spirit was still intact. She was still a fighter. "No, it's nothing. She got out of bed to scold me for asking my father about their financial situation. It's nothing." She waved it away. "I have to give them some money, though. My mom reminded me that I borrowed money to buy the house in D.C."

"How much?"

"Eighteen thousand."

"Whoa!"

"Yeah, I want to give her half now and then a little each month." Venus tilted her head a little, confused. "Why are you acting like $18,000 is a ton of money? Aren't you the rich entrepreneur?" She ran a finger across the point of his nose.

Airic blinked hard, brushing her hand away from his face. "It's your money we're talking about, not mine."

She was speechless, staring into his sharp profile. "Yours, mine? And we're talking about marriage?" She held up her hand with the ring that had caused so much trouble a few hours earlier. "Since the day you put this on my finger I've felt like there was no yours and mine. I've always felt like we were in this thing together." The firm lines around his mouth remained in place. "Airic?" She waited, still poised for his reply.

"You're right. No, absolutely. That's not what I meant. *We*," he emphasized, "need to pay your mother back."

She wasn't satisfied. "Is there something going on?" She searched his eyes. "Tell me."

"Venus, you know better than anyone that here today doesn't mean here tomorrow. I can never get lax. I have to be careful, always. If something goes down, next year, or the year after that, I won't be able to walk into a bank and ask for a helping hand. Black-owned companies get rejected nine times out of ten. A white company could be floating by the seat of its pants and it'd get cash thrown at it."

She stroked the new gray hairs trailing in his hairline. "I love you. You know that?" She kissed him hard, on the lips, pushing herself up, straddling him with her open robe. "You think they'd know you were black?"

He rolled her over. She cried out a giggle. That was their running joke, that Airic could pass if he wanted to. His creamy pale complexion, his fine curly hair that he kept so short it lay flat against his head.

"I'd know," he said, kissing her deeply.

She pulled his shirt off. She held him in her grasp, clinging for dear life, listening as the phone began to ring.

"You want to answer that?" Airic whispered into her ear, new life recovered in his erection.

"Venus, hey it's..."

Her foot "accidentally" looped around the cord of the answering machine, pulling it out of the wall. Jake's voice cut off in the middle of his sentence.

"Who was that?"

"One of the guys I'm working with. I'll call him back later." Venus closed her eyes, blending in with the rug under her back, feeling as low as the floor beneath her. She tightened her grip around Airic's neck, pulling him down. The weight of his body wasn't enough to shut out the thought of Jake, his sweet face filled with worry sitting at home, wondering what was going on. The phone rang again and again while Venus pretended to be in such ecstasy that she had no mind to answer the caller, sinking into the movement of Airic pulsing inside of her. With each ring trying desperately to close off thoughts of Jake.

FRAYED EDGES

THE sound of her Reeboks slapping the pavement sent a flurry of starlings into a frenzy. They flew in a trail straight up to the sky. She ran fast and hard, her breath flowing in and out at a rapid pace. Her palpitating heart was a sure sign that she hadn't exercised in days, maybe weeks. She couldn't remember. All that mattered was now. What she'd done, or hadn't, was of no consequence. She had decisions to make. Hard ones.

She stretched the corner hard, her strides long, picking up speed as her apartment building came into focus. She considered circling one more time to have another conversation with herself. Jake Parson was merely a distraction. Clint showing up like a mirage was just another coincidence. She felt like she'd come to a crossroad with signs posted in four different directions, four different names—her own, Jake's, Clint's, and Airic's. The signs were meant to confuse her, but she knew what was best, what was right.

A stream of sweat tickled before dropping from the edge of her brow. She slowed, then stopped, bending over to catch her breath. The morning air smelled faintly of last night's traffic. It hurt her nostrils to take in as much oxygen as her heart and lungs requested. She stood up and tried to stabilize. She immediately saw the car from the corner of her eye. The bright red sports car pulled up. Jake stepped out coming toward her, his mouth open with questions before she could meet him halfway.

"What happened? I was worried. I tried calling all night, then I came over and you still didn't answer the intercom." His breath came in spurts as if he'd been the one jogging.

"Airic's here," she blurted out, then looked up at the building, grateful her apartment window faced the rear.

He blinked in confusion.

"*Honey*," she clarified.

Jake backed away. "Got it." He swung the car door open then got in and slammed it shut. He started the engine.

She watched his car skid around the corner. She felt like she was going to be sick. Her mouth filled with liquid; she turned so he wouldn't see the expulsion of water coming through her lips. She'd overdone it, using her sleeve to wipe the traces. The early morning silence filled the street, a nuisance of buzzing that she couldn't shut out even with her hands pressed over her ears.

.   .   .

VENUS submerged the plate in the hot sudsy dishwater. She wiped with an intensity that thickened the foam. She tried to drown out the voices and intermittent laughter of her father and Airic in the living room. They were having a conversation that spaced in and out, Airic promising to find a company her father could invest in that produced miniature trains.

She pressed the nozzle, pushing out a jet stream of water to rinse. Airic came and poured the last bit of coffee from the pot. "How much longer do you plan on staying?" He leaned on the counter, sipping from his mug.

Venus continued to wash, spraying a skillet to rinse. The water splashed on her chest. "Shit."

Airic dumped the bitter brew down the sink. "I have to get back to the apartment and get some work done."

"Take the car. Dad can bring me later, or you can come back and pick me up. I want to cook dinner for them." It didn't matter that her aunt had precooked for a week. She couldn't handle spending the full day with Airic.

"So you plan to stay here for dinner?"

Venus stopped to look at him. Observations from a chaotic mind . . . his Adam's apple double-rippled when he swallowed, his eyebrows were growing sparse grays to match his mustache, his white shirt was buttoned almost clear to his throat, allowing his Adam's apple to stick out prominently.

"No, I'm going to prepare so they'll have something to eat for later. Why? Did you have something in mind?" Her wet hand rested on her hip. Observation, he couldn't look her in the eye.

"I didn't come here just to work. But it's important that I finish this work for Monday. I should be finished around five, so I'll pick you up then and we can decide what we're going to do for dinner."

"Don't rush." She squeezed a tight smile. "I have plenty to do here. I'll probably start on the laundry after this." Venus turned back to the sink, ignoring the cold soggy feeling on the front of her T-shirt.

"I'll say good-bye to your dad; I'm sure your mom's already back to sleep." He went to kiss her on the lips and she extended her cheek. He walked away confused but he didn't take the time to ask what was wrong.

Venus stared out the small kitchen window, daydreaming. The earlier run-in with Jake had left her raw and frayed like the edges of unfinished fabric. She was alone in the kitchen, standing in one spot. She'd spent many days looking out of the small square window to the hill covered with ice plant. The ever growing succulents found Southern California canyons irresistible. A few times a year her parents hired workers to dig it up by the root, landscaping with wild poppies and ivy. The ice plant always managed to grow back, stronger than ever.

"Hey, Precious, Airic says he's taking off." Her father's touch surprised her. He took the dish towel out of her hand. "You don't have to stay here. He came all this way. Get on out there before he's gone. Your mother and I are fine."

Venus never felt it necessary to lie to her father. He'd told her several times in several different ways, there's nothing worse than lying no matter what the sin or failure. Not that she was stupid enough to volunteer information out of the blue. She'd acted out the usual teenage rebellions. Sex. Experimentation with alcohol and drugs, but she hadn't been stupid enough to confess. Though if he'd asked, it would have been a different story.

She leaned her head on his shoulder. "Dad, do you like Airic? I mean really like him, or do you just act friendly because he's my fiancé?"

He pulled back. "What kind of question is that?"

She hunched her shoulders.

"Why are you asking me now? You've never asked before." He moved to the dinette and pulled out a chair. "Come here, sit down."

He waited until she was squarely in front of him. "Do *you* like Airic?" He scooted his chair closer to get her complete attention. "Now, hold on before you answer that. We love people and connect through time and events in our lives that bond us forever. We call it love, loyalty, and re-sponsibility toward that person... but liking someone, feeling a sheer joy just to be in their company, that's a whole lot different and seems to me, you should be asking yourself that question."

He leaned his head down to follow her eyes. "Nothing to say? You're having doubts about our friend Airic?"

She shook her head up and down.

"Is it about the young fella you brought to the hospital?"

Venus finally let her head move into her palms. The headache that had been threatening to burst forward was now making itself comfortable be-tween her eyes. No matter if they were open or closed, the red and black spots continued to dance before her.

"You just met this fella?"

"Since I started working in Los Angeles, not long enough to feel the way I do," she muttered downward.

"You can't measure it, Precious. There's no way to measure everything. I know you've spent a lot of time trying to get people to measure up to your expectations."

That got her attention. "What's that supposed to mean?" She looked up. It hurt to raise her eyes.

"You know, like what you went through with the young doctor fella."

"Don't mention him." The thought of Clint asking her if she still loved him made her headache worse.

"My point is you can't keep believing things happen exactly as you map them out. Not like the business you're in where you sit down and plan, strategize, then go out and make it happen. Love, or in this case, like, doesn't happen that way. You can't know when it's going to hit you, you just have to be ready for it."

"Does being ready include already being in a relationship with some-one else?" She put her head back down.

"Life is full of choices; nobody says they all have to be right. Sometimes they just have to feel good. A little joy never hurt nobody, Precious."

Venus' eyes watered from the pain in her head. She felt miserable. "Taking joy for yourself and hurting someone in return, that's not right."

"You're measuring again, trading in one thing for another."

"That's the way life is, Daddy. You can't have it all. If you do one thing here, it affects the other over there; there's consequences, it's the law. Cause and effect."

"Yeah, but what if making your move over here gives way to a positive, stronger result way over here"—he pointed his finger on the table, as if they were playing an invisible game of chess—"results better for you than you ever imagined; how will you know if you never try? You can't predict it all, it can't always be planned out." He stood up and stretched, making a few cracking sounds in his neck. "I know you've got a lot of thinking to do, but for once, I suggest you stop thinking and just do it, like the Nike commercial says. Get on out there and take some chances. Life is full of risk and danger but living is much more fun." He started walk-ing out of the kitchen.

She squeezed her eyes closed, talking more to herself than to him, but it came out anyway. "How would you know?"

She heard her father's footsteps stop. She lifted up her hand. "I didn't mean that, Daddy. My head is killing me. I—"

"I know what you think about your mother and I." He was moving back toward her. "What most anyone thinks who has spent more than five min-utes in the same room with us. Pauletta's here, I'm way down here, doing whatever she says. That's the way it looks, and that's fine by me. Only thing that matters is what's going on in here, and here." He pointed first to his heart, then to his head. "That's your perfect example of how I would know. I never listened to one single person or paid attention to any rules that said this overbearing, controlling, loving, sensitive woman was not for me. That's right, she's all those things, and I love her and, got news for you, like her a whole bunch too. The chance I took was that I married her anyway. Now you better start taking some chances or you gonna end up unhappy and alone." This time he left the kitchen and didn't turn back.

*   *   *

THE rapid pulse in her ears and head began a trail, increasing in intensity as it moved down the sides of her neck and through her shoulders. She found herself upstairs in the small bathroom she'd shared with Timothy growing up. She pawed the medicine cabinet for Excedrin or aspirin. An expired bottle of Tylenol fell into the sink. She popped the cap open, then swallowed two at a time, then two more. She went back and found an almost empty bottle of Sleep EZ. The expired date didn't deter her from pushing the last two into her mouth and sticking her mouth under the faucet, gulping air and water.

Her old bedroom was within crawling distance. It had been years since she'd had a migraine of this magnitude. The only thing she could be thankful for was that they didn't come often enough to cause alarm. She accepted the staggering pain and submitted to the total breakdown of her body and mind as a call for her to stop and rest.

She knocked over the pile of stuffed animals and pulled back the flowered bedspread, curling up and pushing her face into the pillow. Her mother kept her room just as it had always been. Bright yellow walls, pictures of herself when she was a child. Awards she'd won. First-place ribbons hung in chronological order from the spelling bee competitions, four years in a row until she was dethroned in the sixth grade by George, a big bootie boy with a terrible sinus condition. Pictures she'd drawn and painted still in the white laminated Kmart frames. Her mother had been proud of her artistic talent. It came natural to Venus, always had. But she'd ignored pursuing it after her mother said there were more than enough starving artists, the world didn't need one more.

What chances had she ever taken? She couldn't even follow her heart to do something she'd loved. She tried going down the list, the risk-taker list. Things she'd done that were against the grain. She'd cut off all her long straightened hair and started over au naturel. That was huge. She'd changed jobs voluntarily, without having been downsized or let go. No one could claim that was easy. She'd moved lots of times, leaving family and friends. Relocating to a new city was a symbol of being able to change, take chances. She met people every day who had never left the city they grew up in, living in the same neighborhood, near or with their mamas. She rolled her eyes in her head and immediately cringed from the pain.

She took chances. She did! Why should she risk blowing her relationship with Airic when she was so close, so close to finally getting married?

The sleep medication began to take effect. She felt like the swaying branch outside the bedroom window making shadowy movements. Her lids were heavy. Henry's words began to slide off into oblivion, to a place where defending herself was no longer necessary. A place where the truth was self-evident. Where it was risk free. She could take chances in her dreams where everything would turn out all right. It was safe to feel Jake's arms around her, his breath in her ear, holding her close. It was safe to close her eyes and experience the sweetness. She could take chances in her dreams.

⌐   ⌐   ⌐

SHE awakened to the sound of howling winds. The dark room was comforting, even with the sound of ghosts swirling outside. She sat up blinking in the twilight. Her head still thumped mildly, but nothing like the pain earlier. Her body yearned for a long stretch and deep yawn. She stood up, extending her arms over her head, remembering how she'd found her way to the bed in the first place. She had decisions to make. It was time to face Airic. To face herself.

She peeked in on her mother. She lay sleeping comfortably. Venus leaned on the bed and kissed her gently on the lips. "I love you, Mom," she whispered near her face.

Airic was already waiting when she came downstairs. Henry shook Airic's hand and patted him on the back. "You take care now." He walked away without saying good-bye to Venus. Airic didn't catch the tension.

"So, did you get all your work done?" Venus kept her eyes on the hood of the car, trying not to look at the road. Airic drove with an East Coast mentality, heavy foot and lots of swerving, which made her uncomfortable.

"Enough. Definitely enough." He braked hard at the light, sending her head forward with a jolt. Sharp pain stabbed between her eyes.

"Please take it easy; I've been fighting this headache all day." She pressed her fingers to her forehead. She rolled the window down, desperate for fresh air. Airic's aftershave was suffocating.

He lifted a hand and rubbed her neck and shoulders. "Whoa, haven't seen you feel this bad in a long time. What brought this on?"

"I don't know." She removed his hand and placed it back on the steering wheel. "I'll be okay, just watch where you're going." She stared straight ahead, the shine of the hood glaring in her eyes.

Maybe she did know what brought it on. Her body had a way of punishing her when she didn't release and acknowledge. Her conscience was screaming guilt, fear, and confusion. She thought of the rush of emotion she felt when Jake showed up looking so vulnerable, standing before her admitting with his actions that he cared more for her than he wanted to. Worse, there was nothing he could do about it. She'd sent him away, hurt, and now she was absorbing the pain.

"I'll pick up some takeout. We can eat inside."

"Yeah."

She'd dozed off. Before she knew it, they were idling in front of the apartment.

Airic nudged her shoulder, then stroked the side of her face. "You go on up, I'll get the food and be back in a flash." He leaned over and kissed her temple. The scent of his cologne, the very same he'd been wearing since she'd known him, now nauseated her. She got out of the car, begging for the clear air that the strong winds had brought. He waited while she let herself in, then he accelerated heavily, screeching off.

＊　　＊　　＊

THE apartment was filled with Airic, his scent lingering like a fog settling over the land. She moved through the house, opening the sliding door and side windows. The curtains blew up and swirled around her. An immediate chill from the outside, but anything was better than the sickening cologne in the air.

Venus walked to the answering machine, checking for messages, and saw no life. She held up the unplugged cord. At least she hadn't lied to Jake. One out of two ain't bad.

She made her way to the bathroom. She turned on the water, full pressure. The tub began to fill. The steam sometimes helped her headaches.

She stripped herself of clothing and sat on the cold toilet seat, her bare bottom oblivious to the discomfort. She was numb at this point, feeling nothing but the desire to sink as low in the tub as she could. She stepped in when it was half full, letting the water continue to run. All she had to do was say it, put herself out of her misery. Even if Airic didn't hear her, the universe would. She will have told the truth and freed herself. How does one just walk away? She'd witnessed it enough times, even partaken in the morbid behavior as a youth, but as an adult, having respect and compassion for another loving, kind human being, how did one go about the act of crushing them for no good reason, stepping on their backs and staying on a merry course without a break in stride? A good person to ask would be Clint.

Her hearty laugh bounced in echoes throughout the bathroom. Clint would know firsthand how to destroy someone and keep stepping. He'd easily carried out the act with her underfoot. It should be vivid and recent in his mind. The way he simply held up his hand and said, I'm through, enough, I'm going to do what I want to do. *To hell with you, Venus.* She could still see him, Clint's lips moving, telling her, he was glad they'd finally cleared the air so they could always be friends.

Friends.

The laugh again. This time she took in a mouth full of water, almost choking. She turned the knobs off before the tub overflowed. She leaned back into the frothy suds, letting her hair get soaked.

Airic didn't deserve the same treatment as Clint had shown her. No one did. Putting in time and effort with someone, planning a life together, then suddenly smacked down, eliminated, and put to the curb like Saturday's trash. She'd put in four long years with Clint and supported him mentally, physically, financially. Yet the tally sheet showed zero balance. Nothing owed, nothing due. Maybe that was the lesson she hadn't learned. You give because you want to. You love because you want to. Always looking for the payoff was the wrong way to tread through life. She wondered if Airic had already had this revelation. Maybe he *would* understand.

"Hey, where you at? Got the food."

With the sound of Airic's voice she stood up dripping. Her wet hands pushed the door to a solid close. "I'll be out in a few minutes," she yelled.

The door creaked back open. "Thought you might need this." He stuck his hand through the entry holding a small bottle of extra strength pain medication. He shook the bottle a little, then came inside, unscrewing the cap. "Sometimes opening these things will give you a headache in and of itself."

Venus held out her palm, cupping the two small capsules. He handed her a glass of water.

"So, is it an imaginary friend you're talking to in here?"

"Just thinking out loud."

He sat on the edge of the tub. "Anything you want to share, or do you like talking to yourself? I've heard only geniuses talk to themselves. Whenever you see those ranting homeless people, muttering to the air..." He made a smirk on his face that emphasized his own exhaustion.

"So you're saying I'm next. Pretty soon I'll be pushing my little cart around, genius that I am?"

"Not as long as you have me." He scooped a fingertip of bubbles and put them on her nose. "Don't be long. You know how mushy Thai food gets if it sits too long." He stood in the doorway for a few extra seconds. For a moment he looked like the man who had rescued her two years ago, lifting her up when she'd been so far down. There was no mistaking, it was him. Her knight in shining armor who'd made her feel wanted and safe. So if he was the same, it must've been she who'd changed. He shouldn't be punished for that.

She sunk deeper in the tub. "Okay, five more minutes."

DOUBLE SHOTS

MONDAY morning Venus sat in the corner, drinking her double espresso. Having coffee so readily available made it impossible to resist. But she'd done good, a whole weekend without caffeine, or alcohol. But Mondays required a jolt of java, plus she needed an excuse to talk to Jake.

She saw him walk in, his soft-fitting sweater pushed up on his forearms. His slacks were well creased as always, the cuffs hanging over his thick leather shoes. He moved into the Starbucks line. She got up, stepping closer to him. "Coffee, sir." She smiled, holding out the cup. "Please. Take it." Her arm getting tired while he only stared.

Jake took a deep breath and took the hot cup out of her hand. He took a sip and handed it back. "It's really not what I had in mind this morning, but thank you anyway."

Venus watched as he stepped to the counter and ordered the exact same thing, "Tall, whatever's on tap."

She walked past the trashcan and dropped both coffees, hers and his, inside. This day was going to be long and difficult. This business with Jake, plus her mother's doctor appointment—just thinking about it made her tired. She ambled up the steep winding staircase.

She walked into the conference room and sat across from William. He was the only one there. "Hey, how's it going?"

"Beautiful. I had an intense weekend." He stayed quiet, waiting for Venus to inquire, but she had nothing to add. "You know what? I'm thinking about staying here after this project. Los Angeles has some major happenings. I'm digging this town." He wasn't really talking to Venus, but more to himself.

"What's so great about it?" She wasn't really talking to him either. They were both determined to answer their own questions. "Too many dreamers here. Everybody thinks something great is supposed to happen. Sometimes life just is. No miracles."

William smiled. His honest boyish charm seemed to shine through only when Legend wasn't around. Nothing to prove, no image to maintain. "I met someone," he confessed.

"Did you say something?" She adjusted her sight to see him and not the crystal ball filled with her and Jake laughing and running on the beach.

Jake walked in carrying his coffee with Beverly Shaun right behind him.

Legend walked in and slapped hands with Jake. "Was that a party last night, or what?"

"Off the hook, slave. Off the hook," Jake agreed with a full dreamy cast, replaying his role in whatever happened last night. He sipped on his coffee.

"And Beverly, girl you gonna put somebody's eye out with all that." Legend made an imaginary slap go near her backside. "Was that the move, Jake?"

Venus felt like pinching herself to wake herself from this nightmare. She looked at Jake, then Beverly. Neither had anything else to say on the subject. She was dying to ask what Legend was talking about. Dancing? Last night? She regretted not paying closer attention to what William had to say. They'd all been together, partying? She had no right to be jealous.

"All right, man, it was definitely one for the memory books, but now it's time to make things happen. We've got exactly twenty-six days till the Magic Show. No more testing grounds, it's got to happen." The tone was infectious. Everyone began to sit up straight and focus on what he was saying. "Beverly, how're we doing with the breakout?"

"I'm on schedule, but we're going way over budget with the overtime. The models' weight fluctuates from one day to the next; it's like we're constantly starting over."

Jake had a disbelieving look on his face, something edging toward "Have you lost your mind?" He readjusted, letting his first response slide away, replacing it with something more civil, "Beverly, is this a common problem?"

"Well, it happens, but not every one of them at the same time. It's like today, they're all size 8, tomorrow they'll be back down to 4's and 6's. That's hard to work around."

"Sistahs got to stay away from those fries and shakes," Legend chimed in, grinning with his bold white teeth.

"I'm not one to be biased against our own people, but he's right. If I had my regular girls, this wouldn't be happening."

Venus felt compelled to speak, but not before giving Legend a hard criticizing look. "Take control, Beverly. Call a meeting with your fit models and explain that we have a major deadline and they have to stay consistent with their weight. Let them know how important it is."

"It's not like we're dealing with professionals here." Beverly shifted her eyes to Legend. "Somebody picked them out of a lineup of a wet T-shirt contest, bringing them in talking about, oh here are your new models."

Jake stood up, leaning on the desk with his arms firm and flexed. "Beverly, make it happen. Twenty-six days. That's all."

"Well, you were the one that asked how we're doing, and I told you." She crossed her arms over the two midgets hiding underneath her sweater. Even Venus felt it hard to resist staring.

"Call a meeting, Beverly. I'll talk to them." Venus looked at Jake so he'd understand it would get taken care of. "The proposal, how's that coming?"

William volunteered the information. "All points are covered; there's not one reason for the royalty not to see this as gold. Lila Kelly is worth about twelve million in unit dollars. We're asking for a hundred thousand shares at market value, which translates to $2 million. If this thing flies, her gain could be upward of $5 million, easy."

Venus leaned forward in her seat; it sounded like an offer neither party could refuse.

Jake, who was still in a full grimace, said, "That's a lot of money to stand around smiling." He held up his hand and started counting down. "She can't sell the shares for six months. When and if she does decide to sell, it can be in increments no larger than five thousand per quarter. Her contract is for a full year. Nine different shoots. Concert appearances in that span all in Feline and JPWear rags." He leaned back. "Damn, for $2 million, she needs to be putting something else out, too."

Venus found the comment offensive, but the rest of the group erupted in laughter.

"Fax it over, Legend." She stood up gathering her things. "We need to get the ball rolling."

"I think that's something you can handle, don't you?" Jake leaned back in his chair, still carrying his devil-may-care attitude. The room became quiet. The others obviously noticed the tension between them.

"This meeting is over. Beverly, take care of your floor." Jake left the room without another word.

Venus felt the sting of his resentment. She followed him out the glass doors. She knew Legend, Beverly, and William were watching with amusement and wonder. It didn't stop her from grabbing Jake's arm. "Wait a minute. We can't work together like this."

"You know what, you're right about that. I think we can take it from here."

"We? That's my team. If I go, they go."

He raised his shoulders, giving a shrug. She followed him down the stairs, trembling behind each of his heavy steps.

"This is ridiculous. What is the problem, Jake? It's not like I didn't tell you the truth. I told you from the very start I was seriously involved with someone. Why..."

Jake stopped at the bottom landing and faced her. His eyes went soft for a moment, then sharp again. "This is neither the time nor the place. You want to talk to me, you know where I am." He walked off, leaving Venus feeling like the last leaf on the tree. Any slight breeze would send her spiraling to the ground.

Legend came from behind, his black-coffee skin glistening, his eyes dancing with expectance. "You two got issues?" He let one leg ride the stair, while the other stayed straight and grounded. His locks looked freshly twisted, hanging past his shoulders. "Mixing business with pleasure? Now what?"

"Now, none of your business."

"Smart. Very well thought out on your part. I expected better of you, Ms. Johnston," he called after her while she did an about-face and headed back up the stairs. She restrained her middle finger from riding up. She'd expected better from herself as well.

*   *   *

BEVERLY was still in the conference room, overlooking the sample floor. Her soft long mane was pushed up into an *I Dream of Jeannie* ponytail. She turned to face Venus when she heard the door swing open. A smile, or something that resembled satisfaction, settled around her face.

"He's a handful, huh?"

"Who?" Venus gathered her notes and case. It was too late to ignore the high school drama scene everyone had witnessed. Still, she was old enough not to have this conversation if she didn't want to.

"Jake. He can be a little testy." Beverly pulled out the chair she was sitting in earlier, ready to get a full story in return.

"I wouldn't know." Venus closed her case and secured the strap over her shoulder. "Is now a good time to call your models together?"

Beverly checked her watch, disappointment replacing the satisfaction from earlier. "Actually, they're probably all in the snack room."

"Well, there lies the problem." Venus followed her out, determined not to leave the building without a gained ally. "We'll unplug the vending machine for the next couple of weeks." They both let out soft nervous laughs.

"I didn't mean to be nosy." Beverly offered an apology with the tone of her voice. They continued walking side by side. Venus slowed down as they passed the stairs. "There's an elevator over here."

Venus followed, now having to skip to keep up with Beverly's long strides. The red octagon-shaped door opened to a cool interior of white shiny walls with chrome trim. Her reflection next to Beverly made her immediately feel small and unimportant.

When the doors closed, Beverly wasted no time getting to the point. "How long have you known Jake?"

Venus adjusted her bag on her shoulder. "Since this launch. I know it probably looks like we've known each other a lot longer. I was thinking the exact same thing. I actually feel like I've known him forever, like a brother. You know the way a brother and sister take each other for granted, not getting along, but then they make up and forget what the fight was about." She checked Beverly's face to see if she was buying the brother-sister excuse.

"When I first started working here, Jake and I had our share of problems. Sort of like what I witnessed today between you guys." The elevator came to a smooth stop. The two women stared at each other, wondering what the other's real story entailed. Venus wondered if Jake had held her hand while they walked on the beach or had run a hot bubble bath for her with lit candles and soft music. She wondered if he'd slathered Beverly's feet with rich warm cream, then held her in his arms all night while she slept. Venus easily pictured the two of them together. A perfect couple like the ones between the pages of magazines, laughing, heads thrown back with gleaming white teeth and noble chins.

"It looks like you guys get along now," Venus said with no real proof for the statement. Their signals were as mixed as a can of Planters nuts. The only way she would know what she wanted to know was to ask. "Were you ... the two of you ever more than working colleagues?"

Beverly stuck her hand out to stop the doors from reclosing. Venus followed her out, the gravity of information pulling her along like a leash attached to her neck.

"Jake and I have an understanding. A mutual promise to keep a safe distance from each other."

"Why?"

She cut her eyes to Venus walking by her side. " 'Cause I'm a match and he's gasoline. Very dangerous." Beverly would have won if there was a staring contest. Her large almond-shaped eyes traced with liquid liner did not waver. Venus was the first to turn away. They finished the length of the hall to the sample floor without another word on the subject.

*   *   *

AFTER lecturing the models for fifteen minutes on maintaining weight and exercise, Venus went straight to the vending machine and grabbed a

Snickers bar. She needed a burst of energy to go back and tackle Mr. Jake Parson. She couldn't let the day end on this note. There was too much work to be done.

She stood at his closed office door, knowing he was inside, as if she could hear his heart beating where she stood. She put a hand to her chest to see if it was her own rhythm she detected. No. Not nearly strong enough, not nearly passionate enough. She took a step back; she wasn't ready for someone like Jake Parson. Someone willing to pour himself whole into a relationship. She was used to doing the chasing, being the one who wanted more than she would ever receive.

*   +   •

"Venus." Legend's voice caught her off guard. She took a wobbly step backward, when the door opened. Embarrassed but still grateful it was the wall and not the floor she fell into. He grabbed her arm, "Hey now, you all right?"

"Fine." She gathered her balance. "Is Jake inside?"

"I'm right here." They both turned around to see him standing in the open doorway. The bright sunlight settled around him in his office. His face was a silhouette, offering no hint as to his mood.

"Can you spare a minute?"

She felt Legend watching, enjoying her humbleness.

Jake stepped aside, making room for her to enter. He closed the door before Legend could reenter.

"I didn't want to leave things the way they were, from earlier."

The shades were down in his office windows, but light still pushed through. The walls weren't white, she was happy to see. A soft touch of green, beaming energy and fuel for the brain. He walked around to the center of his honey-wood L-shaped desk. On top sat matching accessories. The pen holder, calendar, and clock were all trimmed in the same deep wood hue. He sat down and leaned back in his chair, then twirled around so his back faced Venus.

She stood up, then sat back down on the leather couch. "Jake, I'm sorry. I treated you wrong."

"Past tense is the key here."

Venus leaned her face in her hands. "I should've called you, somehow. Left some type of cryptic message... anything, instead of having you worry." She let her eyes drop to the plush Oriental rug when he didn't respond. She looked up and had an intense urge to turn his chair around to face her. She missed him, sitting less than a few feet away and having no view of the delicate lines of his slim beard, the honest square of his chin. "I'm sincerely sorry, that's all I can say." She stood up and moved her feet with great effort to the door. She should say more, that it was all her fault. What he'd taken as a sign to pursue her was real but her heart and mind had sent out conflicting signals. She wanted nothing more than to feel the warmth of his touch.

"I just wanted you to know how bad I felt. Okay," she said again, as she reached the door.

She felt the heat of his body come up behind her. "You don't have to go." He put a slow, careful arm around her, followed by the other, wrapping her tightly. He managed to turn her around without loosening his grip.

She pulled away briefly, to look into his eyes, and there it was. Venus had scratched it off her list, accepting simple things in its place, honesty, understanding, and compassion. But to feel weightless, empowered but still light as a feather, she had relinquished that to the sickening fairy tales and romances on the big screen. But now, right here, she felt it. Now she understood those moments when the heroine looked into her man's eyes announcing whole and complete submission, because here she was safe, protected. Loved and needed.

Jake kissed her softly on the forehead, then the bridge of her nose, and was heading for her lips when a knock at the door spoiled the moment. Venus moved swiftly and found a corner to concentrate on while she strained to hear the voice of the visitor.

"Hey, can I talk to you?" Beverly's mellow tone crept past him. He stood between any view she may have had of his office or of Venus.

"Now's not a good time. Give me a call in about an hour." The door closed. Jake was back by her side. His hands cupped her shoulders without reserve. He no longer felt like a trespasser on someone else's territory. He was now in his own garden, inhaling the sweet scent of her neck, trailing the line of her collarbone.

"Don't start thinking too hard," he whispered behind her ear before turning her to face him.

"That's what I do. I think."

"Sssh," his finger touched her lips then pressed to the center of her eyes.

She understood what he was saying. She could think her way into an ending, an inevitable bottom line. What he hadn't known was that she'd already played out the complete scenario, in those short seconds when the door opened to Beverly. She'd seen the beginning, the middle, and the end.

"I better get going. I still have time to make it over to the hospital for my mother's appointment with her new doctor." Venus had begged her mother and father to let her come; it wouldn't make sense to be late, or not to show up at all.

"Let me drive you." Jake held her hand while he walked her out of his office, stopping in the middle of the corridor.

"No. That's okay. I'll be fine."

"Do me a favor and call as soon as you get a chance. Give your mother my well wishes." He lifted her chin, kissing her lips lightly.

"Someone might see us." She pecked him one last time. "I'll call as soon as I'm done." Her legs were moving, but she couldn't feel them. Intoxicated. She twisted around and gave him another wave because she knew he was still watching.

She staggered out of the JPWear studio still high from his kiss, from his touch. The noise of street traffic, cars, and people all filtered down to a low hum. She could only hear Jake in her ear, whispering that he'd see her later. Couldn't bear the thought of waiting till tomorrow. *Call me as soon as you possibly can.*

"Nice."

She looked back to see a homeless man grinning at her with bared yellow teeth. The man's voice was enough to bring her back to reality, knock her off the cloud she'd been sailing on while walking to her car. He was still staring at her when she got inside and put her key in the ignition. With all the dirt and grunginess around his face, his eyes still managed to gleam, light bouncing off his pupils.

Venus pulled off, her stereo blaring loudly. The man was still smiling as she drove by, as if the two of them shared a secret. Misdeeds and malice. Wrong against Airic. Wrong against her own good sense. Wrong. She knew she was, and all things done in darkness would eventually come to light.

SMALL THINGS

THE waiting room was sparsely populated. Smooth classical music played through the hidden speakers, and the long couches pushed against the wall benefited only a young woman with wispy hair and deep-set eyes sitting alone staring into space. Venus saw the receptionist behind the partition, sitting in the middle like the chair umpire of a tennis match. She stood up with a look of recognition as Venus came toward her.

"Your mother is here. She's waiting for you." Her pretty dark eyes stayed wide with her smile. She came around and opened the entry door. "I didn't introduce myself the first time; my name is Lettie." She stuck out her hand to shake. Venus hugged her instead. It was becoming a habit, reaching out for confirmation, holding on to another person, close to her heart, to know she was alive and well and that life could be as wonderful as she made it.

"I'm Venus. I guess I never told you my name either." Venus followed her to the doctor's office. Lettie knocked before opening the door. Pauletta and Henry were sitting in two chairs pushed close together, holding hands, shoulder to shoulder for support.

"Mom." Venus squeezed her face between the two of them and kissed her mother on the cheek while hugging her father.

"Hi, Precious." Henry squeezed her shoulder. "Glad you came."

Venus checked her mother's face to see if she felt the same way. Pauletta revealed a weak but genuine smile.

"Dr. Lamb will be here any minute. Mrs. Johnston, you sure I can't get you anything, water, decaf tea, juice, anything?"

Pauletta shook her head no, but Venus leaned into Lettie's ear, "Bring her some water."

"How you feeling, Mom?"

Her head fell back on Henry's shoulder. "I'm missing *The View*, sitting up here. They're supposed to be interviewing that girl's mother, the one that's missing. I swear, this better not take all day."

"Mom, *The View* comes on in the morning, you already missed it."

Henry tightened his grip slightly, kissing the temple of her forehead. "I taped it for you, you were sleeping."

"Okay, the gang's all here." Dr. Lamb walked into the office, the lapels of his white coat neatly pressed down, his tie straight and perfect. This man dotted his i's and crossed his t's. Her mother was safe with Dr. Lamb. He extended a hand to Henry. "How's our young lady doing today?"

The use of the word *young* got a smile out of Pauletta. She lifted her head for the doctor.

He went over her file, then closed it as if there was a simple solution. "This is an exciting time, Pauletta. These days we've narrowed down what to do for someone like you. You'll be able to skip the experimental side of drugs and therapy. After going over your file, I'm thinking the best route is chemotherapy and forgo the radiation."

Venus let out an audible gasp. The room was silenced for a moment. She took the opportunity to ask a stupid question. "Is that going to be enough?"

"Chemotherapy, in this case, will be a strong start."

"If it's that strong, won't she be sick from that, really sick?" Venus rubbed her itching palms.

"There's two types of therapy, light chemo, CMF, and there's the heavy hitter called CAF. Because Pauletta's lymph nodes tested negative, which means the cancer never left the station, CMF is the best treatment for her. The side effects are mostly limited to exhaustion. With exhaustion comes its own set of problems, irritability, restlessness, that type of thing. CMF isn't the type to do damage to your kidneys or make you lose your hair," he said to Pauletta, as if she had asked the question. "It may thin it out a little, but that's about it." He slipped his reading glasses off.

Henry and Pauletta stayed quiet. The presence of authority stifled her parents, which came as a shock, knowing how opinionated they both were, especially when it came to Venus, but here, before Dr. Lamb, they were docile creatures.

"So, after the medicine, the chemo, will she be cancer free, rid of it for good?" Venus spoke up again.

"The word is *remission*. Once someone has cancer, it's better to always stay on alert, always watching. It's like a war with a million enemies. You can destroy 999,999, but that one small thing surviving could create havoc and destruction all on its own. Once the chemo is complete, I'll run more tests, then make that declaration."

Venus felt something tapping through her, an anxiety, a pressing stab. She swallowed and asked, "So there's always a chance it will come back?"

Dr. Lamb looked at her mother and father. "That's why we're going to fight, with everything we've got. Pauletta has to feel confident, have faith, and believe that she will beat this." He smiled, then looked to Venus. "To look on the positive side, to know she's going to be well and live a long full life...to see a couple of grandbabies go to college and do some extraordinary things." He took a deep breath. "I want to do Pauletta's physical exam, then we'll do the CAT scan and MRI today while she's here and start the chemo as well."

Venus didn't mind so much when Dr. Lamb spoke in we's. This was a *we* that felt like they were all working together.

He stood up, straightening himself as he rose. Dr. Lamb's warm hand landed on Venus's shoulder. "You have to keep your side of the bargain. If Ms. Pauletta over here is going to outlive us all, you'd better get to work on those grandchildren."

"Yes, sir," Venus said, trying to express lightness in her voice, all the while trying to stifle the urge to break down. Venus held it in, escorting her mother to the exam room.

She helped her mother undress. The bandage was still wrapped tightly around her chest, neat and precise. This was her father's work. He'd probably taken his time, putting all his concentration into the intricate detail of matching each layer of the gauze with the last, using the same time and concentration it took to put together one of his trains. Venus held the cotton exam robe in front of her mother, then slipped it down to go up her arms so she didn't have to lift. Her mother sat down on the tissue-covered table. It hurt to see her this way.

A nurse pushed in with a wheelchair while Venus was kissing her mother's cheek.

"Are we ready to go?"

"Oh, I thought she was supposed to get examined by Dr. Lamb."

"Tests first, then exam." The nurse was helping Pauletta into the chair. "We'll come out and get you as soon as we're done."

They wheeled out first, Venus followed, detouring when she saw her father through the cut out receptionist hole. Henry was sitting in the center of one of the long couches. He put his arm out for her to take the space beside him.

"You did good, Precious." Henry secured the arm around her shoulder. "She's going to be fine. I know it. Do you know it?"

Venus didn't dare speak, didn't dare disturb the lump in her throat; she took tiny gasps of air, while nodding her head.

"Tell me how you're doing with the little problem we talked about." She didn't respond, only kept her face against his shoulder. "I call it a little problem 'cause things have to be put into perspective, don't they."

She nodded, unable to speak, not able to tell her father that the little problem was wrecking any salvageable mind she had left. Unable to think or walk straight, she, a grown woman, was not able to see where her heart and mind belonged—with someone she'd just met, or with a man who'd been by her side for the last two years. Her father had warned her not to measure, but life was nothing more than measurement and contrast, good and bad, right or wrong. There was no way not to see them side by side. Jake or Airic.

"It's all under control," she lied. Such a small thing compared with what they were all going through right now. Small on the scale of things.

Like the white dot on the gray slide of her mother's mammogram. Almost undetectable. Tiny. But the consequences, the destruction, critical.

She kissed her father, still holding her breath, still unable to chance breathing for fear of releasing the dam of confusion and guilt she carried. She held on to her father, wishing he could give her the answer, simply tell her what to do.

BONES

VENUS came into her apartment and threw herself on the couch. The day had been spent sitting with her mother during her first chemo treatment. It may as well have been Venus who the nurse pierced, her arm taped to the needle that delivered the liquid fire. She held her mother's hand the entire time, feeling her life move through her fingertips. The television had kept Pauletta's attention while Venus watched her mother for signs of anything out of the ordinary. Occasionally Venus faded in and out of mock scenarios with Airic, how she would tell him. She'd promised herself as soon as she got back to the apartment she was going to call, at least lay down the groundwork, *I'm questioning our relationship, the commitment doesn't feel strong enough. Why didn't you marry me when you had the chance?*

She picked up the phone next to her bed. Every ounce of strength she had left went into dialing Airic's phone number. An appointment of fate. A change of path and destination.

"Airic Sanders." His voice startled her.

"I didn't expect you to answer." Venus steadied herself, trying to pronounce her words even and clear. "How's it going?" She rolled her eyes to herself... *how's it going?* "Airic, I'm coming to D.C. on Friday."

"That makes sense."

"We have some things to work out and I need to talk to you... in person."

"Exactly."

She paused breathlessly. What did he know? She relaxed when she heard him carrying on a secondary conversation. Preoccupied, he was orchestrating something else while a small part of him paid attention to what Venus had to say.

"Sorry about that; now, what were you saying? Friday?"

"I'll be there in the late evening. I'll meet you at the house."

"I'm looking forward to it. You don't know how much I miss seeing you padding around here."

Venus squeezed her eyes, a vivid picture of her and Airic lounging in the living room in front of the fireplace sharing the Sunday paper. Soft mellow jazz playing on the stereo while the snow melted and drizzled outside the bay window.

"My mom started chemo today." She changed the subject quickly. "She has to go every week for the next month and a half. She did good, better than me. I was a nervous wreck."

He didn't respond. She guessed it was TMI, *too much information.*

"So...I'll see you Friday." She wanted the conversation with herself to be over.

"Can't wait, love you," he blurted out on cue.

She held the phone against her face; the words wouldn't come. She pushed the button, hanging up before he figured out she had refused to say "I love you too." Although she did love him, in the same way her father had broken it down for her—commonality, bond, and friendship. But do you feel sheer joy just to be in his company? It had never been like that with her and Airic.

It was more like a comfort zone of ease, nothing complicated. Neither had demonstrated passion about anything beyond their own careers. Their relationship had to fit around their work schedules. The same way they couldn't secure a simple wedding date. Deep down Venus knew it was more than schedules that kept them from closing the deal. What would it have cost them, three, four hours tops on a quiet Saturday in a small church? Northern Virginia had plenty of them, one on every corner. They could have been back in their respective zones by sundown, Airic reading from the financial section of his business journal, Venus surfing magazines and reports looking for new trends. Two people who understood the ABC's, Always Be Closing, and yet they couldn't close the deal of their relationship, couldn't or wouldn't make it stick.

The phone rang as soon as she hung up. She had no choice but to answer. If it was Airic asking what happened, why she'd hung up without saying I love you too, she would look more guilty by not answering at all. Less than thirty seconds later, obviously she would still be within arm's reach of the phone.

"Yes?" She answered cautiously.

"I'm here."

"Here, where?"

"In Los Angeles, at the airport." Wendy sounded like a cheerleader. The Los Angeles excitement around her was already taking effect.

"Wendy? You're here, oh my God, I was planning to come to D.C. this weekend."

"The weekend's a whole three days away. Look, I know I should have told you, but you were going to be like, no, no, I'm fine. When you're not fine. So I'm here." She repeated impatiently, "So I'm here. Are you coming to get me or not?"

"I'm coming. Which terminal?"

"United."

"Okay, half an hour, maybe an hour. Keep your cell phone on, I'll let you know when I'm there, otherwise, stay inside."

"Think someone's going to kidnap me? Yeah, you're probably right. I am looking pretty cute in my Cali gear. Not a turtleneck to be seen. But I do need some sun . . . yes I do."

Venus smiled with the thought of Wendy in town. Her gal pal was like a perfect cool breeze on a hot humid day. She needed her friend to help her through this decision and not a minute too soon. Surely they'd laugh about it all, put it into perspective. Life and its funny way of working out. Wendy had become a good friend when they worked together in D.C. Venus thought Wendy went a little dramatic on the makeup in addition to her long silky jet black hair and honey clear eyes. Contacts, Venus had presumed, a weave, definitely. Once their friendship was solid, Venus asked as politely as possible. "Is all that yours?"

"Is all that yours?" Wendy replied with the same trepidation. Venus grabbed a handful of her own (then straightened) hair, realizing that she must've looked the same way to Wendy. The long silky hair parted on the side, hanging past her shoulders. Miss America in black. They both had made assumptions about the other, not realizing that they were staring into the mirror.

And, yes, Wendy's light eyes framed by her dark chocolate skin were a hundred percent natural, no additives. The hair she indeed had grown out of her head, each and every beautiful strand.

She threw off her sunglasses the minute she saw Venus pull up in the car. "No, you didn't go out and get a BMW, with the top down. Oh... no... you... didn't. I knew you were up to no good out here." Wendy fastened her seat belt after throwing her one suitcase into the back.

"I missed you, too." Venus hugged her while she was still talking.

"Ooooh, I know you're up to no good. Don't lie."

Venus put the gear in drive and sped off, happy to have her buddy by her side. Finally someone to help her see the error of her ways.

            "   »   »

THEY sat across from each other in the Killer Shrimp restaurant at Venice Beach. Wendy and Venus ate in the small cozy booth exchanging catch-up details. The kids, Tia and Jamal, were doing well. Jamal was beginning to wear his pants sagged on his hips and Wendy had threatened to make him wear suspenders if he couldn't keep them up right. Her husband, Sidney, was trying to get on with the fire department since Washington, D.C.'s, police department was like being on a hit list. A report of an officer down was on the news at least twice a week.

"Worst of it all, is that sometimes I wish it were Sidney."

Venus put her iced tea down with a thud on the table. "Please don't say things like that, Wendy."

"I know. I know it's wrong. But sometimes, I think, just get it over with. We've been married seventeen years, and I can't remember not worrying about that man. Constant. I have to go in for color touch-ups every other week just to hide the gray hairs. It's sad. You know how many times I wonder how my life would have turned out if I hadn't been so desperate to get married? To anybody. Nineteen years old and wanting to be married, can you imagine?"

"I can imagine. Would you rather be in my shoes?"

"Your shoes are looking pretty good." Wendy sipped on her margarita.

"You and Sidney have two beautiful children. Beautiful," Venus reemphasized. "You're lucky, in more ways than one." She leaned in, capturing the attention of Wendy's intense eyes. "While I was looking for information about breast cancer, I read that women who have babies before the age of twenty-five reduce their risk of getting breast cancer in the future."

"What kind of crap is that? That's the most ridiculous thing I've ever heard." Wendy scooped a fork full of pasta with shrimp.

"It was in black and white, not just in one book either, the same thing in a few books. A hormone is produced once you give birth that sends out protective enzymes in the breast. Then when you breast-feed, it also helps clean out the toxins, the ones they think are responsible for the cancer."

"That is so nasty." Wendy scrunched up her face. "The baby cleans you out?"

"Something like that; whatever it is, it doesn't hurt the baby and it's supposed to be good for the mother."

"So because I was fool enough to marry the first man who looked my way and dropped two babies before I had the sense not to, I'm good to go?"

Venus took another sip from her straw. A flash nearly made her choke. She'd forgotten, but here it was, the memory, icy cold and flat as the liquid going down her throat. She'd been pregnant. Venus remembered her mother sitting beside her humming a small erratic tune, nothing in particular, rubbing and stroking her back while she filled out the paperwork. Venus Johnston. Nineteen. Status? Unmarried student. Number of times pregnant? Once. Venus could see the medical paperwork plain and clear as on the day she'd filled it out. The smell of the waiting room, stale and unemotional. Girls, younger than her, lined the walls in the waiting chairs, some with mothers, some with boyfriends, most with no one at all.

She remembered being grateful for her mother, being able to tell her, "Mom, I'm pregnant." Her mother had nothing to say that day, simply opened the yellow pages and went down the list, dialing numbers, asking about availability, the words *as soon as possible,* then the spelling of her daughter's name and "thank you, we'll be there."

Venus and her mother had squeezed past the pro-lifers who carried picket signs with pictures of bloodied babies and torn wombs. Inside the waiting room she'd filled out papers on a wooden clipboard. The chipped edge left a splinter in her polyester pants. She'd picked at the annoying edge pushing against her skin to no avail, it was too small to find. The turmoil outside made it nerve racking to sit and wait. It had been a terrible time of violence. Bombings by people that claimed to care about saving human life but doctors and nurses could die. It made no sense.

Venus had checked her watch continually every few minutes, anxious to get it over with. She realized she'd been waiting nearly two hours. Still, there were more women that had been waiting even longer, far more anxious, far more desperate. She remembered one in particular, a girl no older than fifteen who'd rushed through the door after being escorted by two sheriff's deputies. Her protruding belly attracting the pro-lifers like fresh meat thrown into a lion's den. "I'm late. I know," she cried. "But I can't wait." She rubbed her rounded stomach while holding another child, leaning on her hip. The receptionist told her that wasn't the problem. Children were not allowed in the clinic. She had to leave.

"But I can't. I don't have any more time."

"Sorry. No children." The receptionist shook her head with the apology. "You can come back later today, I'll hold your appointment. But we have a strict policy against children in the clinic."

"If I had somewhere to leave her, I would have. I can't wait! She'll sit right here. She won't be no problem." The little girl twisted in the young mother's arms, facing Venus. They caught each other's eyes.

Before Venus knew it, her feet had guided her to stand next to the girl. She took the child out of her arms as easily as a pickpocket, sliding away something that didn't belong to her. "Go. I'll take her outside."

Pauletta stood up, "Unh unh, Venus. No." The look she gave made it clear she was already at her wit's end.

The young mother took her daughter back. "Thanks anyway." She pushed out the doors letting in the outside screams of... muuurrrrderer.

After all that waiting, the abortion took less than twenty minutes. No words exchanged on the way home. A silent pact between her and Pauletta to never speak of it again, to forget, and Venus had, conveniently, effortlessly forgotten. A weekend visiting home from college like any other. The following Monday she went back to school, picked up where she'd left off, except for the partying. The late nights *studying* came to an end. From then on she focused on school, focused on surviving and graduating without another piece of herself being removed and left behind.

Wendy stopped chewing and put her fork down. She took the glass out of Venus's hand. "What happened?"

"Nothing." Venus now trying to swallow the lump of regret in the back of her throat; she had to work fast to bury the memory, put it back in its rightful place. "Just thinking how lucky you are." She lifted up her glass to toast. "And me, I still can't get it right."

"What do you mean? You've got Airic. He wants to have kids, doesn't he?"

"We've been engaged for two years and haven't even set a wedding date. Sound familiar?" She reached for Wendy's frosty margarita glass, but Wendy pushed it out of reach.

"What happened to your healthy resolve?"

"I've met someone." Venus blurted it out as if she'd been dying to say it since the moment she'd picked her friend up from the airport.

Wendy's hands slapped the table. She leaned forward like she'd known all along. "Who?"

"Jake Parson. He owns—"

"JPWear...Jake Parson?" Wendy's eyebrows raised to one arch meeting in the middle.

"You've heard of him?"

"Duh... who hasn't... luscious hips and fat juicy lips."

Venus laughed, "...luscious *lips* and fat juicy *hips*."

"What-eeever. Eeew, an ex-rapper. How in the world—"

"I'm contracted with his company through Chadnum."

"Hold it right there. Do you know what you just said? You're messing with somebody you work with. That is the cardinal sin, girl. No, no, no."

"We don't work together; it's temporary."

"Exactly. That's exactly how I would define an office romance. You're around each other day in and day out and you start confusing that with a true relationship. You're brought together for a project or something but soon as it's over, so is the relationship. I know you're not risking your thing with Airic based on an office fling."

Venus looked around the restaurant, slightly embarrassed. Wendy had just reduced her starry-eyed love to an office fling.

"Especially, not right now. Look at you, you're a mess. Completely vulnerable, with your mom sick and this circus that's happening to Airic. I know that's got to be hard. The investigation into his company is probably making him a little hard to deal with, but you guys are solid."

Wendy kept talking without noticing the shock on Venus's face.

"What are you talking about?"

Seconds went by with silence between them. "You don't know?" Wendy whispered.

Venus shook her head, no.

The story came out slowly, not Wendy's usual snappy prose. "The Securities and Exchange Commission is investigating Airic's company. Actually, my cousin Jasmin is the one who pointed it out to me or I would have never noticed it in the *Post*. It wasn't headline news or anything. She remembered meeting Airic and you at Tia's birthday party. They talked a lot about the Internet and programming since she works for AOL and he said he was always interested in new talent, so she was shocked when she read the article. Made it sound like the company was near death. Airic had been reporting false quarterlies to keep his stock price solid so his investors wouldn't run."

Venus was still in the same position, stone-faced, her body supported by her elbows on the table.

"But it's just an investigation. They haven't proven anything yet... I think." Wendy paused, seeing the red veins overtake Venus's eyes. "I can't believe he would keep something like that from you." This time she slid the melting margarita toward Venus. "I'm sorry, girl. I didn't want to come here bringing bad news. I thought I was coming here to help you deal with it. God, I'm sooo sorry."

.   *   *

WENDY fought with the wind and the wind won. She got out of the convertible car, strands of dark hair twisted around her face. It was a small price to pay to absorb the sun's rays. On the East Coast this time of year it was a blustery thirty degrees, raining or snowing.

They walked through the enclosed parking garage in silence. The heavy brass elevator doors opened, giving way to more gold-toned walls. The lobby of the apartment building had fresh flowers on the half-moon-shaped table with an antique brass mirror hanging above it. Venus knew the impression it gave, the same way she'd felt when the realtor showed her the building. The chandeliers, the porcelain vases, and baroque art gave the impression of a Renaissance hotel.

"Nice place." Wendy attempted to break the awkwardness between them since they'd left the restaurant.

"Don't get excited. It's little, it isn't fancy."

"Oh right. You can make a bird's nest look like Taj Mahal."

Venus didn't respond. She was still numb. Her fingers worked the key into the door lock. Wendy followed inside.

"I knew it. Look at this. I love the deep purple. It's almost black."

Venus walked around her and went into her bedroom, then into the bathroom where she closed the door. She sat down on the toilet seat. She needed a minute alone, her face collapsed into her hands. The small shiny tiles seemed to be rising up one at a time like self-playing piano keys. She closed her eyes tight to block out the illusion. How could he not tell her? It explained his reaction when she'd discussed paying her mother back the money for the house. He was sinking. All this time, telling her how well the company was doing, he'd been lying. Even to her.

Did he actually believe she wouldn't hear about it, ever? Was he going to tell her about this? It was like swallowing a sharp sword. She'd been stabbed by Airic.

She ran water in the sink, using her hands to splash her face. She took a moment to look at herself in the mirror. She'd spent the last couple of weeks isolated in her own world with her mother's sickness. Maybe he would have told her if she didn't already have enough to worry about. That was the only possible explanation. Airic was not a liar and a cheat. She wouldn't have been with someone who was foul, dishonest. Not Airic. It was her, not Airic, running around like a loose dog who'd managed to sneak from underneath the fence, freed from the yard, the rules. Playing dating games with Jake. And Clint, had she forgotten about him? For the first time in two years, she actually had.

She submerged her face even deeper into the sink, trying to drown the guilt. She'd been the one preoccupied, out of touch. The entire time accusing Airic of not caring, not calling to check on her and her mother, while it was he caught in a nightmare.

"Venus." A knock at the door followed, then Wendy's muffled voice. "Your phone keeps ringing, but it's not a normal ring." She cautiously poked her head in. "Do you want me to answer it?"

"It's probably the security door downstairs." Venus dried her face with a towel, then walked straight to the bedroom phone and picked it up. "Yes?"

"It's me." Jake's voice sent a shiver down her legs, a wash of happiness at hearing his voice, then a heavy plunge of sorrow overtook her. He was downstairs, he wanted to see her. The clock shone with large red numbers, ten-thirty. She could use the excuse that it was late, much too late. That would have been the truth. Plans changed. There's no further reason to talk or laugh together. No reason to touch, slight sideways touches for no other reason than being near each other.

"I have company, Jake."

She could hear him swallow his heart. No questions asked; the line went dead with his assumption.

Venus hung up the phone and looked at Wendy who was looking at her. "Your office mate?"

"Ahuh."

Wendy bolted to the large balcony window that faced only more apartments in the rear of the building. "I wanted to see him." She pulled the curtain back in its place. "Shoot."

"It doesn't matter now, anyway." Venus sat down on the couch looking dejected and lost. Her hand rummaged through the knots that the wind had put in her hair.

Wendy came and sat beside her. They put their heads together. The smoothness of Wendy's slick mane pressed against her own springy curls felt like a meeting of the minds.

"So, what now?"

"I'd already planned to go see him this weekend. I was going to talk to him about us, our relationship."

"You were going to break up with Airic, end it just like that?" Wendy jumped off the couch, leaving Venus's head to manage on its own. "I mean I can understand breaking it off because you're not happy, but... wow... this is a trip. Jake must be something fierce in bed." Wendy shook her head. "He's got you whipped, girl."

"Can I be whipped if I've never even slept with him?"

Wendy's eyes widened, looking for more details. "Please don't pull a Clinton. Sex is sex, doesn't matter if he put it in or not."

"Okay, well, put it this way, we have slept together, but that's all we did. He held me the entire night. I'd never felt more cared for, more loved."

"Venus, love? You've known him, what, a month?"

"I don't know if it's been that long."

"Girl," Wendy sat back down beside Venus. She gripped her hand, holding up the ring finger. "You'd give up a man you've known and loved for someone who just happened to be there to pick up the pieces when you were vulnerable? You better think about it."

"It wasn't like that. Jake had my attention before I had a clue about my mother's illness." Venus got up and shook it off. "It doesn't matter anyway, Airic needs me. I can't just walk away. I wouldn't treat him like that, not with this investigation on his shoulders. The last thing he needs is more problems." She walked over to the purple wall. She was seeing the darkness, a wall of despair. All the color was supposed to make her feel alive, vibrant, now she felt nothing but dread, lifelessness staring back at her.

"You guys are going to get through this, Venus. You can't let something like this come between you. I meet guys all the time who look good, smell good, and I know they would damn well taste good, but I'm not trying to leave my whole world for a little taste, you know what I mean? Good lovers don't necessarily make the best husbands."

Venus thought to say it wasn't like that. She wanted to make it loud and clear that Jake was everything she'd ever wished for in a man...not a taste, not a little bit. Everything. Venus bit her lip while she listened to Wendy go on about the subject of men and all that she knew to be true. Venus wanted to agree; she'd had her share, she'd been on this earth long enough to agree...all true. But not Jake. She closed her eyes and listened while Wendy reenacted the story of Venus, her fall and rise, the days and nights crying over Clint, then finally realizing that she had a good man, someone who loved her right here and now, and that man was Airic. "He was there for you, Venus. Now you have to stick by him."

Venus nodded in agreement. If nothing else, she considered herself the kind that sticks. She'd never just walk away, turn her back on someone she loved.

STARS

THE overcast sky reflected how Venus felt. The morning sun was hiding behind thick gray clouds. Wendy wanted the top down, but Venus explained the dangers of riding around in the city fully exposed. "A criminal sees a single female riding around in a convertible in the downtown streets of Los Angeles, you can believe your chances of being followed and carjacked are very high."

Wendy rolled her eyes. "Well, what's the point of having a convertible?"

"To impress your friends when you pick them up at the airport." Venus pulled her briefcase and leather bag from the backseat and got out. "Be here at twelve so we can go to lunch. If you get lost getting back to the apartment, or anywhere else, call me. I'll have my cell phone on."

Wendy rolled her eyes and flipped her dark hair off her shoulder. "Anything else?"

"Nope. Just keep your doors locked and always watch your back."

"Grand."

"Have fun," Venus said with a little prayer as Wendy pulled off, jerking slightly into the morning traffic. She should have left Wendy in bed and gone back to the apartment later to pick her up, but she'd come all this way to L.A. She wanted her to have some type of thrill.

*   *   *

THE JP Wear studio was quiet. She wanted to be there early enough to get her bearings and stop by Jake's office. She wanted to see him before they were surrounded by probing eyes. Legend, William, and Beverly had enjoyed the soap opera tension from the day before. She didn't want to spoon-feed them any more drama.

Venus knocked on his door and waited, listening for movement. She took out her cell phone and called the receptionist. "Jake Parson, please." She listened intently for his phone to buzz, nearly pressing her face against the door. She heard a light sound, and then his voice, "Jake Parson."

"It's me."

"How are you?" The warmth in his voice, the consideration threw her for a loop. She was sure she'd have some explaining to do before being welcomed back in his fold.

"Jake, I'm standing right outside your office. I knocked but you didn't answer."

Before she could get her words out, the door swung open. His wide hand reached out and pulled her inside. She was still whirling from his disposition, nothing like she'd thought. Where was the pouting and bitterness over yesterday's rejection?

"What happened, did you tell him anything?" The thrill of espionage covered Jake's face.

She pulled away from him and sat down on the nearest chair. "It wasn't Airic. It was my friend, Wendy, from D.C. She came because she was worried about me."

Jake pulled up a chair next to Venus. He touched the side of her face. "Guess that makes two of us."

"Jake, I ... we ... this, I think ..." She put her hand on his.

"Oh, here we go." He stood up and walked around to his safety zone, the other side of the desk where he could be in charge, make decisions and judgments.

"I don't want to ruin our working relationship. We're almost got the deal closed with Lila Kelly. What I would really like is if we could suspend the personal until we're completely done with the business. I mean, like you said, it's countdown. Soon, you'll be Jake Parson in Los Angeles, and I'll be Venus Johnston back in D.C. Do you think we could be in a real relationship with that distance between us? Does that sound realistic to you? I mean, everything is good and convenient while I'm here, but what about when this launch is over? People are different when they're working together—it feels almost like a marriage—but what happens when they stop seeing each other every day? When they don't go with the coffee, like donuts, or the paper, like pens? What happens when the job is over?"

"I don't consider you a job, Venus." He leaned back in his leather chair. "You've put a lot of thought into this, haven't you? What else did you think about? What changed your mind between now and yesterday?" His soft wide eyes blinked concern. She concentrated on the clock on his desk, the repetition of the ticking, from one second to the next. She watched time pass, contemplating the answer.

"I can't walk away from the relationship with Airic right now. I can't." She stood up. "I don't want to make our working together a bad rollercoaster ride. We're going to have to let it go, for now, Jake."

"What changed?" He wasn't letting go without the answer.

Venus nearly smiled, a clumsy nervous smile. She and Jake were so much alike. He needed to understand, to know the why. She shook her head, clearing her mind. "Airic is in trouble. His company. I can't throw this at him too, not right now."

For Jake, it seemed to be enough. He walked around the desk and extended his hand. "If you need me, you know where you can find me."

She bit the inside of her cheek to stop her lips from quivering. A bait and switch of pain. She wished she had the same type of distraction for her fear. For the part of her that wanted to wrap her arms firmly around Jake's wide back. To be swept away and oblivious to the rest of the world, to not care about Airic or his problems. But she wasn't that type of person. She did care, with all her heart, she cared.

"Can I ask what kind of trouble?"

"I'm not sure about all the details. I didn't find out from him. Wendy told me what sounded like hearsay, but serious nonetheless. I'm going there this weekend. I'll find out if there's anything I can do." Venus kept her head low, unable now to watch the muscle tighten around his jaw, or the movement of his lips as he continued to question her.

"What is it that you think you can do?"

"Whether I can help or not, I need to be there. I'm not the type who just walks away; I'm not that kind of person."

"Really?" he said it slowly enough to pique her interest, and infuriate her at the same time.

"What's that supposed to mean?" she asked, now centering on his dark glossy eyes, searching intently.

"Nothing. Forget it. You do what you have to do." He turned and put his energy back into his work.

"Jake." She reconsidered what she had to say. "Have you ever been in love?" She moved across the office floor like a lawyer questioning her witness. Her skirt tapered too close, the fabric swishing against her nylons.

He stopped stroking the fine hairs on his face and rested his hands on the arms of the chair. "Is this one of those trick yes or no questions? If I choose yes, the next question is, explain your answer? Because if it is, I'm out."

"Okay, no need for an explanation."

"Yes." He said it quickly.

"Did it end on a good note, or bad?"

He held up a finger, "When is the end ever a good thing? What about you? Ever been in love?"

She squinted her eyes at him. "Well, of course, I'm in a relationship right now. That's what this whole mess is about."

"But you still have to answer the question. Better yet, let me rephrase it. Are you in love?"

"What's love got to do with it?"

"Hey, you started down that road, Ms. Turner, I didn't." An unexpected smile arose on his face. A mix of triumph and clarity. "Are you in love or not?"

"Yes. I can honestly say I am."

"With him or me?" Jake's smile, unmistakably, was one of vindication. Venus stood up and made her way to the door. "This has been fun.

Really. We'll have to do it again sometime." Jake grabbed her hand as it wrapped around the doorknob.

"Answer the question."

"I can't." She snatched her hand back. "You happy?"

"Ecstatic." And he was.

She'd given him what he wanted. A shred of doubt, a pinch of confusion. Throughout the morning meeting he was confidence personified. Profoundly aware that he knew something the others didn't. This was not at all the reaction Venus expected from the earlier run-in. William, Legend, and Beverly took advantage of his lightheartedness, proposing ideas that ordinarily would have received his veto.

His eyes were bright with vision. Beverly brought in two models for an impromptu fashion show. The clothing was hip and smart. Venus pictured herself in some of the pieces. "I like it, Beverly. You've done an incredible job."

"Absolutely." Jake pulled up between the two as they were walking out. Venus couldn't help but notice that his hand rested equally as comfortable on Beverly's shoulder as it did on hers. "You guys want to do lunch? William has calls to make. Legend's in, so it'd be the four of us."

"I can't." Venus politely removed his arm from her shoulder. "I have a guest," she emphasized so he'd remember their earlier conversation. "She's from out of town... we're meeting for lunch."

"Your friend is welcome. It'll be fun. Meet you guys downstairs," Jake said as he moved through the two of them. "I'll tell the fellas."

Venus took in an exhausted breath as she watched him stride ahead and disappear around a corner. "Give him my regrets, Beverly. I can't stay."

"Oh, no. Unh unh, he's in the best mood I've seen in a long time. I'm not going to be the only woman in the group. Unh, unh." She put her hands on her fully curved hips. "It's just lunch, it's not going to kill you." Beverly was still planted in front of Venus.

"Today it will."

A look of clarity came over Beverly, "You guys are a thing."

"Actually, I don't know what we are, at this point." Venus was too tired to keep up the pretense.

"Come on." Beverly waved her to follow. Venus knew the direction of the secret elevator. It was their private transport. All conversations locked in a soundproof box.

The red doors closed. Beverly faced Venus. "When I first got here I was blown away. Jake Parson. I didn't even care about his past stardom, being a rapper and all that. I was thinking, damn, I'm one lucky woman. I have this fine ass brotha's undivided attention. He was attracted to me as well, for obvious reasons. It's almost like we had to get it over with so we could go on about our business. And that's exactly what happened. Once we ended the mystery, the party was over."

The elevator stopped. "So once, you're saying, once you guys slept together neither was interested anymore?" Venus put her head down, the information too heavy to manage.

"Hey, we were honest. No time wasted. I didn't believe anything more could come of it, so I let it go. I think he felt the same way. Jake is real smart, deep. He thinks of someone like me as a side dish. I think of someone like him as the steak. But I don't like steak, too many requirements for preparation. I like chicken, not too many things you can do wrong with chicken." She smiled and winked.

Venus jerked a smile back. "That's the end of it. No more ... just for old time's sake?"

"I'm done." Beverly held up her hands. "So which do you prefer, steak or chicken?" They walked out the double doors into the busy streets.

"I like 'em both," Venus said, stepping out behind her. "I don't think I could eat either one all the time."

"Well, some people don't have choices. Some people have never tasted a steak in their life. And when they finally do, they wonder what the hell all the fuss was about."

It took Venus a moment to realize they'd just reduced men into two categories. Jake and Airic, meat or poultry. "Wait a minute. What happens when you don't want either, steak or chicken?"

They both looked at each other, spoke in unison. "FISH."

She reached out and tapped Beverly's shoulder. "Thank you."

"Hey, girl, there's more strength in numbers. We need to realize if we don't start talking to each other, we'll forever be in the dark. Men depend on us not talking, keeping everything on the down low. That's how they get away with so much..."

"Shit," Venus finished her sentence. "I can't wait for you to meet my friend. She's going to love you."

•   •   ■

RIGHT on time. Wendy was idling in the loading zone. Venus waved and walked up to the car, sticking her head through the window. "Get out. I'll park it. We're going to lunch... and you get to meet Jake."

Wendy squealed with excitement, as if she was part of a covert operation. "Is that him?"

Venus looked behind her to see Legend talking with Beverly. "No!" Wendy jumped, startled at her tone. She got out and Venus quickly introduced her. Legend seemed exceptionally polite. Beverly took her in like a newly discovered cousin.

"I'm going to park my car. Keep an eye on my friend here," she said to Beverly, but it was Legend who responded in his deep smooth voice, "I will."

By the time Venus returned from parking the car, the three of them were full of conversation and smiles. Venus had practically run back to the group, picturing nightmarish images of Wendy slapping Legend for his brashness, or worse, finding it appealing.

"Where's Jake?" She was slightly out of breath.

"Still waiting," Beverly said, looking at her watch. "He said twenty minutes an hour ago."

Legend whipped out his palm-sized phone and pushed speed dial. "Man, you got three fine ladies down here waiting for your eminence. Wassup?" He directed his comments toward Wendy, giving her an obvious wink. She reciprocated with a one-dimple smile. "Okay, five minutes, slave, or I'm taking all three of them for myself." He closed the phone and slipped it back in his overcoat pocket.

Venus nudged Wendy. "So what'd you do this morning?"

"Not much. Everything was closed. California is on slowpoke time. I finally stopped and just had a cup of coffee and a bagel."

Legend interrupted, "From here on, consider me your guide. Can't have you coming all this way with nothing to do. Ms. Johnston here is all work and no play, but I on the other hand, will guarantee you a good time."

"She's not going to be here that much longer; I think I can handle it for the next couple of days."

Wendy put an end to the dissension. "Maybe we can all do something together."

"You like to dance?" Legend asked, taking in Wendy's long legs and wide hips with his eyes.

"Dancing?"

"See what I mean." Legend pointed in Venus's direction. "All work and no play. Don't worry, I got you covered." Wendy's one-dimple smile appeared again.

"Sorry 'bout that." Jake came out, still adjusting his coat over his shoulders. He immediately spotted the newcomer. "Jake Parson, how you doing?" He stuck out his hand.

Wendy acted like she was meeting the pope, her hand slowly rising to meet his. "Nice to meet you." Forgetting about all the assumptions she'd made the day before, she looked toward Venus and mouthed, *Oh my goodness.* Venus rolled her eyes.

The sky was clear, and the the air was chilly. Jake led them to a restaurant not too far away. The five of them walked and talked in patches. Venus drifted behind, waiting for Jake to work his way back to her.

"Miss me?"

"Always."

"Everyone's talking shaking their butts tonight. Are you in?"

"Definitely not." Venus kept her resolve. "I'll leave that to you guys. I have way too much on my mind to be out shaking my ass."

"I can help get some of it off your mind."

"I'll pass."

"There's no law that says you can only have one night of fun per week, is there?"

"No, thank you." Venus ignored him and his shoulder that continually bumped against her while they walked. Ignored his light scent that filled her nostrils, making her slightly off balance.

"You mad at me, for this morning?" Jake asked, humbly.

"Why would I be mad at you? I'm the one bearing the bad news."

"Right." He said it slowly. "I appreciate your honesty."

She looked up at him. Cautious. It was a dangerous move, watching his soft eyes, the smooth neat line of hair that framed his face. Jake grabbed her hand and trotted up ahead of the gang when he saw the restaurant approaching. "Right here, guys."

Venus felt all the attention zooming in on their union and wiggled her fingers free of his grip. Jake held the door open for everybody while Venus remained at his side. Beverly passed with a smile, still entertained from the earlier follies. The words *steak* or *chicken* hung between them. Salad, Venus thought back. Beverly winked good luck. Nobody dies a vegetarian.

*　　*　　*

THE flirting between Wendy and Legend was enough to make Venus lose her appetite. The crab cakes sat untouched, next to the barely nibbled artichoke salad. Four out of five people were having a good time. Venus looked around the table and corrected herself—a great time. Her mind was saddled with thoughts of Airic, his business. Every minute that ticked by, she wondered if he was drowning in lawyers and false accusations. How he could go this long without telling her? Secretly, she held on to the hope that he would call before she got there, tell her everything. Secretly, too, she wished that he wouldn't. That way she could hold it against him. The final straw of discord.

The decibel of laughter rose all at once. Venus drew a blank, the only one who didn't have a big smile on her face.

Jake noticed, sliding his elbow against hers on the table. "Didn't your mother teach you, no elbows on the table?"

Venus dropped them down in her lap. Obviously right where he'd wanted them. He reached underneath and grabbed her hand, squeezing it softly, then tight again. There were no words to describe the torment, the guilt. She rose. "Wendy, are you coming with me? I've got to get back."

The conversations stopped, everyone staring at Venus. Her heart was beating loud enough for them all to hear, she was sure. Did they know, could they see that sitting next to Jake had made her blood pressure rise to the point of making her dizzy? That his touch made her want to cry, break down and surrender? She picked up her purse and drew the strap over her shoulder. "I have to go," she said it more quietly this time.

Wendy's expression was considerate, but decided. She was staying. Venus could go off and deal with her demons alone, in the privacy of her own space.

Jake stood up, grabbing his coat off the chair. "Beverly, take care of this, I'll reimburse you."

"Sure." Her wide-eyed gaze fell on Venus. "See you later."

Venus swallowed and nodded, waving weakly to them all.

The sun was bright and unyielding. The icy cold bit through her face and hands. How could she call this weather cold, Wendy had asked, while Venus piled covers on the sofa? This was mild, compared with back home. But all things were relative. All things were based on perception. Here where she'd spent the last month, her body had acclimated, warmed, and become comfortable. She looked into Jake's profile while they walked. Here she'd allowed herself to open up and absorb the heat that surrounded her. But now it was bitter cold, and she was going to have to say good-bye sooner or later.

She and Jake made it to the studio without exchanging one word. He stopped to look up and down the street for her car. Venus kept walking, he followed. The wind pushed against her eyes, causing them to burn and then water. She didn't wipe the moistness away, letting it cool underneath her eyes. After three flights of stairs in the parking ramp, she pushed the door open to the floor her car was parked on.

"Wait a minute. Wait, just stop." Jake grabbed her arm. The echo of his voice in the distance, carried off by the wind whirling around them. "I see what you're doing. Is this it, really? I need to know. I played with you before, Venus. I'm not playing now. I need to know if you're really the type of person who would pretend to love someone you don't. That you'd actually go to D.C., pretending you could make everything all right. Tell me now if that's the kind of person you are."

Venus stood there feeling shallow and predictable. Easily read. Of course, she was exactly that type. She would stick, through thick or thin. Loyalty, dedication, those were supposed to be good things. Her nose was starting to run from the cold. She wiped, then crossed her arms over her chest, still not sure how to answer his questions. No. Yes. She'd never been the type to stand passively by and let things happen as they may, and yet, things always seemed to be happening to her. Who was responsible for that? Fate.

"You're going to go to D.C. and you're going to stay. For a minute I was so sure this was a formality, a small-print detail that had to be wrapped up, so you'd have closure and then we could move on." His breaths started coming in short hurried spurts, "I was so sure...but now I see, you're going to let it ride. You would actually follow." He paused, trying to catch his breath. "You'd go down that path and let life be as it may...forget that you would be unhappy. Forget that you're unhappy right now...you're going to try and make it work. You'd walk away...." His voice was hoarse and jagged.

Venus reached for him. "Jake. Oh God." He stumbled back but caught his balance. He reached into his pocket and pulled out a small white plastic casing. He snapped off the cap and put his mouth to it. He inhaled, squeezing it twice. She held firmly on to him.

"I'm all right."

"You have asthma." She sat with him on the concrete divider. "I can run and get some water, something. Are you sure you're all right?"

"No, Venus, I'm not all right." His words came out slow and easy once again. Back to where they'd left off.

She didn't turn away, afraid to be labeled further, coward, right along with predictable. "It's more than that, Jake. I do care about him. I do. It's more than feeling obligated, or feeling like I have no choice with the hand I've been dealt. Airic has been there for me."

"Until now?"

"Right. Exactly, until now. So that means it's my turn." She took care before she began, but it was the story that needed to be told. She started from the beginning. Her relationship with Clint Fairchild, her wish for a happy life, her need to be married before the clock struck twelve. She told of the breakup, what felt like the ending of a marriage when in truth, they'd never even made it to engagement. Four years of her life, she'd felt like she'd wasted. Humiliation. Then there was Airic, waiting patiently for her to reawaken, to understand that all was not lost, she had him. She had a great career, and most important, she had herself. Airic hadn't solved all her woes, but he had made them bearable. She admitted that once in a while she'd drifted, believing that she'd settled for second best. He was a workaholic. He didn't have time for her, but she was too busy to notice. She was a workaholic as well.

Venus turned his face toward her. "I really don't know what's going to happen when I go there. One part of me is furious that he didn't tell me about his company, but on the other hand, I was here dealing with my mother. Maybe he didn't want to burden me. I don't want to assume anything."

Jake stood up. "You don't understand." He stared off, Venus honed in on his breathing, light and effortless. She let out a sigh of relief.

"What don't I understand?"

"I want to know where I fit in. So what, if he forgot to tell you, or wanted to spare your feelings, what's that got to do with me? Me and you? God, I haven't felt this way..." He stared off again, frustrated.

She stood up and pushed her head under his chin, she wrapped her arms around him. She closed her eyes, listening to the rapid pulse of his heart. "I haven't felt this way either." She moved to her tippy toes, kissing him lightly on the chin, testing. He kissed her back on the lips, softly at first, then holding her tight. She could hear the wind move through them, seeping through the light open spaces. She pressed herself closer, hoping to seal the gaps. To mend the heart that she had broken.

SAFETY FIRST

THE huge picture window that overlooked the water was a square of blackness, studded with sparkling diamonds. The stars danced and dipped in the midnight sky. She'd known better than to follow him home. She knew they would end up here, where she lay beside him, her head resting on his chest while she studied the scar at the center of his throat. She traced his brow with her finger, then let it follow around. He awakened, taking hold of her hand.

"How did you get this scar?"

"I thought I was dreaming, and that you weren't really here." Jake touched her hand that was trailing around his neck. "I had a close call when I was younger."

She grimaced, picturing him being threatened with a knife by a gang of thugs.

"I came in contact with grass. The kind that grows on the front lawn."

"You fell in grass?" Venus asked, still stretched out across his bare chest.

"My mother used to tell me each and every day, stay out of that grass, Jake. You know you're allergic. Can you picture a childhood where you can't even run through the sprinklers in the summertime, or play a game of touch football? Well that day, I watched all the guys load up on foot, heading for the park, like they usually did, leaving me all alone like the last survivor in the neighborhood. At that point, I was so pissed off, I didn't care what my mother said, didn't care what my punishment was going to be. All I wanted to do was play some ball. I told the guys to wait up, I jumped in and went full steam ahead. Everybody on the street knew my mother, heard her always yelling out the window, 'Stay outta that grass, Jake!' like she had radar. They even made me quarterback, 'cause they knew it was something of a holiday, just having me play. It was a good game, too. I threw two touchdowns for my team. Hadn't hit the ground once. Then on the last play, this bulldozer named Eddie Demoy came at me from the side and took me down, face first into the grass. I ate it big time. At first nothing happened. I stood up, shook it off, and thought my mother had been pulling my leg all this time... all this time, telling me to stay out of the grass, keeping me from playing Pop Warner football for three years in a row, probably just so I wouldn't get hurt. Next thing I know, my whole body broke out in raw itch; it felt like somebody had stuck me in a fiber-glass sheet and wrapped me up. I scratched like nobody's business. By the time I got home I was a walking mummy, covered by my own skin, swollen, my eyes nearly closed, my throat constricted. I couldn't breathe.

"My mother opened the front door, saw me, and screamed. She was in a fit of tears, crying the whole time while she drove me to the hospital. She just kept mumbling, 'I told you to stay outta that grass, I told you to stay outta that grass.' When I woke up in the hospital, I had a tube stick-ing out of my throat." He paused, touching the scar. "Tubes in my arms."

He stopped again and waited while Venus kissed him on the lips. "After that, I never questioned another thing she said."

The rhythm of his voice had stirred something deep inside of Venus. When she first lay down with him, it felt like a dying man's last wish. She could at least fulfill this one part, so even if he was right about all the things he'd said earlier, about her staying with Airic, she would have this one moment. They would have a memory so precious and splendid. But now, she carried a ferocity to make love to him that had nothing to do with what tomorrow held. More to do with the ache and need growing between her legs. A pull working its way through her body, through her core. She wanted him inside of her, full and thick the way he'd been a few hours ago. Curing her, with long even strokes. She wanted her head to swim, lost in a hapless dizzy whirl when he teasingly stopped, slipping out to ask if she missed him.

YES. Yes, she did. She missed him terribly. The void was real. The emptiness of having him near but not completely inside of her made her dizzy with anticipation. She straddled him as politely as possible, fearing she could hurt him as desperate as she felt, as hungry and needing as she felt. He lifted her up by her waist and gently positioned her to slide the length of his penis. The room felt like it was spinning. The bed was a magic carpet that was above ground, floating with no direction. She lost herself in his grasp, holding on for dear life. "Baby, sweet, sweet," she whispered into the air. Into his chest, tasting the salt on his skin, perspiration from his earlier working.

He cradled her, pressing her down until she was sure she couldn't bear another inch pushed inside. Surely she could scream louder than the crashing waves outside. So be it, she thought while the air left her lungs. So be it. Her own voice was foreign to her. The thick lull that turned into a martyr's groan with every push, every stroke. She wanted him to use her, break down every barrier, then rebuild her again from scratch. Then his moan blended perfectly with hers. A sigh so perfect, like a sad sweet song. She stopped and touched his face. The only movement between them was from their eyes, blinking, quiet.

"I love you." He said it slow and deliberate. "Do you understand?"

Venus let her head move up and down. Yes. She understood perfectly. He held her face, kissing her, sucking her tongue. She understood that she never wanted to let him go. She didn't want to wake up tomorrow or live another day. She wanted to stay in this time and this place without dealing with the consequences. The ones that Venus Johnston would have to answer to when the sun rose or the die was cast.

How do you know you love me? You don't even know me. What does that mean, anyway? You love me? What prize does that hold? She closed her eyes and waited for him to wash through her, clear the last puzzling thoughts, the last speculation from her mind. His body tensed, turning solid and hard against hers. He held her intensely while he throbbed one last time inside of her. I love you, too, she thought, lying on his chest, and thinking about all that tomorrow would bring, and all that she would lose.

*   *   *

IT hadn't dawned on her that they'd skipped the use of a condom for the second round, not until she crept her way to the bathroom in the dark and felt the uncomfortable trickle of fluid running down her upper thigh. She stood there, paralyzed by the sudden realization. A chill ran through her naked body. The choice of standing there and freezing or grabbing a towel. She pulled the soft thick towel off the bar and wrapped it around her shoulders, then went into the bathroom and closed the door.

She sat in the dark as she thought about all the possible outcomes of acting irresponsibly. HIV, AIDS, STD—the initials were like hieroglyphics in her mind, crazy mixed-up imagery. She calmed herself down. If she feared any of those things, she wouldn't have been here with Jake in the first place. Besides, it worked both ways. She and Airic stopped using condoms over a year ago. Neither of them had been tested, going in on blind trust. She closed her eyes and let her head fall in her palms. At least she was on the pill.

A hush clouded her brain. Pregnancy. She couldn't remember the last time she'd taken a pill. The last few weeks had melded into one thick blur. Eating, sleeping, driving to see her mother, driving to work to see Jake, a big file of numberless pages, no order. Had it been a day, two, or three? She couldn't remember.

She finished in the bathroom and felt her way back to the bed, sliding under the covers next to Jake. Her heart was still racing with the discovery. She was too old for this, wasn't she? Too old to be worrying about an unwanted pregnancy or the possibility of a disease.

Jake rolled over, letting an arm find its way around her waist, pulling her in close to him. She tried to relax, commanding each breath to be slowed, each trickle of doubt to be erased. Worrying wouldn't solve anything right now. She closed her eyes, then opened them just as quickly. Wendy. She'd forgotten about her friend. She didn't have a key to the apartment. Venus had taken the keys right along with the car.

She touched Jake's arm, then shook it. "Jake." He was slow responding but she had his attention. "I have to get back. I forgot about Wendy."

"I'm sure she's fine."

"I didn't leave her a key to my place. Where's she going to go?"

"She'll be fine, Venus. We left her in good hands."

"Legend," Venus whispered to herself, letting her head fall back against the pillow, "no." She removed his arm. "I have to go, Jake."

His arm tightened. "Look, it's"—he leaned across her sheet-covered breasts and looked at the illuminated clock—"three o'clock. You're not running out of here at three in the morning. Check your messages, see if she called. If there's nothing, I'll give Legend a call."

"And Beverly, will you call her, too?"

"What?" He detected a swipe, a modest accusation.

Venus sat up. "Beverly, she told me about you two. Slam bam, no thank you, ma'am."

"What are you talking about? Where's this coming from?"

"We didn't use a rubber, Jake. Now I've got to worry about Beverly, and who knows how many countless others you've slept with."

He rolled out of the covers. He pulled on his boxers that lay at the foot of the bed. "Venus." He yanked open the drawer in the nightstand. He dumped the entire contents on the bed next to her. It looked like Halloween candy. Condoms in brightly covered packaging in more variety than she knew existed. "I always use protection. Why I didn't with you? I don't know." He weighed what he was about to say next, taking his time. "Some things are worth taking a chance for. I never doubted for a second that we weren't going to be together. It wasn't in the back of my mind that I was taking a risk. With you, I felt safe. I thought you felt that way, too."

She did. She had. Safe was truly what she'd felt in his arms. But here, now, they were in reality. Consequences and repercussions. "It goes both ways, Jake. I should have said something. It's my responsibility as much as it is yours." She scooted to the edge of the bed, pulling the sheet with her. "I have to go."

He moved to her side, kneeling down. "Tell me why. Is it about your friend, or do you just want to get out of here?"

Venus looked out at the black sky. The stars that hadn't yet given up, still dancing with the same twinkling energy. The moonlight allowed her to see half of Jake's face, the side shadowed in darkness. "I'm scared."

"What are you scared of?"

"It feels like I'm falling down this huge hole, and it just keeps getting deeper and longer where I can't get out. I'm out of control. This is the perfect example, me here with you. I have sense, I keep telling myself, I'm thirty-six years old, I keep telling myself. I should know better than to fall for this..." She looked away.

"Fall for this?" his voice changed, indignant. "You mean me, like I'm putting something over on you?" He stood up. "I told you I didn't want to play anymore, Venus. If that's what you want, you got it." He stepped back, his chest heaving with every breath.

She quickly turned her frustration to concern. She didn't want him losing his ability to breathe, not because of her. She stood up to touch him. "Are you all right?"

He backed up, avoiding her hand.

Venus moved past him and went into the bathroom and closed the door. She listened intently, trying to hear a change in his breathing rhythm. A shift in the air. She heard him pick up the phone, the tone of dialing, then paused.

"Hey, man, it's me. I know, I know, I'm sorry to wake you, but Venus was worried about her friend. She asked me to call, see if you knew what was up." A pause. "What... I heard that, you guys had a good time then, cool, cool. I'm glad she's all right. Do me a favor, have her call Venus as soon as she wakes up, she's worried. All right, check you later, man." He hung up.

Venus felt momentarily lighter. Wendy was safe, if being with Legend could be called safe. She leaned her head against the door. Her married friend Wendy. She hoped one of them at least used a condom. She slid down the length of the door and sat in the crumpled bed sheet wrapped around her body. Surely, they'd laugh about this one day.

THE room was empty when she came out. Still only lit with the moonlight that bathed the right side of the room. The door of the bedroom was open, where Jake had fled the scene. She peered out and could see a corner of light from downstairs. Music played, jazz, the kind that gave her a headache with its jagged, uneven beats. Carrying herself along in her toga made of the top sheet, she followed the sound into the softly lit living room. Jake sat on the oversized couch, shirtless, wearing only draw-string pants. He held a brandy snifter in his hand, swirling it around in front of the candlelight glowing in front of him. Venus felt an intense urge to curl up next to him just to inhale his scent. Soft, light, open like his heart.

He still had not looked up to acknowledge she was standing there, draped like the Statue of Liberty in her sheet. "Can I sit with you?"

He took a sip of his drink. Venus wanted to kiss the moistness from his lip and taste the rich liquor for herself. "I freaked out. I'm sorry about that blowup."

Now she could see his youth. In the way he held his head, slightly tilted to the side, like a pouting child. Men were already far more imma-ture than women; why she had to fall for another young one, like Clint, spoke volumes about her own personality. Maybe she was longing to take care of a child. Even one over six feet tall with abs of steel.

She made her way to his side uninvited, slowly at first, then snuggling up. She leaned her head on his bare shoulder. "Hi." She took the glass out of his hand and set it on the table. She waited patiently for him to accept her apology. She preoccupied herself by staring in her hands, the busy lines that creased her palms. So many lines going in every which direc-tion. Once a friend in high school opened her palms in class and said, "Let me see your future." Venus was excited. She'd seen the other girls with predictions of two children, maybe three, the long thin one the span of their palm crossing the two shorter ones, a long happy marriage. Not Venus, her palm read like a schizophrenic treasure map.

"Well, what do you see?" Venus had asked, anticipating so she could pick out the names of her first- and secondborn. Her friend stared, and stared, twisting her hand to take sideway, upside-down, and back again views. "I don't know," she'd said, "just a lot of lines. I guess you're going to have a busy life, a lot of different—"

"Different what?" Venus had asked, panicking. "Different experiences," her friend answered, trying not to show her disgust.

"What's on your mind?" She felt Jake's hand near her neck, massaging gently. His touch filled her with relief even though temporary. The treasure map of her palms told the story, short erratic lines like tiny razor cuts. Each and every one of them leading to nowhere. Always close, but no cigar. She knew Airic didn't want to marry her. She knew he didn't want any more children as much as they'd talked and planned. And now, here she was with Jake, another short line in her hand. One more stop. She could hear her mother's voice, all the work, all the prayers, asking for a happy life. *The only thing you do with all that thinking is take the long way.*

"So I guess you're next."

"What?"

"You." She leaned on him. She opened up her hand, pointing at her palm. "That's you right there." She picked out a faint line, short, light, secretly woven into the others. "One project, then on to the next. I'm never going to be married, have children. Just a constant one-stop wonder."

He closed her fingers one at a time. He encircled her now balled fist in his warm hands. "I'm bigger than that, Venus. I couldn't possibly fit. Ignore all your little superstitions and tarot cards when it comes to me, okay?"

"You're bigger than fate?"

"I'm bigger than your assumptions."

"No one is bigger than fate."

Jake opened his own palms, showing her. "See anything familiar?" So many busy lines, congruent, adjacent, parallel, almost identical to hers. She traced them with her finger, until he couldn't take the tickling sensation any longer. "Guess we're two lost souls that found each other. So what do you make of that?"

"Maybe we're related, same gene pool. What'd you say your daddy's name was again?"

A strong deep laugh burst out of him. He stroked the thin hair on his manicured goatee. "Believe it or not, I know people who have lived that nightmare. That's not one to be messed with." He pulled her onto his lap. "All I'm saying is, if you're going to use that excuse, use it for everything, don't pick and choose. Some things are meant to be ... or all things are meant to be. You'd have to include me in that equation either way." He opened her hands placing his flat on hers. She attempted to slap them before he snatched his hands out of the way. Before it was over, her hands and knuckles were stinging. Not fast enough. She'd only gotten a smidgen of his thumb, and that was because she cheated by grabbing a hold of it while she swatted with the other.

"What's next, rock, paper, scissors?" She peeled back a broken nail, an injury of the battle. "You don't like to lose, do you?"

"That's why it rarely happens." He pulled her across his chest and cradled her close in his arms.

Venus smoothed a finger across the arch of his lips, "Have you ever asked a woman to marry you? Have you ever been that far in a relationship?"

"Nope, and I have no shame admitting it." He nipped at her fingers until he caught one in his mouth. The warmth of his tongue wrapped tightly around her finger made her moan. He sucked lightly before letting it slip past his lips. "So you want to be married?"

"I do. Absolutely. It's expected, it's tradition. I want a family. Kids. Plus, married people live longer. It's a proven fact. Not to mention stability, constant love, constant companionship."

He pushed the sheet away that was draped over her legs. "You can get all that from a dog, or a cat, constant companionship. There must be something more." His fingers trailed gently across her pubic line, down to the fold of moistness between her legs.

Her breath rose with his touch. "A dog or a cat can't talk back, they can't tell you that they love you or give you a hug at the end of the day." Venus wanted to say more, but unable to think clearly once his fingers pushed inside her.

Jake tilted his head, still smiling. "You're right about that. I know what else they can't do." From where she was lying, his long dark lashes fanned out in perfect even length over his almost closed eyes. He brushed closer, his face finding a home against the coolness of her breast, closing his lips around the thick skin of her nipple. He pulled the sheet completely away, pulling her body into position. He kissed her first before disappearing into the center of her thighs. His tongue moved softly, searching for the tip of seduction. Stroking and lapping with gentle affection, lingering on the smooth firm surface that grew more sensitive with each pass of his tongue. She closed her eyes, clutching him near his ears, under the smooth line of his jaw. Her breath rose higher. Her mind soared, then sailed back to easy. She would take it like a woman, even though her hands were digging into the fabric of the couch. He worked her over, silently, effortlessly, as he tested and trailed in search of new information for the next time, and the time after that.

There, right there. Venus threw her head back.

A dark low hum escaped her lips. She wanted to run, save herself before it was too late. She held on while the helix rose, her hands pressing his face deeper into her center. She couldn't stop to care if he was receiving oxygen, breathing for life, because she was in her own world, her own selfish, hungry world. She rumbled, her body shook, involuntarily, bringing her to a melting spot. She could understand how it could all get confusing. Love, lure, lust. They all started with L, four letters, easy on the tongue. The tongue so sweetly dipping into her sex, moving up and down. She throbbed with relief against his mouth.

He only gave her a moment to recuperate before starting over where he'd begun. Making her understand there was more that she needed. Companionship? Stability? But there was so much more. He turned her over, pulling her to the edge of the couch. He slipped inside of her from behind. His arms wrapped tightly around her waist pulling her hips flush against his pelvis. She twisted around to watch him, the sheen of moonlight glistening on his chest. The sweetness of her sex still fresh on his lips.

The rhythm of their dance changed rapidly. From slow and methodic to fast and dangerous. Every nerve, every cell in her body screaming his name. The message was clear, he didn't want her to ever forget that it was he at her center, moving through her core. Driving harder with each stroke. There would be no room for doubt or confusion. "Where are you? Tell me..." he breathed in her ear. He wanted to hear her say it.

"With you, Jake. I'm here with you."

His hands spread wide, controlling the angle of her hips. He moved with her at his mercy. He slid out, pulling away for only seconds, which felt like an eternity.

"Please." Her whisper quickly fell into a whimper. "Please, baby."

He took his place and began again. Starting over once again. It had to be clear and understood. With each blow of reason, Jake was telling her where she was, who she was with and why. She would never forget, he made sure.

When she thought she couldn't take any more, he fell into her body, taking her with him, melding himself into her. Their bodies collapsing in unison.

"What was that game called?" Venus asked, breathing hard, needing air.

"I don't know," he said as he rolled over, perspiration coating his chest as it rose and fell, "but I think you won."

STORM WATCH

EXHAUSTED, she drifted off to sleep. It wasn't a deep, lost sleep. She could still feel the world around her. Hear the sound of the ocean as it rolled and landed in the shore. Feel the rambled beat of the music coming through the walls.

When she'd awakened, cold surrounded her. She was on the floor in the living room with a blanket and sheet wrapped around her. Venus looked up and saw the shift of daylight, but it was gray, dark. Fog low and heavy hovered over the beach. She looked at her watch, realizing Jake was probably gone. She cleaned up and got dressed with more speed than the mornings she'd overslept in college, rushing out of the dorm wearing her shirt wrong side out, or the same thing from the previous day because nothing else was clean. Funny how time moves but nothing changes. She rushed back down the stairs, and called Jake's name one last time. The house was quiet, missing an integral part of its appeal, its owner.

She drove on the freeway, faster than what was reasonable in the downpour that covered the city. The rain fell in huge pellets, thumping the hood and the cloth top of her BMW. The window wipers worked feverishly to keep the surface clear. She turned the music down when she thought she heard her phone ringing.

"Venus Johnston."

"Girl, it's me."

"Wendy, where are you?"

"I'm sitting in your friend's living room, well, I guess you can call it a living room. There's no walls, but it's where the couch is."

"Legend," Venus said with more disdain than she wanted, "is not my friend. He's an associate. He works for me, although he wouldn't admit the later part without a gun to his head. What happened? You two do the watoosi?"

Wendy laughed, then clearing her throat, said, "We'll talk about that later." Her voice lowered. "He's getting out of the shower. And where were you all night?" She chuckled. "Oh yeah, I remember...how's Mr. JP himself this morning?"

Venus ignored the quip. "Go with Legend. He's coming to the studio, then you can take my car back to the apartment."

"He asked me to stay here and wait for him until he got back."

Venus swerved, nearly running into the back of a Continental. "What the hell? I don't think so."

"Right. What am I thinking?"

"I don't know. Something in the air." Venus flipped the switch of her windshield wipers, making them go as fast as they could. What the hell had gotten into both of them?

"I'll see you in a few." Wendy hung up the phone.

Venus pressed the gas even harder. She wanted to use the very same foot to deal with Legend. The arrogance, to think Wendy had nothing to do but sit around and wait for his return like some concubine. Venus knew he wouldn't have made an offer like that if there were any chance he couldn't get rid of her. Married with children was always more appealing. If she was single and free he would have been escorting her to the door at the break of dawn.

She had no choice but to come to a dead stop. The traffic had piled up, probably an accident.

Men. She thought again. No, not all men. Not Jake. Yes, Jake.

She parked and got out, trotting and splashing in the small puddles to cross the street. The building was open, but empty. She wondered if Jake was even inside. Just because he wasn't home didn't mean he'd beelined it to work. He could've gone to work out. A body like his wasn't maintained by doing pencil-and-paper push-ups all day.

Jake's office door was slightly ajar. She listened for a second before knocking. She pushed the door open and stepped inside. Empty. Venus walked around his desk and looked for a sign of life, a steaming cup of coffee, his briefcase, but saw nothing. She sat down in his chair and scooted close to the front of the desk, letting her hands run along the edge. The drawer handle was calling her name. She pulled it lightly, expecting it to be locked. It rolled out easily. She looked at the doorway before looking down into the contents of the drawer. Office supplies, pens, notepads, paper clips. She shut it and moved to the next one. She rummaged with her hand, lifting up from the bottom. The weight of a picture frame between her fingers. With one jolt, she pulled it out from underneath everything else. It was Jake and a woman. They were outdoors in the snow. Ski gear, hats and gloves. She was soft and beautiful. They shared the same perfect smile, the same warm eyes. Her skin was a tad bit lighter, but still the same toasted brown.

Venus almost dropped it when she heard Jake's voice.

"Did you find everything you were looking for?" He walked around the desk and took the picture out of her hand. "That's my mother. You would have found better stuff if you hadn't rushed out of the house. I pulled up as you were taking off." He held up a small white bag. "Breakfast."

Venus moved to sit on the edge of his desk and watched what must have been his routine, taking off his jacket, opening up his calendar, settling into his chair. Venus opened the bag and pulled out the cinnamon twist. She took a deep breath and then put the donut to her mouth and took a bite. A small dust of sugar remained on her lips while she chewed. Jake stood up and kissed her, taking the sugar with him. He opened the drawer and put the picture back.

"Why do you keep it hidden?"

"Because everyone thinks it's my girlfriend, gets kind of annoying."

Venus smiled. She'd thought girlfriend, only because she knew he didn't have a sister. "She looks so young."

"She was young when she had me."

"You made her sound like an old battle-ax, yelling at you through the window."

Jake smiled. "She reminds me of you. Strong, opinionated, smart, but really a softy on the inside, just doesn't want anyone to know it."

"So, I remind you of your mother, exactly what I needed to hear. What about your dad. Where's he?"

"He's here, in L.A. He and my mother split when I was about seven or eight. Never really saw much of him after that. What are you trying to figure out?" he asked, slightly annoyed.

"Who you are," she answered point-blank.

"You know that song' 'If you don't know me by now...' " He threw up his hands, in aggravation. "... guess you'll never know. Why can't you trust what's happening here, between us? What makes it so unbelievable?"

"I know you're real." Venus put her hand out to him. She felt his lips kiss the smooth ridge trailing from her wrist. She closed her eyes while he pressed his face to the center of her palm.

"Then don't run."

She stood up. The air was still moist and cool, even in the confines of his office building, sealed away from the rain and wind. A quiet grayness moved over them, probably a cloud swelling above the city, ready to unleash more of the storm.

He took tighter hold of her hand. "After last night, you're still going to go?"

"I have to" was all she said before walking out of his office and closing the door quietly, as if she could stop from disturbing him. As if she could leave him the way she'd found him.

Venus went straight to the conference room. The building was starting to fill up with people. She put her head down and perused her handheld organizer, looking over her schedule. Wendy's flight was changed so they could fly out together in the morning. Her mother's next chemo appointment wasn't until next week. She wondered how it was affecting her.

Henry answered on the first ring. He sounded full of energy, she tried to pump herself up so not to bring him down. "Dad, how's everything?"

He explained that Pauletta had been sleeping nonstop for the last twelve hours. Good for her, Venus thought. No one else had. "I'm going to D.C. tomorrow. I just wanted to let you know, but if you need to reach me, call my cell phone. I mean for anything, Dad."

He was tinkering with his train, she could tell by how long it took for him to respond. "We got it covered around here, Precious. You go do what needs to be done. Take care of yourself, me and your mother aren't going anywhere."

"Okay." Venus looked up and saw William and Beverly go by she quickly put her head back down. "Tell Mom I'll be back Monday. Give her a kiss for me."

"Will do."

She dialed Chadnum next. She hadn't checked in for a while. William had been the liaison, essentially covering for her while she dealt with her family drama. After Venus finished leaving messages and giving updates, she focused on what she was going to say when she saw Airic. She didn't want to accuse him of anything. He'd probably had enough of that with the Securities and Exchange Commission.

She couldn't help herself, her fingers started dialing, easily, without the assistance of her brain. He answered on the first ring. "It's me." Venus pressed her knees together to keep them from shaking.

"Hey, you." Airic didn't sound like a downtrodden man, beaten by the system of unjust accusations.

"Wendy's here, she told me about your company, Airic. About what's happening to you." She blurted the words out like a four-year-old tattle-tale. There was a long pause. She gripped the phone tighter, frustrated that he had nothing to say. "Airic, what's going on?"

"You'll be here tomorrow. Can it wait till then?"

The same anger and humiliation she'd felt when Wendy brought it up, the same slap of astonishment fresh as it had been that day, crept like a needling itch all over her body. "No! I don't want to wait until I get there. I want to talk about it now."

"Tomorrow, Venus." The line went dead. Venus was cut off. She threw the phone back in her purse stood up and paced along the long glass wall of the conference room.

"Hey." Wendy came in smiling. Legend was right behind her, the classic smugness all over his face. He was dressed in a suit Venus hadn't seen before. His long dark locks cascaded over his shoulders like ivy.

"Delivered in one piece," he said to Venus, all smiles. His dark skin was supple and healthy, and his eyes shone light, the same glow radiating on Wendy's dark skin. They sat side by side, their shoulders touching.

"We had the best time...dancing," she added deliberately. No one would guess Wendy wore the same clothes she had on yesterday, her hair and makeup still in place.

"Here are my keys." Venus tossed them over the table. "The car is right out front. You probably should go and get some rest, a nap or something." Venus pulled her collar away from her skin searching for relief. "You know what, I'll walk you out." She checked her watch.

Legend stood up. "I got it. Relax."

"No, I'll go." Venus stood up.

Legend looked at Wendy as if he expected her to side with him. There was no contest. Venus rolled her eyes, sucked her teeth. "Ssssh." Walking out the door, she didn't look behind, hoping Wendy knew better than to leave her hanging.

.   .   .

"WHAT was that all about?" Wendy caught up to her side. They stood in front of the red-doored elevator. It was time for secret conversations.

Once inside, Venus looked Wendy in the eye, "He's an arrogant jackass, and now my best friend finds him appealing. Makes my skin crawl."

"Well, what'd you leave me alone with him for?"

"I didn't know you were going to be screwing him by nightfall. You're married, Wendy."

"Oh, right, and you're not?" The elevator stopped.

"No, I'm not." They both pushed out at the same time.

"You may as well be and that didn't stop you from falling for what's his name, Jake. By the way, I see your dilemma." She tried to add a touch of softness. The click of their high heels echoed in sync on the hard enameled floor.

"Still, I'm not married. You are," Venus said while they walked out the double doors. The wind and rain sprinkled their faces. She welcomed the coolness.

"I plead temporary insanity." Wendy held up her right hand. "But I had a good time. Once in a while, it keeps the doors from closing in on you, the difference between being locked up like a lunatic in your own mind."

"So, you've done this before?" Venus asked, trying not to show shock.

"Seventeen years…honey, please." Wendy said, leaning in to hug Venus when they reached the car. "You'll see what I mean when you get married."

·   *   ▪

You'll see what I mean when you get married. Those words stuck with Venus throughout the morning. No. She wouldn't know what Wendy meant once she was married. Venus shook her head while she sat in the conference room. No. Once she was married, there wouldn't be a need for any extracurricular behavior. She wouldn't be lonely in her marriage. That was the point of finding a partner in the first place. Someone she wanted to spend the rest of her life with, someone to grow happy and hairy with, accepting the good with the bad, the highs with the lows. Sticking together against whatever trouble may come. That was her ideal of a happy and fulfilled life; why would someone risk a lifetime of love for a one-night stand?

Before she could contemplate the answer, Jake walked in holding two Starbucks cups. He set one down in front of her before sitting next to her. "You didn't get your morning coffee." He didn't do his usual distance routine, trying to maintain a professional atmosphere. He remained in the chair next to her and even rolled it closer.

"Thank you," Venus said, clearing her throat. Her eyes darted to check the look on Legend's and William's faces. Nothing, not even a question mark appeared over their heads. They simply had taken it for granted that Jake would know whether or not she'd had her morning coffee since she'd obviously awakened with him. Was she being paranoid?

Venus took a sip, ignoring her instantly scalded tongue. "Where's Beverly?"

"She's downstairs, she's got deadlines," William answered.

"I think she should be in this meeting. I'll go find her." Venus was geared up to remove herself from the table.

"Trust me, she's got her own problems to handle." Jake touched her arm. "I'll fill her in later. I just got a call from Lila Kelly's manager. Seems she has other offers on the table similar to ours."

The first thing Venus thought of was the T-shirts that probably had landed on every competitor's front porch like the daily news. "I knew it." Her eyes went into one heavy line. "I knew this was going to happen." She faced Legend. "This is the last time, you hear. I'm sick and tired of you trying to undermine me. I'm sick of the disrespect. I'm sick of your attitude. Once we're through here, you're out." She said it with a finalized thumb over her shoulder.

Legend stood up, pushing the chair back into a roll. "You don't have to wait. Every minute I have to sit up here and deal with your bullshit is a minute too long."

Jake stood up, covering the door before Legend reached it. "Wait a minute. This is crazy. Come on."

"You want to deal with her, you deal with her. I've had it. How's she going to sit here and point the finger directly in my face, like I went out and waved a bull's-eye?"

Venus stood up too. "You may as well have. I told you that T-shirt idea was wrong. I told you, but you and William are so busy trying to prove me incompetent, you're smarter, you're better. Legend and William, the incomparable duo," she mocked.

William made an adjustment in his chair, facing Venus with incredulousness. "How're you going to include me? This mess is between you two. Has been from day one. Some kind of unhealthy sexual conflict, I say."

"Oh, I'd have to be deaf, dumb, and already dead!"

Jake's voice went up a notch. "Calm down!"

Venus fell back into her seat feeling like a cornered animal, no way to get out. "Fine." But she wouldn't be responsible for the consequences. She'd have no choice but to react the same way a trapped animal would, snipping and biting at whoever came too close. Fine, she found herself repeating in her head. Everything would be fine. She sat back in her chair and took hold of the situation. Deadlines were looming.

Venus did the natural thing and began to suggest Plan B and possibly even a Plan C. Jake was quick to dismiss other options.

"Other offers are on the table, doesn't mean she signed anything. Nothing is done until the deal is signed. We'll just have to make a personal call. Go see her like we did before." Jake sat down next to Venus. "Quick hop to New York, remind her how much she liked you."

Venus held her breath, unable to speak. He knew she was planning to leave in the morning to see Airic. "At this point it's probably all about the benjamins, Jake." She let her eyes cut to Legend. "Competitors are making offers, exactly what we didn't want to happen. They're probably putting up cash instead of stock. Money, that's what it's all about, not personality contests."

"I wouldn't mind going." William's grin full of mischief. "A personal visit with an offer she can't refuse."

Jake kept his focus on Venus, waiting for her to concede. She could feel his eyes unwavering.

"How do you even know there are legitimate offers?" Legend felt calm enough to enter the conversation.

Jake leaned forward, "I know."

Venus spoke up, unable to hold up to the pressure. "It's simply time to negotiate." She faced him head on. "I'm sorry." She said quietly, implying more than the small two words could carry on their own. "I think the dynamic duo can handle it from here." She picked up her bag and left the conference room with a stunned Jake and a victorious Legend staring at her.

She hurried down the unstable stairs, feeling free and clear once her heels rested solid on the enameled floor. At least that's what she thought until the sound of Jake's voice caught her.

"Venus." He was standing at the top of the stairs. His soft eyes cool, but still telling her what she didn't want to hear. *Please don't go.*

And her eyes returning the message he didn't want to hear. *I wish I didn't have to.*

She pushed through the large glass doors and didn't dare look back.

*   *   *

WHEN Venus came through the door of the apartment, Wendy was carrying on like a schoolgirl. She held the phone in the crook of her neck while she peeled potatoes. The stereo was on. She talked loud over the bass and guitars of Carlos Santana.

"No, you will not call me when you get to D.C." Wendy giggled again, before catching Venus standing across the room chewing on her nails. "I have to go. No. No. Okay. I'll call you back." She placed the phone back in its cradle.

"Let me guess who that was." Venus rolled her eyes.

"He's sprung, girl. What can I say?"

Venus turned up her nose in disgust.

Wendy turned off the radio. The apartment became quiet. She was preparing for her job as superfriend. "Come on, sit down." She pushed the red velvet pillows off to the side. Venus did as instructed, sitting down and taking off her shoes.

"Tell me what's going on." Wendy's concern always transferred her back to wife, mother. The responsible one. It didn't matter that not less than a minute ago she was on the phone talking to Legend, loud and silly.

"It's not obvious?" Venus sunk deeper into the couch.

"Jake?"

"No. I don't think I need to worry about Jake." She'd poked enough holes to ruin his sail, this time she was sure.

"Then Airic? What'd he do?"

"I point-blank asked him what the hell was going on, and he wouldn't answer me."

"Why'd you ask him over the phone? He can't talk about something like this over the phone, Venus." Wendy gave her the don't-you-know look.

"You want to hear another one?"

"You got a million of 'em?"

"Yep." She went to the kitchen and picked up Wendy's glass of wine and took a long swallow. "I don't care anymore. I don't care. I'm going to D.C. and hand him back his ring, tell him good luck and have a happy life."

Wendy put the knife down.

"I'm not going to fight it anymore. I'm not meant to be in union. Till death do you part and all that shit. I get it. I give." Venus threw up her hands. "I'm out."

"You have to give Airic a chance to explain."

"Why? This isn't something I'd put up with. Not the old me. This new me is pathetic. Letting shit slide, ignoring the bigger issue. We're supposed to be partners, best friends. How could he not come to me?"

"Did you consult with him before you spent the night with Jake?" It was Wendy's job to ask the tough questions. Venus was shocked into silence.

Wendy tried to soften what she'd said, "People mess up all the time. That's what a marriage is about. Maybe that's why you can't get there, Venus. Nobody has any leeway with you." She went to the kitchen and resumed her vegetable chopping.

Venus stood across from her, separated by the kitchen island. "Well, maybe if you had half as much of the no-bullshit detector as I do, you wouldn't be in the situation you're in. You wouldn't need to be messing around."

"Situation?"

"You're married, unhappily married, as far as I can tell," Venus continued, unable to reel herself back. "I don't want that. I'd rather walk away and be single for the rest of my life than deal with someone who claims he's working all hours of the day and night, when we really know what that means." Venus felt her body quaking. Her temper beyond reach to pull back. "I'd rather put it all out on the table, now, and walk away, than live like that." Venus said it with disgust. She didn't want to be mad at Wendy, she wanted to be mad at herself, at Airic. At every past mistake she'd ever made that brought her to this point. But she couldn't help it.

Wendy unwittingly pointed her chopping knife in Venus's direction. "I have made mistakes. Everybody makes them, Venus. Do you hear yourself? Self-righteous, sanctimonious crap. If I didn't know better, I'd think you'd been to church. But it's worse than that; this is deeper than that. This is built in. Your perfection radar zaps everything that crosses your path. If it doesn't pass inspection, you try to stomp it out."

"That's not true."

"Yes, it is."

"That's not true. I put up with crap all my life...from men, in relationships. In friendships. I let people hurt me."

"Yeah, but they only get one chance. That's it. No middle ground with you."

Venus's head was starting to hurt. A montage of events and partings, friends and lovers who'd come and gone. She saw the door close, shutting tight, blocking things out when they didn't go her way.

"So now that you found out I'm not perfect, am I banished from your kingdom, too?" Wendy's eyes watered slowly.

"I'm sorry. I didn't mean to say those things. You're one of the sweetest, most caring people I know. I'm so sorry. I don't know how you put up with me."

"That's what people do when they love someone; they accept the good with the bad." She threw a piece of raw potato and hit Venus square in the nose.

"I'm sorry," she said again, coming around to Wendy's side and giving her a hug. They walked to the couch. Venus closed her eyes letting her head fall against the backrest. "I thought Airic was everything I would ever need."

"Then give him a chance." Wendy pulled her long legs underneath her, getting prepared to help her friend sort it all out...once again.

"It's too late."

"It's never too late." Wendy breathed out frustrated, tired of giving unused advice. She left, then came back with the box of Kleenex, handing it to Venus with a here-we-go-again attitude.

"How could I fall for someone else, if I was so secure in my relationship with Airic? How could I have gone out with Clint if everything was supposed to be solid?"

"Clint!"

This was another wrench thrown in the dilemma. Wendy jumped up, "What are you talking about? You saw Clint?"

Venus nodded her head up and down. Wendy snatched the box of tissue back as if she didn't deserve it. "You saw him when?"

"He's here in L.A., working at the hospital where my mother had her surgery. We went out."

Wendy's mouth fell open. "And?"

"And nothing, he wanted to know how I felt about him, about us. It's safe to say, I'm completely over him. I was home free, doing so well." Venus dabbed her eyes. "Now I'm just lost. My heart is scrambled, like bad data." Venus got up and studied the purple wall. It looked lifeless and dark. The sound of rumbling thunder outside filled the room. She walked to the curtains and pulled them closed.

Wendy came and stood next to her. "Would you have had doubts about Airic if you'd never met Jake?"

Venus made a questioning face, like isn't it obvious. Then she decidedly backed down. "I don't know. Airic not telling me about the investigation into his company, that's huge. Even if everybody deserves one mistake. It's huge."

"Oh sweetie." Wendy put a long slender arm around Venus's slight shoulders.

Venus could barely breathe pressed against Wendy's shoulder; she managed to pull away long enough to speak. "I'm just tired, that's all. I'm tired of trying to get it right."

"Anything good takes time."

Venus pulled back again. "Have you been hanging around my mother? Sounds like something she would say."

Wendy let out a howl. "Speaking of which, I was hoping to see her. Do you think she'd be up for a visit?"

"She had chemo a couple of days ago. She's still sleeping it off."

"That's cool." Wendy blinked her light brown eyes. "Maybe next time. So what are you going to do?"

After all their mishmashing and teeth pulling, Venus never made it clear. Loose ends refused to be tied. "I don't know. I wish I did."

"I know one thing...don't you dare tell Airic about Mr. Good Lovin'.

You do that, and you guys are through. Do you hear me?" She took Venus by both shoulders. "Don't you dare!"

Venus bit the inside of her cheek, "I wasn't going to. I would never be that selfish. I think confessions just clear your own conscience. It doesn't make the other person feel any better. If I told him, it would crush him."

CORNERS AND
CROSSROADS

THE plane took off on time, a rare and momentous occasion. Wendy sat next to her, reading a magazine. Venus closed her eyes, tired from the late-night sharing session into the wee hours of the morning. "Maybe it's not that you don't forgive, maybe you're just always waiting for the out." Where would she be without Wendy with her big eyes on the outside looking in where things always appeared clear, basic, and simple? "Maybe you're afraid, deep down, afraid to be with anyone, so you push them away first. First chance you get." Who needed a therapist when you had friends?

"Maybe you're right," Venus whispered to herself before opening her eyes to see the airplane's steward giving emergency directions and pointing to the exit signs. She'd contemplated not getting on this flight at all, because she knew Wendy was right. Any excuse would do. It would have been safer to stay in Los Angeles and let it all flow under the bridge. But it was a must. She and Airic had to talk. They had to clean out the bad to make room for the good. She wanted to make it work.

Sitting on the phone last night with Jake, she'd already made her decision. "I know what I feel for you is real, I know it with all my heart. But I'd be no good to you, believing as I do, that I can't finish anything—that everything I start ends in failure. I'd come to you the exact same way, with a word on the outside of my package written in big black letters, IR-REGULAR, like the sheets, or the socks in the clearance bin."

"You know the funny thing about that... even if they're irregular they still work," he'd said, trying desperately to end her excuses.

"I think that people are put into our lives for a purpose; they come and they go, but something is always left behind. Something we can use to make us better. You have made me a better person. I believe in love, Jake. I believe in all its possibilities." The rain still had not stopped falling. She pictured him sitting in the middle of his living room in front of the windows facing out to the shore, bare-chested, candles burning. "Thank you for taking the time to care for me. I don't think I would have gotten through any of this. Finding out my mother was sick, nothing near that bad or frightening has ever happened to me in my life. It brought me to my knees, I have to tell you. I'd never felt so vulnerable, so completely helpless."

"If it had been another time..."

"Hey!" Wendy's voice snatched Venus away from the memory of Jake's last words. "Did you see this? Did you know he was married?" She opened the entertainment magazine to the center pictures of the actor who'd been making women swoon for the last couple of years. "Look at her. She's not even cute."

"Wendy, please." Venus pushed the magazine away.

"Still thinking hard, huh?"

"I'm through thinking." Venus adjusted herself in the uncomfortable airplane seat. They weren't made for short people, regardless of what tall people thought.

Wendy closed her magazine. "I'm impressed with your decision-making skills. Do you know how many women would have just kept both of them on the line? One on the West Coast, the other on the East."

"That's way too much work." Venus put her head back, feeling the altitude pressure surge in her ears. "I barely have enough energy for one."

The plane landed five hours later. Venus woke up, pulling and swirling pieces of her hair, trying to put the shape back into it. She had reached a crossroads where a decision was necessary, to either cut it all off again or put it into twists.

"I'm surprised you haven't given up on this natural thing. It looks like way more trouble than it's worth." Wendy simply ran her fingers through the ends of her shiny straightened hair and instantly looked fresh and new. She pulled her jacket on and zipped the leather clear to her neck. "Get ready. You're going to feel what real cold is."

"It's okay." Venus was preoccupied with thought as the passengers started moving off the plane. Her nerves were on edge. Time was closing in on her. She wasn't worried about her hair, the weather, or anything else. Only what she was going to say when she finally saw Airic.

*　　*　　*

THE house was empty. Sandy, her little cocker spaniel, had been staying over at Wendy's house, being taken care of by Tia and Jamal, mostly Jamal. Tia didn't like the way Sandy bit into her doll's leg, pulling until the tug-of-war ended with a limb missing.

Venus flipped up the Honeywell cover and pushed the thermostat up. She walked around the house. It was built only six years ago, but the old-fashioned Tudor style stayed true to its heritage with hardwood floors and narrow square-paned windows; several in a row lined the front of the house. The wooden blinds were raised, as if no one had touched them in days. Venus dropped the blinds one at a time and felt instantly warmer.

She wanted it to be nice and cozy when Airic arrived, the best possible circumstances for him to lay his burden down. He needed to know that she was through playing perfectionist. That's what she understood now. Airic was simply afraid of her. Afraid of what she'd do if she found out about the company's woes. She'd proven herself to be consistent. Foul me and you're out. No three strikes, only one.

She filled the steel kettle on the stove with water. The gas flames were a welcome sight compared with the electric stove in Los Angeles; electric heat and appliances, all so cosmopolitan and fake. Temporary. This was a real home. She opened the cabinet and pulled out the tea container. She inhaled the scent of peppermint before dropping the linen bag into a cup.

She sat at her round kitchen table. There was an empty bowl, edged with dried milk and cereal. Airic only ate Corn Puffs in the morning, the strangest thing she'd ever seen in a grown man. Cold cereal of any kind completely grossed her out. She shoved the bowl farther away. The chair beside her was pushed against the table, stacked with newspapers. Wendy had mentioned that's how her cousin knew out about the fraud investigation. The dates went only as far back as this past Sunday. She pulled out the financial sections of each paper, folding them neatly in chronological sequence.

Companies were being hit hard by the Internet crunch. The craze that had swept the country was now responsible for hundreds of thousands of people being out of work. She skimmed over articles, one after the other, of dot-com demise. Did anyone really think a site selling dog food was going to make millions? She set it aside and went to the next one, reading, slowly looking for any information on Airic's company. She turned to the stock page, looking for the symbol VPNS, Virtual Privacy Network Solutions. Airic believed the name of a company was everything. Second only to location, location, location. The price on this date was $46 a share, less than half of what it had been a month ago. The news of the investigation must've hit hard. She put her arms down and let the paper crumple in her lap. Airic. She shook her head. She hurt, but not out of anger. Hurt for him. This was a nightmare.

She finished her tea and started cleaning up. The kitchen first. She soaked dishes in the sink that had sat untouched too long, swept and mopped, then started the dishwasher. Next was the bedroom. She grabbed her overnight bag, carrying it up the stairs right along with the vacuum from the hall closet. Their bedroom wasn't as bad as she presumed. The blankets and comforter were hanging off the side of the bed. Clothes were draped over the large chaise in the bay window, but nothing drastic. She gathered his pants and shirts to put in a pile for the dry cleaners. Instinct pushed her hands into each set of pockets. On the last pair, she pulled out a folded piece of notepaper. Venus walked to the edge of the bed and sat down, still holding all the clothes.

She knew before she opened the paper fully. Her mouth went dry, a wretched taste, sour and metallic all at once on her tongue. She folded it back up, her hand shaking. How could he know what the price would be at future dates? She remembered asking herself that question when she'd found the file in her apartment. She remembered thinking that she could help. Probability and analysis were her specialty. She remembered. She knew. Now she understood. He'd done exactly what he was accused of.

Airic. She put her face in her hands still hugging his clothes close to her chest. His shirts smelled of his aftershave. The scent that had sickened her only days ago, she now relished.

Airic.

It had taken all the strength left in her body to continue moving about the day. She'd driven to the dry cleaners, stopped at the grocery store. Gone to Wendy's and finished Act I, Scene 2, of crying on her shoulder. She took Sandy home, needing someone who loved her unconditionally. Her little cocker spaniel didn't know about her weaknesses, her unfailing ability to destroy anything good that came in her path, whether directly her fault or not. It was exactly the reason she couldn't stay with Jake. He was too good to be exposed.

She came back to the house and cooked, just as she'd planned to do. The scent of baked red snapper with bell peppers and rosemary hung in the air. She heard the door unlock, then Airic coming inside. She listened while he hung his keys on the metal rack near the door, along with his trench coat.

Venus dried her hands on a towel, walking directly to Airic. He'd lost weight. Sharp wells showed underneath his cheekbones. His pale skin was dull. She hugged him. He held on to her while Sandy danced around their legs.

"You made it." His heart was thinly beating underneath his shirt.

Venus pulled away. "I cooked dinner." She went back into the kitchen before he noticed the puffiness underneath her eyes, the signs of defeat in her face.

"Smells good. I'll wash up and be right there. Hey, little girl." He bent over and played with Sandy. Airic liked the cute bundle of fur and wagging tail but couldn't make any promises that she'd get fed regularly, which was the very reason Venus had taken her to Wendy's while she worked in Los Angeles.

The plates were already on the table, the food sitting in the center. Airic walked in and sat down. "This looks good."

They ate and drank, clinking forks to ceramic, ice to glass. Venus swallowed with difficulty every bite, clearing her plate. She didn't remember how the food tasted. Sure it was delicious. She didn't do anything differently, and it was Airic's favorite. His plate was cleaned, too.

"Am I that bad, Airic?" The words rushed out. Venus couldn't stay silent on the subject any longer. "Am I such a harsh horrible person that you couldn't trust me, couldn't depend on me?"

He took a long heavy breath. "What can I say? It didn't work out." His eyes lifted up to hers, the first time he'd looked her directly in the eyes since he'd been home. "I didn't want you to know. I thought I could fix things. I thought I'd have time to fix the company, put it back in the black, then you'd never have to know." His shoulders slumped, his head leaning back. "I didn't want to lose you. Your respect, your admiration."

"Please don't say that. Please, no. Don't you see what you're saying?... that you thought so little of my capacity to love, to see you through this, that you couldn't trust me. That's what it means when you say you were afraid. That I'd turn my back on you, walk at the slightest bit of trouble. That's what you're saying. God. I didn't want you to feel that way about me. I wanted to finally be right, to finally be the person that someone could count on, through thick and thin. I wanted to be that person for you, Airic. All my life, it seems like I've let someone down one way or another. I lacked whatever it was that made other people stick. Made other people stay. Conviction, forgiveness, compassion, whatever it's called. I thought you saw that in me. I thought you trusted me. But it is so obvious...there's something seriously flawed here." She pressed her bent fingers into her chest. "I will spend the rest of my days trying to figure it out."

He stayed silent only for as long as it took for him to become angry, too. His narrow chin jutted out. "You know what, you're right. I was never sure about us. From the day we met, I felt like you had better things to do than be with me. Like no matter how much time we spent together, your mind was somewhere else. I never stopped feeling like your second choice, your fall guy. I knew you weren't over him, Clint. You think I didn't know you were still wishing for him instead of me? You spent so much time telling me that you loved me, but whenever I looked up, you were gone, New York, Chicago, Philadelphia. Then, you're in Los

Angeles." He slapped the outside of his hand into the other. "Could you have run any farther?"

Venus shook her head. "You acted like you didn't care if I left."

"We both did a fine job of not caring. Honestly, by then I was far too wrapped up in this mess; you could have stabbed me with a poker and I wouldn't have felt it. Don't you understand? I was scared. Ten million dollars of other people's money, and I screwed it up. I didn't have the energy or the inclination to keep chasing you, to keep hoping that one day, you'd wake up and be happy it was me by your side."

"But, I was..."

He shook his head. "No. You were scared to lose me, like I was scared to lose you. Like this was our last chance so neither of us wanted to blow it. That's not happiness, that's survival."

She'd never looked at it that way. Complacency. Merely surviving. It was the way of the land. She'd watched her mother and father do it for over thirty years, or at least that was how Venus had perceived it from her mother's side. Only recently, she'd seen her father's point of view. It was more than survival for him, he'd loved Pauletta...*and liked her a whole bunch, too.* But she was sure her mother had come to that point out of sheer wear and tear. Time. Venus believed in time. With a little time, she'd feel as deeply for Airic as a wife should feel for a husband. But now it seemed they'd run out. The hourglass was empty.

"What happens next?" Venus tried not to look at her palms, ignoring what she knew was already history, written and preordained.

He shook his head. "I don't know. I can't deal with us right now. I've got to prepare to go before the board in the morning, convince them that the company is still solid, solid enough to operate without me. That's part of the deal. The SEC wants me to resign, give my shares of the company over to a trust. But the deal will only work if they don't bust up the company."

"I'm so sorry, Airic, I hate to see this happening. I know how hard you worked, what this all meant to you." She too shook her head, a slow turn of incredibility. "I just can't believe what's happening." She gently bit the edge of her knuckle. "I can be your test board. Present your case to me. Tell me what you're going to say tomorrow."

"Haven't figured that out yet, but I wouldn't mind a little help." He rubbed his tired eyes. Venus stood up, next to him. He pulled her close, leaning his head against the firm flatness of her stomach. "Believe me when I tell you, I'm sorry."

"I'm sorry, too." She wrapped her fingers around his neck. "Let's go make this board of directors understand what they might be losing." He stood up, surrounding her with his long slim arms, a conciliatory hug. They would always be on the same side, she understood; nothing would ever change that.

BABY

THE following days were long and exhausting. Venus went with Airic to the hearings. She waited outside sitting on the hard, shiny wooden bench for hours at a time. Airic's lawyer always looked as if the end of the world were near, shaking his head with doom when Venus would ask how it went. "You can never tell with these things," he'd respond. But this time, he pushed through the heavy double doors, smiling. Venus stood up, scared to move her feet.

"We did it, baby." Airic picked her up, hugging her.

What mattered for Airic was that they didn't dissolve the company. He didn't care if he was a part of the business. He'd worked hard, committing years of his life to its inception; more than anything he simply wanted to see it stay alive and grow.

Airic shook his lawyer's hand. "Thanks, thank you." He turned facing Venus. "Let's go celebrate."

Venus felt like a child being led out of the building, down the long tier of steps to the street. "Airic, wait. Stop." She couldn't take another step, staggering from the constant swell of nausea she'd experienced since morning.

"You all right?" He touched her face. "You don't look good."

If she looked anywhere near how she felt, he spoke the truth. Venus sat down on the concrete stairs, her face tilted up to the bright sun. Her eyes closed. "I think I'm pregnant." She wasn't searching for a response. She'd simply blurted the statement out to see how it would stand on its own. She'd harbored the fear, the thought, quietly, but it was burning a hole in her mind.

Airic sat down next to her on the steps of the federal courthouse.

She kept her eyes closed, absorbing the heat of the sun. Ironic that she'd had to leave California and move back home to D.C. to feel it.

"Venus." Airic's hand glided up her back, across her shoulder. "You think or you know?"

"I know." She turned to him. She opened her eyes, not at all surprised to see the look of mortification on his face. "When I was dealing with my mom's health, I guess, everything got away from me. Days kind of melted into each other. I slipped up on the pill a couple of times."

"Okay. Okay, wow. That's great."

Venus shook her head no. "It's not great. I can see it in your face. But it's okay, it really is."

"It's just…I am happy, absolutely." Airic took her hand. "Guess we better set that date, huh?" He brought her palm to his lips.

A car had passed, barely escaping being hit by a taxi. The driver's horn went off at the exact same time as her response. "What do you mean, no?" Airic stood up, blocking the sun so Venus would have no excuse for not looking him directly in the eyes. "When are you going to forgive me? You think I don't know what you're feeling? I know this has hurt you. The trust, the faith. I know. But we will get past it. I'm sorry. I'll keep telling you until you believe me."

Venus put her head down. The wave of fullness, then a crash of emptiness in her belly. "It's not that simple."

"Why? Why isn't it? It's a choice, Venus. Yours. It's that simple."

"I can't." She swallowed hard to get the words out. "I've gone over it in my head, over and over, again and again, and I can't. It has nothing to do with what happened to your company. Nothing to do with you not telling me." Venus took a deep breath, waiting for the nauseating spell to pass, not wanting to add insult to injury by actually throwing up on his suit.

"What is it, then?" He stood up, knowing the answer.

"I do love you, Airic. I do, but it's not enough. I wish it were."

"Does that make any sense? Listen to yourself. We're having a baby,

Venus. No more games. No more time to play. We've got to work with what we've got."

Venus stood up; that was it. He'd said it in a nutshell, something she'd been trying to articulate. She didn't want to *work*. She didn't want to make it work, forcing herself into living a lifetime of regret. "I can't. Not even if I wanted to." It was true. For the first time she didn't feel the need to follow a path, a divine set of circumstances. She was pregnant. Airic was the father. She'd already confirmed that with her calendar. It happened on his last trip to L.A. The scary part was that she'd hoped it was Jake's. That would have given her a reason to go back that didn't require her to make the decision on her own.

But she had made it. She'd cared for Airic too much to let him go through his trouble alone, the breathless waiting, hoping no one sued him in addition to the legal fees and fines. The loss of his credibility and name. She'd promised herself that she would wait until the crisis was over before ending their relationship.

He picked up her hand and pressed it to his lips. His eyes squeezed tight, as if he could change what she was about to say, change time and space and all the alignment of the stars. It doesn't matter, he would have said if the weakness hadn't clogged his throat. If the fear hadn't marched all over his heart. It would matter, because she needed more than a father for her baby, she wanted it all. All the love, all *the whole bunch of like,* the passion, the soul. She wanted it all. She didn't want to settle for less, she wanted it, she deserved it, and he would have to understand.

          ʁ   *ʁ*   *ѡ*

AIRIC didn't move out right away. He had nowhere to go. After months of calling in favors and promising he'd learned his lesson to anyone who felt inclined to ask, he was finally offered a teaching position at a small college in Boston. He'd accepted. But by then, Venus had already felt like she was only half of herself, a thin shell, walking around afraid of breaking. She'd been sick to the point that she'd only gained twelve pounds by her seventh month of pregnancy. She'd blamed it on the stress. Worrying about Airic. Worrying about the new life she was carrying. She spent the better part of her days cursing her decision of depriving her child of a father. All she had to do was say the word and he would stay. But she couldn't do it.

Even though they'd agreed and had planned the day of his leaving, Venus was overwrought with jitters and exhaustion. She wept at the sight of his jeans, faded, folded up on the bed, along with his flannel shirts, the red and blue one, the orange and black one, her favorite. She'd finally collapsed in the middle of the hallway. Airic knelt over her, touching her face. She saw him spinning above her like an old 45 record. His eyes, his nose, his nose she remembered because she could see the hollow interior of his nostrils. The blackout didn't last long. Airic had moved her to the bed and was dialing the paramedics when she came to.

"Airic." She sat up, rubbing her stomach. "We just need to eat something." He hung up the phone. "Are you sure? You scared me." He rushed out of the room. Venus heard the rumblings in the kitchen, cabinet doors opening and closing. He came back with peanut butter slathered on two pieces of wheat bread and a large glass of milk. He sat next to her on the bed.

"I hate this... it doesn't make any sense."

Venus swallowed the milk in large gulps. She chewed the bread slowly. He patiently watched her before he tried again.

"What are we doing here, Venus?" Airic's sideburns had turned completely white but blended well with his ash brown hair and fair skin. He stared straight ahead while he spoke, "How did we get to this point?" He picked up the large teddy bear that sat against the wall. He squeezed the plush toy lightly in his hands. "I wish I could go back in time," he said, flipping the small card attached to the bear's neck. He read the signature. Venus read it too even though she knew exactly what it said. *You deserve the beary best. Love, Jake.* She felt both the desire to smile and cry. There were more where that one came from. All five sat on the bed where she slept each night. One stuffed teddy bear a month since she'd told Jake about the pregnancy. She hadn't told him right away. After talking to him on the phone almost daily about everything under the sun, she felt deceitful. Scared he would end his ritual of calling every night, soothing her with his words while she lay in bed rubbing the growing roundness of her belly. When she'd finally told him, the truth, the circumstances, he simply said, "Thank you." For what, she'd asked. "For trusting me," he replied. She explained that she only wanted his friendship, the same as from the start. She explained that Airic was sleeping in the downstairs guest bedroom until he could find employment and a place to live. She explained that she was scared, and to that Jake said, "Without fear, there would be nothing to conquer." So wise to be so young was her response before crying herself to sleep.

Now Airic was asking how they'd come to this time and place. She wished she had wise words of her own.

"Is he the reason why?" Airic snatched the card off and balled it in his hands. Venus reached across to take the teddy bear out of harm's way.

She faced him. "It's us. It has nothing to do with anybody else. The only thing meeting him accomplished was bringing it to light sooner rather than later. Remember the heart-to-heart we had five months ago? You said it in plain English. You said you never trusted that I loved you, not from day one. So for two years we were pretending. I don't want to pretend for the rest of our lives. I don't. I've seen it. Hell, I've lived it. And I wouldn't wish it on anyone, let alone my own baby."

"*Our baby,*" he corrected her sternly.

She guided his wide hand to her stomach, placing it on the growing life inside her. "*Our* baby," she agreed. "I'll never question your love for *our* child. But I would always question your love for me."

THE last month of her pregnancy made the others look easy. She experienced the worst gas and bloating, not to mention the ankle swelling and sleepless nights. She was a walking zombie and had no one to take it out on. Airic had to leave for Boston for his new teaching position. He'd wanted to wait the pregnancy out with Venus but the new semester was going to start with or without him. His career limitations offered him no room to negotiate.

It was for the best. At least that's what she kept telling herself, her mother as well, who'd called to ask her to move back to Los Angeles. She didn't like her so far away, all alone.

"I have Wendy, Mom. And I need to be alone, to sort things out." Venus sat on the couch with her feet propped up.

"You've been alone long enough. If you haven't got it figured out by now, you never will. You need to come home. What are you doing out there? You're not working. It's not like you need to be there. Just come on home." Pauletta was in the kitchen, which was obvious from the sound of dish clatter and water running. She was back to her old self but had recently taken up swimming. She claimed to feel better than ever.

"This is my home."

"Well then, I have no choice but to come there."

"Mom...oh, that would be nice, especially after the baby's born, but not now. Okay?" Venus did her best to fight back the urge to cry. She was alone, frightened. Yes, this is what she'd asked for, to be able to take a minute and say, *"I'm all right."* To know that she was blessed and take nothing for granted ever again, whether with someone or alone. Each moment in a day was a gift. But it was hard work, a constant self-convincing battle.

Venus returned from her daydream to hear her mother concede, "Okay, but I want to know the minute you go into labor, the very minute. No, forget that, I'll book my reservations for a couple of days before the due date, that way, I won't miss anything."

"I kind of just had plans for Airic to be in the delivery room. I mean, it's important for him to bond with the baby early."

"Right..." Here it would start again. Pauletta saw nothing to be gained by the single mother strategy. The rules were simple. Baby makes three...not two. "You need him in the birthing room but you don't even plan to let the man live with his own child? Does that make any sense?"

Venus rolled her eyes to the ceiling. "I better go...I've got a doctor's appointment."

"Do what makes you happy, Venus."

"I try, Mom. I really do. I'll talk to you tomorrow." Venus tossed the phone to the other end of the couch. Making herself happy was what this was all about, wasn't it?

The baby's due date was around the corner. She'd officially been on maternity leave for the past few weeks but had stayed out of the office once she started showing conclusive signs of unwed motherhood. She was far too old to be embarrassed, but it wasn't something she was ready to discuss with her colleagues. The who. The what. The *How*. Especially with Legend—he was the last person she'd wanted to bump into. Although these days, that would no longer be an issue.

Legend and William had decided to give the entrepreneurial fight another try. She admired them for their persistence and courage to be independent. Legend had even boldly offered her a piece of the pie as if he hadn't taken every opportunity to make her life miserable when they worked together. "I'll give it some thought." She'd smiled and winked at him, but in her head she was screaming, *Are you insane... why not just stick a pin in my eye?* But she did wish him well. Someone with that much arrogance had no limits on how high they could soar.

Venus stood up, the most painful part of her day, and stretched. Her doctor's appointment was hours away. Wendy planned to come over and take her to The Baby Store first, a perfect place for some retail therapy since her true vice of shoe shopping had come to an end. She couldn't fit into any of the shoes in her closet and had resorted to wearing Dearfoam slippers.

Going up the stairs was the second most painful part of her day. She waddled directly to the room across from hers, complete with bright yellow walls and a faux blue sky with clouds, all the painting accomplished by Airic under her strict supervision. The pristine white baby furniture was fit for a prince or princess. She made the doctor promise not to let the cat out of the bag. She wanted to meet her new baby face-to-face and let him or her define his or her own future. For now she was off to get more stuff that the baby probably wouldn't need.

Wendy arrived nice and early with Tia at her hip. The little girl had yet to be corrupted by the entertainment and media world. She had two pigtails and wore a pink jersey running suit with little pink and white sneakers.

"I brought you something," she said, holding the secret behind her back.

Venus stood at the front door, her round stomach protruding. "What? I hope it's cookies."

"Nope," she said, smiling with her two front teeth missing.

"No cookies, then I'm closing the door."

Wendy stuck her hand out before Venus could pretend to close it all the way. "You better move. I have to use the bathroom." She pushed past Venus quickly.

"Uh oh, you pregnant too?"

"That's not funny."

Tia came in and did a sidewinder walk to the couch. She kept her hands behind her back. "Close your eyes."

Venus stood and put her hands over her face. "Okay, ready."

"Now put out your hands."

"I might peek."

"You won't," Tia said. "I trust you."

"Okay, ready." Venus slid her hands away from her face and extended them to receive her surprise. She felt the smooth pat of Tia's hand brush into hers and then nothing. She opened her eyes to confirm that her palms were empty. "Oookay, well thank you, Tia." She was perplexed but felt compelled to play along.

"It's a wish."

"Oh, a wish," Venus said, relieved. "Yippeee. I love wishes." She stared at her open empty hands.

"But you only have one," Tia said, concerned she was being misunderstood.

"One wish."

"So it has to be good. Mommy said when she was pregnant with me all she wished for was a happy healthy baby...and she got me." She smiled wide, her gums glistening in the front. "What're you going to wish for?

No, don't tell me." She put up her hand in a stop sign. "Mommy says if you tell it won't come true."

A surge Venus had been fighting all day threatened to come, giving way to a stream of tears falling down her cheeks.

Tia hugged her as tight as she could. "Don't worry, Venus, you'll get your wish."

WISHES

V ENUS woke up, hearing her mother's voice. "Be careful what you wish for, you just might get it." She raised up not seeing her mother at all, but the sterile white walls of a hospital room. She shifted the weight of her body, on wobbly elbows.

"You're awake." The nurse came in carrying a small tray. Too small to be of any use. The paper cup was filled with orange juice and the saucer with a small stack of cookies.

It took Venus all of that time, from the moment she'd awakened, till the nurse set the tray in front of her, to remember. Yes. She indeed had to be careful what she wished for. She had been sitting in the car, Wendy driving and Tia in the backseat, pulling into the doctor's office parking lot when she'd blurted out, "God, I wish I could just have this baby today. I'm so tired." Five hours later, Wendy was screaming, "*Puuuussh*," and her wish was granted.

"We'll bring the baby in as soon as you get that juice and cookies down." The woman was one big blur of green, her top and pants without separation. She walked over to the other side of the room, pulling back the curtain. "How're you doing, Mrs. Cotter?" Venus heard another woman respond. The nurse told her the very same thing . . . as soon as she ate her cookies.

Venus did as she was told. It helped that she was starving, thinking to herself, if the woman in the next bed didn't eat her cookies, she'd go after those too. She swallowed the last gulp of orange juice and sat up, eagerly waiting.

"Here she is." Another nurse, a short black woman, came in pushing the small square cart with the swaddled baby inside. Venus had to breathe, count backward. She couldn't afford to keep crying every time she saw her. It depleted her of liquids, the hydration she needed to produce milk for her baby. She wiped her eyes, promising not to cry, threatening herself not to cry. She held out her arms, anticipating the weight, the warmth. Five pounds, seven ounces.

"She's mine," Venus confirmed, putting her face to the baby's head and inhaling. Her breast swelled immediately with her simple presence. "I love you, sweetheart. I love you." Her tiny mouth opened as wide as it could go in a twisted yawn. Her tiny fingers stretched out over her head.

"Okay, remember what I showed you early this morning. This is your last free lesson." The nurse laughed at her own joke. "Her head goes in the crook of your arm, tilt her head, that's right. Stroke her cheek on the side, now put it in. There you go. I know, it's not going to hurt like that forever, just until she stops sucking." The nurse amused herself again, leaving Venus to her own pain.

It hurt, but it was okay. Everything was okay; from the minute she'd found out she was pregnant, it had been okay. Venus looked down on her small pinkish-brown face. Her coal black eyes, looking around, informed, curious like she'd been on this earth before and wondered if things had changed.

Venus slid her finger to the edge of Mya's mouth, breaking her suction. She moved the baby to the other side. The swelling of her breast felt like someone had sewn bowling balls underneath her skin, tight, heavy, stretched to the max. She'd always dreamed of having big breasts but this was ridiculous.

"How's she doing?" Wendy crept in, whispering. "There's our baby." She came to the side of the bed, kissing mommy and child. "She's even prettier today, and so are you."

"I'm a mess."

"You're glowing."

Venus let her hand slide to the roundness of her cheek. "You have to put some makeup on me. He's coming today."

"Got it." Wendy put the pouch on the edge of the bed and unzipped it. "This is what you call makeup? I use more than this just to do my lips." She shoved the three small items to the side looking for more.

Venus looked at the plastic makeup case she'd carried since college. It held what she needed nice and compact. "Did you bring the spray and comb?"

"Good grief, child, you just had a baby. He's not going to be expecting you to look like a princess. But I just happen to have Wendy's deluxe save-the-day kit." She propped the big silver box on the edge of the bed and pulled out a comb. She started working on the massive spread of hair.

"Ooouch." She pulled her head away from Wendy's offending hand with a comb full of hair. Venus bit down on her lip, while the baby seemed to be biting down on her, too. She used her finger and broke the suction, pulling Mya away. "Ouch, and you too. God, that hurts."

"Beauty costs and so does motherhood." Wendy commenced taming the sprawl of hair. "You know, next time you get pregnant you might want to get a perm. Hair gets thicker when you're on those prenatal vitamins, and thicker hair is not what you needed, my dear."

Venus turned her face back toward Mya. She was quiet, but still awake. "She's so amazing."

"Just like her mommy." Wendy went to work pulling the hair back and collecting it into one big scrunchie. A stray curl bounced out. She used a bobby pin to secure it with the rest. She applied a little blush and eyeliner, then the lipstick.

"Conservative," Venus ordered. "I don't want to look like Bette Davis in *What Ever Happened to Baby Jane?*"

"I got it."

"Ease up on the blush."

"I got it," Wendy exclaimed again, dabbing the brush for a reload of color. "So when's the last time you talked to him?" Wendy asked as if they'd been on the subject all along.

"You mean besides when I called to announce I'd just given birth."

"Yeah, exactly."

"A few days ago."

"C'mon...details."

"We talked like we always talk, about everything, nothing in particular. We try not to get too heavy."

"What exactly are you expecting from this little visit?"

"I don't know. I don't expect anything." Venus couldn't look Wendy in the eye.

"Good, I don't want you to be hurt."

"I'm not going to be hurt," Venus said with obvious fraud in her voice. Who was she kidding? She was most definitely expecting something to happen. She was spoiled rotten with expectation. Yes, every day was a gift, she told herself, and she was responsible for making sure she made the best out of it...period. But always, in the back of her mind, was expectation.

"I just don't understand." Wendy was still stuck. "Is he the one you want to be with? I mean, this isn't another prince-to-the-rescue reenactment? Then you get him home and realize he's a toad."

Venus took Wendy's hand and snatched the blush brush. "Just forget it. I don't need this."

"What? What're you mad at me for? I'm just trying to get it straight. I mean, you do this all the time. You make these decisions—"

"I just told you that I'm not expecting anything. Zilch, nada, nothing. He's my friend. He'll always be my friend. Just like you and me, friends."

Wendy took the makeup back. "You don't try to look cute for me, *friend.*"

"The truth." Venus looked in her best friend's golden brown eyes. "The truth is, I'm not depending on him to love me. I don't need it. I'll survive just fine, but she..." They both looked down at Mya, who slept peacefully in her mother's arms. "She needs a father's love."

◦   ◦   ◦

WENDY left after having stalled long enough to bump into him when he arrived. Only problem was that he never showed up. Venus and Mya lay together watching reruns of old sitcoms, trying to look adoringly like a mother-and-child Kodak moment. A commercial popped on. A bright smile of recognition came to Venus. Lila Kelly was in concert wearing the colorful JPWear clothing. When she kicked her leg out, Venus recognized the boots. She had to admit she was proud, even though it had been left to the guys to make it happen without her.

The commercial came to a close, Lila Kelly did a high howl, threw up her hand and yelled, "You can make a difference." A caption appeared on the screen: *Your Support Goes to the Breast Cancer Foundation.* She covered her mouth, overwhelmed; he'd done this for Venus, for her mother. The clothing line was a big hit. Jake kept her updated at every turn, but he never mentioned anything about the Breast Cancer Foundation. At least two things had turned out right. She looked down on Mya, glad she was one of them. By late afternoon Venus had given up complete hope. She was exhausted, needing to really sleep, especially since she was on Mya's feeding schedule.

Venus didn't want to put Mya in the carrier next to the bed but knew it was the only way she could sleep, without being fearful of rolling over and smothering her precious baby. She placed the tight bundle in the carrier, turning her on her side, with a couple of blankets behind her for support as she'd seen the nurse do. She leaned back into the bed, grateful to get her feet off the cold acrylic floor.

She stretched the cover over her shoulders and watched Mya until her own eyes fell like heavy shades. It was always the same dream. Jake. In this one, his strong arms held her, cradling her like she was the baby in need of care. Safe. She wished she could stay there forever. But no, was it time already? She struggled to pull herself awake, hearing Mya's soft airy cry. Venus fought to get to consciousness. She was so tired.

"I'm coming, sweetie," she murmured, still unable to raise her head, raise her eyelids. She felt a hand stroke across her face, pulling the hair away that had freed itself again from the bobby pin. It tickled enough to raise her blood pressure with panic. She quickly opened her eyes, still blurry. The carrier was empty. "Mya." She sat up, ignoring the pain ringing in her stretched full breast.

"Right here." Airic bent over and kissed Venus on her forehead. "She's beautiful."

"She is," Venus agreed, smiling at the picture before her. Airic looked studious in his brown suede coat and tweed trousers. Back to the picture of health. No longer stressed or overworked. He held Mya, the blanket dangling past his arm.

"I'm sorry to have missed it. I couldn't get here yesterday; I tried." He swayed side to side, rocking her in his arms. "She looks like me." He smiled, almost in relief as if before now he hadn't been truly sure.

His confirmation suddenly made Venus feel guilty. Somewhere in the back of her mind, she'd wished for the opposite, that the doctor had estimated incorrectly, giving her a chance to proclaim *Jake, the winner*. It would always be lurking in the back of her mind. An awkward silence followed. Airic simply held her.

Now would come the difficult part, expectation. She tried to let the moment be as it was...father holding daughter, father wanting to love daughter as much as she already did. Venus sat up as straight as she could, the weight of her breast pulling down on her. He instinctively leaned over to give Mya back.

"You can hold her longer, if you want," she said, proud of her first venture into unselfishness.

"No. I can't stay. I just wanted to see her, and you. Make sure everything was all right." He walked to the window and twirled the miniblind wand. Sunlight flooded into the room. Airic was nothing more than a silhouette now, his sharp profile reminding her of the third grade assignment to sit in front of the projector while her teacher outlined the black paper.

"I'm not in a position to pay a lot right now, Venus. I can do something of course, but not as much as I would have normally. I'm starting over with my new career teaching. Let me tell you, it's not for the person on the fast track. Money is sparse."

Venus was too busy being shocked by his chosen topic of conversation to respond.

"I was in the beginning stages of my career when my two girls were coming up, just like now." He turned away from the window for a moment and looked back at her. "This is déjà vu. Wanda made things difficult for me, you know all about that. We talked about that. I didn't want to go down this road ever again."

Venus swallowed hard dry gulps, still unable to respond. This road ... children?

"If we could just agree to do the best we can, together."

"Of course. Of course, that's what I want, total agreement—"

"You say that now. But I know how it's going to go, I'll get the phone call one evening, you not feeling like things are equal. You'll say I'm not doing my share. Day-care costs. Medical, preschool, it all adds up, Venus."

"Airic, I can take care of Mya on my own. You know that. I want you to—"

"What, Venus? You want me to, what—pick her up every other weekend, take her for walks in the stroller while you're working, show up on birthdays and holidays with a pretty box that has something she's not even interested in because I'm so out of touch with her life? Is that what you want?"

"Yes. Absolutely. I want you to be there. Memories, Airic, that's it, that's all we have. When it's all said and done ... in the end, memories are our most priceless possessions." She swiped the tear that escaped down her cheek. "I want her to remember her father, her mother, grandparents, friends that came and went. But money? It's not about money. I'm so far past that. Possessions and time clocks, trying to keep up the pace with what other people have or what they think I should have. Been there, done that." The baby jerked in her arms like she was having a bad dream, then a half smile formed on her small lips. Venus thought she was too young to know the meaning of a smile, but who could say for sure?

She turned her attention back to Airic. "It's just about her, now. That's it."

"Don't fool yourself, Venus. This magical world you've dreamed of, the children, and family, it doesn't work without money, and lots of it. The happy memories won't happen without someone paying for them. All I'm saying is I fully plan to meet my obligations. I just don't want it to turn into something ugly."

"Me ... turning it into something ugly?"

"Yes, you. This could have all been so simple."

"Simple? How? How was any of this simple? You never wanted to marry me... not until you found out I was pregnant and don't stand there pretending any different."

"I'm not pretending. At least I have the decency to be straightforward. You seem to think there's a fairy-tale world out there where people fall madly in love and stay that way." He sat on the bed and pulled out his checkbook and pen.

"What are you doing?" Venus felt like kicking him off the edge of the bed but knew the jolt would shake Mya awake. She tried to stay calm. The rhythm of her voice skipped high and unbalanced. "This child is more than an obligation, do you understand? And if you're going to make her feel that way in your presence, then you don't ever need to come around."

He stood up, pushing his wares back into his jacket pocket. He took a deep breath and exhaled relief. "One day you're going to have to grow up."

"If you're an example, I don't ever want to get there," she said through clenched teeth, conscious of her tone. She didn't want Mya to experience one moment of uncertainty. She watched as his brown loafers moved to the door. It swung open, then he was gone. Venus closed her eyes. Expectations, such a filthy word. She wiped the tears before they made it past the wells under her eyes.

"Way to tell him." The voice came from the other side of the curtain. Then the blue fabric shifted to one side. Mrs. Cotter had eaten her cookies and was well on her way to recovery. She smiled, tired with sympathy. "Can I come over?" The neat line of cornrows tight against her scalp pulled her eyes back a bit. "Ain't it a shame? We used to say, sperm didn't make a daddy, we needed the money too; now we're calling them checkbook daddies and that's not enough. We want full partnership, well maybe a third." She moved closer to the bed, leaning in to get a better look at the sleeping child. "What's her name?"

"Mya."

"I just had my third, a boy. No breast feeding for me. I'm taking advantage of my rest while I can. Make sure you do the same, 'cause you're looking at at least three months of sleep deprivation."

"Yeah, I'm already feeling it." Venus yawned wide and unmasked.

"Okay, that's my sign to let you nap. She's beautiful," Mrs. Cotter added. "Don't worry, he'll come around." The curtain went back to its closed position. Venus never got a chance to add her own two cents to Mrs. Cotter's statement about the checkbook daddies. She knew for certain not to hold her breath for Airic to change the way he felt. She'd witnessed it all along but had ignored the signals. He'd kept his distance from his other two daughters, basically feeling there was nothing for him to do but write checks and send unfeeling gifts. Most people saw what they wanted instead of what was really there. Venus was most people.

Once again she closed her eyes, not meaning to fall into a deep unshakable sleep, one that included a blissful dream, one of Jake smiling down on her, asking, "Did you miss me?" The slow rhythm of his words, the honest tone of his voice, she would have guessed it was all too real, especially when she felt his smooth lips on the bridge of her nose.

Yes, she'd missed him. She curled up the same way she did on the many nights they talked on the phone, his voice soothing and caring. Yes, she missed him deeply.

"You know what this means, don't you?"

"What?" Venus found herself sitting up in the dream. He sat on the edge of the bed holding a soft mound in his arms wrapped in a blanket. So many things he was good at, so many things his natural ability. She couldn't resist reaching out, touching him, tracing the line from his ear to the wide stance of his shoulder.

His smooth palm cupped her face "Means you finished something. Those lines in your hands... guess they finally connected."

"What about yours?"

He put up his hand showing her his palm. She felt her hand rise in a high five, their fingers interlocked. "Finally met their match. A line for a line." He looked down on the sleeping child. "Guess we'll have to warn her when she grows up. Life isn't always simple. Straight lines may be the quickest way to a destination, but think about all you'd miss in the middle."

"So wise to be so young," Venus chided, the tears swelling underneath her closed lids. She wanted to open them, but feared... it truly was only a dream.

"I love you," he whispered in her ear.

"I love you, too."

"Can you look me in the eye when you say that?"

Venus opened her eyes slowly. It was real. He was real. He held Mya in his arms as if she were his very own. This time it was she who breathed out a sigh of relief.

"You really are here." She sat up slowly, pulling the sheet over the two large wet circles on her hospital gown.

He smiled, taking her hand in his. "Nothing works without you. I jumped on a plane as soon as Wendy called."

"She called?"

"Early this morning. Don't be mad. I struck that deal weeks ago."

Venus couldn't afford to cry. She needed every liquid in her body right now especially since every ounce seemed to be excreting from her engorged breasts. She'd made deals, pacts, and promises not to cry another tear, but one look into his tender eyes and she fell into a pitiful sob. Tears of joy, she wished she could explain, but there were no words that would come.

"I see I have work to do." He rubbed a thumb across her face, clearing the constant stream.

No, she shook her head. The work was already done.

"Hey, c'mon now. You're supposed to be happy to see me." He squeezed Mya within their embrace, holding on to both of them.

"I am, I'm happy." She held him tight, then pulled away, concerned about Mya between them.

He pulled her back into a soft embrace, "Uh uh, I got you now . . . I'm not ever letting go."

ALWAYS THE
BRIDESMAID...

Aftered the breakup with Clint three years ago, Venus couldn't have predicted the way her life was going to turn out, not even with a wild guess. But when she'd met Airic, it all seemed to fall into place. She'd gotten back on schedule for finding her perfect mate and living in her perfect home with her perfect two point five children. It had been a work in progress since the age of five. She'd always been a planner, but how things actually ended was another story.

She'd thought about it a lot over the past six months, from the moment Wendy had announced she and Sidney were planning to renew their vows. After seventeen years it was time for a re-do. "We need this to put things right, things that have been wrong for a very long time," she'd said to Venus while they searched the rack at Neiman Marcus for an elegant gown that didn't scream foul play. "First thing Sidney said was, I already married you once, the deal is sealed. Then I broke it down for him...the seal had a leak, a huge one, and it needed to be repaired."

Venus didn't bother to tell Wendy that the leak she was referring to needed addressing at the nearest marriage counselor's office. She didn't see how a ceremony could fix anything. Ceremonies. Rituals. Beliefs of happy ever after.

Yet, here she was again, a bridesmaid, standing to witness a union, till death do they part, a solid oath of love and commitment that had an expiration date. Or worse, an out clause called boredom, gridlock, or just plain old-fashioned contempt. She tried to stay focused, knowing one lapse in attention; she'd see Vivica Fox at the back of the church. Her eyes drifted away from the preacher over to the bride and groom. They really did look happy. Wendy had her thick long hair pushed back and held in place with a diamondlike tiara fit for a queen. She'd ended up buying the gown at a small bridal boutique. It even had a train, something she hadn't had the first time around. Being five months pregnant prevented formalities seventeen years ago. Wendy and Sidney had opted to carry out their ceremony in a judge's office.

Wendy caught Venus looking her way and winked at her. For some reason that brought an anxiety she'd tried all afternoon to suppress. Venus held her breath, hoping the pastor had a closing in sight. He seemed to not want to end his performance, enjoying his nice white robe with the golden trim and tassels and all. How often did he get to wear his special robe? Venus closed her eyes with a special prayer for him to wrap this baby up, and quick.

"Wendy and Sidney, God offers us as many chances as we need to get it right. Even when it seems you've come to the end of your rope, never underestimate the power of God. Never feel like this union has no place to go. You have my complete admiration for knowing all things can be healed in God's house. Today, you've become proof for all who stand before you that this *is* the doctor's house. Now, if you will, please turn around and face your family and your friends as a testimony to the will of God."

Venus was hoping that meant her, too; she didn't remember this part from last night's only rehearsal. She watched as Sidney's brother, the groom's man, turned slowly to face the crowd.

Yes, freedom was approaching. She just wanted to hold her baby. She looked out and zeroed in on Mya, her curly head taking in the sights, singing her own tune of life. She had a lavender dress on to match her mommy's.

"Please repeat after me," the pastor directed the order to the audience. "May God bless this union...in sickness and in health...and for all the days of their lives...Amen." After the last bedraggled amen, he announced, "You, Sidney Westcott, may kiss your bride."

Venus wore a huge smile that had nothing to do with the cameras' flashing on and off. For the first time the nightmare, or day-mare in this case, hadn't happened. An entire ceremony with no imagery of Clint leaving her at the altar. An excitement expanded around her chest. She was free. This time she was truly sure. The scar on her heart was healed.

She felt Wendy's hand curl around hers. "I couldn't have done this without you. Don't worry, next time, it'll be me standing by your side and you'll be the bride."

"Don't worry about me." Venus looked Wendy in the eye. "For the first time in my life, I know where I stand. There's no alarm about to go off on this clock. I've got everything I want." She wrapped her arms around her best friend. "Throw the bouquet to somebody who needs it, okay? To someone who *really* needs it, 'cause I don't." She let Wendy out of her embrace. "See that man over there holding that precious little girl..." They both looked out past the sea of people. Mya had her open hand against Jake's mouth. He pretended to take a chunk out of her palm, sending the baby into a fit of giggles. Next to them were Pauletta and Henry; they'd flown out just for Wendy's nuptials, happy somebody was getting married these days. "It doesn't get any better than that." Venus squeezed Wendy's hand. "Just promise to visit often."

"You know I'm going to be out there checking on my goddaughter." Wendy blinked back tears. "I'm going to miss you that's all. You're going to have your mother and father, not to mention the best part." She nodded at Jake and Mya. "I know you're going to forget about me."

"I couldn't survive anywhere without you, especially not in L.A. Don't you dare cry. Your makeup is going to be ruined and you still have a full night ahead." Venus kissed Wendy on the cheek. "Go. Sidney is getting pummeled over there." She turned the bride in the direction of her husband.

Wendy was effortlessly swept away by the crowd. Venus looked again in the direction of her small family. They were no longer sitting in the same spot. She looked around and began to nudge her way through the crowd, eyeing everyone until she reached the outside of the church.

It was a perfect day for a wedding. The sun shone directly overhead in an endless blue sky. She saw no one except the limo driver smoking a cigarette. He threw it down and stepped on it when he saw Venus. "Time to roll?" he said, straightening his tuxedo jacket and adjusting his sleeve cuffs.

"Soon," Venus yelled before turning to go back inside. She picked up her dress and hiked up the long stairs of the chapel. When she reached the doors, they were locked.

She'd just come out this way, hadn't she? She leaned her ear against the smooth wood. There wasn't a sound to be heard, no buzz of happy people who had free champagne and cake to look forward to. She stepped back, confused. These were the same doors, she was sure. She pushed them again and they gave way.

What she saw shocked her. The audience was sitting down again, half on one side and half on the other. The pastor was standing at the end of the aisle, his arms resting at his sides with the open Bible in one hand. Wait a minute. This had already happened. Like a strange glitch in *Matrix,* she blinked again, trying to put herself back into real time.

"Step inside, young lady, we're running over schedule." This seemed to amuse the crowd. A few snickers echoed in the front of the church.

Venus looked around dumbfounded, her mouth still hung slightly open. A renewal of the renewal...had Wendy or Sidney fallen off the wagon in less than ten minutes? She tried to sort through the faces staring at her. She blinked, trying to focus on her mother and father. They were sitting in the front, smiling. Her feet began to move as the pastor had insisted, we don't have all day, young lady. One unsteady step after the other, he continued to wave her toward him, signaling her to speed it up. Before Venus reached the end, Jake came out the side door carrying Mya.

Oh, right, it was a perfect time to take advantage of a church full of people and a pastor eager to keep the party going, a baptismal ceremony. Her mom and dad were here. Why didn't she think of it? Venus smiled and stretched out her arms. Mya jumped, her little body landing firm against her breast that had shrunk to disappointing AA's, one cup smaller than she'd started out.

Jake kissed her on the lips a little too passionately for her taste in front of this group...*for a baptism?* Venus wobbled on her thin high heels. She felt Mya being lifted from her arms and turned to see her father smiling. "I'll hold her for you, Precious. You're going to need your strength for this one."

Now she was scared.

"Venus," Jake said as he took hold of both her hands. "Since the day I met you I've never been happier. I've never felt like I had more to live for than myself, until you came along." He paused and moved a finger across her face, lifting the weight of her hair and putting it behind her shoulder. He reached into his pocket. The small black box appeared. Venus cupped her hand over her mouth. Stay calm, she screamed in her head, but she knew her knees were about to give way.

Jake opened the velvet box to a gold band with three diamonds across the middle. "I don't want to wait another day, not even another minute. I want to know that every morning I wake up will be with you. I couldn't imagine this life without you in it. Will you please do me the honor of becoming my wife, right here, right now?"

Venus felt her mouth move, but no sound came out. She felt a nudge at her left elbow. "Say yes," Wendy whispered.

"YES!" Venus shouted too loud. Chills ran up and down her body. She threw herself in his arms and hugged him fiercely. "I love you." She said it again and again so he would understand, so he would know it was more than a reply. A declaration she wanted to make to him and to the world. "I love you," she whispered over and over. She pulled back and looked him in the eye... "Jake, you didn't have to—"

He put a finger to her lips. He understood about her doubts, her questions. Why now? That was the beautiful part about it; she was willing to spend her life with him whether he signed on the dotted line or not. She trusted him, wholly and completely. And he trusted her. There was no ulterior motive... no underlying fear... no hidden goal. Just love.

"Well, all right. That's what I'm talking about." The pastor was pleased with his opportunity for an encore. "I've only met this young man today, but when he told me his story, and the story of Venus Johnston I knew... I knew immediately this young man wasn't messing around. He was on a mission to love this woman and her child, to be a husband, to be a father, to reap the rewards as well as the sorrows...yes. So we stand here before you today, to witness the love and dedication before God. Can I get a witness?

"I said, can I get a witness!" The crowd responded in full union. Venus smiled when she heard her mother's voice behind her, "Yes, Lord...on a mission," and the many voices that followed.

"But like in every good story, there's two sides," the pastor continued. "Now I've heard this young man's side. He is ready if I've ever seen ready. Now I want to hear the story of Venus. You see, it's a pastor's duty to make sure there are no reservations in the heart and mind. It's my duty to present a strong union before God, a union that won't easily be strayed or fettered by temptation...by trials and tribulations...by life's ups and life's downs." The pastor stopped abruptly. All eyes were on Venus. Speechless at first, she didn't know what to say. She was quickly searching her mind for something as poetic and beautiful as what Jake had said. Something about his way...his gentle way. No, maybe about the way her mind and heart fluttered with anticipation when her phone rang. She could mention the fact that she loved him. What more was necessary? Wait, no. She could tell about the time she felt like a complete and total failure for still not having Mya trained to sleep more than two hours at a time...waking up hungry and cranky. How he'd flown from Los Angeles and landed on her doorstep armed with lullabies and determination. He held Mya for four solid hours, just so she would stay asleep and Venus could get some rest. No, no, that was small compared with him offering to move JPWear and the building itself to the East Coast, just so he could be by her side.

She felt the impatience of the crowd, and then something wonderful happened. A quiet calm came over her and she knew exactly what to say into those soft loving brown eyes. "My heart was yours from the moment I met you. You gave me space, you gave me time to listen to my heart. For that I am grateful, because without that time, I wouldn't know for sure that what I feel for you is real. Not a figment of my imagination. Not a fairy-tale fantasy, but real. The kind of love that comes when you feel a sheer joy just to be in that person's presence." She nodded in her parents' direction but her eyes fell quickly back on Jake. "The kind of love that makes you want to wake up every day to see the sunrise 'cause you know there's just going to be more of you." She bit her lip, hoping she could stop the line of tears that were about to fall. "You...you make me happy. That's all." She'd said it as plainly and truthfully as it could possibly be said. She knew all about fulfillment of id, defining her own purpose and loving herself, and all the other practices of the self-help gurus. But all it took was one man. One strong loving man who wasn't afraid to carry the weight of one strong loving woman.

"Now that's what I'm talking about." A smile of satisfaction lit the pastor's face. He lifted his arms. "Rise with me. Say a prayer for this couple." Everyone's head bowed. Venus closed her eyes too but she couldn't shut the little voice going off in her mind. So this is what her mother meant by taking the long way. All the thinking and worrying in the middle, falling victim to the trap of stress. Trying to figure out a future that's designed to work out right no matter what. She listened to the pastor's words, but she had her own private prayer. Her own need to be thankful for every high and every low. Without them she wouldn't be who she was. She wouldn't know real joy and understand it and respect it. She wouldn't have Jake. She felt his smooth palms touch her face. The ceremony was proceeding without her.

She spoke the words "I DO," right on cue.

"You know what to do now, young man."

The kiss. You may kiss the bride. Those five magic words. So many times she'd heard them as a witness to someone else's grand day. Stood idly by watching with hope and reverence. Not this time. She grabbed her loving new husband around his neck, pulling him close and plunging into the deepest, most gratifying kiss that either one had ever experienced. If not for the sudden sound of hand clapping and cheering from the crowd, Venus was sure it could have gone on forever.

She blushed from embarrassment and pushed her face into his chest.

"It's all right, baby. We've got a lifetime," he whispered. The crowd still hadn't calmed down, and neither had Venus. Her heartbeat was brisk, her face flushed. The warmth encapsulated her entire body. Is this what every bride is thinking on her wedding day... *let's get on with the honeymoon?* There was nothing she wanted more than to sink into his loving touch, skin to skin, heart to heart. She forced herself to ignore the quivering ache and fell into a band of well wishers. Pauletta was the first, her smile wide, her eyes glistening with tears.

"Oh, Mom." The sight of her mother, now the picture of health, and remembering what Timothy had said, sent Venus into a fit of hiccuping sobs. *You know Mom will refuse to leave this earth before both of us are neatly tied in matrimonial knots.* She hugged her tighter, not ready yet to let go.

"Now you ladies are going to have to break it up so somebody else can get a hug." Henry squeezed between them, having gained back all of his weight plus a few extra pounds. He grabbed them both. "You done good, Precious."

Venus kissed her father on the cheek before realizing he was missing something. "Where's Mya, Dad?"

"She ran off with some good lookin' fella," he chided. Henry lifted a finger and pointed to the new groom. Mya was hoisted on his hip, hanging on while he swung from one handshake and hug to the next. They were a match, for sure, in their element as the center of attention.

Venus reached up on her tiptoes and gave her father another good long hug. "Thanks for making me understand the difference between love and true love, Daddy."

"I think you already knew the difference." He gave her a knowing smile. The part he didn't say was that she'd known all along but was afraid to face the truth. Being with someone for the sake of not being alone, settling out of fear. Guilty as charged. It would have made her miserable in the long run. Venus now considered herself one of the lucky ones. She escaped over the narrow fence of obligation and predictability and made it to the other side of sheer love and a whole buncha like. There was no place she'd rather be than in the arms of the man she loved. She knew it from the first time she laid eyes on him, but she'd told herself that it was all make-believe. A figment of her warped imagination. Fairy tales don't happen to you, Venus.

Says who?

"I guess we'll be sharing the first dance," Wendy said, as she came up from behind. Venus turned around and immediately hugged her friend.

"Oh, God. Did you know?"

"Girl, it was truly a shock. That man over there was just too serious. He was determined, okaaaay."

"But I'm sorry we stole some of your thunder. This was your big day ... well, your second big day."

Wendy handed Venus her opulent bridal bouquet. "It was the best day of my life. And I got to share it with my best friend, and I do mean share. Do you know how long I've wanted this for you, just to see you happy, truly happy? Not but a minute ago you were telling me that you didn't need a ceremony to make your life complete, but sister friend, you are glowing. Do you hear me? Glowing."

"It's just the cherry on top," Venus said.

"And here comes that chocolate sundae now."

He came and hugged Wendy and reached around and shook Sidney's hand. "Thanks, Wendy, thanks for letting us intrude."

"Long as you don't expect to share the honeymoon suite we've got over at the Watergate," Sidney said with a devilish grin. "Wendy makes too much noise to be sharing rooms."

"You guys are nasty." Venus feigned embarrassment.

"Not necessary. I got big plans for this lady right here. Your mom and dad are going to keep Mya. We're headed to the warm blue seas of the Caribbean." He kissed Venus on the top of her head. "You know what would be cool is if you guys came with us. This place is huge—six bedrooms. You guys take one side, we take the other, hook up when we wanted, stay invisible when we didn't. For letting us take over your day like this, I'd even spring for the airline tickets."

Wendy's eyes got big, then came back down to earth. "Work. Us working folk have to pay the bills, but I'm going to hold you to that offer for sometime down the road."

They said their good-byes. Venus was all cried out. Her nose was stuffy, but it didn't stop her from inhaling Mya. All the goodness and warmth in her baby's coal black curly hair and warm soft cheeks. "Take care of Grandma and Grandpa, okay?" She acted as if she understood, wrapping her chubby arms tighter around Henry's neck. Venus would see her again in seven days. Don't panic, she told herself, but it was hard. They hadn't missed one day together in her nine months on this earth. Venus had even done the unthinkable, quit her job and started taking independent projects just to make her own hours with her daughter.

She settled into the passenger side of the car, spent and exhausted. She turned her head sideways and watched the man who'd just whisked her away. "You want to know something?"

"What," he said, picking up her hand and putting it to his full moist lips.

"I love steak. There's a lot you can do with steak."

A perplexed frown fell on his face. "You hungry?"

"Oh, if you only knew. Famished." She smiled, wide and open. "Good tender juicy steak. Steak with mushrooms, grilled, sautéed. Steak with gravy. Steak into burgers." She continued singing the praises of beef while he drove, looking back and forth at her, clueless.

"There's porterhouse steaks, rib eye, New York cut fajita style...ummmmm and have you ever tried it in mango salsa..."

ACKNOWLEDGMENTS

Becoming a published author has been my dream for quite some time, and three books later, I still feel the same excitement and joy. I will always be grateful to Ayesha Pande for giving this opportunity to fulfill my dream and for the simple words of advice that continue to empower me—always stay true to your characters.

A giant acknowledgment and appreciation hug to my literary agent, Marie D. Brown, who knows how to make hot soup out of all the hot water I find myself in.

Thanking everyone who has touched my life and shown support would probably take as long as it took me to write this book. But like a true Gemini, I gotta try the impossible, so here it goes: Diane Burns, Rita Beasely, D. Lynn White, Dana London, Lillian Lewis, Tonya Johnson, Kim Roby, Victoria Christopher Murray, Karen Logan, Vernon Logan Jr., Vernon Logan Sr., Anne Thomas, Dwayne and Lanita Logan, Ingrid Lincicome, Janice and Cornell Harris, Bill and Lynn Crandall, Carol Mackey, Patrik Bass, Jewel Parker Rhodes, Patricia Elam, Debrena Gandy, Nana Collins, Lucille Logan, Tameka Mullins, Monique Greenwood, Ruby Deloach, Vivica A. Fox, Tananarive Due, Cynthia Hollis, Nicole Holomon, Gail Stewart, Rachel Mackey, Sharon Sobers...hold on, there's more...John Marshall, Jacquese Silvas, Erma Branch, Evelyne Branch, Celeste Branch, and all the Branches on the family tree, Evelyn Hosch, Tonya and Marlon (aka Wendy and Sidney), don't forget to invite me to the wedding. Yes, I can see the future.

Seraphine Kinlow, hairstylist extraordinaire, thanks for making me shine, nappy or straight. Diane Guilford of the Lambda Kappa Omega Chapter AKA, you have given me motivation and inspiration to be the best person I can be.

To the dreammakers—Amy Schiffman, Angela Dejoseph, Halle Berry, Vincent Cirrincione, you've given me a gift of a lifetime that I will always cherish. Tina Chism, glad we agree that there's a little bit of Venus in every woman regardless of race, class, or culture. To my kids who never let me forget my day job. Tiffany and Quinlan, thank you for keeping me grounded and happy! Thank you to all the readers who have made this magic happen for me. For all of the Aha! moments, letting me know through e-mails, letters, and hugs that all the hard work has not been in vain, but really touches each and every one of your lives. As well to the many booksellers and event planners: Pamela Walker Williams, Jan Emanuel, Lauretta Pierce and Mary Jones of the African American Book Club Summit, Mari Mitchell and Tena Ivory of the Seattle African American Book Festival, Yasmin Coleman, Martina (TeeC Royal), Curtis Bunn, Cydney Rax, Robin Green-Cary; and Rosalind Bell, to whom I am especially grateful. Much gratitude goes out to Rachel Kahan and the Crown family for nurturing all three of my novels.

Most important, to my husband, Cameron Thomas, for giving me the freedom and inspiration to write. Without you, there would be no me. Last, but certainly not least, a gracious bow to my courageous mother, Rena Logan, for challenging every test result, mammogram, and doctor's opinion with determination and faith. There is no greater power than being informed... to all the mothers, sisters, and daughters—we owe it to each other to be healthy and strong, physically as well as spiritually.

Peace and God bless,
Trisha R. Thomas

Reader's Group Guide

Venus Johnston is a walking, talking success machine. She's got the perfect job, the perfect fiancé, and she's on the road to a perfect life, complete with a checklist of perfectly checked-off goals. Sort of. The truth is that a secret, nagging doubt is preventing Venus from setting a wedding date, and when she finds herself hiding the diamond on her left hand from a handsome new partner at work, she realizes that it's time to reevaluate her journey before she makes a mess of everything.

Then terrible news throws a wrench in the works. Venus discovers that her mother is battling cancer and suddenly she feels like an angry, scared kid, alone and in need of back-up. And when back-up arrives in an unexpected guise, driving a fast car, Venus faces the challenge of a lifetime. Where does a sister draw the line between love and loyalty, temptation and blessing, happiness and habit, and when is it time for a fresh start in life?

The sassy heroine of Trisha R. Thomas's award-winning novel *Nappily Ever After* is back in this stylish, romantic, and long-awaited sequel. Here is a guide designed to direct your discussion of *Would I Lie to You?*

Questions for Discussion

1. The novel opens with Venus's recurring nightmare: she is abandoned on her wedding day when Clint is lured away by a glamorous actress who tells him, "You know you need a real woman, someone who's going to love you and take care of you and put you first at all times." Is Venus afraid that she is truly incapable of putting someone first, or merely afraid that Clint thinks so? Why do you think this dream features Clint rather than Airic as the groom?

2. Venus does not hesitate to take the job in Los Angeles, and, in fact, is packed and ready to roll when she springs the news on Airic. However, she is irritated that Airic does not put up a fight. He is "a little too excited for her taste.... Part of her wanted him to throw drama, plead for her to stay, maybe even pout a little. What would it hurt to show that he cared, needed her? He didn't always have to be so understanding, so mature." What does this double standard tell you about Venus? Would she have canceled her plans if Airic had begged her to?

3. How much of Jake's allure is due to the fact that he is a refreshing, baggage-free distraction from Venus's family crisis? How does Thomas set up tension with her descriptions of Jake? Are you surprised to find him a trustworthy, loveable character by the end?

4. Venus is deeply conflicted about her career: "What was she doing here in Los Angeles? She'd asked herself that question numerous times. Her answer always straight from the pages of *Essence, O,* and *New Woman* . . . unleashing her career potential, setting goals, and overcoming fears. She was, after all, the Millennium woman . . . Underneath it all, she simply wanted to be loved. . . . A husband, a baby, a home with a cuddly little dog." Is Thomas suggesting that some women are pressured by the media to strive for career success against their own gut instincts? To what extent do you think magazines like *Essence* and *O* affect women's ideas, both positively and negatively, about what they should be doing with their lives?

5. How do you explain Venus's fury at her mother's doctor? Are her feelings directed at the illness itself? The medical field for being inadequate to the task? Her mother for being mortal, or possibly passing a flawed gene on to her? Is any of this emotion aimed at Clint?

6. Alienated from her parents and confused about her men, Venus ends up relying on the kindness of strangers. Who helps her in unexpected ways? What point do you think Thomas is making with these encounters?

7. What is the significance of Venus's memory about her college boyfriend, Tony, and the tumultuous end of their relationship? What fears about herself does this memory dredge up?

8. When Jake turns on the charm during their first meeting, Venus acknowledges, "the fun was always in the chase." When she feels overwhelmed by his ardor, she admits, "She was used to doing the chasing, being the one who wanted more than she would ever receive." And when she is late to visit her mother at the hospital, she berates herself: "Always a step behind . . . a true sign that she was never going to catch whatever she was chasing." Discuss Venus's obsession with "the chase." Is she able to let go of this cat-and-mouse mentality in the end?

9. Venus tells Jake, "I learned a long time ago not to blame others for my

unhappiness, or happiness for that matter. Either way it's my responsibility." Has she internalized this lesson? Where do you see examples
of her having achieved this clarity?

10. Henry and Wendy offer Venus clashing advice about her relationship.
Henry insists that *liking* someone (Jake, for instance) takes prece-
dence over loyalty or even love. He tells her that "life is full of risk
and danger but living is much more fun," and urges her to "start taking some chances or you gonna end up unhappy and alone." Wendy
urges her to stay loyal to Airic. "You'd give up a man you've known
and loved for someone who just happened to be there to pick up the
pieces when you were vulnerable? . . . [Airic] was there for you . . .
Now you have to stick by him." Both Henry and Wendy claim to be
happily married. Whose advice do you agree with?

11. When Venus confronts Airic about his agonizing secret, she turns the
conversation toward herself, rather than comfort him: "I wanted to finally be right, to finally be the person that someone could count on,
through thick and thin. I wanted to be that person for you, Airic . . .
Conviction, forgiveness, compassion, whatever it's called. I thought
you saw that in me. I thought you loved me the same way I loved you.
I thought you trusted me." Is Venus being fair? Is she honestly feeling injured here, or has this situation merely provided her with an
easy "out" from the relationship?

12. After all her hard work on the JPWear account, Venus capitulates to
"the dynamic duo" during their last meeting in LA, but not until she
has a temper tantrum and balls out Legend. This is not her first loss
of control in a professional setting. How do you feel about Venus
abandoning her career ambitions so quickly, and in such a firestorm?

13. Discuss Airic's assessment: "Most people saw what they wanted instead of what was really there. Venus was most people."

14. Venus is delighted by the sabotaged wedding that closes the novel. Is
this what she has needed all along in order to make a decision—a
forced, public accounting of her own feelings? How would the novel
have been different if Venus had freely chosen the timing and cir-
cumstance of her wedding?

Venus Johnston's story begins in Trisha R. Thomas's witty and wise first novel, *Nappily Ever After.*

Praise:

"A smashing debut . . . lively and engaging."
—*Essence*

"*Nappily Ever After* is the vibrant tale of a young woman's journey to independence. It's an exquisitely passionate novel from an immensely gifted new author."

—Pamela Walker-Williams,
the Page-Turner Network

Wherever books are sold

Three Rivers Press
CrownPublishing.com